THE
SWEETEST SIN

Other **AVON ROMANCES**

Coming Soon

And Don't Miss These
ROMANTIC TREASURES
from Avon Books

MARY REED McCALL

THE SWEETEST SIN

AVON BOOKS

An Imprint of HarperCollins*Publishers*

AVON BOOKS
An Imprint of HarperCollins*Publishers*
10 East 53rd Street
New York, New York 10022-5299

For the members of Central New York Romance Writers, past and present, who helped me in honing my very first vision of this story so many years ago—particularly authors Maggie Shayne and Cara Summers, whose support and encouragement with recommendations and formal critiques were invaluable . . . you are all the best of the best.

And to Angela Bartelotte—when your car broke down in front of my parents' house after the CNYRW Holiday party in 1992, it was one of the most serendipitous moments of my writing life. Thank you for sharing your knowledge and your friendship . . . none of this would have come about if it hadn't been for you!

Acknowledgments

I offer my gratitude:

To the generous people affiliated with the real Eilean Donan Castle in Scotland, who sent me pamphlets and documents concerning the castle, its grounds, and its history, including information on the hereditary constables and overlords, the MacRaes and the MacKenzies . . .

To all those who offered me their time and a thorough critique of this manuscript at various stages, including Kat Simmons, Theresa Kovian, Annelise Robey, Meg Ruley, Ruth Kagle, Lyssa Keusch, the "Erie Gang", and David and Marion Reed . . .

To Dr. Wayne S. Harrison D.D.S., for professional service above and beyond the call of duty, which allowed me to finish the revisions of this book of time . . .

And finally: In memory of Amber Schalk, a faithful friend and fellow CNYRW member . . . your sunny smile and "never-quit" personality will live forever in my heart.

Prologue

Eilean Donan Castle
The Highlands, 1545

She wouldn't wake up.

Duncan MacRae crouched over his bride and stroked her cheek, his hand trembling. In all of his nineteen years, he'd never felt so afraid, so helpless. Crushed rosebuds clung to the wreath in Mairi's hair, a profane reminder of the life they'd promised to each other only moments before the MacDonells' attack turned their world upside down. The blooms' faint, overripe fragrance made him want to retch.

His bride.

Why hadn't he been able to protect her? He was heir to the mighty clan MacRae, guardians to the Dukes of Ross. He should have known that the enemy would attack— should have known that Morgana MacDonell wouldn't rest until she'd gained her vengeance.

Closing his eyes, Duncan breathed deeply. His head throbbed, and his heart ached. Christ, how had it come to this? The MacDonells had overcome the castle guards, helped by his own traitorous brother Colin in sneaking past the gate. In the battle that followed, he'd fought to lead Mairi to safety. But then he'd been struck from behind. Something must have happened to her after he'd lost consciousness, for he'd woken next to her in this cell, in the dungeons of his own keep.

And she wouldn't wake up.

Panic gripped him. His heart hammered as he stroked her cheek again, leaning close to feel her breath against his skin. Tearing a strip of his plaid, he soaked it against the wet stones and dabbed her face with it, desperate to revive her.

She made a rasping noise. The sound barely fluttered from her lips, and Duncan's heart felt as if it would explode. He wanted to clasp her to him, let his strength drain into her . . . to bring the light back into her laughter-filled eyes. Instead, he smoothed his fingers across her brow.

And then he saw it. The bloody bruise that spread back into her hairline. He breathed in sharply, a curse frozen in his throat. His touch to the spot was light, disbelieving. The hard core he'd built inside himself began to crack.

"Mairi, my God . . ." His fingers threaded into the pale silk of her hair, and he buried his face against the curve of her neck. She stirred, and Duncan went still with hope. He felt her deep shuddering sigh, and then . . . *nothing*.

Shock lanced through him, followed by a surge of denial and agony. Frantically he searched her face, holding his breath to hear any hint of hers, pressing his palm to her breast to feel the reassuring rhythm of her heart. But all was still. Silent. *Dead.*

With a cry he pulled Mairi up and held her close, rocking her back and forth, until the sound of the cell door grating open raked through him.

"See you found your prize, young MacRae."

Duncan stopped moving, his shoulders tensing. Gently, he laid Mairi back on the rotted pallet and stood up. He wanted to grab the unknown MacDonell cur and swipe the smirk from his face, but a wave of dizziness made him veer into the wall. Pain lodged in his skull, sending arrows of agony shooting into his eyes and neck. He bit back a groan, trying not to appear weak as he shook his head and steadied himself against the damp stones.

The man picked dirt from his thumbnail with a knife. "That isn't your only surprise, though." He stepped aside, and Duncan squinted in the light that streamed through the doorway.

He heard the tread of light footsteps. An elongated shadow moved across the opening, followed by its owner, a young woman, who stepped into the slash of torchlight. In the moment it took his eyes to adjust, the image of her hammered at his senses. Tall, slender, with long, fiery hair and seductively curving lips.

Morgana MacDonell. The temptress who'd destroyed his life.

"Ah, Duncan. You're not looking well." She grinned and tilted her head; the movement made a curl slide away from her breast, exposing the gilded pendant that hung round her neck. Duncan started; she wore the *Ealach* amulet. His amulet.

As if she'd read his thoughts, Morgana raised her brows, her eyes cold, flat blue. "It's mine now. It would have been ours, had you kept your promise to me." Her gaze deepened to azure, shining with excitement. "But never fear. I know the *Ealach*'s powers, and be I your wife or no, I'll be wearing it well."

Anger and the recent blow to his head prevented Duncan from speaking at first, but when he did, his voice grated with bitterness. "I never pledged myself to you, Morgana."

"Liar. I was to be your bride. You and the *Ealach* were both to be mine."

"I belonged to Mairi. You said you understood my oath to her."

"Aye, but I never accepted it." Morgana fingered the amulet again. "Now with you or not, the *Ealach* is mine, brought home after a century of possession by your cursed clan." Her eyes gleamed in the light, and Duncan was struck with the intensity of her gaze. "I'll be using it to impose my rule over all the Highlands."

A knot of fear curled at the base of his spine, temporarily masking his anger and pain. He knew the *Ealach*'s powers, though for generations none had invoked its might. Legends abounded of how it had been used in the dark times. Of its force to control the mind, to deaden the soul . . . even to kill. But no MacRae would use it for ill; each clansman took the vow before battle. Their amulet was a harbinger of prosperity, used only for good, which was why God had gifted them with possession of it.

Duncan wanted to argue with Morgana and deny her clan's claim of ownership, but he clenched his jaw, refusing to let her goad him further. It would do no good to reason. Morgana believed whatever she pleased. She always had. And that was all the more reason why he should have expected this of her—why he would never forgive himself for failing to see her plan.

She shrugged when he didn't respond and strode farther into the cell. "English guards await you above, in the hall. King Henry paid me well to deliver a fine Scottish morsel to him." She looked him straight in the eye. "While you're rotting in London Tower, I hope you think about what might have been if you had not spurned me."

She paused and stroked the amulet, her eyes sharpening to sapphire ice. Then she blinked. "Oh, and allow me to offer my condolences on your wedding day." Her lips curved with malicious pleasure. "Was it as disastrous as I've heard?"

Duncan felt his entire body tense as her high-pitched laughter tinkled over him like shards of glass. He watched mutely as her gaze took in Mairi's still form on the bed. Looking back at him, she laughed again, and the sound of it made all of the hurt, all of the helplessness and anguish he'd been feeling since this began, converge on him in one blinding flash of pure emotion. But as he lunged for her throat something slammed into the back of his head, driving daggers of pain into him, before dropping him into darkness.

Chapter 1

Thirteen years later
Dulhmeny Castle
The MacDonell stronghold

"The MacRaes! God help us, it's the wild MacRaes come upon us from the north!"

Aileana MacDonell sat in her familiar spot at her bedchamber window, twisting her hands and trying to still her heart as she looked down at the frenzy taking place below her. The woman who'd shrieked the warning ran past, apron flapping, to scoop up a child in each arm. Various other clan folk darted in the direction of the bailey tower to grab spears, shovels, and chipped swords before rushing off to join in the battle cries Aileana heard burgeoning in the distance.

For the past quarter hour, since the early morning attack began, she'd been straining to see something, to understand what was happening. And now she knew the name of their attackers.

The MacRaes.

She'd thought them all dead; they'd all but vanished from the Highlands, as far as she knew. Standing up, she paced her chamber and dug through her memory, trying to recall the last battle her clan had fought with them.

She'd been a child of nine—only a year after Morgana had died in banishment for consorting with the English. The *Ealach* amulet that her sister had stolen from the MacRaes had been the root of that last war with them. But the enemy had been vanquished. The *Ealach* had done its rightful work, bringing her clan peace. Bringing them prosperity . . .

And ensuring that Aileana remained isolated from everyone for most of the past thirteen years as its appointed keeper.

Pushing that thought aside, she paced to the window again, looking for some sign of her brothers. If only one of them would climb the wall outside her window to release her so that she could take a weapon and join in the defense of her home. Gavin and Robert used to sneak her out when Father was away. They'd run with her and tease her, never seeming to tire of plaguing her with tales of their bravery. Oh, how she craved some of their good-natured boasting now. If only Gavin would come to—

A sudden breathlessness made her sink to the edge of her bed. She clutched her stomach, awareness spreading thick in her veins, even as her fists clenched until the half-moons of her nails bit into her palms.

The amulet. Something had happened to the Ealach.

Doubled over now, she gulped breaths of air to quell the ache. When the sensation passed, she pushed herself upright. Her instincts had never been wrong before; as the amulet's keeper, her connection to it was strong. Something was amiss, but how? It rested secure as always in her chamber's specially built hiding place, having never left the haven of Dulhmeny's walls in nearly a decade and a half. Racing over to the gilded door that marked the recess in the wall, Aileana tested its lock. It held.

Curses. There was no other way to reassure herself of the amulet's safety. Unless . . .

Ignoring a mental warning that reminded her of the punishment to be had for leaving her chamber without attendants to accompany her, Aileana ran out into the hall and then to her father's rooms. Retrieving the silken cord and key from a chest near his bed, she rushed back to her chamber and fitted it in the lock. The door swung wide, revealing the sacred hollow. Its velvet cushion was empty.

"Oh Father, how could you?" Aileana's horrified whisper echoed the empty feeling in the pit of her stomach. How had he taken the *Ealach* from its place without her knowing?

Her bath. Aye, everyone knew that she was allowed to leave the main portion of her bedchamber each day at dawn to bathe in privacy. She'd heard battle sounds beginning just as she was stepping from the washtub this morn. Father must have learned of the attack sooner—

Heaven have mercy, but he'd taken the amulet from its hiding place and onto the battlefield for protection.

Aileana felt faint as she considered what would happen to her clan if the *Ealach* were lost again. She'd been told of how it was in the past, of the darkness that surrounded them when the MacRaes still held it in their evil grip. Father had reminded her more than once that her own mother's death, brought about by birthing Aileana, might have been prevented, if only the *Ealach* had been near.

A familiar pain twisted her insides, and she sat down hard on her bed. From her very first breath she'd brought grief to everyone. So it had only been right that when the amulet came back into her clan's possession, she be groomed as its keeper. She'd accepted it long ago. Learned to swallow the resentment that swelled whenever she allowed herself to consider all of the time that was lost to her forever—the normal rhythms and flow of life amongst her clansmen that she would never enjoy.

The *Ealach* provided security. It brought the Mac-Donells good fortune. Without it, life was unpredictable and terrifying, and she knew that she'd spill her own blood before she'd allow anyone or anything to threaten her clan's security again.

Bolting out into the corridor, Aileana descended the curved staircase two steps at a time. She slipped into the great hall, her gaze darting round the piles of possessions others had left behind in their hurry to seek safety or a place in the battle raging beyond the keep. She knew she risked Father's wrath in doing this, but the amulet was at stake. Her hands trembled as she stripped off her over-skirt and tunic before donning a lad's garments that she found in a heap of belongings abandoned near the hearth: a shirt, leather vest, and leggings. Lastly, she tied a plaid at her waist and tucked her long hair beneath a helmet.

Her breathing slowed, calming to a rhythm of grim determination as she walked from the keep. The sounds, scents, and tumultuous sights of the yard assailed her senses, but still she continued on. Past the gate and up the crest of the brae, she strode, in the direction of the battle sounds.

She had to find the *Ealach*, whether she risked her life

or no. It was in great danger, God help them, and the salvation of her clan depended on her ability to bring it to safety again.

Morning mist drifted across the field, blanketing the dead and dying like a mother's cooling touch. It obscured much of the carnage from Duncan MacRae's view, but nothing could block the groans and screams echoing off the cliffs. All around him moans of pain swelled in eerie chorus, making his mount stamp and snort. Glendragon skittered sideways, and Duncan tensed, pressing his knees into the stallion's sides.

His gaze swept the field with predatory efficiency. He clenched his ruined, twisted fingers within their leather gauntlet, savoring the aching wound. Its throbbing had intensified today from wielding his claymore against so much resisting bone and flesh. The threading scar on his cheek—another token from his English captors—tightened as he clenched his jaw, and he fought the urge to stroke his fingers across its whitened flesh.

Where was the devil's spawn? The MacDonell chieftain had fallen, of that he was sure. He'd seen one of his men strike the fatal blow only moments ago, straight through the MacDonell's black heart. Yet there'd been no time to search the body. The man's legions had swarmed around them, preventing Duncan from gaining his just reward.

Glendragon jerked at his bridle, demanding Duncan's attention; the stallion's powerful muscles rippled, his nostrils flaring at the scent of death. His might was leashed and awaiting his master's command, but Duncan kept him tightly reined, even as his own frustration grew.

Through thirteen years of hell in the English Tower,

he'd stayed alive for this day. Through the beatings, the cold, the pain . . . the crippling of his hand. He'd endured all of it to taste this one moment of triumph. With this attack, he'd finally initiated his revenge against the MacDonells. Now he hungered to take back the *Ealach*, to steal it from this nest of vipers and return it to its true home.

Mist floated from the cliff's edge, revealing several corpses sprawled on the field. *There.* The bitter tang of vengeance filled Duncan's mouth, and savage joy flared through him. The MacDonell chieftain's body still steamed from the heat of battle; it lay in a death-pose next to his shield.

But as Duncan spurred Glendragon toward the remains, a young soldier darted forward. Without a moment's caution the intruder leaned over the body and embraced it before pulling open its shirt to grasp at something inside.

"Nay!" Duncan's growl of rage rolled across the battlefield. The thief looked up, startled, then stood and wrenched off his helmet . . . freeing a cascading mass of red-gold hair.

In that instant disbelief washed over Duncan, and his blood beat faster. *Morgana? The murdering bitch was here on the battlefield?* But he'd learned that she was dead, brought low in banishment not long after betraying him to the English. Nudging his stallion closer, he stared down at his mortal enemy, unwilling to accept the truth his eyes beheld. That face, exquisite as ever, the slender build, the flaming hair . . .

Raw hatred spilled into the battle lust surging through his veins, igniting it with lethal potency; his sword arm tensed as he raised it in preparation to swing the death blow that would finally bring Morgana MacDonell to her just reward. But before he could act, she took several steps toward him, stilling him as effectively as if she'd shot an arrow through his heart.

Dark honey eyes stared up at him—eyes as golden brown as Morgana's had been piercing blue. They shone luminous with grief that the bloodthirsty sorceress would have been incapable of feeling. This wasn't Morgana, but a stunning likeness of her . . . all but for the eyes and the emotions that played freely across her delicate features.

"May you roast in hell for what you've done here, murdering MacRae!"

Duncan's impression of tender femininity vanished.

Her body shook with pent-up feeling. "Come and finish it then. You've killed the chieftain, now slay his seed as well!"

Calm filled Duncan. *Morgana's sister*. Of course. This one had been no more than a chit those years ago—too young to have taken part in the massacre against his clan. Sweeping his gaze over her, he scowled. "I seek not your life, woman, only the amulet. Give it to me and go in peace."

"Peace?" Her face twisted into a mask of fury. "What know you of God's peace?" The gilded talisman dangled from her grip, swinging on its golden chain as she taunted him. "I swear on the blood of my father that I will forfeit my life before I relinquish the *Ealach* to you."

A dangerous cold seeped from Duncan's chest to the tips of his gauntleted fingers. The amulet was his. He'd be denied no more. "Cease, woman," he thundered. "Give it to me or face retribution when I take it from you." He urged Glendragon forward, threatening to fulfill his words with action.

"Then do your worst, MacRae. But I'll not be standing by for the kill." Her eyes glowed with defiance, and every muscle of her slim form seemed to go rigid. Tense.

Too late, Duncan realized her intent. He followed her gaze over the cliff's edge, down the precipice to the cold, gray surf that crashed to the rocks below. Suddenly, she whirled and raced toward the ledge. Duncan's wordless roar filled the air, and he launched himself off Glendragon, charging forward to catch her.

But she was too quick. He reached out, trying to grab her, desperate to stop her from going over the cliff . . .

And wound up holding nothing as she threw herself from the bluff.

The moment seemed to spin itself out into eternity, slowing to an agonizing string of images that burned forever into Duncan's soul. Tightness filled his chest when he saw her graceful arms stretching out, saw her hair streaming behind her like a wave of silken fire. In the next instant he glimpsed her face with its wide-eyed, haunted expression, her mouth opened in a soundless shriek of terror as the wind tipped her over, and then over again in her plummet toward the deadly surf.

And as she fell, a shaft of sun burst through the clouds. It glinted for just a moment off the amulet she held tightly in her hand, before it disappeared with her beneath the punishing, pounding waves.

Chapter 2

Duncan's senses exploded, his emotions coiling into shock as he peered over the rocky ledge. The woman chose death over relinquishing the *Ealach*? Waves surged, and white foam rolled with crushing force against the narrow band of jagged rocks lining the beach. There was no sign of her.

The salty air burned his nostrils as he stalked the precipice, and he felt a grinding sensation in his stomach. *Those eyes.* Those wide, haunted eyes. He couldn't erase the image of them from his mind. He told himself it was just the aftermath of battle. But the sensation snaked at his gut, relentless, harping.

Curse her. She was a reckless harridan, a witless shrew . . .

A frightened, helpless female.

He fought the swell of guilt twisting his belly. She'd resisted, damn it. And she was the enemy. Morgana's sister. The thought stilled his uneasiness, settling ice into his veins once more. He had to regroup. His mission here was unfinished.

Swinging astride Glendragon, he rode onto the battlefield. The day was won, but chaos stilled reigned, and it took time to find Kinnon. His cousin sat with several other warriors on the bluff, his tunic stripped from his torso to tend a wound to his shoulder. Blood seeped from between his fingers, and he looked up in surprise, wincing when Duncan pushed his hand away to tie a makeshift bandage with a strip torn from his shirt.

"This should hold for an hour or two. Come. We've work to do."

Kinnon frowned and ran his hand through his sweat-dampened hair. Even matted from battle, strands of it shone white-blond in the sun that had burned away the morning mist. "God's head, cousin, do you never rest?"

"Nay," Duncan muttered, quelling his impatience with action. He grasped Kinnon's good arm and pulled him to his feet. "Now find Gil, Ewen and Hamish, and meet me at the base of the bluff. I'll explain when we get there." He tossed Glendragon's reins to a soldier and began to stalk across the field, pausing only long enough to half turn and growl, "Hurry."

There was no time to waste. For sure as the English were bastards, he and his men had a long day of searching ahead of them. And he didn't intend to give up his quest until he had his prize in hand.

Warmth radiated up her palm to the rest of her body. Cautiously, Aileana opened her eyelids a crack. The sun glistened, fat and yellow in the robin-egg sky, so beautiful that for a moment she forgot what had brought her to this place. Then memory slammed home, making her breath catch and her head throb.

The Ealach.

A tingle against her fingers made her hand clench, and she felt the amulet's reassuring weight. Thank God she'd managed to hold onto it. It had saved her, sure. Just thinking about her bold action on the battlefield made her feel like swooning again.

Struggling to a sitting position, Aileana pushed the damp weight of her hair from her face and stared at the *Ealach*. Its intricate gold setting remained unharmed but for the wet of the ocean, and the opalescent surface of its stone winked back at her with a thousand colored lights. It seemed to know something, though she remembered little after the sensation of falling through the air and into the cold embrace of the water.

She should be dead.

But she was alive, and she had to move quickly to protect herself and the *Ealach* from the marauding MacRaes. Aileana toyed with the idea that they would think she'd perished in the fall, but she couldn't take any chances.

A thrill of fear ran down her back at the expression she remembered seeing in the MacRae leader's cold gray eyes. He'd used his gaze to pin her, his aura of unyielding power magnified by the jagged scar that ran down the length of what otherwise would have been a face of almost flawless masculine beauty. He'd seemed an unholy, avenging angel, his shoulder-length, golden hair swirling wildly around his face.

Shuddering, she shook her head and stood as she slipped the *Ealach*'s chain around her neck. The pendant nestled between her breasts for only a moment before a dizzying swirl of images spun her into a vision of the amulet's last resting place. Screams of agony and moans of death . . .

Father. Turbulent emotion swelled in her heart. In her mind's eye she saw him lying there, mangled, his dignity stripped away as surely as his lifeblood soaked the ground beneath his body. He'd been snatched away before his time, before she'd been able to make him see that she wasn't like Morgana. That she could be worthy of his love and pride.

Her jaw clenched with a fierce, welcoming burn. She pressed the amulet close, feeling the metal heat upon her skin. One thing was certain; the MacRae devil could rot in hell before she'd let him steal back what Father and her clansmen had died to protect.

A new energy flowed through Aileana's limbs, spurring her on in her task. Ignoring the ache in her legs, she clambered up the bank. Tufts of hardy grass sprouted among the rocks, and she glimpsed splashes of purple as well. A violent shiver shook her. Wrapping her arms round herself, she peered into the intense blue of the sky. It spread above her, wide and open.

The countryside was beautiful, just as she remembered from her days of childhood freedom. But where would she go? She had to hide the *Ealach*; that much was certain.

Struggling to regain her sense of direction, she squinted and surveyed the landscape. The area seemed familiar. If instinct served, she wasn't far from an ancient rowan grove that Morgana had shown her long ago. She'd been just a little girl who'd idolized her older sister, then. It had been shortly before the crisis, before Morgana had stumbled into the temptations of sorcery— a time when they'd often found time to wrap cold partridge and bread in cloths and carry it out to eat in the shelter of the rowan trees.

If she could find the grove again, she could dig a recess there to hide the *Ealach*.

Then, once the amulet was safe, she'd search out one of the clans friendly to her people, to the east of Dulhmeny. But she'd have to find them soon. For summer or no, the gusting winds shook the trees like an old woman's bones.

Aye, she needed to hide the *Ealach* and gain refuge with another clan before nightfall, or she knew that the MacRaes would soon be adding her lifeless body to their bloody list of dead.

Duncan cursed under his breath as he knelt to examine the prints below him. A female's step, small and light. His men had scoured the beach, looking for her body washed up to shore, but it seemed she had eluded him again. This was all that remained, her footprints leading up the beach and into the woodland.

The MacDonell woman was alive.

A spark of relief lit in Duncan's chest, but he extinguished it with brutal force. She held what was his, and he didn't relish the cat and mouse game she played with him. He stood, grasping a handful of sand, and flung it into the lapping maw of the ocean.

"Kinnon, take your men through the wood from the northern point. Hamish, approach from the south. I'll be taking Gil, Ewen, and the others to follow her trail from here. We need to flush her from her hiding place."

The men nodded, their faces solemn. The air crackled with tension, as if each warrior sensed the importance of this hunt to his chieftain. Everyone began to disperse, and Kinnon directed his men to retrieve their horses. Then he came toward Duncan.

"Perhaps it would be better for me to be coming with you, cousin. You've the look of the Tower in your eyes right now, and it wouldn't serve for you to be too rough with the woman, be she a MacDonell or no."

Duncan pulled his gaze up to Kinnon's face, reading the worry couched there. He didn't blame him. They were of an age, and Kinnon knew him well. Truth be known, he was the only person that Duncan would consider trusting with his life.

After Morgana had ravaged their clan in the attack, Kinnon had approached their overlord, the MacKenzie Chief, for help. The MacKenzie had refused, wanting to keep the peace, and so Kinnon had moved on his own, pulling together enough surviving MacRae clansmen to try to free Duncan from the English. But he'd only been captured himself for his pains.

The English bastards had imprisoned Kinnon at York, and by the time he'd gained his release, it had been too late to do Duncan any good. Kinnon had had to focus his attention on rebuilding the clan, on trying to make it strong and whole again. Eventually, Queen Elizabeth had taken the throne and released all of her Scottish prisoners, Duncan among them. He'd returned home only months ago to find his clan still struggling to regain their fortunes and their pride, but alive and safe, thanks to Kinnon.

Unblinking, his cousin pressed his point. "What say you, Duncan? I can appoint one of the men to lead my group so that I can ride with you."

Duncan shook his head. "Never fear. I'll not be harming the woman . . ." He paused to check Glendragon's bridle before glancing at his cousin again, ". . . unless she refuses to give me the amulet."

Kinnon blanched. The wind ruffled through his sunbright hair, making him look younger, and he moved as if to stop him. "Hold, now, Duncan. You know I cannot let you do something you'll be regretting later."

Grim satisfaction lifted the corners of Duncan's

mouth, and he slapped his cousin's back. "Ah, Kinnon MacRae, what would yer own mother be sayin' about havin' as gullible a man as ye fer a son?" He savored the feel of the brogue rolling off his tongue. In the Tower he'd been beaten senseless more than once for speaking Gaelic outright. It had incited the guards to a fury, and many of the other Scottish prisoners had learned to confine themselves to English if they spoke at all. But Duncan had refused. It had been the only method of rebellion open to him, and no matter what the physical cost, it had helped to keep his soul free.

Kinnon stood still, stupefied for a moment; then he threw his entire weight against Duncan, knocking him off balance. His chuckle rumbled from deep in his belly. "Sure the evil fairies had a hand in makin' a worthless wretch like ye, Duncan MacRae. Take yourself off, then. But dinna say you were lackin' the offer of my help."

Duncan righted himself and gave a quick nod, more pleased at Kinnon's concern than he'd ever admit. He took a deep breath of the clean Highland air, filling his lungs, as if its freshness could remove all memory of the Tower's stench. Looking up, he checked the position of the sun. Just past noon. There was still plenty of time to pick up the scent and hunt down his prey. With a glance at his men, he started up the stony embankment.

Intense pride burned in his breast. He was Duncan MacRae, chieftain of his clan. Kinnon was fiercely loyal to him, as were all of these warriors. They'd risked their futures to come together once again under his leadership. They were counting on him.

And that was all the more reason for using any means necessary to seize the *Ealach* back from the thieving MacDonell wench who'd taken it.

* * *

Aileana tried to scrape away the dirt that clumped cool and gritty beneath her nails. Straightening to her knees, she stretched her back for the first time since her escape from the MacRae leader more than two hours ago. Her work here pleased her. No passerby would guess that behind the leaves and moss rested a secret grotto, or that within the shallow cave lay the precious *Ealach*. Wiping her hands on her rumpled clothes, she edged back into the brush, promising herself that she'd return to get the amulet later when she was sure she wasn't being followed.

She moved quickly from the spot, careful to avoid leaving cracked branches or crushed vegetation. But after several minutes of ducking and hiding, she failed to see any sign that she was nearing an allied clan. Spotting another leafy copse of trees ahead, she decided to creep into the shadows to reconsider her plan.

Bark scratched her as she crouched near a trunk, then she settled onto the soggy earth. Peering through the branches, she could just see a sliver of blue sky above her. When she looked ahead, however, it was as if a magic transformation had taken place in the forest. Sun slanted into a tiny glade less than twenty paces away, beckoning her with warmth. Her heart rolled with a sickening thud. It was an accustomed sensation, just like being back home, gazing from the confinement of her chamber to a freedom she wasn't permitted to enjoy.

She struggled against the temptation to dart into the little clearing. To just this once dance in the sun or scamper in the leaves. A niggling voice echoed in her head, reminding her that she could do whatever she wanted now. There were no walls to hold her, no barriers now other than those of her own mind. With the *Ealach* concealed, she was free to go where she chose.

But what if it was dangerous? She chewed her lip, trying to weigh the harm in indulging herself. A swift glance in either direction assured her that nothing was amiss. In truth, she most likely feared for naught. The MacRae devil couldn't possibly think her alive now.

A flare of excitement shot to the ends of her fingers and toes. She would do it. Ignoring the quaking of her stomach, she scrambled into the clearing and sat in the middle of it, soaking up the sights, sounds and smells of the woodland as if she'd never get enough. For this one, perfect moment she was free! Free to move and explore. To dig in the dirt or lay in the sun. Free and—

Alone.

A hollow ache bloomed in her with that grim reminder, quelling her enthusiasm. She pulled her knees to her chest. Saints above, what was she thinking? She had nowhere to go, no one to protect her. And it was still possible that she was being followed. Sitting in this clearing left her exposed. Vulnerable.

Aileana threw herself back into the cover of brush at the clearing's edge. Only then did she allow herself to take a breath. She'd been so foolish! Never again could she forget her circumstances. Father was dead, and Gavin and Robert might well be, too. Who knew if any of her clan had survived?

Heat prickled her eyelids. Her brothers had been the only spot of joy in her life. She couldn't bear the thought of them lying crumpled and wounded. *Or slain like Father*. Her breath came faster, and the pressure behind her eyes swelled.

Swallowing hard, Aileana rubbed her hand across her nose. She wouldn't cry. She had to be strong to make her clan proud. She'd figure out what to do. She'd go and—

A tingle shivered up her spine, despite the protection

of her hiding place. She'd heard footsteps on the ground nearby, she was sure of it. A twig crackled to the left of the clearing, and Aileana's gaze darted to the spot. Something flashed in the sunlight. Something metallic, long and sharp. Her heart thudded in her chest as she tried to inch farther back into the concealing trees. Her cursed hair would be like a beacon in the light. She might as well jump up and down and wave her arms.

Something dug into her thigh as she slid along the ground, and she tasted blood as she bit her lip to keep from yelping. Dragon's breath, how could she have been so stupid? *Never underestimate your foe.* The words rang shrill and clear in her head, Gavin's warning from their childhood games with claymores echoing too late to be heeded. She'd broken a fundamental rule, and now she would pay.

She felt blood, warm and wet on her leg from where the stick had gouged her, but she ignored the sting as she inched toward the copse. Hair rose on the back of her neck and her breath froze.

"There she is!"

The cry pierced the glen, and Aileana's muscles bunched into a knot of energy an instant before she shot to her feet and ran.

She'd never make it. At any second she expected to feel the cutting rip of an arrow between her shoulder blades. But then, somehow, she was within the shelter of the trees . . . and flat on her face. A lancing pain shot from her ankle up her leg, and she rolled to her side with a gasp. The root that had caught her foot looked innocuous, but its gnarly strength had been enough to make her see stars.

Biting her lip, Aileana dragged herself through the damp leaves, groping her way to a hollowed-out trunk that was tipped on its side. If she could just wedge herself inside it, she might remain undetected. Her blood pounded and her breath came ragged as she started to dig her way into the hiding place.

The fertile smell of rotted wood filled her nose. She didn't hear anything but her own labored breathing, until a deep voice behind her echoed, "I'd hate to have my men shoot that pretty backside of yours, but if you don't stop burrowing like a hunted fox, you can be sure you'll be serving as their trophy for the day."

Chapter 3

Duncan watched her go still with a twinge of regret. But the warmth caused by the sight of her wriggling bottom began to recede as he focused on the green and blue bit of plaid draped over that delectable portion of her. She was a MacDonell and his enemy. He couldn't allow himself to forget it.

Though he stifled the urge to help her up as she struggled to stand, the sight of the blood smeared across her leg gave him pause.

"You're bleeding." With a nod, he sent Ewen for a dampened cloth. When he returned, Duncan held it out to her. "Here. Clean it so we can assess the wound."

"There is no wound," Aileana mumbled. "It's only a scratch."

Duncan studied her. She looked much different from the shrieking force of nature she'd been on the battlefield; now she stood still before him, tight-lipped and pale, though struggling to appear unshaken by his formidable presence or that of his men. Still, she wasn't as good at pretense as he was at reading people; his years in the Tower had honed that skill razor sharp. She was favoring one ankle, and her eyes were dimmed from pain and fear.

He held out the cloth again. "Clean the *scratch*, then. Now."

Clamping her mouth tight, she grabbed the rag and began to dab her thigh. He heard her hissed intake of breath as it brushed across the cut. Though his jaw tightened, he refused to assist. He'd probably get nothing but the sting of her nails down his cheek if he tried.

When she finished, she looked up, holding the soiled cloth between her finger and thumb. "What do you want me to do with this, then?" Her voice lilted with sarcasm, though the effect was ruined by the dirt on her face and the dead leaves hanging from her hair.

Duncan took the rag and tossed it back to Ewen. "We have unresolved matters between us, woman. Give me the amulet. I'll wait no longer."

"I will be addressed by my proper name. I am Aileana of the Donells."

Irritation filled him at her retort, only to abate when her eyes welled with restrained grief.

"My father was chieftain of our clan before you slew him, and I am the keeper of the *Ealach*. No one will be touching it save me." She swept a glance over him and added with a reckless tip of her chin, "Especially not the leader of the wild, murdering MacRaes."

He might have admired her rash courage in other circumstances, but not now when she was withholding what was so clearly his. Taking two steps forward, he grasped the front of her tunic and pulled her to him. His voice was dangerously quiet. "Hear this, *woman*. I tire of your insults. The amulet is mine, and you'll be giving it to me now—or I'll be forced to find other means of getting it from you."

"Then you'd be spitting in the wind, because even if I wished, I could not give it to you."

"Why?"

"Because I do not have it."

"You lie."

She cast a bitter smile at him. "I learned long ago not to lie, MacRae. And I make this vow . . . as long as I have breath, your murdering grasp will not be touching the *Ealach* again."

Cold fury swept through Duncan, and he thrust her away from him. She thought to mock him? It was a dangerous game she played, far more dangerous than she knew. For thirteen years he'd endured taunts and insults from his English captors. He'd felt the slashing degradation of their words even more often than the sting of their fists, and he'd never bear the brunt of it willingly again.

Utter silence fell over the glen as his clansmen shifted uneasily. Duncan willed his rage to ebb enough to speak. "If you do not give me the *Ealach* right now, Aileana MacDonell, you're going to be a very sorry lassie."

After a moment Aileana's chin tilted up another fraction, but she shook her head nay.

Duncan stared at her in disbelief. She had to be bluffing.

And his bluff would be better.

He paused for only an instant before motioning for Ewen to approach. "Strip her for a search."

Duncan watched Aileana's gaze dart to Ewen and then back to him, as if measuring his intent. He allowed the cold, hard look he leveled at her to hold a flicker of interest and was gratified to see the careful mask she'd made of her face begin to disintegrate.

But the fear that replaced it made his fists clench and his teeth grate. Hell's fire, he'd not wanted it this way, but she'd left him no choice. Still, when she made a choking sound and squeezed her eyes shut, it sent a sickening stab into his chest. Cursing himself under his breath, Duncan struggled to remain firm as Ewen took hold of the length of plaid wrapped round her torso. When her tunic was unlaced, her eyes snapped open.

She remained silent, her stare fixed upon his face. He tried to focus on that part of her as well, struggling to calm the disturbing feelings that rose in him as the rest of her clothing fell away. Except for the cut and some smudges of dirt, she was perfection. He felt an involuntary surge of desire when his gaze fell on the pink tips of her breasts, tightened to succulent raspberries in the open air. His gaze slipped lower.

It was a mistake.

The dusting of cinnamon-hued curls at the joining of her thighs made him shift to accommodate the sudden, heated swelling of his manhood. He snapped his stare back up to her face, trying to force his mind to a different tact . . . a more rational plane of thought. The Mac-Donell wench had thwarted him again, he reminded himself; she was undaunted by his attempt to subdue her. And the *Ealach* still wasn't his.

That knowledge killed the last remnants of lust. His blood cooled, and he crossed his arms over his chest as sanity returned. Tipping his head mockingly, he said, "Well done, lass. Your display is worthy of the most sought after harlot in the land." He curled his lips in a wicked smile. "But like any bit of Eve's flesh, you're heir to deception. Perhaps I'll be instigating a more *thorough* search to—"

"Duncan!" Kinnon rode hell-bent into the glen, his horse sweating and panting. He pulled the stallion to a halt and swung to the ground, calling out, "Gavin Mac-Donell's been taken at Connor's Crossing. He's wounded, but he's alive and under guard at Dulhmeny."

Gavin MacDonell. The name cut through Duncan's heart with the swiftness of a sharpened blade. Behind it rose the choking hatred so familiar to him now. Having revenge on that deceptive whelp would be almost as fulfilling as it would have been to see Morgana's head on a pike. Gavin MacDonell had been his sister's willing supporter in the attack that had taken Mairi's life, and Duncan wouldn't pass up the chance to see him pay for it.

Turning sharply, Duncan strode toward Kinnon. His cousin's stallion pranced and pawed, but Duncan took hold of the reins and stilled him. He saw Kinnon notice Aileana's condition, saw the look of pained embarrassment flick over his features.

"Have you no shame, man?" Kinnon muttered hoarsely, his blue eyes snapping with anger. "She's standing there naked for all the world to see!"

"It was necessary."

Duncan handed Kinnon the calmed horse's reins and walked to Glendragon, tethered at the edge of the glen. "But I've no time to discuss my lack of morals, cousin. My meeting with Gavin MacDonell is long overdue." Duncan nodded for Ewen to return Aileana's plaid and tunic before mounting Glendragon. "Bring the woman back with you to the castle."

He didn't trust himself to look back as he wheeled Glendragon around and thundered from the glen, concentrating instead on the rhythmic beat of his stallion's hooves. This first battle for the amulet might be lost, but Gavin MacDonell was his. For years he'd imagined the pleasure he'd get from running a claymore through the man's heart; now that the moment of reckoning was here, the thought filled him with nothing but a grim sense of purpose. He was counting on the act to ease some of the pain that ate away at his heart . . . pain from his own brother Colin's betrayal, pain from the memory of Mairi's lifeless body—pain from his constant feelings of helplessness and rage.

Revenge would surely bring balm to the bitterness in his soul. When every last guilty MacDonell had been made to pay, he would find freedom from the tortuous memories. He had to.

It was the only means of salvation left open to him.

Aileana watched Duncan storm from the glen, and she shuddered. Her limited knowledge of the man told her that Gavin's confrontation with him was going to be much worse than what she'd just endured. Still, she felt a wild flash of joy in knowing that her brother lived. And he might remain unharmed, if she could just reason with the MacRae. With a yank she tied the ends of her plaid, voicing no protest when Kinnon helped her astride a horse. The sooner she got to Gavin, the better.

Soon the rounded turrets of Dulhmeny's outer walls loomed over the hillside. The keep rose square, straight and tall from the center, jutting proudly in the afternoon sky. Without pause Kinnon motioned for his men to follow, and in single file they rode through the castle's massive, curved gatehouse and into the yard beyond.

Aileana maintained her silence until they reached the great hall. It looked as it always had, the crimson wall hangings impressive under vaulted ceilings, fresh rushes on the floor, clean and sweet smelling. An ache settled in her heart. How could everything appear the same when their lives had changed forever? Father would never again preside over the annual festivities here. The familiar rhythms of her clan and her community were vanished forever beneath the MacRaes' brutal carnage.

A movement at the end of the hall caught her gaze. Duncan sat in the banquet seat of honor, his muscular legs jutting from beneath his tunic, his leather-covered feet resting on the table with casual disregard. Her hands tightened to fists. The insolent wretch thought nothing of defiling everything he touched.

"You and your kind might favor the habits of beasts, Duncan MacRae, but my clan does not," she snapped from across the hall. "Kindly remove yourself and your filthy boots from the head of our table."

"It is all right, Aileana. I invited him to sit."

Gasping, Aileana swiveled in the direction of the voice; a shock of relief thrilled to the ends of her toes. Robert! Both of her brothers lived. With a stifled cry she ran to him.

"You're safe! But where's Gavin? I worried that you might be on the field like Father . . ." Tears overwhelmed her, and she cupped his face in her hands. Robert smiled, his eyes tired, his cheeks still smeared with the dirt and blood of battle.

Taking her hands in his own, he gently pressed them to her sides and indicated that she should face the MacRae. She argued against it with her expression, but Robert's calm won out, and she finally clenched her jaw and turned to the hated intruder.

Duncan remained in the same infuriating position as before, feet up and relaxed, seemingly oblivious to the affront she'd offered him and his people; he even rocked a little in the chair. But when he saw that he had their attention, he eased his legs from the table and stood with slow, arrogant grace.

Though his gaze bored through her, he directed his comment to Kinnon. "When I told you to bring the woman to the castle, I should have mentioned that you'd be wanting to gag her. She has the annoying habit of harping like a shrew, with no wit for when to be silent."

"You've no need to insult my sister, MacRae," Robert grated.

"If she'd keep a civil tongue in her head there'd be no need to say anything to her at all," Duncan retorted.

Aileana bit her lip until she was sure it bled, held back by the gentle pressure of her brother's hand on her arm. A familiar, impotent fire filled her chest. She wanted to wipe the smirk from the MacRae's face and to put him in his place—preferably in the vat of pig swill out in the yard where he belonged. But she quelled her emotions as she always had, masking them behind a blank expression.

"But insulting your sister isn't why I'm here, as well you know," Duncan said, nodding to two of his men near the door, and they exited, only to return shortly with another man between them. Aileana's stomach dropped at the sight. Gavin looked more dead than alive, half-standing between the two MacRaes. Blood ran down his face to soak his plaid.

"I've a score to settle with your brother. I'll be taking him now, and I'll return to finish what remains between us when the deed is done."

"Hold, MacRae, in the name of peace," Robert said, taking a step forward as if to forestall him. "Take a share of what is in our coffers. Take that portion of land which abuts your own holdings. But leave Gavin with us. He'll do you no more harm, I promise you."

"His is a blood debt and cannot be satisfied with such things."

The cold in his voice tingled through Aileana like ice.

As the MacRae started to exit the hall, she lunged forward. "Hold, please! At least allow us to prepare ourselves for a moment before you take our brother out to be slaughtered."

Duncan stopped, suspicion clear in his stormy gray eyes.

"It cannot hurt you to wait another few minutes, man," Robert added, picking up on her lead to stall for more time. "You've waited thirteen years already."

With a scowl, Duncan finally nodded his acquiescence.

Moving with Robert to a place out of everyone's hearing, Aileana took his hands in her own, almost too overcome with grief to concentrate on anything else. "Why?" she whispered. "Why would he want to harm Gavin so? It's a cowardly thing to fight a wounded man when the battle is finished!"

"There is much you do not know, Aileana . . . much we kept from you." Robert's expression darkened. "In truth the MacRae has cause for dispute against Gavin. Our brother joined Morgana those many years ago when she attacked his clan. You were but a wee lass, and I was away, getting schooled in Edinburgh when it happened. Can you recall any of it?"

Vague memories flickered in Aileana's mind. They'd always troubled her enough so that she'd pushed them away when she happened to think of them before. Now she wished she'd been more vigilant.

"I—I recall bits of what happened."

Robert cast a glance at Duncan. "We do not have much time. The MacRae wants our brother's life as payment for the wrongs he committed."

"But we cannot let him take Gavin to be murdered!"

"I confess I know not what to do," Robert said, looking pale and suddenly ill-suited for the role of laird so recently vacated by their father. "Our men have been defeated on the field, and I—"

"I have an idea," Aileana interrupted in desperation, her stomach twisting with the thought, even knowing as she did that there was little choice in the matter.

"What is it? Quickly, Aileana, tell me."

She swallowed. "Perhaps we can establish a peace between our clans."

"How? The MacRae rejected my offers of wealth and land."

"It can be achieved through a marriage. A wedding between the MacRae and a MacDonell would go far in compelling him to be more reasonable about this."

"*Marriage?*" Robert looked at her as if she'd grown a third eye. "What self-respecting MacDonell woman would be fool enough to agree to marry with the leader of the wild Mac . . ." His voice trailed off as understanding hit him, and he pulled back as if she'd struck him. "Please, don't say you're thinking of *yourself*, Aileana. Bind yourself to the MacRae?" He was reacting as if she'd suggested he let her stretch her neck on the English king's block—something she supposed might not prove to be all that much more awful than what she was proposing. "I'll not allow it. It would be shameful—especially for you, the laird's daughter and keeper of the amulet."

"And yet our brother will die if you do not at least consider it."

Aileana's quiet reminder seemed to stifle Robert's remaining protests. His mouth clamped shut, and he looked at her as if seeing her for the first time. "God, Aileana— marry the *MacRae?*" he echoed, as if he couldn't believe she was truly considering the possibility.

She nodded, steeling herself to see this through. It was always the same; she would make a sacrifice for the sake of her family and clan, though even she had to admit that marrying the MacRae went beyond what she'd ever dreamed would be required of her. Her mind almost refused to grasp the concept. Yet if the clans declared peace, Gavin's life would surely be spared.

She twisted to view the cursed subject of their conversation. He leaned against the table, his arms folded across his chest, an expression of annoyance darkening his features. He was a formidable man, tall and powerful-looking, with the gold-flecked hair and chiseled jaw that marked most of his kinsmen. From what she'd seen, the MacRae was a force to be reckoned with. Life would be nothing but misery with him, to be sure.

And yet their choices seemed few. If nothing was done, Gavin would suffer a terrible fate; married or no, she could at least survive. And there was a slim possibility that she might prosper as Duncan's wife, if he could be convinced to take their bargain.

At that moment, the object of her thoughts clenched his fists and pushed away from the table's edge. When he stalked toward them, she got the distinct impression of a thundercloud about to burst.

Her chance at prosperity suddenly seemed remote.

Before the MacRae could reach them, Aileana faced Robert again whispering her insistence that he accept her plan. Revulsion almost choked her, but she reminded herself that Gavin's life hung in the balance. She would survive as the MacRae's wife if he agreed to have her. At least she hoped that she would.

When Duncan reached them he growled, "Enough. It's time to finish this."

"That you deserve repayment for the harm that was inflicted on you is clear, MacRae."

Duncan's gaze snapped to Robert, uncertainty and distrust written in every hard, sculpted line of his face. "You're *agreeing* with my claim against your brother?"

Robert nodded. "I know you were wronged. But Morgana was a dark influence upon the youth that Gavin was those many years ago. Because of that, I'm asking you to have compassion, though I would not ask you to go empty handed. I have a proposition."

"Explain," Duncan said. Aileana saw a muscle jump in his cheek, and she would have sworn that his gaze grew several degrees colder.

"A peace between our clans would help to undo the wrongs that have been committed on both sides. You were attacked most unfairly those many years ago. Today, we mourn the death of our chieftain, my father, along with countless other loyal and true MacDonells."

Duncan clenched his jaw again, but said nothing.

Aileana watched Robert's fingers twisting behind his back. Sympathy filled her at the knowledge of how difficult this was for him; he was trying to forget his own concern for Gavin's safety, while suffering the frustration of knowing that he was going to offer her as bait to their sworn enemy. Pride surged in her breast. Her brother displayed strength of spirit in front of the evil tyrant, and it helped her to stand bravely beside him.

"I propose an offering for peace." Robert paused, and then spoke each remaining word as if it was a precious pearl. "I will give you our Aileana's hand in marriage in exchange for Gavin's life."

There, it was said. Aileana lifted her chin higher, her even expression calculated to show that she knew full well her bride-value. A man like Duncan MacRae would need to search far and wide for a willing woman with bloodlines more noble than her own.

The MacRae remained silent, his face immovable granite, his eyes deepening from gray to icy flint. The only sign that he'd heard came in the twitch of a muscle near his temple. For a moment, Aileana thought that he would ignore Robert's offer and add to the insult by walking from the hall without another word. But then she watched in fascinated horror as his expression changed—to what, she wasn't certain. Perhaps sharpened was the best way to describe it.

With careful, measured steps he approached her and cradled her chin in his firm grip. His leather glove felt warm and smooth against her skin, making a tingle of raw sensation sweep through her. Her gaze fixed to his sensual lips as they edged upward. But instead of relief, his smile made her feel captured. Frozen in place.

Wordlessly, his hand drifted from her cheek to her shoulder; he raised a tendril of her hair and rubbed it between his finger and thumb. Through the numbness, a dark thought began to edge its way into the recesses of her mind. It wriggled and twisted, forcing itself into her consciousness until it became too strong to ignore. Then it burst upon her with the turbulence of an impending storm.

The bastard was inspecting her like a sow at market.

Aileana gasped and her cheeks burned. But before she could react, his hands slid down her sides to her hips, his touch bold, testing her flesh with unmistakable meaning. It was a show put on for the others, she knew; he had already seen her unclothed in the glen, and that made it all the worse.

With a guttural cry, Aileana shoved at him and stepped back. He didn't move. His eyes glinted with laughter, a deeper smile quirking his arrogant mouth . . . and her temper snapped. She whipped her arm upward, intending to slap him hard enough to make him see stars, but he reached out and grabbed her hand, stopping her.

"Not a very docile sacrifice, are you, lassie?" Duncan murmured for her ears alone, though his deliberate movements could be seen by all as he pressed her arm to her side again firmly.

Robert looked ready to throttle him, clearly struggling to hold himself in control for Gavin's sake as he paused before muttering again, "So what say you, MacRae? Will you be taking my sister to wife or not?"

So great was Aileana's fury that she almost didn't hear Duncan's response. But his answer gradually seeped through, making the blood in her veins congeal.

"Your sister is attractive enough. My own eyes told me as much earlier today in the glen. And it's true I need a woman to warm my bed."

With a nod of decision, he leaned forward and directed a glare at Robert. "Agreed, MacDonell. I'll spare your brother's life in exchange for taking possession of your sister. But I'll not take her as wife." He flicked his silver gaze to her. "I'll take her as leman."

Robert's stupefaction matched hers, it seemed, though his lasted but an instant. With a bellow of rage, he lunged at Duncan, only to be yanked to a stop by three MacRaes who'd been standing behind him. Aileana watched the struggle as if in a dream; she shifted her gaze and saw Duncan shrug, saw him nod for his men to drag Gavin from the castle, saw him move toward the huge, arched portal at the end of the great hall . . .

Her palms felt clammy. The image flashed through her mind of what her life would be like as a social outcast, reviled and scorned, isolated by walls more impenetrable than those erected around her as the *Ealach*'s keeper. Yet she knew she must speak before the MacRae vanished through the door, taking Gavin with him. Swallowing the dry ball in her throat, she took two steps forward.

"Wait," she whispered.

The MacRae didn't hear her. He kept walking, his stride inexorable, his hands clenched into fists of violence and hate.

"Wait, I said!" Her command bounced from the stone walls of the hall, its echo fading to utter silence.

Duncan had stopped at the authority in her voice. Now he turned with slow deliberation. His head tilted slightly down and to the side, and she felt a sharp piercing sensation in the area of her heart when his gaze locked with hers.

"You dare to forestall me longer?"

"I stopped you because I—" she faltered, twisting her fingers in her plaid, "—because I wish to accept your terms of agreement."

Duncan stiffened, staring at her in silence, while Robert clamored protests. Aileana simply shook her head and held firm.

Shifting his weight forward, Duncan bridged the distance between them. When they stood less than two paces apart, he came to a halt. "The agreement is for you to come with me as *leman*. You will hold none of the privileges of wife, though I will be taking a wife later. You will still be required to remain with me, to use or discard as I see fit." He knew his words were harsh, but he wanted them to be, to ensure no misunderstanding in their bargain.

Aileana didn't answer right away. She was looking at a point above his shoulder, and as he waited, he saw the color of her cheeks intensify. Finally, she nodded. "I understand."

Duncan stood still, unable to pull his gaze from her; shock swept through him, mingled with disbelief, hostility, and desire. He'd never thought she would be so bold as to accept the offer. A tiny flicker of respect for her courage filled him, but he quenched it. This was revenge, pure and simple, though it meant he'd have to forego the pleasure of killing Gavin MacDonell. But Gavin would suffer endless agonies over his sister's humiliation, and that kind of living hell would be almost as good as the death he'd planned to inflict on him.

"Very well." Looking over his shoulder, he called to the men holding Gavin, "Release him." Then he gestured Robert toward Aileana. "Say your farewells. We're leaving."

As he waited, Duncan struggled to control the warring emotions that besieged him. He didn't like the turn the day had taken. It created a host of new problems. But Aileana MacDonell had called his bluff on the challenge he'd been so reckless to throw at her, and honor demanded that he go through with the deal.

Her proximity to him would have one added benefit, though; she would be under his power, making it easier for him to force her to reveal the *Ealach*'s location. Images of the methods open to him, of her beauty and the pleasures she could provide, drove lancets of desire through him. But then thoughts of her kinship to Morgana doused the flames in a shower of ice.

Facing her again, he issued the order to leave. He forced himself to remain impervious to the wrenching loss painted across her delicate features, trying to ignore the worry so obvious in Robert's eyes. It was what they'd agreed to, damn it. And there wasn't another instant to waste. It was time to go.

"Come. We've miles to cover before sundown."

Aileana fixed her grief-stricken face forward, refusing to meet his gaze. As he took her arm and led her through the door, Duncan closed his ears to the soft sounds she made as she clearly struggled to hold back tears. But at the portal she twisted round in his grasp, craning her neck to see her brothers for as long as possible until the solid wall of stone blocked their view. Still he led her on, pushing ahead until they reached his stallion.

He hoisted her in front of him astride Glendragon's saddle. As they began to ride, a coppery wave of her hair slid across his face, and, annoyed, he brushed it aside. But not before its fragrance wafted to him, sweet honey and clove. The pure simplicity of it twisted a knot in his gut and played havoc with his senses.

As if she somehow discerned his reaction, Aileana stiffened. Duncan watched the signs of grief fade from her face as if by the stroke of a wand, masked by that bland expression she seemed to wear so often. Even her tears dried quickly under the snap of the wind.

Gritting his teeth, Duncan urged Glendragon to a gallop. Aye, sure as the sun rose, he'd taken trouble for a ride today. But he would tame Aileana MacDonell once they reached home. She could rail and rant, or shroud herself in silence; either way he would bend her to his will.

And yet somehow, he couldn't rid himself of the persistent voice deep in his mind. The voice that churned a dire omen with every beat of Glendragon's hoofs, urging him to take heed and prepare before it was too late . . .

Because, it warned, his lion's share of tribulation had only just begun.

Chapter 4

Aileana stretched her aching muscles and inched closer to the fire. The night spent huddled on the ground, protected by nothing but two thin plaids, had confirmed one of her long-held beliefs.

Men were senseless idiots.

The idea that they could wage war on each other after sleeping in such conditions seemed addle-minded at best. If they thought to gather piles of leaves or nice, thick pine boughs to lay beneath their plaids, they'd be much more comfortable and agile in the morning. At the very least, it would warm them while they slept.

But when she'd suggested as much to the MacRae last night, he'd leveled such a look of masculine disgust at her that she'd clamped her mouth shut. The beast had even denied her the privilege of gathering her own makeshift mattress, snapping an order for Kinnon to keep her under control and near the fire when she ventured toward the copse of pines at camp's edge.

Aileana supposed she should be grateful that the MacRae had chosen to remain aloof. Yesterday, after the first, grief-numbed hour of riding, the realization of what she'd actually done began to sink in. She'd agreed to a life of virtual slavery, sure to be ostracized and rejected for her status as the MacRae's leman. And being his leman meant more than just helping to serve his meals and clean his castle keep.

It meant sharing his bed.

A shudder slithered down Aileana's spine. She'd not allowed herself to fully contemplate that part of the bargain yesterday. Now that the prospect faced her in the clear light of morning, she had to purse her lips to keep her teeth from chattering. All kinds of images danced through her mind, making her think. Making her feel. It was enough to make her stomach ache.

With a start, Aileana stopped herself from imagining any further. The pain was too great. Gone forever was the wedding night she'd dreamed of her whole life. Duncan MacRae wouldn't attempt to satisfy her maiden curiosity with tender touches and exciting, whispered words of love. Tonight when they reached Eilean Donan, he would bed her, pure and simple; he would slake his lust on her body and then leave her until the next time he felt the need. She'd be his leman, nothing more . . . an outcast to his clan. Reviled. *Scorned*.

Swallowing the ball of fear in her throat, Aileana stood and adjusted the plaid at her shoulder. Instantly, seven suspicious male gazes trained on her. She went still, having almost forgotten that her every move was now watched and studied. Except for the few moments of privacy allowed to her earlier for tending to her personal needs, her life was no longer her own.

She almost laughed at the irony of it all. She'd gone

from being a solitary, virtual recluse as the *Ealach*'s keeper to being surrounded by enemies under order to note the slightest change in her breathing. She fought a sudden, unthinkable impulse to shake her hair into wild disarray, dance in crazed abandon, and keen to the rising sun.

But then she caught sight of Duncan across the clearing. He'd turned from a discussion with his men to fix his gaze on her. His silver eyes held a feral gleam, an unmistakable glimmer that made her look down and cross her arms over her chest.

It was apparent that, just like Father, the MacRae was a man used to being feared and obeyed. With him watching her there'd be no chance of disobedience. She turned her back on him. Then, secretly making a face that mimicked his glower, Aileana twisted her hair into a makeshift braid and crouched again near the fire. Let him stare all he wanted. Right now, she was hungry. Picking up the crusty bannock and hunk of hard cheese Kinnon had left her, she broke her fast with relish.

All too soon, the call came to mount up and continue the ride to Eilean Donan. Aileana breathed a sigh of relief when she saw the MacRae ride out of the clearing with a group of his men. She would be allowed to walk with the others, away from him. Bending down to retrieve the trailing end of her plaid, she tucked it into her belt and draped it into acceptable pleats. It would be good to get back into her women's clothing, she thought, as she started toward the men traveling on foot.

When she passed the last, doused cook-fire, she sent up silent thanks that she wouldn't be made to ride with Duncan again, to bear his impossible closeness or feel the warm pressure of his thighs on her hips. It had been a terrible burden, remaining impassive in that position yesterday. Each jolting movement had made her more aware of him and his claim on her. His nearness had made her want to grit her teeth. It made her stomach clench. It made her want to scream—

"Give me your hand."

Aileana jumped. She snapped her gaze up to see Duncan astride his steed, one gloved hand extended to her. His other gripped the reins, keeping the stallion's powerful energy contained enough for her to approach.

Even so, the breath seemed to leave her lungs, though she refused to appear weak in front of the MacRae. "Nay, I'd rather walk." She eyed the stallion's massive hooves as they gouged the sodden earth near her feet. His nostrils flared, and he snorted as Duncan reined him into tighter control.

"Give me your hand and get up now." He gave her a look that would wilt a daisy. "Unless you're telling me that MacDonell wenches need footstools to get their dainty arses up into a saddle."

Heat rose to Aileana's cheeks and with it a fear-numbing burst of animosity. Grabbing his outstretched arm, she leaped up, landing sideways on the stallion's back. As she wriggled astride, she accidentally kicked Duncan's shin.

When he growled in irritation, she snapped, "So sorry, milord, but my dainty arse needed adjusting."

Aileana thought she heard a choking sound behind her, but when she hazarded a glimpse over her shoulder, she saw nothing but the tight, grim line of Duncan's mouth. Perhaps he'd missed her comment, she reasoned. But then the low-pitched timbre of his voice filled her ear, quiet and cutting.

"You will confine your prattling tongue and your wayward feet, or I'll be forced to truss you up and carry you gagged and bound into the castle yard of Eilean Donan."

She remained silent, and so he did nothing—until she clenched her fingers in his steed's mane so hard that she made the beast toss his head and let out a snorting whinny.

"Damnation, woman, he'll throw us if you don't stop clinging like that. He's a stallion, not a bed sheet!"

Aileana stilled. She waited, tension building, before working up enough courage to twist around and look at Duncan's face. He was scowling and his eyes were steely gray, but he didn't seem in the midst of any preparations to tie or beat her. Relief spread in a blessed flow to the ends of her fingertips, and she turned forward again. Taking a deep breath, she thanked God for the reprieve she'd been granted. All of her life she'd struggled to curb her tongue and hide her emotions. Father had tried to punish it out of her, but it hadn't worked. Now it was more important than ever that she concentrate on controlling herself.

For Duncan MacRae was an unknown entity, and that made him all the more frightening. And more dangerous.

This couldn't be her new home. It couldn't.

Aileana sat straight as a claymore as she viewed the castle; it was nestled at the merging of the three lochs opposite the Isle of Skye, a dark, square structure, reflected ominously in the waters. She swallowed hard as Duncan pulled Glendragon to a stop on the bluff overlooking the sight; all of his men rode into formation behind him.

"What . . . what happened to it?" she murmured without thinking. The castle looked as if animals and wild things had inhabited it for a long time. Her gaze took in the crumbling tiles of the roof, the uneven window openings in the main tower, and the gaping holes in the wall where piles of stones had fallen to the ground.

A tense silence followed her question, and from the corner of her gaze she saw Kinnon shift uncomfortably, while Ewen and the others darted uneasy glances at their laird. Aileana didn't need to see Duncan to know that his eyes bored shafts of gray flint into her back. She swallowed again.

"Thirteen years happened." His voice was dangerously soft. "Thirteen years spent living in hell, courtesy of that bitch you called sister."

Aileana felt his arms tense when he gripped Glendragon's bridle as if he wanted to strangle the thin strips of leather . . . or her neck. Then without another word, he pressed his knees into the stallion's sides, and they continued on, down the sloping path toward the ruined castle. Aileana's heart thudded in her chest, seemingly in time with the thumping cadence of the horses' hooves, as each man followed Duncan in solemn procession.

Soon they entered the courtyard. No cheers of villagers greeted them, no smiles or shouts of happy wives and children. Several bedraggled waifs and a few women gathered in the yard to meet their men. Their expressions of grim relief struck a chord in Aileana, and she felt an answering swell of sympathy.

She knew what it was like to feel completely at the mercy of outside forces, especially the everlasting impulses and intrigues of men. She remembered all too well days spent in seclusion, evenings passed restricted to the confines of her bedchamber because Father thought it best to keep her spirit pure and free from distraction. Gavin and Robert had sometimes stolen into her chamber to entertain her, but their visits were brief. Father had wanted her thoughts only on the amulet, and whenever he left for a journey or hunt, it was always with orders that she be kept confined to her rooms. It was at those times that she'd wished him dead.

And now he was.

The odd hurt lanced through her again, but she was given no time to nurse it. Several of the men had already dismounted and disappeared into the keep, and Duncan was waiting for her to slide from Glendragon's back. She tried to ignore his hands at her waist as he helped her down, but their warmth seared through her tunic to brand her skin.

It reminded her of the inescapable fact that she was his possession now, property much the same as a goose, or sheep, or sow he'd purchased. Except that those creatures were free to live in peace on the land. She would be forced to share this man's bed. Gritting her teeth, Aileana stared straight ahead and walked into the castle with as much dignity as her boy's garments would allow.

The interior of Eilean Donan wasn't much better than its outward condition. Her nose wrinkled at the stale smell as they came into the great hall. The floor rushes looked as though they hadn't been changed in months. Only a few dogs lounged in the hall to collect the bits of meat, bread and other leavings that fell from the tables, ensuring that the rotted food would remain until someone removed it.

"Bridgid!" Duncan's bellow shocked Aileana's attention from the floor. She hazarded a glance at him. Displeasure shone in the grim lines of his mouth, the hooded scowl of his brows. When a red-faced, angry-looking woman burst into the hall, Duncan grasped Aileana's arm and pushed her in that direction.

"Take her to the kitchens with you, Bridgid, and see

that she has something to eat. Then set her to some tasks." As he started up the stairway opposite Aileana, he yelled back, "And send up some water for my bath. I cannot stand this filth any longer."

Aileana looked after Duncan in surprise. Neither of her brothers or father had ever asked for a bath that she could remember. And yet she recalled that Duncan had insisted they stop at one of the small lakes they saw on their journey. She'd thought he wished to rest the horses, but when he'd returned to the fire, his golden brown hair and tunic were damp, and she'd realized that he'd taken time to bathe in the lake.

"You going to stand there all day, missy?"

Aileana snapped out of her thoughts. The woman Duncan had called Bridgid faced her, hands on her hips. Wisps of frizzy black hair stuck out around her face, and she glowered as if she'd just swallowed a swarm of bees.

"My name is Aileana MacDonell. And no, I don't intend to stand here all day. I'd prefer not to be here at all."

Bridgid grimaced. "I know very well who and what you are, missy, by the message sent here ahead of you. But I'm the *bailie* of this castle, and since the MacRae trusts me with the managing of it, I'm going to see that his wishes be obeyed. So you're coming with me, quick or slow, but you're coming. We've plenty of work to do." With that, Bridgid turned on her heel and stalked back to the kitchens.

Aileana looked around her in distress, hoping to find even one ally among the men, women and children who filled the chamber. Surely someone would understand and intervene on her behalf. She was the keeper of the *Ealach*, and with the exception of Father and the MacRae, no one had ever treated her with such heavy-handed disrespect in all her life.

But when she gazed round the hall, she received reactions ranging from mild disinterest to barely concealed animosity. Blinking back the renewed prickling behind her eyes, Aileana squared her shoulders and started after Bridgid.

Quick or slow, Bridgid had said. Well she wasn't going to be quick, but she'd not be slow either. Duncan had ordered that she attend to some tasks after eating, and she kept her mind focused on that prospect as she walked into the cavernous, smoky kitchens at the end of the corridor. The chores would be a welcome refuge from the fears that were beginning to consume her.

For far more quickly than slowly, night was coming, and when it did, there'd be no shelter left for her. She'd be forced to face Duncan MacRae—and become his leman in truth as she had in name.

With a sigh, Aileana sank deeper into the round wooden tub. It was the largest vessel of its kind that she'd ever seen, and the sheer volume of the warm water surrounding her was heavenly. She wiggled her toes as she rinsed the soap from her hair. This was the first rest she'd had all day; Bridgid had worked her to the point of exhaustion, taking pity, finally, when she saw her nodding to sleep over a bowl of apples she'd given her to pare.

But when she'd been led to this room at the top of the stone steps, her sleepiness vanished under a fresh onslaught of terror. This was *his* room. It was *his* tub that Bridgid helped her fill. At first she'd resisted, arguing that she'd rather wash from the basin near the window. But Bridgid had just given her the annoyed, impatient look she was coming to recognize and stomped from the room.

Once she was alone, the lure of the tub proved too much to resist. Now she gazed around as she soaked, curiosity overcoming her fear. Unlike the rest of the castle, Duncan's chamber appeared spotlessly clean, though cramped with furniture. More than a dozen candles filled the area with mellow, luxuriant light. Such wanton waste astounded her; at home two or three tapers sufficed to brighten a chamber.

Aileana noticed other extravagances as well. Rich tapestry hangings covered the windows, though Aileana imagined that when they were tied back, the spill of sunlight would be breathtaking. On the floor were numerous woolen mats and furs, to help keep drafts away.

Finally her gaze shifted to the imposing, curtained bed, and a shiver ran up her spine. Its framework was elaborately carved and solid, made to last through many generations. The coverlet was thick, the mattress soft and inviting. It was a massive bed. A bed made to be shared. A bed for begetting children . . .

Water splashed over the floor as Aileana lurched to her feet. She had to get dressed. Duncan would be walking through that door at any moment to claim his rights, and she'd spit pebbles if she was going to allow herself to be sitting here naked when he did.

With lightning speed, she dried herself and pulled on the long sleeved, white chemise that Bridgid had left for her. It was too large—someone else's clothing—but she didn't mind. More material meant more security, or at least the illusion of it. Her breath came fast, and she trembled as she hurried to the fire.

By the blessed angels, how had she ended up in such a shameful position? The ordeal ahead of her would be the worst she'd ever faced. She knew little of what happened during the intimate act between men and women . . .

nothing more than bits of whispered stories she'd heard when the maidservants gossiped. She gathered that coupling was painful for the female, unless the man was very gentle, and that a larger man meant more pain and perhaps even bleeding. Bleeding from where she wasn't certain, but she had an idea, and it made her stomach churn. Duncan MacRae was a very large man, and she would wager her teeth that he wasn't the gentle type.

A cold draft swept up Aileana's back, making her stiffen. He was here. She felt his presence as surely as if he was running his hands over her naked flesh. Turning slowly from the wall, Aileana wrapped her arms round herself and faced the man who would take her innocence this night.

Duncan stood massive and imposing in the shadows of the doorway. His gold-flecked hair waved to his shoulders; the chiseled set of his face was unreadable. With slow, even steps, he walked closer to the fire, loosened his shirt, and sank into the chair perched before the blaze, still facing her.

Aileana's gaze slipped to the expanse of sleekly muscled chest that showed through the parted edges of his shirt. Firelight danced over his skin, honing powerful ridges and contours and illuminating several jagged scars that rippled from the top of his chest to the flat planes of his belly. He looked casual and relaxed, his clothing impeccably clean and well crafted, and as unlike his war gear as this embroidered chemise was to her borrowed soldier garb.

"Come here."

His soft command sliced the silence, and Aileana's gaze jerked up to his face. The jagged scar that ran along his cheek seemed faded in the shadows. But his smoky gray eyes studied her in the firelight, making her heart beat in staccato and her breath catch. Vaguely she noticed that he still wore his leather gloves; they matched a dark stripe in the swath of plaid draped in folds round his hips. Forcing herself forward, she walked step by step until she stood in front of him, steeling herself for what would come next.

That inscrutable silver gaze drifted up from where her bare toes peeped beneath her smock, along the outline of her legs, belly and breasts, finally lingering at the burning expanse of her face. Aileana clenched her hands in front of her, willing herself to be strong, to resist the urge to fall at his feet and beg for mercy. He'd surely laugh and humiliate her more if she did.

"You're trembling."

His quiet statement caught her off guard. She thought she'd heard a hint of concern in his voice. Her breathing slowed, and the panic receded a bit. Perhaps he was not wholly without honor or sensitivity. He might treat her with tenderness, or at least some—

"But you're wasting your virginal show of modesty on me, for I'll not be taking my pleasure with you as my leman, this night or any other . . ." Duncan leaned forward, lacing his fingers together as he rested his forearms on his thighs. ". . . because I will not risk the possibility of breeding my *bairns* on a MacDonell wench."

Aileana gasped at the insult. He'd played her for a fool, bringing her all the way to Eilean Donan only to stand her before him like this to debase her further. Her hands balled into fists at her sides. Her gaze darted round the chamber, but her clothing was nowhere to be seen. As she willed calm to fill her, she walked over to the bed, grabbed a blanket and wrapped herself in it before heading to the door.

"And where do you think you're going?"

The arrogant tone of his question freed her tongue. "To find where Bridgid's hid my clothes, so I can get them and go home."

"If you do that, your brother will die."

The harsh words slammed into her, and Aileana whirled from the door, throwing caution to the wind as she flung her anger back at him. "The agreement between us was to spare Gavin's life if I came with you as leman. I fulfilled my part of it—it's your change of heart that frees me to go home!"

"There's been no change of heart. If you leave, you will be casting off our terms and our pact."

Frustration bubbled over in Aileana. She stalked to him, the blanket dropping to the floor, forgotten, in the heat of emotion. "Dragon's breath, MacRae! You just said that you did not—"

"If you'd cease babbling for the space of two breaths, I'd tell you the way of it between us."

Aileana's mouth clamped shut, her arms crossed in defensive pose over her chest. Being interrupted reminded her, suddenly, that she'd lost control of her emotions. Stiffly, she prepared for the punishment that should follow—that had always followed such outbursts at home. Father had drowned out her opinions all the time, and then, when he'd finished his tirade, he'd delivered her correction with heavy-handed stoicism. But Duncan just stared at her in silence.

Feeling more than a little reckless at the freedom his reaction allowed, she abandoned her training in docility even further and let her brows arch in mocking question as she waited for his explanation.

Duncan gestured to the stool opposite him. "Sit."

"I prefer to be standing when I hear your twisted thoughts."

He grimaced, his reply matching her sarcasm. "As you wish. But know you that our agreement stands as before. Your brother's life will be spared, provided that you serve as my leman, in every way but in the sharing of my bed."

He shifted back in the chair, lounging in insolent confidence. "However, my clan and yours must think our arrangement true. You will sleep in my chamber, on that pallet over there," he indicated the ticking on the floor in the corner, "except in the wee hours, when you will come into my bed so that Bridgid won't suspect anything amiss when she comes in to feed the morning fire."

Silence fell thick and heavy between them, the added disgrace of these new terms wounding her deeply. "Why are you doing this?" she asked at last, her voice quiet with hurt. "It piles the sin of falsehood on what is already an abomination. Do you really hate me so much that to torture me like this gives you pleasure?"

Duncan's silver gaze wavered, then hardened again. "Your *torture*, as you choose to call it, need not be forever. You could go home tomorrow, if you wish."

"Of course I wish it," she retorted. "But you're speaking in riddles."

"Not at all. It's very simple. Your humiliation and the dishonor to your clan will end on the day you reveal the location of the *Ealach* to me."

"Give you the amulet?" Shock, anger and relief blended in a torrent as Aileana stared aghast at him. "But we made no such condition in our agreement. You're changing the rules to suit yourself!"

"That's the way of it, Aileana MacDonell. Give me the amulet and you go free. Keep it and remain bound to me."

A hissing log on the fire popped and fell to the coals,

flaring sparks. Aileana glared at Duncan. He sat composed as he awaited her decision. She averted her gaze. Giving him the *Ealach* meant she could return home tomorrow. Back to the only home she'd ever known, but as a failure, perceived a fallen woman by her clan. Or she could continue to protect the *Ealach* and suffer the indignity of appearing to be Duncan MacRae's leman for the rest of her days.

It suddenly dawned on her that either way, she faced the same trap. Whether in the MacRae's bed or out of it, she was ruined.

She glanced beneath hooded eyes, studying the lean, muscular grace, the golden, scarred skin and chiseled features of the tyrant sitting before her. Bitterness rose hot and full in her throat. Because of him she would never savor the pleasures of home or hearth or the joy of her own children playing round her feet. She'd be scorned by all who saw her as Duncan's cast-off whore. The issue was moot; even if he allowed her to remain pure in body, no one would believe it. It would seem impossible that this bold, virile animal had denied himself full use of his leman. And because of that, no self-respecting man would ever again consider her for a wife.

Aileana straightened and clenched her jaw. Her dreams of a normal life, of companionship and family, fluttered away like ash up the chimney. But if she stayed at Eilean Donan, she could at least ensure that her suffering had purpose. The amulet would remain safe.

It was settled, then. Duncan MacRae could chew nettles; she'd not tell him where she'd secured the *Ealach*. He'd drawn the battle lines against her with his cruel treachery, and now he'd pay the consequences. He'd pay dearly.

"I've made my decision, MacRae. I'll be staying."

With a flap of her chemise, she scuffed toward her pallet, adding, "May your sleep be full of ghosties and evil fairies for the bargain you struck with me tonight."

Refusing to look at him again or react to the weight of the silence billowing at her from where he sat, Aileana stretched out on the soft ticking and burrowed deep. Prickling heat stung her eyes, but she blinked it away. This was no time for tears. She needed to make plans. Duncan MacRae would get his fair reward for this, by heaven. And now she had all the days for the rest of her life to enact every plot she could envision against him.

With that comforting thought, Aileana squeezed her eyes shut and tried to let her mind drift into dreams of satisfying revenge.

Duncan rolled over and tried to find a comfortable position. Sleep had eluded him for several hours. He'd watched the fire burn down to glowing embers, watched his remaining candle melt to nothing. And more often than he cared to admit he'd sat up to look at the fiery-haired, stubborn wench curled into a sleeping ball on the corner pallet.

Aileana MacDonell surprised him at every turn. He'd been certain that, granted the possibility of going home, she'd give him the amulet without clamor. He'd ordered Bridgid to work her hard this day to add to the entice-ment of leaving. But she'd stood her ground. And now he was faced with a prospect he'd not allowed himself to truly consider. She would be living here for the devil knew how long. Every day he'd have to contend with her chattering tongue, her annoying female ways, her pointed stares . . . and a constant view of her creamy-skinned beauty.

With a groan Duncan punched a lump on his bed.

Comely or not, he couldn't take her. Morgana's blood ran in her veins. Her clan had slaughtered his people. *Slaughtered Mairi.*

Cold seeped into his chest. He didn't want to see the picture in his mind again, didn't want to remember. But it was there. It would always be there—the sight of the woman he'd loved, still and lifeless at his feet.

Closing his eyes, he rolled onto his side. No further reminder was needed. Aileana MacDonell was a forbidden temptation, his opponent in this battle of wills. And if he had to work like hell, he'd get her to tell him where the *Ealach* was. Soon. But he had a sinking feeling that until he did, he'd be spending much of his time immersing himself in the distractions he might find in the great hall.

Or anywhere else that the accusing, seductive gaze of one honey-eyed, flame-haired temptress might not be able to reach him.

Chapter 5

The smell of warm oatmeal pulled Aileana out of sleep, making her smile with satisfaction an instant before she remembered where she was. At first, she stiffened under the covers, her mind blurry with images of the horrible day that had changed her life. Pictures of the battle, of Gavin wounded and bleeding, of hiding the amulet in Morgana's secret grove. Then she remembered last night and Duncan's casual, infuriating comments. *You will sleep in my chamber on that pallet over there, except in the wee hours, when you will come to my bed so that Bridgid won't suspect anything amiss . . .*

Satan's fire, she was in Duncan MacRae's bed.

She gasped and peeped from beneath the thick blanket, cheeks burning as she realized that he must have carried her from the pallet while she slept. Her gaze darted around his chamber. Thank the saints, but he'd left already. Relaxing again, Aileana scrunched down, pulling the covers up to hide the tip of her nose. Then she froze.

She sniffed, scowling in concentration. It was a pleasant scent, light and clean. With a start she'd realized that it was *his* fragrance coming from the bedclothes . . . the same sharply sweet smell as the square of hard soap Bridgid had taken from the tub last night before she'd tossed her a pot of soft lye soap from the kitchen. The realization was enough to propel her out of bed and into a chemise and kirtle that she found draped across one of the room's carved chairs. The garments were of serviceable weave, coarse but well crafted. Aileana felt a twinge of regret for her own gowns back home; they were of fine fabric and woven in colors to suit her.

Home. She had to stop thinking of Dulhmeny like that. This was home to her now, whether she liked it or not. And today was the first full day of her new life here. Her usual good nature tried valiantly to reassert itself and failed. Her mind kept straying to the revenges she'd conjured up last night to play against Duncan. How could she feign a peaceful demeanor? Life as the *Ealach*'s keeper had been difficult enough with its isolation and loneliness. But she'd only traded one kind of captivity for another, and this one was decidedly less tolerable.

Biting back a scowl, Aileana tried to ignore the growling of her stomach as she finished dressing and walked down the stairs to the great hall. Several tables jutted at odd angles round the room; they were full of men, some standing hunched over trenchers of steaming oatmeal, others sitting on the benches and ripping off hunks of dark bread and stuffing them in their mouths. Many of them looked unkempt, their flowing hair and beards snarled, their bare legs dirty beneath wrinkled plaids and tunics. Aileana sniffed at the vulgar display; it was becoming ever more apparent why everyone called this clan the wild MacRaes.

A prickle of apprehension slid down her spine an instant before she saw him. He sat at the far end of the hall, his silver gaze fixed on her, penetrating. Unlike his clansmen, Duncan exuded a sense of clean, calm orderliness. He looked refreshed from his night's rest, though she thought she saw a glint of annoyance in his eyes before he turned to Kinnon, sitting next to him.

At that moment Bridgid huffed up to Aileana and dropped a heavy iron pot into her hands; it was empty, smeared with the jellied remnants of cold oatmeal.

"It's about time you showed your face this morning, missy. Here. Take it back to the kitchens and have it filled again." Bridgid shook her red face at Aileana, muttering, "There's no time to dawdle with a room of hungry men. Get about it." She stalked away, charging at whirlwind speed toward a table whose occupants were banging their fists in a rising crescendo of complaint.

Aileana gaped at Bridgid's retreating back. *Serve* these animals? But Bridgid had already turned away, waving her toward the kitchens. With a sigh, Aileana let the pot dangle from her grip and did as she was bid. The sound of women's voices spilled from the warm chamber beyond the hall, rising and falling, punctuated with laughter. But as soon as she stepped into the chamber, the chatter tapered off and fell to silence by the time she'd reached the middle of the room.

"Bridgid told me to have this refilled," she murmured, holding out the empty pot. The only sound to break the quiet came from the bannock cakes hissing on the hearth-fire.

Finally, one of the women sauntered forward. She was tall and dark-haired, her ample curves filling a kirtle that was a shade too tight. She reached out and grasped the pot between her finger and her thumb, clearly being careful not to touch Aileana's hand.

"Here, Maggie," she said to the small, blond girl behind her, though she kept her gaze only on Aileana. "Wash this out before you fill it again." She fixed her with an insolent expression. "We don't want our men catching anything from the MacRae's new whore, now, do we?"

Aileana stood her ground, but a sick, hollow feeling unfurled in her belly. Someone jostled into her and pushed her roughly aside.

"That's enough out of you, Nora MacKenzie." Bridgid jabbed her finger into the woman's shoulder. "If you want to spend the day wailing about being misplaced from the MacRae's bed, then do it on your own time. That, or I can send you out to the pig trough, to muck and mumble by yourself." Bridgid glared. "Make your decision."

Nora's gaze sliced across Aileana once more before she grumbled under her breath and moved back to the cook pots. One by one, the other women went back to their tasks, their sideways glances leaving Aileana little doubt about the meaning of their whispers.

Pursing her lips, Bridgid took a pot of fresh, hot oatmeal from the fire and wrapped the handle in a cloth before handing it to Aileana. "Take this to the MacRae's table. His was running low."

Aileana just looked at her, surprised at her intervention. With a tentative nod, she said, "Thank you for what you did just now. I won't forget it."

"What I said wasn't for your sake, missy, believe you me," Bridgid snapped, angry red mottling her cheeks. "Work needs to be done, and that was the quickest way of getting Nora back to it. I'll not be defending the likes of you with my breath." She tilted her head with a sharp gesture to the door. "Now get moving and take this in before it gets cold."

Cheeks burning, Aileana turned away without another word and strode from the kitchen. She reached the MacRae's table almost without looking, but as she prepared to set the pot of oatmeal on the broad wooden surface, she heard a hissed conversation right next to her that stopped her cold.

"The MacDonell lass has a nice twitch to her arse when she walks, eh, Dougal?"

"Aye, and a fine lap for resting in as well, if you ken my meaning," the other said, chortling. "Do you think the MacRae'll be sharing her anytime soon?"

Aileana's gaze snapped up. The two men sat an arm's length away from her at Duncan's table, one as broad as the other was lean. They stared, the lanky one grinning. Her stomach sank to her toes. When she set the pot down, her hands trembled so badly that some of the oatmeal sloshed onto the table in front of them.

"Ach, watch it there!" the portly man hooted. Then he winked. "But clumsy or not, you're a fine piece with that red hair. The MacRae's a lucky man."

"Not bad," the second one admitted, smacking his lips. He reached out to pinch Aileana's hip. She gasped and backed away. "Though I think she needs a lesson in the manners of a serving wench. Spilling half the oatmeal is no way to feed a man!"

Aileana's gaze flew to Duncan; she expected him to at least upbraid his men for their rudeness. But he simply returned a look of level contemplation before leaning back in his chair.

Heat crept from her neck to the roots of her hair. How

dare he sit there and let these ruffians abuse her without speaking nay against it? Impotent fury wound through her, so strong that her throat felt squeezed shut with it. But the rage was quickly followed by a swell of desolation. She'd gain no help from Duncan MacRae; she was foolish to have even hoped for it.

Duncan watched Aileana's reaction, seeing her emotions clear in the depths of her eyes. An odd ache unfurled in his belly at the fierce color in her cheeks and the sight of her hands twisting in her skirt. The surge of satisfaction he'd expected to feel when his plans for her humiliation began to bear fruit failed to surface. And it annoyed him. She was supposed to take the place of Gavin MacDonell in his revenge, and yet how could she, when he wouldn't allow himself the pleasure of her discomfort?

Disgusted with himself, he averted his gaze and broke a piece from the chunk of bread that had served as his trencher. He popped it in his mouth and concentrated on chewing, pretending not to notice when Aileana slipped from the hall, as soundless as a ghost. The conversation around him continued at low pitch, though the two men who had insulted her had finally gone quiet in favor of nudging each other and grinning. Duncan felt someone's stare boring into him, and he turned to see Kinnon; his cousin's head was tilted, his brow raised in a condemning expression reminiscent of that moment when he'd first noticed Aileana's nakedness in the glen.

The bread lodged in Duncan's throat, and he stopped chewing. Kinnon's accusing stare grew more intense.

Duncan muttered a curse, throwing down the last bit of trencher. "What did you want me to do, then? Cleave them in half for speaking to her?"

Kinnon only looked at him, reproach heavy in his

eyes. Then he shook his head with a snort and went back to his food.

Duncan tried to shrug off the gloom and concentrate on his meal, but he found that the crude conversation that had begun again between the men at the end of the table suddenly irritated him to the point of distraction. Throwing a baleful glare at Kinnon, he lurched to his feet and growled, "Enough! You two—" he pointed at the plump Dougal and his wiry companion. "Get out to the courtyard and polish the rusty swords. Now!"

The men leaped to their feet, bits of bannock cake and oat broth dribbling from their beards. They had the temerity to look ill-used, blinking and mumbling in feigned innocence, until Duncan followed his command with a wordless bellow that sent them tripping and scuffling out of the great hall.

Sitting back in his chair, Duncan picked up his bread again. He paused with it halfway to his mouth, then threw it down again. Tilting his mug to his lips, he drank deep before slamming it to the table.

Kinnon brushed a few crumbs from his fingers, taking time to sop up the last of his broth before tilting his gaze to Duncan. "A bit testy today, are we?"

Duncan made a scoffing sound. "Eating tasteless food tends to have that affect on a man." He cut him a glare. "Of course you're an exception to that."

Kinnon skirted the gibe. "It's not Bridgid's fault that the larders hold little more than oats and kale. The men have become lazy for the hunt. And the MacLeods have not been properly intimidated by your return. They keep stealing our livestock, to test us. We must take action against them soon." Kinnon swung his leg over the bench and stood up. "And yet much as those clans be thorns in our sides, it is not they, nor the poor food that be chafing at you this morning, Duncan."

Duncan contested Kinnon's cool gaze with a lift of his brow. "Nay? Then pray sit back down, cousin, and give me the true reason."

"I do not need to sit to tell you what any eyes but your own can see. MacDonell or no, you took in yon girl as your leman, and you're not in the habit of allowing anyone in your service to suffer mistreatment—unless you be the one offering it, of course. You didn't help her when she might have used your influence just now, and that's what's sticking in your craw, cousin."

With that, Kinnon nodded and started toward the door, but as he strode away, he called over his shoulder in challenge, "Then again, you're the laird. Think on it as you wish."

Duncan scowled and stared back into his empty cup as Kinnon left the hall. *Laird.* Aye, he was the leader of the wild MacRaes. But his men were more apt to carouse than fight, and as added insult he'd been cursed with a slip of a woman who looked the picture of her depraved sister while behaving like either a shrewish magpie or a timid mousie.

Just then Bridgid charged by with a platter of steaming oat pudding. Before he would let himself think too much more about what he wanted to do, he pulled her aside.

"Get the MacDonell woman back here. I need to tell her something."

"Ach, don't we all! But I don't know where she's taken herself off to." Her voice thick with sarcasm, Bridgid added, "One of her kind, perhaps she's taking a *beauty* rest—or could be that she's out wandering the edge of the loch to let the sea breeze flow through her hair."

Duncan sighed and pushed himself away from the table. It was clear that he'd not be getting much assistance from his *bailie*. He tried to look stern. "When you see her, tell her I need to speak with her tonight."

Bridgid nodded and started away to her tasks, but Duncan stopped her again. "And keep her occupied in the kitchens today. Somewhere away from the men."

Rolling her gaze skyward, Bridgid stomped off, muttering about coddled brats under her breath. Duncan scowled as he set off to find Kinnon. He stepped out into the misting rain and breathed deep, flexing his hand within its leather glove to ease the ache that the damp brought to the poorly mended bones.

He could waste no more time on troublesome women. His cousin had been right when he'd warned of the unrest among the neighboring clans. He needed to contact the MacKenzie soon and make plans for stemming the growing problems, or it seemed likely that the question of how to handle Aileana MacDonell would soon prove to be the least of his worries.

Shadows had fallen over the waters of Loch Duich by the time Duncan allowed himself to consider taking his rest for the day. The rain had dissipated by late morning; now the setting sun tinted the billowing clouds pink and gold, finally fading to smoky violet as he called a halt to the sparring and war practice he'd overseen for most of the afternoon.

The evening meal had taken place in virtual silence. Kinnon was wrapped in his own thoughts, and the others were so exhausted from the day's activity that they'd barely kept their heads steady above their venison stew.

Duncan smiled wryly and chewed the end of a narrow bone. At least his frustrations had had one positive result today; he'd managed to incite a sort of terrified enthusiasm for the hunt. Many of the men had chosen to take to the wood rather than face him in the hand-to-hand fighting he'd pressed on any that decided to remain at the castle. The reward had been three fine bucks and a doe, with meat aplenty for Bridgid to make several hearty meals in the kitchen.

Yet for all of his efforts, the most difficult task still lay ahead of him. At the top of the curved steps, in what used to be the haven of his bedchamber, Aileana MacDonell lay in wait to ruin his sleep for a second night in a row.

He stole a wistful glance toward the end of the hall. Several of his people sat around the massive fireplace to hear the clan *senachie* tell tales of battles fought during times of old, when the MacRaes had first pledged their allegiance to the great MacKenzie overlords.

The bard painted a glorious picture of Duncan's ancestor, Lachlan MacRae, who'd joined in a bloody battle when the MacKenzie was protecting Wester Ross from the MacDonalds; Lachlan killed many in the conflict, crowning his victory by slaying a MacDonald chief. Then he sat on the body in the middle of the battlefield. When the MacKenzie saw him there and asked why he fought no more, Lachlan had replied that if everyone killed as many MacDonalds as he had that day, the MacKenzies would win the day.

Duncan frowned. Would that he'd been so sensible in his response when Robert MacDonell had asked him if he wanted to take Aileana in payment for Gavin's crimes. His mouth tightened. But stubbornness had prevailed over common sense, inciting him to meet the challenge with one of his own. Greedy for revenge, he'd added insult to the harm he was about to inflict. And now he was stuck with Aileana MacDonell because of it.

There was nothing redeeming about this mess. He couldn't even bed her. Memories of the evil her clan had wrought made that unthinkable. Yet at the same time, Kinnon was right in believing that his conscience wouldn't allow him to stand idle while others abused or insulted her. Revenge or no, he couldn't stomach it.

He clenched his jaw and looked down at his right hand, flexing it against the warm, smooth leather of his glove. Aye, it was a fine mess. And there was no way out of it that he could see, save finding a way to make Aileana MacDonell give him the *Ealach* and go home.

The sound of laughter pulled him from his thoughts, and he looked again toward the gathering at the hall's end. One of the village wenches had hopped onto Angus's lap and was winding her arms round his neck in invitation.

A pang shot through him. For thirteen years in the hell of the Tower he'd longed for such warmth. Not only for the release to be found in a woman's softness, though that need drove him the same as any man. Nay, more, even, he'd ached for the simple want of touch, the peace to be found in a loving woman's embrace. He craved the perfect sense of belonging he'd been so close to knowing with Mairi before she'd been killed.

He'd loved Mairi in the way of youth, the emotion sharp and sweet, but it had never come to full fruition. When he'd returned from captivity, he'd sought out female companionship, eager to feel again, to have something other than the grinding pain of regret and vengeance twisting in his gut. But every time he looked into their faces he'd seen it. The shadow of fear. His scarred face and ruined hand made them shudder.

Nay, being with women only left him feeling more alone and more aware of the truth—that if Nora or Tyra or any of the other women warmed his bed, it was due to their respect for his position as the MacRae or the pleasure he might give them, nothing more.

More laughter and cheers rose from the *senachie*'s corner, and Duncan pushed himself to his feet. He had to leave. Self-pity was an emotion he rarely indulged, and that he had just now surprised him. But he couldn't afford to dwell on the past; his present difficulties demanded attention and would wait no longer.

By the time he reached his chamber, he'd decided on how he would approach Aileana and what he would say to her. He wasn't a heartless man, and that was going to make this conversation unpleasant for him as well as for her. But she was too upsetting to the balance of his life, and if getting her to admit where she'd hidden the *Ealach* meant that he'd have to appear unfeeling, then so be it.

He gritted his teeth and nudged open his door, prepared for a confrontation. Yet the sight that greeted him almost took his breath away. Aileana sat curled before the evening fire, a needle in her hand; her arm moved in rhythmic motion as she darned one of his tunics.

Duncan's throat constricted at the utter serenity, the picture of domestic tranquility she embodied. The firelight caught her hair, setting her cinnamon tresses to gold, and he watched in fascination as she nibbled her lower lip. For the briefest moment he allowed himself to revel in the vision and to imagine what it would be like if she were truly his woman . . . if she were his wife.

Then she looked up and dropped her needle with a gasp. Her cheeks paled. And he saw it, the cursed whisper of fear—or was it revulsion?—shadowing her expression.

Pain wrenched through him, and he strode into the room, muttering, "What do you think you're doing in here?"

"I—I'm mending your clothes." Aileana retrieved the tunic she'd dropped, her gaze shifting nervously between him and the small mound of his clothes that she'd already repaired.

"Why?"

"I thought it my responsibility, and I'm skilled with the needle." She set the work aside, curling her hands on her lap. He'd noticed that she fell to it often, that anxious, twisting of her hands. Another twinge rippled through Duncan's gut, and he realized suddenly that her constant, fearful reaction to him bothered him more than anything else did.

Anything except the knowledge that he'd done nothing to prevent her from feeling it.

Striding to her, he scooped up the garments she'd stitched and shoved them in a basket. When he spoke, he tried to sound normal, as if he hadn't just allowed another MacDonell to twist the knife deeper in his belly.

"Your efforts to appear biddable are wasted when none but I can see them. In future you will confine your domestic work to the hall or other areas where the clan can bear witness."

He thought she might argue, but at the last moment she held back. Her cheeks reddened to a furious blush, and he couldn't help but think that she looked like a woman drowning, too frightened to reach for the branch that would save her.

The nagging pain jabbed him again, and he surprised himself by asking suddenly, "Well, what is it? Do you wish to say something to me?"

Aileana swallowed, and, amazed, Duncan watched her demeanor change. She unclasped her hands and sat up straighter, as if his question had unlocked some magical door.

"Aye, I do have something to say. I have reason for wanting to remain in here," she said. "And it's ill-mannered of you to bar me from it without first knowing why."

"Heaven forbid that I be ill-mannered," Duncan answered, folding his arms across his chest. "What is it, then?"

Aileana blushed again, only this time the coral dusting of her cheeks banished the last traces of that awful frightened look. She stared directly at him, and her accusing eyes pierced him to the heart. "I know you heard what your men were saying to me while you were breaking your fast. But you did not see what happened in the kitchen just before that."

He raised his brow. "You're right, I did not. Tell me."

"The details are of no matter. But it made clear to me that your clan despises me. And while it's true that I've agreed to endure your spite because of the agreement between us, I will not be the object of all the mistreatment and hatred your people decide to heap upon me." She nodded. "That is my reason for wishing to keep to this chamber when I'm not needed below, and a good one it is."

"It's not acceptable," he argued, shaking his head. "You must learn to get along with the others if you're going to be living here." He shrugged. "Of course, if you want to return to Dulhmeny, just tell me where you've hidden the *Ealach* and off you'll go without another word from me."

"So you're still resolved to use cruel bribery, then?"

"I'm not trying to be cruel, lass, just realistic," he said, steeling himself to drive the lance home. "If you're going to stay, you must keep in mind why the others resent you. It's because of all that your kin did to us. We're still suffering the effects now. There's a chance that if you work at it, you might win them over—but you cannot be doing that hiding in this chamber."

"*Win them over?*" Aileana's hand clenched in her skirts and her eyes narrowed. "I've no care what that barbarous lot you call clansmen think of me!"

Duncan turned away from her. "Have it your way, then, Aileana MacDonell. But I'll not be taking steps to make your stay here easier." He took up the basket of clothes as he swung open the chamber door, calling over his shoulder, "You know what needs to be done if you want to leave. Until then, you'd be wise to follow me down to the hall to continue your work. I'll give you a few moments to comply—but there'll be no more re-treating to this chamber from now on."

Duncan heard her gasp as he left the room. Slamming the door behind him, he set off down the hall. That hadn't been easy. The woman was sharp as a blade and soft as butter all at once. She left him at odds, no matter what the outcome of their infrequent discussions. Yet he'd done what he intended to, hadn't he? She would come out of his chamber, as he'd bid her—she hadn't argued further. But the unsettled feeling remained.

Then, from the corner of his eye, he saw something peeking over the edge of the basket he carried. Something that swung with every step that he took. It was the tunic that Aileana had been mending when he came into their chamber.

Emptiness unfurled with sudden ferocity in his stomach. He stopped in the middle of the hall, setting his burden down on the floor. Temptation came over him, too powerful to resist, and slowly, he stripped the gloves from his hands to touch the tunic, to feel the quality of her stitching with his fingers. Her work was fine and even. Worthy of a noble lady.

Or a loving wife.

A tingle of longing shot up his arm to lodge in the area near his heart. He closed his eyes and breathed deep, willing his resolve to remain intact as he tucked his tunic back into the basket. But the hollow feeling gnawed deeper.

He clenched his jaw and kept walking. Damn Aileana MacDonell. Damn her sweet, innocent gaze and her bursts of temper. And damn the effect her presence here was having on him. He'd planned to put her in her place just now. Planned to show her who was in control. But it seemed that she'd gotten the better of him once more, and simply by gazing up at him with those wide, honey-brown eyes as she sat mending his clothes. For in that instant, she'd made him thirst for something that he'd been allowed to taste for one, brief moment in his life, but could never have again.

He stalked into the great hall, tossing the basket of clothes on the floor before continuing through the huge chamber and out the door to the yard. He didn't pause to acknowledge any of his people. He needed to get some air, needed to get away from his thoughts and his tumultuous feelings. And yet he knew that no amount of walking would help him to escape the knowledge that was burning a hole in his chest—the sad truth that pummeled him from the inside out.

Nay, he couldn't deny it. He'd been defeated once, years ago, by a MacDonell woman, and though he'd vowed never to let it happen again, in this latest battle of wills with Aileana, he couldn't deny that it felt like he was losing once more . . . only this time the forfeit seemed to be a tiny piece of his already ravaged heart.

Aileana stared at the unyielding panels of the door, sure that the wooden beams were no more hard and dark than the soul inhabiting Duncan MacRae's human form. Whirling away from the reminder, she felt her knees give way, and she sank down, struggling to resist the urge to dissolve into tears.

Ever since she'd first set eyes on the leader of the wild MacRaes, she'd felt in a constant state of turbulence. It was unsettling, especially after all of the years spent schooling herself to appear calm no matter what her inner feelings, even in the face of Father's most humbling wrath. But Duncan seemed to have the ability to strike at the most vulnerable part of her, to make her feel exposed and raw. Wrapping her arms round her stomach, Aileana tried to focus on something—anything—to keep her from sliding into the morass of feeling that meant losing control.

The Ealach.

Aye; she'd concentrate on the amulet and the good that would come from protecting it. If only the opalescent pendant were here with her. If only she could feel its weight and warmth in her palm and sense the reassuring power that throbbed through her when she touched it. But it wasn't here, and it never could be. She needed to keep it safe, keep it hidden.

Until when?

The question ragged at her, but she refused to answer. She couldn't. Not now. Not yet.

After a time, her breathing began to slow, and she felt her heart ease its pounding. But for all her trying, she couldn't summon the vision she needed. The *Ealach*, mercurial as always, refused to appear in her mind's eye. And it troubled her. Rarely did the amulet refuse to respond to her call.

Opening her eyes, Aileana sighed and stared into the flames that glowed and popped in the hearth. She knew she shouldn't let it disturb her; her failure was probably due to the devilish MacRae's constant goading.

When I'm more calm, the image will come.

Sitting back on her heels, Aileana let the fire's warmth soak into her skin, feeling it bathe her face and arms. The dancing flames were hypnotic, but her uneasiness remained. It was almost as if she'd lost the *Ealach*, somehow.

Though she knew it wasn't possible, she couldn't resist that frightening, renegade thought. It was a dark image, full of shadow and enchantment, telling her that her hold on the amulet was slipping—and that if she didn't take care, all of her work and sacrifice would be for naught, and it would vanish from her life forever.

The Northern Highlands

It was hot. The heat from the conjure fire rose in silky, undulating waves to caress Morgana's naked body. She hunched motionless over the flames, murmuring the incantation, her gaze fixed as she concentrated on the image beginning to form from the depths of the glowing ash; a ball of blue light rolled to the surface and burst forth, spinning and taking shape. For an instant it hung suspended there, a perfect replica of the amulet. Then it dropped back with a faint popping sound and a release of stinging, acrid smoke.

Shaking herself from the trance, Morgana uncurled her body from the cramped position of meditation and stood. She stretched, catlike, and reached for the silken robe she'd draped over the only chair in this ruined castle's tower room. The fabric slid cool and smooth over her heated flesh, and she knotted the belt before summoning Iona. Only after the serving girl left did Morgana allow herself the briefest of smiles. Her visions were powerful and rarely wrong; the *Ealach* was vulnerable at last, outside of Dulhmeny's walls for the first time since she'd been banished to this forsaken place. It was unprotected by a keeper and there for the taking.

The creaking door interrupted further musings. Colin strode into the room and grimaced. "How can you abide this heat? It's like roasting in Hades."

Morgana said nothing as she walked over to him, smoothing her hands up the powerful length of his arms and across his chest to weave in the golden tangle of hair at his nape. He gave a low growl and bent to kiss her neck, murmuring, "Iona didn't tell me it was loving you were after."

Arching her back, Morgana leaned into him and closed her eyes. If she kept them shut it was easier to pretend that it was Duncan who held her, that it was his strength supporting her, loving her . . . quenching the burning desires that beat with every pulse of her blood. For thirteen years she'd satisfied herself this way, with Colin none the wiser. But now was not the time. Pulling back, she pushed his groping hands away from her breasts.

Colin frowned, making the scar that disappeared beneath his eye patch whiten. She stared at the patch, remembering. Reliving the moment when Duncan had struck down his brother before he himself fell senseless on the altar during their attack on his wedding day.

Colin had lost his eye because of that blow.

Running her finger lightly above it, along his brow, Morgana let a slow, sweet smile curve her lips. Then she tilted her head to meet his gaze. "Finally, Colin. The needing, the waiting . . . it's all over. The *Ealach* is to be ours once more."

Raising herself on tiptoe, she pulled his head closer until her lips brushed against him, her breath whispering over his ear like a lover's caress. "It's time, my darling, for vengeance."

Chapter 6

Aileana brushed the last bit of vegetable peelings out into the yard with vicious jabs of her broom. Two pigs and a goat thumped over on cloven hooves, snorting and rooting for the scraps as if their lives depended on it.

"We'll be needing to gather more rosemary before the morrow, missy. See to it after breakfast," Bridgid said as she passed by.

Aileana nodded, maintaining the virtual silence she'd taken up with everyone at the castle during the three weeks she'd been here. Her method seemed to be working. Except for the occasions when she caught some of the women whispering behind their hands, the insults and mocking had diminished. Even Duncan seemed to be complying with her unspoken wishes; he'd been busy leading raids on the neighboring clans that pestered them, but when he was at Eilean Donan, he maintained his distance.

And she was more miserable than she'd ever been in her life.

The fact that she couldn't blame her gloom on him made it even worse. In truth, his behavior confused her. Although she'd always pretend to be asleep when he took her to his bed in the wee hours of each morning, she'd found it impossible to ignore the gentleness of his touch. He'd move quietly, so as not to disturb her rest, lifting her in the secure strength of his arms before tucking her under the blankets. Though he never laid a hand on her once they were under the covers, his body's warmth but a palm's breadth away made the hours till dawn creep. The vulnerable, open expression she caught on his face every now and again while he slept made it even more difficult.

Lately, she'd found herself struggling against the impulse to roll over and curl into the curve of his embrace. Desperately, she'd resorted to recalling every insult, every humiliation that he allowed to come her way during the day. She relived every time he'd commanded her and insisted that she wait upon him at table. But no matter what she tried, the other visions would eventually steal in to torment her. Visions of him standing next to her pallet, the dying embers of the fire casting his lean, muscular body in relief as he stripped off his tunic and his plaid . . . the quiet, somber expression in his eyes as he carried her to his bed.

Those moments in the middle of the night showed another side to Duncan MacRae. He befuddled her mind, and she felt at a loss about what to think of it—of him.

"I do not have to think of him at all," she mumbled as she plunked her broom down behind the kitchen worktable.

"Talking to yourself, are you?"

Aileana turned to face the person who'd spoke so sarcastically. Nora MacKenzie leaned back against the table, her breasts straining against the fabric of her tunic. "Mayhap you're coming down with one of them pestilences that be spreading up from Edinburgh. Feeling a bit delirious are you?"

She isn't worth answering. Aileana swept her gaze up the length of Nora's well-endowed frame before looking away in dismissal. But as she attempted to move past, Nora stepped away from the table to block her path.

"One thing I know for certain—poor sleep isn't the cause of your trouble."

Aileana scowled, but she refused to answer.

Nora seemed not to care, her smile widening. "I have eyes, you know and it's clear that the MacRae isn't keeping you up nights. He's always in the hall with us . . . and then later in my chamber with me." She raised her brow, taunting. "You must know very little about the ways a woman can help a man, so that he gets a good night's rest."

Stung, Aileana couldn't help retorting, "I suppose such talents come naturally to a woman like you, Nora MacKenzie."

Nora flushed, but the smile never faded from her face. "All that matters is that Duncan enjoys the satisfaction I give him. Every blessed night." She pushed herself away from the table and grabbed a basket. "I should be thanking you for your lack of skill. It's not often that a leman cannot hold her laird's interest for even a few days." She tossed her head and looked over her shoulder as she left. "So sleep well. I'll be making sure Duncan does the same!"

Aileana watched her go, a strange ache working its way up her belly to settle in her heart. Nora had to be lying; Duncan had no interest in her. She'd watched him ignore the woman's overtures time and again at table. He'd even nudged her off of his lap, once, when she'd tried to get him to drink more ale.

But then what *had* he been doing until the wee hours each night? Aileana swallowed hard. She thought back over the past weeks, her mind racing, wanting to grasp some bit of truth that would prove Nora a liar. But her claims rang true. Everyone had left Aileana alone. Including Duncan.

And the women snickering behind their hands . . .

Anger swelled in Aileana's chest. Dragon's breath, what if it was true? What if Duncan was bedding Nora, and so openly that the rest of his clan couldn't help but know it?

Aileana sank onto the bench that flanked the table. But why? Why would he deliberately compromise the ruse he'd created himself? He'd wanted everyone from both his clan and hers to think that she was his leman in truth. And she'd agreed to it. Agreed to remain here at this cursed castle in exchange for Gavin's life. How dare he add insult to injury, then, by permitting the others to witness his distaste for sharing her bed?

Aileana lurched to her feet. Her heart beat wildly, and her nails bit into her palms and she tried to hold herself back, knowing she was spiraling into an abyss of raw emotion. *The wretch.* That he chose to slake his lusts on some other unfortunate woman was a blessing, but the way he was doing it gained nothing but further humiliation for her. Marching out of the kitchen, Aileana set off in search of the man who appeared bent on destroying her life. He wasn't on the sparring ground or in the hall. She even worked up enough courage to ask Kinnon if Duncan had joined the day's hunting party in the glen.

He hadn't.

Finally, at a loss as to where else he might be, she stamped up to their bedchamber. Perhaps the fiend was fetching another pair of those cursed gauntlets he so loved to wear; along with his scowl, they seemed his favorite way of intimidating people. But she wouldn't let him dominate her this time. Duncan MacRae was as accountable as the next man, and she would force him to admit that he'd nullified their agreement. That he'd broken his own rules concerning her appearance as his leman.

With a shove that sent the door slamming into the wall, Aileana strode into their bedchamber. Then she stopped with a gasp. Someone had pulled back all of the curtains, and sunlight spilled into the chamber like a glittering waterfall. It blinded her for a moment, but a splashing sound warned her, an instant before Duncan's rich voice rang through the chamber.

"Hand me that cloth, will you?"

Aileana's heart rolled in her chest as her vision adjusted enough to make out the form of the giant washtub. And Duncan was clearly sitting in it, submerged in bubbles up to his chest. His eyes were squeezed shut against the lather covering his head, and his left hand waved back and forth in the general vicinity of a folded linen towel that rested on the stool beside him.

By the time Aileana found her tongue, she could only stutter, "What did you say?"

Duncan's hand ceased to wave. A slow grin split the bubbles on his face. "Ah, my loyal leman." Eyes still closed, he tilted his head back. "It's very simple. Either you can hand me that cloth over there," he gestured again toward the stool, "or I'll be needing to get up in all of my naked glory to fetch it for myself."

Aileana felt the blood rush in her ears. The renewed splashing sound shook her from her stupor, and she lunged forward to shove the cloth into his hand before he managed to pull himself to a standing position in the tub.

"Thank you, lass," he murmured as he wiped the soap away and smiled again. "I thought that my proposition might make your choice easier to make."

Aileana clutched her arms round her middle and stepped back. Easier wasn't the right word. Panicked had been more like it. There was something disconcerting about standing next to Duncan when he was in this . . . this state of undress. He'd shaven recently, and his smooth skin glowed so that she hardly noticed the scar on his cheek. His hair looked darker when wet, though the sun still lit the flecks and streaks of blond in it as if they were touched by a sorcerer's wand.

Her gaze drifted to his tawny chest, and then down his abdomen to where bubbles obstructed her view. But as she stared, she realized that the shiny spheres were vanishing one by one, leaving patches of clear water in their wake. And if she let her gaze drift down a little farther under the water she could just barely see . . .

Skittering back another three steps, Aileana began to pace. "Perhaps you'd better be getting dressed now. I've something of importance to discuss with you."

"Aye, the water's taking on a bit of a chill—though the room seems warmer, somehow, since you came in to see me."

His eyes sparkled quicksilver, and the lilting quality of his voice sent a tingle up her spine. If she didn't know better, she'd guess that Duncan MacRae was dallying with her.

Heat rose in her cheeks. *Ridiculous.* She heard him get out of the tub behind her. Careful to keep her gaze averted, she walked toward the windows and began to unloose the ties that held the curtains back, intending to let them fall shut and give him some privacy.

"Do not do that."

His piercing tone made her jump. She whirled to face him, surprised to see that his usual hard expression had returned. He'd wrapped the linen towel round his waist, though water still dripped down his chest and from the ends of his fingers. His right hand was hidden beneath the plaid and tunic he held in obvious preparation to don.

"Why not? Do you prefer that the entire clan watch you dress in front of your extravagant display of glass?"

"Just let it be."

Impatience shoved at the already tattered remnants of her composure. She stared at him. Why would he take issue with something so simple? Throwing up her hands, she walked over to the one open window and prepared to close it, so that he at least wouldn't freeze from the chill air as he dressed.

"Nay!"

She snapped her gaze to him again, incredulous. "Now you wish to catch your death of cold as well as lose all modesty?"

Though his eyes hardened further, Duncan didn't answer; he turned from her to pull his long-sleeved tunic over his head. The linen towel slid from beneath the garment to fall damply on the floor. He didn't respond to her question until he'd knotted his plaid and slipped on his familiar, leather gloves.

Then his voice was quiet, full of some emotion Aileana couldn't identify. "I like the light. I like the fresh air." His expression darkened, and he glanced away. "There is much that I could command as laird of the MacRaes that I do not ask for. But this I need. Leave it at that."

He turned to gather his leather bag of provisions, along with his claymore. *He was going to go away again, curse him!*

Aileana snapped her mouth shut and stalked over to him. "I do not wish to talk with you about your privileges as laird. I came here for another reason entirely, and you'll hear me out before you go off on another one of your endless excursions to raid the other clans."

Duncan swung slowly around, weariness and something else—was it acceptance?—weighing down every inch of his taut, muscular frame. "Get on with it, then, Aileana. I've much to attend to before we set out against the MacLeods this eve."

"I'm sure you do, though in matters not related to *fighting,* I'd wager." Facing him with hands on her hips, she fired a look at him that would melt iron. "I'm here to tell you one thing, Duncan MacRae. I'll put up with your crass treatment of me in front of your clan and your bitter silence behind closed doors, but I will not allow you to humiliate me by bedding Nora MacKenzie every night that I'm forced to live in your accursed holding as your leman."

Fingers of shock threaded from the top of Duncan's skull down the rest of his body. *Bed Nora MacKenzie?* The last time he'd lain with her or any woman had been at least a fortnight before his attack on Aileana's clan. Why would she think otherwise? He narrowed his gaze.

"My bedding Nora or not has nothing to do with you."

"Aye, it does." She glared at him. "Even without considering the shame you hope to bring on me by openly favoring her over me, we cannot very well convince both my clan and yours that I'm your leman in truth, as you insisted we must, if you're spending every night with her."

Slowly, Duncan set down his bag and his claymore, and the blade made a clattering sound against the floor. He straightened again, thinking all the while. Aileana believed that he'd taken another woman to his bed, and it angered her.

The thought sent a strange tingle of pleasure through him. *She was jealous.* He forced himself to push the thought aside, trying to focus instead on the matter at hand. Of course her argument held no logic. He spent enough time with her in the early hours of each morning to make intimacy between them not only possible but also likely to anyone who cared to notice. Still, nettling her sense of fairness might work to his advantage. He could use it to prod her into telling him where she'd hidden the *Ealach*.

Leaning back against an oak table that had been in his clan's possession for five generations, he said, "Bedding Nora MacKenzie or anyone else does not nullify your position as my leman. I'm fully capable of satisfying other women and still taking my pleasure with you." He raised his brow, nodding. "Any of my kin, and likely yours as well, are aware of that fact."

Aileana gasped, but Duncan continued, "I told you when you came to Eilean Donan that I wanted the *Ealach* back. You're hiding it. And I'll do whatever it takes to make you tell me where it is—including shaming you by openly seeking my pleasure with other women, if need be."

He shifted his gaze so that he wouldn't see her reaction, forcing himself to keep talking and staring into the flames of the fire to distract himself. "We're locked in a game you cannot win, Aileana MacDonell. Just tell me where you've hid the amulet and be done with it. Then you can leave in peace, and this humiliation will be over."

"My disgrace will continue long after I leave, MacRae, as well you know," Aileana answered flatly. "You've ensured that with this unholy bargain between us." All the passion had left her, and her voice echoed cold and hollow like the whisper of a ghost.

Duncan couldn't stop himself from looking at her then, feeling a jab in his gut at the desolation he saw in her eyes. He hadn't allowed himself to think about that, but of course she was right. By living with him as leman, even if only in name, she'd never again be considered fit as another man's wife. He struggled against the urge to comfort her, to reach out and fold her into his embrace. To quell the feeling, he moved past her and gazed at the breathtaking view of the loch beyond his windows. *Don't be a fool,* he told himself. She'd never accept solace from him. Not when he'd been the very cause of her disgrace.

But he'd had good reason for what he'd done. Her sister and her clan had brutalized his life and stolen what was his, and Aileana was adding to the injury by continuing to keep the *Ealach* from him. All of this pain, all of this unpleasantness never had to be if she wasn't so stubborn and unyielding.

Duncan willed his anger to take hold again. He could not let kindness drive him, couldn't let pity keep him from his goal. Though he'd never permit physical harm to fall upon her, Aileana must be made to reveal where she'd hidden the amulet. And if shame and underhanded tactics were needed to achieve that end, then he would use them.

"Giving me the amulet will make your life easier, if

nothing else, Aileana," Duncan said with grim finality. "You'll be better off in the bosom of kin who love you and want to protect you, rather than here, surrounded by people who wish you harm." He bent to pick up his bag and his claymore. "Think on it while I'm gone."

The hurt in her eyes was too great to bear. Grief shadowed her face, and he couldn't stop the renegade thought that such a thing was wrong, terribly wrong. That a proud, loyal woman like Aileana MacDonell should know nothing but joy and love.

Gritting his teeth, Duncan strode to the door. He couldn't allow himself to reconsider anything that had passed between them. He wouldn't.

So then why did he hurt like hell right now?

Before he could make the mistake of answering his own question, Duncan did the only thing he could think of doing—he pushed open the door and left, refusing even to nod to her in farewell.

Aileana rolled over on her pallet the next morning, restless, waiting for the cock in the yard to crow. It was almost dawn, yet she knew she didn't need to move into Duncan's massive bed. Whenever he was away, Bridgid left her alone to make a morning fire or not as she chose, using the opportunity as another way to show her disdain. She was never outright neglectful, but her coldness spoke volumes nonetheless.

Duncan was right. His clan hated her and wished her ill. All day yesterday and into the night, his words had churned in her mind, prodding her to a decision she'd been dreading to make. It certainly might have the power to change her life, she trusted for the better, but at what cost?

She allowed herself a grim smile. It wasn't the choice

Duncan had been hoping for; oh, no, she'd not reveal the hiding place of the amulet to him anytime soon. Nay, she'd decided on a plan that he'd suggested himself on her second night here, though she'd known even then that he'd said it only because he thought her incapable of accomplishing the task.

She was going to make the wild, murdering MacRaes like her.

Rolling onto her back, Aileana pulled the covers to her chin and stared into the gray quiet of the chamber. Silence and docility hadn't worked with his obstinate clan. Since her arrival she'd tried to behave as the calm woman that Father had worked so hard to create of her. For all of her life, it had been a struggle for her to comply—a fight against her true nature—but where meek obedience had pleased Father, the MacRaes were using her efforts to be accommodating as simply another reason to overpower and isolate her.

How to make them like her, then . . . ?

She was woefully inexperienced where such things were concerned. At Dulhmeny, she'd been kept apart, treated with a kind of innate respect by anyone who saw her, regardless of whether or not she deserved it, thanks to her status as the keeper of the amulet. She'd had no real chance to learn the skills required for friendship with others; anything she knew of human concord had been learned at the hands of her brothers or father, and her mother's death had left her with little in the way of female guidance, except for Morgana. After the Troubles and Morgana's banishment, Father had tried to remove any remnants of her influence on Aileana with steely focus, using his own will to beat her into submission.

Sighing, Aileana moved her thoughts from the past to

the here and now. What about someone here at Eilean Donan to pattern her behavior after? If she wanted to garner this clan's respect, she'd do well to choose someone who'd achieved it already. There was Duncan, of course, but he was their laird and a man as well. Not the best comparison, for her purposes.

Was there a woman who might serve? There were many females at the castle. Too many, where Duncan was concerned. But there was only one that Aileana knew to be respected and obeyed by one and all.

Bridgid.

Pulling the covers over her head, Aileana groaned. With the exception of Nora, Bridgid was the last person she wanted to emulate. The woman barked orders, ran around in a fury and seemed annoyed most of the time.

Yet there had to be more to her than that. Rolling from her pallet, Aileana scuffled to the hearth and rekindled the fire. She ruminated as she worked, mulling the possibilities.

Bridgid was good with children. Aileana remembered her surprise the morning she'd seen Bridgid's face wreathed in smiles because little Tom had brought her a posy from the glen. Bridgid had patted the boy's head and given him a cake from the larder when she thought no one was looking. Then she'd scooted him off to play before reverting to her usual self and snapping an order to one of the kitchen workers.

Chewing her lip, Aileana eased herself into the chair in front of the now brightly crackling flames. Bridgid occasionally showed other softer qualities as well. Many in the clan came to her when they were sick, and she always made time without complaint. She even seemed to know some of the healing properties to be obtained from certain plants and foods.

Here was a connection, Aileana thought. She herself had been a sort of healer at home, and the herbs from her garden, along with her status as keeper of the amulet, had inspired many of the folk to bring their sick up to the castle for her treatments.

Perhaps emulating Bridgid wouldn't be as difficult as she feared. The *bailie* was like anyone else—a blend of prickle and puff. She helped those around her, but she also wasn't afraid to vent her feelings and frustrations.

It was settled, then. Bridgid was the one. Aileana dressed with an energy she hadn't felt since she came to live with the MacRaes. It might be the hardest thing she'd ever done, but she'd make them like and respect her. And she'd have the double satisfaction of watching Duncan swallow his words, along with the gall that was sure to accompany it.

Anxiety fluttered in the pit of her stomach, though, as she prepared to descend to her fate. The results could be no worse than what she'd been forced to endure already, she reasoned. With any luck she'd be successful, and Duncan would see his extortion attempt had failed. That, in and of itself, was a worthy goal.

And it was exactly what she needed to remember, she thought, as she took each step from the safety of her bedchamber toward the staring, unfriendly faces that waited for her in the kitchen below.

Chapter 7

As usual, when Aileana entered the kitchen all conversation ceased. Looking around, she weighed
her options. She'd decided to begin her new life at Eilean
Donan by enlisting some of the women to help her start
a collection of herb pots, as she'd used at home. But
she'd need baskets for gathering, and some clean, well-
shaped pots in which to store the roots, leaves, and flowers she collected.

Pushing up the sleeves of her tunic, Aileana steeled
herself for her first trial and started toward the scullery
area. There she approached two women bent over a vat
of steaming water, rinsing some of the morning's breakfast bowls.

"I'll finish this," she said firmly as she nudged them
aside. "And while I do, I want you to find me eight or ten
small clay pots, preferably with lids. You know better
than I where they're kept. Just stack them at the end of
the courtyard." Aileana plunged her arms into the warm

water and began to scrape and rub the bowls with a
handful of scouring twigs from the bottom of the vat.
"Oh, and find a few baskets as well. I'll be foraging in
the wood later today."

Dead silence greeted her command. She felt the stare
of every person in the kitchen boring into her back. Now
was the time to act upon her decision to be authoritative.

What would Bridgid do?

Lifting her arms from the vat with a splash, Aileana
whirled to face the women. "Have I been unclear? It
isn't so hard, I think, and I'd be doing it myself, but I'd
be wasting time, not knowing where to look." She blew
a strand of hair from her face and wiped her brow with
her forearm. The women just continued to stare, though
she saw a flicker of suspicion in the younger one's eyes.

Willing her voice to sound commanding, Aileana
scowled. "It's very simple. You can do it one of two
ways. Either I'll follow you to where the pots are stored
and leave this mess behind for you to clean when you return, or I can finish the task while you do as I bid. It's
your choice." Raising her brows, Aileana waited for a
response.

After another tense silence, the younger one snipped,
"I'm not doing anything until I talk to Bridgid. I think
she'd be interested in knowing about this."

Aileana pursed her lips. *Curses.* She'd counted on
practicing her authority for a while before she was made
to face the master herself. Well, there was nothing to be
done about it. She'd have to deal with Bridgid sometime.

Turning back to the bowls, she shrugged. "Do as you
wish. But if I don't have those pots available to me by the
time I'm finished washing these, I'm going to rip apart
the pantry, the buttery and any other storage place I can
see until I find what I need."

The two women left, and the others in the kitchen slowly resumed their tasks, though Aileana sensed an undercurrent that hadn't been there before. She took solace in the methodical work of cleaning the other utensils, biding her time until Bridgid returned with the women. *Firm and in control.* She repeated the phrase to herself as she worked. But she still jumped when the *bailie*'s rasping voice cut through the low hum in the kitchen.

"What's this, missy? Making demands of a sudden are you?"

Aileana turned slowly from the tub. Bridgid looked especially irritated; she'd obviously been pulled away from some hard work. A faint sheen of perspiration covered her brow, even at this early hour. As usual, her head cloth was a bit askew and her wiry hair had escaped to frame her face in prickly looking curls.

"I'm not demanding anything," Aileana answered, proud that her voice never wavered. "I'm simply trying to accomplish a task. I need pots for storing my herbs, and I don't know where to look for them." She wiped her hands dry on her tunic and glared piercingly at the two women. "If it's that much trouble for them to help me, then I'll just go ahead and waste the time searching out the pots myself."

She started to push by, but Bridgid stopped her. Startled, Aileana looked up and saw a glimmer of interest in the direct gaze that met her own.

"What are you wanting with herbs and such?" But before Aileana could answer, Bridgid's expression hardened, and she stepped back. "You're not using them for deviltry, are you? Because if you do the things your cursed sister did, I'll string you up and light the fire beneath you myself!"

Aileana blanched at Bridigd's reference to Morgana's evil; it seemed that her sister had inspired hatred that went deep. Though it startled her to hear such words spoken, it wasn't unexpected, she knew. Even Father had forbidden the mention of Morgana's name in the years following the Troubles. And it had been because of her that Aileana had spent so much of her life sheltered in her bedchamber, to prevent any dark forces from influencing her in her possession of the *Ealach*, as her sister had been swayed.

She shook her head, keeping her gaze fixed on Bridgid. "I swear I've never used my knowledge of herbs for evil. In truth I learned the beneficial uses of many flowers, roots, and leaves."

But Bridgid still stared at her with stern accusation, and Aileana's temper flared. It wasn't right, and she couldn't accept it—not if she hoped to earn the respect of anyone at Eilean Donan. Letting her frustration have complete rein, Aileana stood to her full height and added, "More important, though, is this: whatever my sister was or was not in the whole of her life, I am not her. I've spent years paying for her sins, and I'll do it no more." Cheeks flushed, she finished with a demand. "Now for the last time, I'm asking for some help in finding what I need. If you won't give it, then get out of my way so I can fetch the blessed pots myself!"

Everything went deathly still in the aftermath of her outburst, and Aileana had the distinct impression that this was one of the few times Bridgid had ever been rendered speechless. When she finally spoke, there was something in her tone that hadn't been there before.

"I suppose there isn't anything wrong in your gathering herbs for storing. We can use them for cooking, as well as for illness." She seemed to consider Aileana for a moment more, studying her with her gaze before finally nodding. "Very well. You can pick what you like to put away, but not until after the noon meal. Ella and Mab . . . they'll lead you now to the storerooms and help you find some pots. Get on with you then," she sputtered, before flapping out of the kitchen to harp at some other unfortunate worker.

The younger of the two women looked pale, and her eyes widened fearfully as she took in Aileana from head to toe. Then she and Mab left the kitchen, heads tilted together as they whispered, likely about her, she knew, from the sidelong glances they kept giving her.

"The pots are stored in there," Mab said, once they'd crossed the center yard. She waved in the general direction of a little wooden door; it seemed to lead to a room that had been added to the castle in more recent times. The stones of these walls looked newer compared to the more ravaged parts of the fortress.

Aileana nodded acknowledgement, and the women scurried away. She hardly noticed their condemning looks for the swell of excitement that bloomed in her breast as she pushed open the door to the cool, dark storage chamber. Rows of little earthen pots lined the shelves—a veritable treasure trove of them. The floor was full as well, the rest of the chamber scattered with several barrels and a few large crates that rested in a random pattern atop soft cushions of hay.

Stepping over them, she examined some of the pots on the shelf. But as she lifted lids to examine the ancient remnants of their contents, her gaze kept straying to the crates. They were large and finely built. Not the kind of boxes she would have expected to find in such a place.

Finally, she could resist her curiosity no longer. Picking her way back to them, she knelt beside the largest of the crates and pulled at its lid. To her surprise, it slid off easily. It was clear that someone had opened it recently, and it looked as though that person had taken great care with it.

She shifted to let the light from the door come in, feeling a thrill of surprise at what she saw. Yards of glossy satin lay coiled inside the box; spun of deep green, it shimmered even in the dim light, and she reached out to touch the buttery-soft material with reverence. But as her fingers brushed over the silk, she felt something hard. Something buried beneath the folds of fabric. Gently, Aileana moved the soft material to see what lay beneath.

A gasp of wonder escaped her. There, in perfect condition, rested a harp of exquisite workmanship and beauty. Its lines were long and elegant, and it was formed of wood that had been polished many times by loving hands. Wood that glowed mellow against the detailed golden comb and tuning pins that held the strings in place. As fine an instrument as this must be worth a small fortune, she thought absently. She let her fingers drift along the massive, carved circle that formed its base, then up along the beautiful, sloping neck, and to the strings. At her touch, a delicate vibration filled the chamber with the richness of angel-song. She was so lost in the melodious sound that she almost didn't notice the shadow edging closer to the doorway. But then it shifted, plunging the room into darkness.

Weak-kneed, Aileana scrambled to her feet. Her efforts to replace the cover on the box failed; her clumsy hands only succeeded in knocking the lid to the earthen floor with a thump.

"Don't be frightened, lass. I've not come to harm you."

Turning to face the speaker, Aileana shielded her eyes

with her hand. The man appeared in silhouette, bright morning sun streaming in behind him.

"It's me, Kinnon. I saw the door ajar and thought to see who disturbed Duncan's storage chamber with him not about the castle." He stepped farther inside, coming into clear focus. His golden hair waved soft to his shoulders, and Aileana was struck again by the brilliant blue of his eyes. As ever, he had a kind look about him, though he was clearly wondering at her presence here.

Her gaze drifted to the bandages wrapped in thick layers round his leg from knee to ankle. "What happened to you?" she asked.

"I split my leg in the exercises yester morn." He shrugged. "It's a hindrance to be sure, but nothing that won't heal in time."

"Is that why you're here instead of raiding the MacLeods with Duncan?"

He nodded and smiled. "Aye. That's my reason for being here. But you still haven't explained yours."

She felt herself flushing, even though she reminded herself that there was no need to feel guilty. She had permission to be here, after all. "I needed some pots for my herbs, and Bridgid had two of the women bring me here to look." She gestured to the shelves. "There seem to be a good many to choose from, and I should have no trouble finding what I want."

"And yet you were not looking on the shelves but in that crate. I don't suppose you found any pots for your plants in there, now, did you?"

This time guilt gripped her more firmly, deserved, she knew, for the snooping she'd been doing. "In truth, my curiosity got the better of me," she admitted. "I seem to have an affinity for hidden places and mysteries."

To her surprise, Kinnon grinned. "A woman after my own heart." He limped over to the harp. "It's quite a find you've made here. An old friend from long ago, this is." He stroked his hand up the curved neck of the instrument, a wistful smile on his lips. But as he looked up his expression turned serious. "I wouldn't let Duncan see you touching it, though, or any of these things." He gestured to the other large crates in the chamber. "It's better to let them lie for now."

Aileana shook her head. "Keeping such a fine thing locked away . . . it seems sinful. If he's not going to use the harp, then why not trade it for gold or cattle—something to aid the clan's prosperity?"

Kinnon shook his head and folded the satin around the instrument again before replacing the lid. "Because it's a part of Duncan as much as his eyes or his heart. He will never allow it to be sold or taken." Straightening again, he turned and looked at Aileana as if he sought something hidden beneath the surface of skin and bone. She began to feel uneasy, as if he was somehow capable of seeing into her very soul. Finally he spoke, his voice softer than before.

"This harp was Duncan's own pride and joy, lass. It was near as precious to him as possession of the *Ealach* was to our clan these hundred years. Mairi gifted him with it—or her family did, as a betrothal offering—but it mattered not. He thought of the harp as being from Mairi, and he loved it as he did her."

Heat filled Aileana's cheeks, and a strange, sinking sensation spread through her. She resisted the urge to fidget. Mairi—the woman she'd been told was the love of Duncan's life . . . his bride, killed in Morgana's attack on the MacRaes so long ago.

"Duncan loved this harp better than he loved some of

his kin," Kinnon added, breaking into her thoughts. Smiling, he shook his head. "He was just coming into his own in those days, Duncan was, a golden lad with a future as laird of our clan ahead of him. Before your sister's attack, he kept the harp near him much of the time, and, by God, he could wring the soul right out of you with the music that he made. Aye, those were happy days, with him and Mairi."

Staring down at the crate, Kinnon paused, and his expression darkened. "I managed to carry it off and hide it once we learned that Morgana had sold him to the English. But I couldn't help what happened after that. Even in the filthy hell of the Tower, he was so damned stubborn. He hasn't been able to bring himself to touch the harp since coming home last year."

Aileana waited, breathless, for Kinnon to explain further, but he brooded in silence. She knew she shouldn't care—knew she shouldn't feel so defensive in response to his memories of Mairi and Duncan—but she couldn't help it. Worse, perhaps, was that a strange urgency to hear the rest of his tale consumed her. More than anything she wanted to know something more about Duncan and the woman who had won his heart, even though it felt like salt on a wound to think of it. Finally, working up her courage, she asked, "What . . . what happened to make him hate his music so much, then, that he chooses to secret his harp in here?"

As if shaken from a dream, Kinnon looked up. She saw the nightmare seep out of his eyes, leaving nothing behind but the hard, bitter truth. His jaw tightened. "Duncan doesn't hate his music, lass; the English just made sure he could never have it again. Of all the tortures they put him through, it was one of the worst they could have conceived for a man of Duncan's gift; they broke every bone in his hand. It healed, but the scars took away his ability to play."

Horror emptied a pit in Aileana's ·stomach. "The gauntlets . . . ?" she whispered.

"Aye," Kinnon nodded. "He wears them to hide the ruin they made. In truth, he's fortunate to still possess the ability of grasping his sword." Walking to the darkest corner of the room, Kinnon began to unwrap a large, bulky object that leaned against the wall. "Duncan refused to bend to his keepers in the Tower, and because of it, they looked on him as a challenge." His voice grated. "The bastards used the whole of thirteen long years to try out different ways of breaking him."

Aileana shuddered. She knew little of what happened to those unfortunates captured by enemies, but she could imagine enough to make her want to forget that such places as the London Tower even existed.

Kinnon finished unwrapping the object and stood back. "This went the way of the old times too, thanks to the English. Once we returned home, he had it removed from his chamber and closeted here. Like his harp, he hasn't used one since, as far as I know."

Aileana stepped closer to get a better view. As with her first sight of the extraordinary instrument, this new discovery startled a gasp from her. The looking glass Kinnon had uncovered was of impressive size—almost as tall and twice as wide as she was. Stepping closer, she reached out and touched the costly object. Its surface felt cool and smooth against her fingertips. Though the elaborate silver frame looked tarnished from years of disuse, such a mirror was an unimaginable luxury.

"Your clan . . . how came you to own treasures like

these? My people claim prosperity, yet I've never seen the likes of this before."

Kinnon's mouth twisted in a half-mocking smile. "Though it may not appear so now, before your sister attacked us, the MacRaes had much wealth and power. Our overlords granted us with lands and estates, and we gained our other possessions in successful campaigns and wars." One blond brow arched in surprise. "I cannot believe your kin neglected to tell you aught of that. Aside from wanting to steal the *Ealach*, a desire for our holdings was what incited your sister to attack us—that and her need for revenge after Duncan refused to marry her."

"Marry her?"

"Aye. She desired the match; he did not. And even if he had wanted Morgana, he was already in love with Mairi by then and pledged to wed her." Kinnon frowned. "They did not tell you that bit either?" When she shook her head in stunned silence, he made a scoffing noise. "You come from strange folk. Did you yourself never question the whys of the feud between our peoples, beyond the possession of the *Ealach*?"

Embarrassment made Aileana's cheeks feel hot as she tried to explain. "I was but a child when Morgana waged her battle against you. When it was all over, Father brought me to my chamber, telling me that from that day on, I was to become the *Ealach*'s keeper. I was his only remaining daughter, and so it was fitting that I fill the role. He said that the amulet would bring prosperity back to our clan, as long as I remained confined there to protect it. A little while after, the council determined that Morgana had committed crimes against our clan, both in practicing the Black Arts and by consorting with the English . . . but she saved herself from execution thanks to having retrieved the amulet for our people. They banished her to the far north instead, where she died a year later."

Aileana swallowed and looked back to Kinnon for understanding. "It's all I know—all I was ever allowed to know."

An expression of disbelief had crept across Kinnon's face as she spoke. Now he just stared. "Are you saying that until you came here you were kept locked in your chamber to watch over the *Ealach* for thirteen years?"

Aileana shrugged. "I was allowed to come down to the hall at certain times. It was the way it had to be. I was nearly eight when the *Ealach* came home. Morgana had been banished, and as the chieftain's only remaining daughter, it became my charge. We had been without its good influence for nearly a century, and Father decided that dedicating me as keeper would aid in achieving a quicker reversal of our ill fortunes. My loss of freedom was a worthy price to pay."

Kinnon continued to gaze at her in silence, and she wrapped her arms around her waist, recalling the hours of loneliness and boredom, standing at her open shutter to catch a sniff of the air or watch the people of her clan living their lives. His obvious pity made her uncomfortable, though, so she added, "It wasn't unbearable. I was allowed freer roam of the main keep on certain feast days and Sundays. And I got out of my chambers at other times as well, mostly when Father was gone; my brothers would sneak up then and steal me out to play."

She thought for a moment. "Oh, and Father allowed me my herb beds for a while. During the space of two years, I was given leave to come down for an hour each day to tend them and learn what I could about plants from an old woman who lived in the village; she was getting too frail to give much help to the sick, and so I begged for the chance to be trained to take her place, eventually—to have something more useful to do. That ended, though, when Father learned I was cultivating centaury; he feared I'd use it for practicing the Black Arts as Morgana had done." Aileana spoke matter-of-factly. "It is true that if given in the right dosage centaury can cause delusion. I never considered using it in so sinister a way, but Father wanted to take no chance that I might be tempted to darkness as Morgana had been."

Kinnon remained silent for a few moments more before saying in a somber voice, "You've been a virtual recluse, lass. No wonder you caused such a clamor when you came to live here."

She looked at him in wounded denial. "If I did, it was wholly deserved. I've been treated with naught but disrespect and loathing since I arrived at Eilean Donan, though I've tried my best to fit in with the whole lot of you."

Shaking his head, Kinnon spoke more kindly. "Hold, lass, I've no wish to kindle your anger. I'm just trying to make sense of it all so that perhaps I can find a way to help Duncan reach an understanding with you."

"He doesn't wish to reach any kind of reasonable understanding with me." She gave an unladylike snort. "The only thing he's interested in is badgering me into telling him where I've hidden the *Ealach*."

Kinnon smiled enigmatically. "Perhaps . . . perhaps not. My cousin isn't as blustery as he seems. There are many layers to Duncan MacRae; it might not be a bad thing for you to try to uncover a few of them."

Flushing, Aileana stalked over to the shelves and took

down three pots, muttering, "Aye, well I doubt I could penetrate a single layer of that man's stony hide, even if I was foolish enough to want to," before adding more loudly for Kinnon's benefit, "I'm afraid I've dallied here long enough. Would you consent to help me carry some of these pots into the keep?"

Smothering a grin, Kinnon gave her a feigned bow and murmured, "At your service, lass."

As they trumped back to the kitchen with her booty, Aileana thought over what Kinnon had told her. She had difficulty imagining Duncan as anything but a harsh and unbending leader. Then again, people weren't always as they seemed; she knew that better than most. Walking into the kitchen with Kinnon close behind her, she gazed boldly at the women who looked up, noticing that, for once, all conversation didn't cease the moment she entered the room.

Aye, her plan to fit in with the MacRaes and make them like her was progressing well.

The future remained unknown, but one thing was certain. She was going to be using her new, commanding persona to full advantage from now on and as often as possible, practicing the skill until the moment the irascible, enigmatic leader of the wild MacRaes finally returned home . . .

Because she knew that when that time came, she'd be put to the test like never before—and she'd be damned if she was going to fail in it.

Chapter 8

Duncan raked his gloved hand through his hair and groaned as he dismounted Glendragon and led him toward the stables with the other men and their mounts. Sleeping on the ground each night after long days spent skirmishing with the MacLeods had left him aching. Some pains sprang from his old prison wounds, while others were signs of age, no doubt. But be it as it may, he wasn't ashamed to admit that he wanted nothing more, right now, than a hot bath and the comfort of his bed.

After settling Glendragon with a double ration of oats, Duncan nodded to the men who were dispersing to find their families, and then trudged to the center yard and into the castle's main keep. His sleep-deprived mind took foggy note of the area; it seemed quiet for this time of the afternoon. Almost deserted.

His steps slowed as he passed the place where the dogs slept. Gone was the pile of bones and refuse that used to surround the animals. Clean rushes covered the floor, the hounds stretched out upon them, snoring in blissful oblivion. Duncan paused in surprise. It looked as though someone had taken a comb to the animals' unruly coats.

Shaking his head, he continued toward the great hall; he must be more tired than he realized. The dogs were never brushed. They just romped in their natural state, happy to be left to their own play and none the worse for wear.

Duncan rubbed the back of his neck as he entered the passageway leading to the great hall. He saw with satisfaction that at least this one command had been obeyed, even in his absence. Every wall torch was lit, illuminating the narrow corridor as if midday sun shone through the stone. But like everywhere else, the hallway was empty, save for several large baskets filled to overflowing with tiny blossoms of purple heather.

Baskets of heather?

This time Duncan jerked to a stop, his stupefaction breaking all bounds as he absorbed the innocuous sight of the flower baskets set on the floor at regular intervals. Walking into the great hall, he peered around like a hawk searching for prey. Where the devil was Bridgid— and what was she thinking with all this feminine nonsense?

And then he began to notice it. The regular clamor of the hall was no more than a genteel murmur; he looked round and saw his men, huddled over cups of ale, staring belligerently ahead, but speaking nary a word; they sat nicely as schoolboys . . . boys with neatly trimmed beards and clean tunics and plaids.

Disbelief threatened to still Duncan's heart. But then

the numbness faded under an onslaught of blistering rage.

"Bridgid!"

He roared his *bailie*'s name, and twenty pairs of eyes turned on him. If he hadn't been convinced that he'd lost his mind, he might have believed he saw a gleam of desperate hope in more than one of the gazes his kinsmen fixed on him. Wordlessly, several of the men lifted their arms to point toward the kitchens, and Duncan stalked in that direction.

There was no one in the kitchen itself, but as he rounded the corner to the kitchen yard, he heard voices raised in anger. One was Bridgid's, another was definitely male, and the third was unrecognizable, letting loose a string of commands that virtually drowned out the other two.

As his gaze took in the sight before him, his steps slowed before stopping all together. He'd not have believed it if he hadn't seen it with his own eyes. Old Callum was squeezed into one of the wooden kitchen tubs, his bony arms and knees poking out the top, flailing and cursing as Aileana stood over him, trying to unwrap the plaid from his torso. Bridgid stood nearby, hands on her hips, managing to evade the water and soap that sprayed up in glistening droplets every time Aileana tugged the fighting Callum's plaid.

"You're going to let me take this from you and wash it, Callum Menzie," Aileana grated, "or you're not going to be allowed in the hall any more. You'll be taking your meals in the stable with the rest of the animals!"

"That's eno' now!" Callum roared. "I got into a tub for ye—and I even let you take shears to me beard, but that's as far as I go! Me plaid stays with me!"

"Has everyone lost their blessed minds?"

At Duncan's exasperated bellow, all activity ceased; Aileana took two steps back, Bridgid whirled to face him, and Callum blinked up at him like a soapy, wet owl. They all stared, dumbfounded, and Duncan charged forward. "Someone had better answer me. I'm in no mood to be making guesses."

"What is it you want to know, then?"

It was Bridgid who'd spoken, somewhat timidly, he noted, but facing her, he growled nonetheless, "Why don't we start with something simple—like telling me why the dogs are combed like cats, why there are flowers in my hall, and why my men are sitting at the table, looking like they're waiting for a sermon!"

At that, Bridgid's mouth opened, but no sound came out. Aileana stepped forward, chin upraised. "Don't be badgering Bridgid, Duncan MacRae. It was none of her doing, but mine. I'll be taking responsibility for it if you've anything to say."

"You're blasted right, I've got something to say. I cannot believe—" Duncan's throat seized up as comprehension of Aileana's admission hit home. His brows furrowed and he directed a hot glare at her. "*You?* You're trying to tell me that *you're* at the root of all this nonsense?"

Did the woman think him daft? Not only was she a leman in the eyes of his clan, but she was a MacDonell besides; she could no more order his men to bathe and shave and be obeyed in it than she could breathe under water. They'd throw her in the loch if she tried. Barking a laugh, he rounded on her, standing between her and the others. "It is my experience that wee mousies squeak, Aileana MacDonell, they do not roar. Now I'll be knowing the truth of all this before I step a foot from this yard."

"Then you can grow roots and plant yourself if it

pleases you, but the truth is staring you in the face. I ordered the changes you see, and if you do not like them, then you can address your complaints to me." Aileana dug her fists into her hips and looked him square in the eye.

Nonplussed, Duncan swung his gaze to Bridgid. His *bailie* gazed back at him with a level expression that bespoke agreement with Aileana. Doubt fell beneath the hooves of swiftly rising anger. It seemed his meek, timid leman hid more than one surprise for him behind that face of angelic innocence; perhaps she *had* created these disturbances. How and why remained a mystery. But it wouldn't be for long.

"You," he said, pointing at Aileana, "will meet me in my chamber in exactly one hour."

She quirked one dainty brow, and her voice lilted to his ears, as sweet now as it had been shrill before. "If I'm free, aye, I'll come. Otherwise I'll be there when I can make the time." He saw a glimpse of pearly teeth before she swept past him and back toward the kitchens.

So great was his surprise at her answer that he felt like he had indeed grown roots, fixing him to the spot. But when Old Callum coughed, he started from the spell Aileana had cast on him. Callum shivered in the tub, his lips tinged blue and his teeth beginning to chatter. "Are you through, MacRae? I'm thinking I'll be needing a glass of spirits afore I catch my death of cold."

At Duncan's nod, Callum surged from the water and grabbed at the length of dry plaid that Bridgid held for him. With a sniff of tattered dignity, he dried his arms and legs and then draped the plaid round himself; but as he wobbled toward the kitchen, Duncan heard him muttering and cursing under his breath.

Callum was right. They'd all been bested by a wee

MacDonell lass. And as chieftain of the clan, Duncan decided, it was his duty to put a stop to it.

Gritting his teeth, he trudged through the yard to the
kitchen, and from there across the hall and up the steps
to his chamber; he looked neither right nor left, uttering
not a word in response to the wide-eyed gazes his people
gave him. His mind twisted with thoughts, alternating
between bafflement at the apparent change Aileana had
made in both her demeanor and his castle, and anger that
she'd done either without asking his permission.

When he finally reached his room, it was with grim
resolution. He needed to prepare for his bath—and for
the reckoning his unpredictable, red-haired leman had
earned this day.

Exactly an hour and a quarter later, Aileana stood at
the portal to Duncan's bedchamber. Clenching her fingers, she breathed a prayer for strength. Duncan would
be her greatest challenge yet, and she knew that she'd be
fortunate to escape this meeting unscathed. Still, these
past days of practice gave her confidence. She'd learned
many things in the process of overcoming his clan, not
the least of which was that to get a desired result, she
had to interpret each individual she faced with careful
scrutiny.

Where some of Duncan's kin responded to her snapping and blustering, she sensed the chieftain himself
needed a more subtle approach. Mild antagonism—such
as her deliberate lateness—would serve to show her inde-
pendence. And though she was certain that he would
shout and attempt to cow her into submission as Father
had done when she was disobedient, she vowed to remain firm once she stood face-to-face with him.

Aileana looked down at her green overskirt, examining it with a critical eye; it still bore a smudge from the rasher of bacon that Nora had tipped into her this morning as they served breakfast. She rubbed the spot to no avail. It would have to do. Her hand trembled as she smoothed her unruly hair back one last time. Then, pushing open the door, she strode into the bedchamber.

Duncan stood with his hands linked behind his back, gazing out at the sun setting over the loch below. Clearing her throat lightly, Aileana waited for him to acknowledge her presence; she knew he was aware of her by the way he'd stiffened when she came into the room. But he remained silent.

"I'm here as you bid," she murmured. "And I'm waiting to hear what you have to say to me."

"Aye, you are waiting," he answered quietly. He swung around to look at her, adding, "And if I wanted to be true to the point, I'd be making you do so for the full quarter hour as you did me."

Aileana felt herself flush; his controlled dignity made her almost ashamed that she'd used such a ploy against him. Almost, but not quite.

She stood straighter. "I came when I was free, as I told you I would. You seem to be forgetting that I'm no fee post, paid to do your bidding at a moment's notice."

"Nay, you're my *leman*, which under normal circumstances requires much, much more."

She felt herself flushing a deeper hue, though she managed to retort, "It is by your command alone that we live a lie."

Duncan's gray eyes warmed to quicksilver. "Then you're saying that you'd be in favor of a true joining between us?"

An image, hot and explicit, raced through Aileana's mind, making her turn away from him. She retreated to the relative safety of the hearth, trying to gather her thoughts, to remind herself of the new personality she'd vowed to project. But the strange feeling that his suggestion had unfurled inside her continued to wind its way through her. It was all she could do to slow her breathing to a normal pace.

Without looking at him she answered. "I'm not saying anything of the kind. I was just reminding you that your complaint about my service holds no weight, since it was you who dictated our terms."

She heard the tread of his boots as he crossed the stone floor. When he brushed by her to sit in the chair opposite the hearth, she shivered. The tingle of awareness she felt was the result of her animosity toward him, she told herself, nothing more.

"Turn around."

His command, uttered in a soft, authoritative tone, spurred her to compliance. But when she faced him, another jolt of sensation swirled through her belly. Duncan leaned back in the chair, studying her, his expression a mix of vulnerability and intensity. The sun's dying glow cast the room in warm shades, accenting the perfection of his scarred beauty.

His golden brown hair fell in waves, to shoulders that were draped with a length of colorful plaid on one side. The setting sun combined with the flicker of firelight to dance across his powerfully muscled forearms, and Aileana resisted the urge to smooth her fingers over his skin.

"You're a sorceress, lass," he murmured. "Different from your cursed sister, but a sorceress nonetheless."

Uncertainty took Aileana's breath away. Did he seek to mock her by invoking Morgana's memory? Was he trying to trap her into saying something to damn herself and expose the *Ealach*? Biting her lip to keep from trembling, she answered, "I—I do not understand what you mean."

Duncan's generous mouth tilted up on one side, heightening her impression of utter, sensual masculinity. "I'm saying that you must have cast a spell on me when you came into this room, Aileana MacDonell, because until then I was ready to wring your neck with my bare hands. And now . . . very different kinds of thoughts are filling my imagination."

Looking down, Aileana twined her fingers together and squeezed tight. Her heart thudded in a heavy cadence. What game did Duncan play? He couldn't be in earnest. Mayhap she misread his intent altogether; perhaps her naiveté kept her from seeing the true meaning behind his enigmatic words.

Either way, it seemed best to withdraw to another, if more dangerous topic of conversation. Glancing back up at him, she stiffened her shoulders and asked, "What think you, then, of the changes I made at the castle while you were away?"

Duncan's gaze cooled slightly, and he sat up from his relaxed position to rest his forearms on his thighs. "I think that you acted with rash disregard. It's the hows and whys of it I cannot figure."

"I assure you, I undertook every change with forethought. None of it was acted upon with disregard."

"Then mayhap you'll explain to me why you felt the need to do anything at all."

Duncan sat composed, quite unlike the obdurate tyrant she'd expected he'd be. She looked down again, toying with the answer she'd planned to give as reason for instigating the changes, and remembering the insults she'd intended to drop on him concerning the sloth and disorder of his clan. But she found that those excuses sounded petty now, even in her own mind.

Glancing at him from the side of her gaze, Aileana realized that Duncan was working a magic of his own on her. Though she'd meant to needle him, to plot against him and keep him at arm's length with her newfound boldness, his calm prevented her from doing anything of the kind. In a strange way he even seemed to invite her confidence, along with something else she'd never experienced before from a man . . .

A request for honest discussion with her.

Warmth filled her, loosening her reserve and pressing her to tell Duncan MacRae the real reason she'd been driven to test her powers of persuasion on his clan. The tripping throb of her pulse beat in her throat, and her mouth felt dry as she waged the silent war inside her. It would be so easy to dissemble, to hide behind the same protective defenses she'd built over a lifetime of domination. But something was pushing her in the opposite direction, urging her to trust, though by all rights Duncan was the last man she should consider trustworthy at this point.

"I—I do not know where to start," she murmured, buying time to think.

He motioned for her to sit on the second chair near the fire. "Make yourself comfortable and start anywhere you like, lass. I'll keep up." His quicksilver eyes warmed again, piercing her with that same vulnerable, sensual quality as he took her hand in his own gloved one and eased her to the seat.

At the touch of the warm leather, all thinking stopped. A strange sensation tingled up Aileana's arm and deep into the core of her, even more startling and pleasurable than what she'd felt when he'd brushed by her earlier.

And then she knew that what had seemed impossible was about to happen.

She was going to tell Duncan the truth.

Moistening her lips, she let the words come. "You told me once that your clan disliked me for the harm my sister and my people had done to them, but that if I worked very hard, I might learn to change their view of me." Aileana wrapped her arms around her middle where she sat facing him. "After you left to raid the MacLeods, I decided to do just that."

The fire popped and crackled in the companionable silence. After a space, Aileana saw the corners of Duncan's mouth twitch as if he wanted to smile. "Am I right in thinking your decision stemmed in part from a wish to spite me?"

A nervous laugh escaped her, and she nodded. "Aye. I admit that was one of my reasons."

"And the others?"

The smile faded from Aileana's lips, and she twisted her head to gaze into the fire. "The other reasons do not concern you."

"Aye but they do, if they pushed you to act in matters of my clan without my knowledge. I demand the complete allegiance of every person living under my roof, Aileana, because I know too well what happens when a viper is allowed to dwell in secret among them. I will not let it happen again."

Duncan sounded harsh, and Aileana glanced quickly at him. His expression had hardened, his jaw set in a rigid line that managed to condemn, convict, and sentence her in one fell swoop.

An answering hurt lanced into her heart, a wound that stemmed from constant lack of trust. Her own father had doubted her strength of character enough to lock her away from human company at the tender age of eight. Bridgid had all but outright accused her of witchery.

And now Duncan. It was almost as if he expected her to leap up from the hearth and slit his throat with a concealed dagger. Was she forever cursed to be judged by the evil standards Morgana had set so many years ago?

Bitterness scorched her as she said, "My sister is *dead*. Wicked though she was, can everyone not leave her at rest? Must you and the rest of your kin fire her sins at me like arrows every time you suspect my loyalty?"

"Your sister ruined many lives, Aileana, and if there is any justice, her soul burns in hell this very moment," Duncan answered. "But I was never fool enough to let your sister abide with me and my people. It wasn't her I was thinking of when I spoke."

"Who, then?" Aileana challenged.

"My own brother, Colin MacRae."

A cold chill slid down Aileana's back. Duncan had a *brother*? She'd never suspected such a thing—never even questioned the possibility in her mind. But what could one of Duncan's own kin have done to earn his hatred on the same scale as Morgana?

"Where is this brother? Why haven't I met him?"

"He's dead."

A horrible thought took hold of her, and before she could stop herself, she blurted, "Did you kill him?"

"Nay. Though I wish the pleasure had been mine." Duncan pushed himself from his chair and paced over to the window. Night had crept across the moors, darkening the waters of the loch to murky gray. He splayed his fingers on the glass and leaned against it, letting its smooth expanse cool his forehead.

Colin. It hurt Duncan to think of him almost as much as it did to remember Mairi. But he wouldn't honor his brother's memory with silence. Better to reveal the whole sordid truth so that no one could deny that Colin was a bastard in action as well as birth.

Pasting a mocking grin on his face, Duncan twisted from the window. "Colin was my father's son, born a year before me of an illicit union Da made with a woman from a village across the loch. Though he was of the wrong side of the sheets, we were raised together like true brothers, and he never gave me any cause to suspect that he resented my legitimacy. We knew our places: I was to become laird, while he would take a favored position on my council. In truth, I appointed him to lead the watch on the day I was wed to Mairi, the woman I loved . . . an honor he repaid by killing some of our guards—his own kin—to provide your sister and her minions unhindered access past the curtain wall of this castle. She and others of your clan slaughtered my bride and many of my people on the day that was to be the happiest of my life."

He closed his eyes against the dark bitterness that still filled him whenever he allowed himself to think on it. "Colin stood next to me as I spoke my vows, aware that the enemy was breaching our walls at that very moment. When I finally managed to figure out what was happening—when I understood, finally, that my own brother had betrayed me—it was too late. We fought, and I wounded him before I was knocked senseless, but he escaped with Morgana. When it was all over, Mairi was dead and I'd been sold as a prisoner to the English."

He stopped talking, and Aileana just stared at him, wide-eyed, from where she sat before the fire. Finally, she whispered, "Is there more?"

Leaning against the wall, Duncan crossed his arms over his chest and clenched his fists. "Not much. In the end, Colin chose to follow your sister into banishment and die a miserable death in the mountains there with her." Duncan lifted his gaze to Aileana, pinning her with intensity and trying to make her understand the consequences to be faced should she or anyone else betray him again. "My only regret is that I wasn't there to choke the life from both of them myself."

Aileana blanched and closed her eyes, breathing in, and for a moment, Duncan just stared at her, the sight of her sitting with the fire lighting her golden-red hair from behind numbing him, sending a horrible image spinning through his mind. He tried his best to resist its deadly pull on him, but it swept over him, its ferocity choking the air from his lungs and making his fists clench. Heaven help him, but at this moment she looked just like *her*. With her eyes closed Aileana looked an exact replica of the murderous bitch who had destroyed his life.

Raw animosity rose up in suffocating waves, and it was all he could do to ground out, "Aileana—please, do not sit like that. Look at me, lass."

Her eyes snapped open then, fear stiffening her features at the leashed anger in his command. But the depths of her tawny gaze dispelled the nightmare from Duncan's imagination. He felt the rage begin to flow out of him as she uncurled herself from the hearth to stand before him.

Her cheeks looked hollow, her expression that of a child who's just learned of a loved one's death. "No wonder you hate me so," she whispered. Her lips trembled, and he could see the fluttering beat of her pulse in her neck.

"Nay, Aileana. I do not hate you. It's just that when you were sitting there like that, I couldn't stop thinking . . . I couldn't get it out of my mind that you looked just like—"

"Morgana." Aileana breathed her sister's name, and as Duncan watched, her jaw tightened and that terrible, stricken expression slid across her features. "I know," she murmured. "I look much like my sister. I was never allowed to forget it. And I cannot blame you for hating me because of it, after hearing for the first time the full truth of what she did."

She smoothed her hands in a repetitive motion over her skirt, her gaze distant, lost in a world of her own making. When she focused on him again, he saw in them the ache of old pain . . . pain that had taken years to accumulate, but to which he had just added, with his unthinking, gut reaction of moments ago.

It filled him with an inexpressible sadness that was as sudden and violent as his response to Aileana's appearance had been. But before he could gather his composure enough to do anything, to say anything, she spoke again.

"I cannot promise you perfect obedience, Duncan MacRae. I *won't* promise it to you." A flash of the defiance he'd seen when he came home shown in her face. "I cannot go back to the frightened, sheltered woman I was forced to be these many years. But I swear to you that unlike my sister, I do not seek ill for your clan. You have my word on that."

Duncan watched her, spellbound, as she walked with quiet grace to the door. "I've several tasks to finish before I retire for the night. I'll return when they're complete. Good night."

And with that she disappeared through the open door. But not before Duncan caught sight of a single tear that had begun to trickle down her cheek.

It seemed as if he could hear his heart thundering in

his ears in the terrible silence she left behind. Swallowing hard, he blinked to rid himself of the dry, scratchy sensation that lodged behind his eyes. Then, wordlessly, he closed them and dropped his chin to his chest, feeling as empty as if someone had just driven a dagger through his heart.

Chapter 9

Aileana pounded the last of the dried marigolds into dust before carefully brushing the powder into the curved stone vessel that rested on the table. Bridgid handed her a flagon of good wine from the storehouse, and Aileana poured until only two finger widths of space remained at the top of the bowl. For the final ingredient she added a bottle of vinegar to the mix and stirred them all together. Word of the plague had spread up from the south, and this mixture was the only one Aileana knew of that might spare the inhabitants of Eilean Donan.

"Cover this and let it sit in a cool place for three days before straining it," she told Bridgid. Wiping the back of her hand across her brow, she shook her head. "With luck, I think it'll last until the threat of the plague passes."

"I don't think it'll matter, missy. Some of the men are saying they'll drink no more of your brew," Bridgid complained. Concern wrinkled her brow. "They're claiming that nothing will be stopping the sickness if it means to take us in its clutches. They rejected my tonics for the same reason."

Aileana's lips tightened. The marigold formula couldn't help anyone if they refused to swallow it.

She thought for a moment. "It is true we cannot make them drink anything outright, Bridgid . . ." She nodded toward the pot of oats bubbling on the kitchen fire. "But we can fix it so they'll be getting some anyway if we don't mind being a bit sly about it."

Bridgid's wiry curls bobbed as she nodded. "I ken your meaning missy, and I think it's a good plan. I've always hoped to find another woman who'd be willing to stand up and help me keep the menfolk in order. Most times they don't know what's best for themselves anyway."

Bridgid heaved the bowl into her arms, heading for the cellar, and Aileana allowed herself a brief smile. That was as close to a compliment as she'd received from Bridgid, but it gratified her to know that she'd made progress in the two weeks since Duncan returned from raiding the MacLeods. And she'd been true to her word with him, making only those changes that she thought would improve the lot of the clan.

He'd seemed tolerant of her decisions, if not appreciative. He'd even agreed to swallow some of the marigold tonic himself just a sennight ago, before he left on another raid against the neighboring MacLennans. She recalled the pleasant surprise she'd felt that morn when Duncan had insisted on viewing her herb collection; he'd listened to her describe each plant's use with careful attention, then he'd complimented her on the variety she'd managed to gather in so short a time. He'd left shortly after that, and she'd realized that she felt empty. Like the sun shone dimmer and the wind blew colder.

Almost as if, God help her, she missed him.

Her erratic emotions were due to the change of seasons, she decided. The skies rumbled with gray clouds more often than not this late part of September, and a chill had settled over the moors.

The early frosts were making forays to the wood and glen more difficult, and she'd been forced to accept that her store of herbs was as full as it was likely to be until the spring thaw. Still, after combining her fresh gatherings with Bridgid's old ones, Aileana thought they'd have enough to get through the harsh winter season and the threat of plague. With a little extra industry, a rich bed of soil could be cultivated in the castle yard before the snow flew, making it ready for a spring planting.

But it wouldn't wait long; more digging needed to be done, and the old bed, unused for many years, thirsted for a proper weeding and turning of soil. Letting her gaze drift over the kitchen, Aileana gathered a bucket and the small basin of live plants she'd gleaned from the forest floor. As she collected the items, she allowed herself a flicker of satisfaction. This room, at least, glistened with cleanliness and order—something it had sadly lacked when she arrived.

But the castle yard called her to more work. Tucking her braid more firmly beneath her head cloth, Aileana trudged outside. And as she dug her shovel into the ground, she promised herself that she'd tease some order from the tangled patch of earth before the sun set on Loch Duich or wear herself out in the trying.

*   *   *

Just two nights later, Aileana heard the cries she'd been dreading; they rose in a frightening crescendo throughout the castle keep, urging her from her pallet. Bridgid burst through the door to the bedchamber moments after she'd pulled her tunic over her head.

"The plague, missy—it's upon us. Come with me if you will, for I can use your help in treating them that's afflicted."

A cold blade of fear pierced Aileana. It was confirmation of what she'd already suspected, but her hands trembled as she straightened her overskirt. "Aye, I'll come. Who's been struck with it?" she asked as she followed Bridgid through the door and down the hall.

"Inghin's boy came down with fever yesterday, but now he's shaking and out of his mind, and he's got the swelling on his neck and below his stomach."

Aileana bit her lip and nodded. It boded ill. She walked more quickly next to Bridgid, silent now in the chill of the yard. If it was as Bridgid described, the disease had progressed rapidly; little would be left for them to do to save the lad.

Worried faces peered out of shutters and doors as they made their way through the castle village, and the smoky scent of banked fires filled the air. Aileana ducked her head to follow Bridgid into a cottage near the far edge of the settlement. In the moment it took to get her bearings, she noticed several things. A low keening rose from the far end of the room, and she saw the laundress, Inghin, crouched there, rocking back and forth over a slender form on the pallet. A few other village women huddled in the dark corners of the hut. They sat peering into the smoky gloom, likely braving the contagion because one of their near kin had been stricken.

"William, laddie, wake up for your mum!" Inghin's voice cracked with desperation. But the boy remained unresponsive except for a faint moan as he thrashed his head on the straw pallet.

Bridgid moved forward. "Let me see him, Inghin. We'll try to help if we can."

The woman twisted around, her eyes red-rimmed with fear and grief, lighting with wildness the moment she caught sight of Aileana standing behind Bridgid.

"You," she rasped. The word rang with accusation. Her brows drew together in a sneer, and she spit a curse. "Why are you here, except to gloat over your work, witch? Damn your soul to the flames, MacDonell. Your cursed sister sent you to finish what she started—it's *you* who's killing my boy, and I'll see you dead for it!" She lumbered up from her knees, trying to lunge at Aileana, but Bridgid darted forward to hold her back.

Bridgid eased the woman onto a stool and murmured to her in soft, soothing tones. At last Inghin bent over and began to sob, and Bridgid hugged her tight. After a few moments, the *bailie* lifted her head to direct Aileana toward the sick boy.

"See what you can do for him, missy, while I care for his mam," she murmured. "Never mind what Inghin said. It is her worry speaking, nothing more. She'll be glad for your help in the morning."

Blindly, Aileana nodded. She tried to force the numbness from her limbs and the nausea from her throat, but it kept closing in on her, the woman's words wounding to the bone with the hatred that filled them.

William moaned again, but this time his entire body stiffened and he started to convulse. Without further thought Aileana rushed forward. Foamy spittle flew from the boy's lips as he jerked and twisted in her grasp;

her hands felt seared with heat where she touched him, and she knew that if they didn't bring his fever down, William would die before dawn.

"You," she called to an old woman huddled near the door, "bring me a bucket of cool water from the loch. Hurry!"

Wordlessly, the woman shuffled to her feet and scurried off, her eyes looking as though they might pop from their sockets. Aileana held onto William until the shaking stopped, then she leaned back on her heels and peered around the tiny room again. Her gaze met the dark eyes of a boy who seemed but a shade younger than the sick lad. But when she looked at him, he skittered farther into the shadows. Aileana gestured for him to come back into the light.

Reluctantly, he obeyed, standing on shifting feet in the smoky fire's glow. His hands twisted behind his back, and he looked down, trying to avoid Aileana's stare.

"What's your name, lad?"

"Evan," he mumbled, still looking down.

"A fine name, Evan," she murmured. She paused before adding, "But mayhap not the name of the man who'd perform the kind of great deed I'll be needing to help save young William here."

At the mention of great deeds, Evan's head snapped up. "I can do many things! Better'n most!" His eyes welled with tears. "And I'll do anything to help my brother. On my word of honor!"

Aileana's heart twisted. She hadn't meant to make the boy feel guilty. But she had wanted to incite him to cooperate, and the quicker the better. Striving for a more understanding tone, she said, "I don't need anything that is bad, Evan, only something necessary to help your brother's heart beat strong. Can you get it for me? It's something you'll be needing help to carry."

Evan nodded, his eyes alight with the understanding that his would be a serious mission.

"Good, then." She nodded back. "I want you to fetch one of the casks of wine stored in the castle. Get another lad and come back with it as soon as you can. Will you do that for me?"

"In a whistle-breath, I can!" Evan shouted, dashing to the door.

Aileana turned back to William after the boy left, biting her lip with concern. His breathing was labored, and when she felt his neck and near his groin, she noticed the hard swellings that Bridgid had warned of earlier. It was clear that the plague buboes caused him pain; he writhed and groaned louder when she touched the swollen places.

She felt a hand on her shoulder. Tilting her head, she saw Bridgid standing next to her. The *bailie* had left Inghin in the competent hands of two of the other women who were trying to persuade her to lie on the pallet near the tiny room's hearth.

"How is he?"

"Not good," she answered quietly. "If the fever cannot be lessened, he will die before morn."

Bridgid knelt down beside her. "I heard you tell Evan to bring wine." Her glance drifted to Inghin, who appeared to be giving in to the women's entreaties to rest. She looked to Aileana again, speaking more softly, even, than before. "But wouldn't the tonic you prepared be better than plain wine for the lad?"

"Nay. The strength of the wine will not be dulled by vinegar and herbs as it is in the tonic."

"You fear for his heart, then."

Aileana nodded. "He needs the stimulation of the wine, but we will need to sponge him continually to cool any heat it might bring to his skin. That is why I've sent the old woman to the loch. It was faster to get and just as cool as the water from the well."

Bridgid fell silent, and Aileana worked to loosen William's clothing. She wanted to make him as comfortable as possible until the others returned. When she finished, she sat back to wait. He seemed at peace for the moment, and all was quiet, but she sensed a strangeness from Bridgid; the *bailie* hung back, wary and guarded, watching Aileana with a vigilance that unnerved her.

Assuming that she simply feared contagion, Aileana said, "Perhaps you should return to the castle now, Bridgid. There is no need for you to sit watch this night."

Bridgid made a scoffing sound. "It is not your place to send me home like an errant child, missy. I've no dread of the plague, if that is what you're thinking."

"I was only trying to say that there is no need for us both to look the demon in the eye. It is only William, for now. One of us is enough to sit with him."

"Then why don't *you* go back to the castle and your bed?" When Aileana started to shake her head, Bridgid burst forth, "And why not? I know I asked for your help, but do you not worry for your own safety, toiling here, in the heart of the disease?"

That strange thought stilled Aileana for a moment, making her pause. It was true that illness floated thick around them. It hung like a deadly cloud over the entire chamber. But she felt little concern for herself. In truth she'd always felt a great satisfaction in helping to heal the sick at Dulhmeny. They'd been the only people other than her brothers that Father had freely allowed her to talk to during the many years after Morgana's banishment and death.

Being here was only a little different. MacRaes or nay, these people needed her, and she found that she was willing to risk contagion for the pleasure of that burden. It would be a chance to prove once and for all that she wasn't like Morgana . . . that she didn't thrive on spreading destruction as her sister had. Nay, just the opposite.

Finally, she met Bridgid's gaze and answered, "I've treated many illnesses in my life and never taken sick because of it. It will be the same for this, I warrant—and if not, then I cannot change the hand of God."

Bridgid shook her head and mumbled, "I do not know, lass. Perhaps Inghid was right—it might not be best for you to be here, though I asked you to come."

Aileana bit the insides of her cheeks. So it came down to this again. *Trust.* Bridgid didn't trust her. Hurt spread dark tendrils through her veins. How could she have been so daft as to let her guard down even for an instant? She'd come no farther down the road of acceptance than where she'd been the first day she walked into Eilean Donan's castle yard.

"I am sorry," Aileana said stiffly. "I did not realize my help was still suspect with you as well." She rocked back on her heels, bracing her hands against her thighs to stand. "I will be leaving now. Send for me if there is anything you feel you can trust me to do."

"Nay, missy, it is not that." Bridgid reached up and pulled Aileana back down. "I've no fear of your honesty. Truth to tell, I know precious little about healing them that come down with the plague; I *need* your help if you're willing to give it."

Aileana's brows drew together. "I do not understand, then. Why were you trying to send me away?"

Bridgid looked down and shook her head; her breathing sounded heavy, as if a burden weighed on her. When she met Aileana's gaze, hers was shaded with kindness and concern. "I was giving you leave to go, missy, because I've thought better of what some of the others might say if the sick die, as many are bound to, under your care. I had not considered that part of it when I called on your aid, but since Inghid spoke, I've seen where it might lead to that."

"You're thinking they will brand me a witch and accuse me of working spells to kill their kin, plague or nay," Aileana said flatly.

"Aye," she admitted. "And not only what they would call you, but what they might do to you as well."

Aileana clamped her lips tight.

"Some might think to use you to ease their hurt. And with the MacRae away on a raid . . ." Bridgid shook her head. "Mayhap it is better for you to retreat to your castle chamber, lass. I can come to you for advice or remedies as needed."

Bridgid's suggestion struck a chord with Aileana. *Retreat to your castle chamber.* The concept sent a shudder of revulsion through her. She'd spent the better part of her life locked in her chamber, and unless she was forced, she'd never do so willingly again.

"I think I will take my chances against the plague."

At Bridgid's stricken look, she grimaced, adding, "I know precious little about people, thanks to the life I led at Dulhmeny, but I do know how to heal their bodies. And besides that, I'm fearing you will need every available helper in the coming days. Where one falls sick, many usually follow."

"It is your decision, missy, though I cannot say I will be sorry for your help," Bridgid answered, looking at her with a new measure of respect before she frowned again, the action furrowing deeper lines at the sides of her mouth. "Do you think it will be laying low the entire clan, then? I do not think we can stand another devastation so soon after coming together again under the MacRae."

"Pray God it will not come to that." Aileana looked around the tiny hut. "But chances stand that any one of these folk will show signs of it next, and then . . ." She placed her hand on the feverish William's brow again, mentally cursing that the water hadn't arrived yet. "Come what may, I will stay with you. That I swear."

Any further chance at conversation dissolved in a flurry of activity as Evan came rushing through the door. Another lad followed him in, the cask of wine leaking from a tiny crack along its side.

"You've got to come! There's another fallen sick. We dropped the wine trying to help her, but in the end we couldn't lift her up from the ground."

"Who is it, lad?" Bridgid asked.

Evan's eyes were filled with tears of frustration as he swung his gaze to the *bailie*. "Old Jehana! She was on the bank of the loch, trying to get the water the lady wanted, but now she is just lying there, and to touch her is like burning yourself with fire. Please, you've got to help!"

An anxious glance passed between Bridgid and Aileana, and they stood as if of one accord. "Evan, get two strong men from the village and show me where Jehana is," Aileana said. "We will help her, lad, best as we can."

Bridgid nodded her agreement to stay behind with William, and Aileana set to action. It was going to be a very long night, she realized, as she strode through the door behind Evan. Two fallen ill in less than an hour, and more sure to follow if the sickness held true to the virulence proclaimed of it in the Lowlands.

She needed to keep her wits about her now, she knew, for she was about to be tested as never before in her protected life at Dulhmeny. And she faced the added pressure of knowing that this clan might hold her personally responsible for any failure to heal the afflicted.

Mouthing a prayer for strength, Aileana trudged onward. Aye, it was going to be a long night. A very long night, indeed.

Chapter 10

Her arms felt leaden. They sagged to her sides no matter how hard she tried to grip the cloth and bathe the faces of the sick. With effort born of desperation, Aileana pulled the basin and dipped the piece of rag again. She let the cool, minted water drizzle over Nora's neck and chest, praying in the never-ending litany of the past four days for God to spare the people of Eilean Donan from further ravages of the plague.

Eighteen had died thus far. Old Jehana had succumbed, as had Floraidh and Fergus and several of the other men who'd stayed behind when Duncan left more than a fortnight ago to raid the MacLennans.

But little William had lived. And if means existed, she'd make sure that Nora and the rest survived as well.

"Missy, why don't you take a rest now? There's some cold mutton waiting in the kitchens," Bridgid cajoled, her eyes looking as weary as Aileana felt. "You need to keep up your strength. You cannot keep working without respite."

"I'll not be leaving you alone to do all the tending." But even as she spoke, Aileana couldn't prevent her traitorous mind from leaping at the prospect of sleep. She shook her head, trying to clear away the fuzzy feeling, and the *bailie* clucked her tongue and muttered.

As Bridgid went on her way to another patient, she stumbled, and Aileana frowned. Bridgid was exhausted, too. Neither of them had taken much rest in the days since the plague struck the clan. There'd been too much work to do, and after the first twelve hours, too many sick to tend.

Pushing back the sleeves of her tunic, Aileana moved on to young Kenneth; he'd fallen sick just yesterday. After a quick examination for swellings, she repeating the cooling process she'd administered to Nora. They'd converted the great hall to a kind of infirmary, since there wasn't already a chamber for that purpose on the castle compound. Aileana made a mental note to insist that Duncan order some new construction for such a room come spring.

Duncan. She missed him, there was no doubt. She knew that now. She missed his warmth and his compelling presence . . . missed his arms around her when he'd carry her to his bed each night. But she would find strength to care for his people in his absence, that she promised herself.

A wave of dizziness washed over her as she leaned down to pick up the basin. Forcing her feet to move, she trudged across the hall, planning to go to the well and draw some fresh water. She picked her way over rows of people in varying stages of disease. Some stared straight ahead, eyes glassy with fever. At the far end were those near death. Those unfortunates Aileana had taken on as her own crusade; she vowed to save as many as she could, even if she needed to go two more days without sleep to do it.

Stopping to pull a blanket over a shivering child near the door, she steeled herself against the helplessness that was beginning to consume her. She knew better than most that it did no good to become emotional. But she couldn't stop the horrible thought that the sounds and smells surrounding her were shadows, surely, of what hell must be like. Groans and coughs battled with wails of pain and grinding of teeth; magnified in the close quarters, the noises exceeded even the hideous echoes of the battlefield on that day Father had been killed.

Worse than the sound, though, was the stench; the foul odors of sickness made the air unfit to breathe. Yesterday, she'd insisted that the hall's shutters be left open. Such ideas were considered dangerous; drafts often led to chills and death. But the need for clean air had overpowered any possible argument, and so the shutters were opened.

A reason to thank Duncan.

Warmth spread through her, her mind latching on to the thought as surely as it had registered complaint about the castle's lack of an infirmary. It was Duncan, after all, who'd insisted that every room be equipped with plenty of windows after his return from the Tower. He'd had them hewn into the stone walls, even, where openings didn't exist already, and it appeared now that his insatiable need for fresh air might be the winning factor in the struggle many of his people waged for their lives.

Aileana brushed a lank wisp of hair from her eyes and continued to the well. The cool outdoors beckoned her, and she tried to concentrate on something positive as she stepped into the chill. At least she needn't fear Duncan falling under the disease's ravages. Bridgid had ordered that a sign be posted on the castle's main gate, telling all who came, to remain outside the wall for fear of contagion; unless he and his men had contracted the plague during their travels, they'd be safe.

Upon reaching the well, Aileana paused, filling her lungs with the clean, crisp air. It was so pleasant that she found herself lingering longer than she'd intended. But soon duty reared its head again, and she walked back to the sick room where Bridgid awaited her.

The *bailie* looked stern as she took the basin of water. Setting it on the table, she turned without hesitation and pushed Aileana toward the kitchen. "Now you'll go, missy. I'll not be telling you again. I'm still *bailie* of this castle, and I need your healing skills for these people. You cannot be doing me or them any good if you're senseless from lack of food and sleep."

Aileana tried to muster the will to fight her order, but she was too tired to resist. Her shoulders slumped, and she closed her eyes and nodded. But as she started to make her way toward the kitchen, a sudden banging and scramble of activity stilled her. She sensed more than saw the figure move behind her, near the door. When the familiar, deep voice echoed through the hall, it sent a tingle down her spine.

"Christ's Holy Blood—what is all this?"

She looked behind her, shivering in response to the ice reflected in Duncan's silver eyes. He pinned her with his gaze, his legs spread in a wide stance, and his hands fisted at his sides.

"Aileana MacDonell, I want to know just what in hell you have done to my clan."

Duncan was losing the struggle, and he knew it. The hellish sights. The sounds. The smell . . . God help him, the smell. It spiraled him into the world of the Tower all over again. Except that these prisoners were all familiar to him. These people were his clan.

His kin.

He took another step forward, clenching his gloved fists as tightly as he could, trying to regain control. His gaze darted from Aileana to Bridgid and back again, and for the first time he observed the strange flush on his leman's face, the dark smudges beneath her eyes—the defeated stance of her body.

"It appears that you cannot read, Duncan MacRae."

Aileana's restrained comment struck him like a slap in the face, blinding him to the weariness in her posture. But it gave him something to cling to, and he grasped it as if for dear life.

"I can read enough to know what is written on the gate, woman. I will not be barred from my own castle."

"Then you are a fool, risking your life for no good reason."

"It is no foolishness to ensure that my people are safe."

"And of course with *me* ministering to them, you're filled with doubt about that possibility."

Duncan glowered, matching Aileana's irritation with his own. In truth, once he and Kinnon had deciphered the sign, he'd feared for everyone inside Eilean Donan, to his surprise, Aileana most of all. In fact he'd been worried almost senseless about her—so much so that when he'd first come in and seen her standing in the hall, thankfully still walking and breathing, he'd snapped out the first cutting words that rose to his lips to mask his overwhelming relief. But he couldn't admit that weakness to her. "I needed to see the condition of my people with my own eyes," he settled on muttering, sweeping his gaze around the great hall. "And this does not exactly reassure me."

Her gaze pierced him, making him notice again her eyes' heightened brilliance and her tired expression. "If the arrangement isn't to your liking, Duncan, it is because we had little to work with. You've no infirmary and many that need tending. What would you have had me do—lay the sick on the ground in the yard?"

The question seemed to drain Duncan's energy, depleting him of any remaining heated emotion. Running his gloved hand through the tangles of his hair, he shook his head and sighed. "Nay, lass. I'd not have that."

Bridgid stepped forward. "I was just telling the missy to rest a spell and get some nourishment. There is plenty of cold mutton and bread in the kitchen for you and your men as well." She looked behind Duncan, seeing no one but Kinnon, who stood quiet in the shadows of the doorway. "Where are the other lads?"

"I made them stay outside." He looked straight at Aileana. "If I am foolish, it is not with others' lives."

She didn't respond to his goad, though, only leveling a strange look at him. "I will go ahead to prepare food for the three of us, then. It is not safe to meet with your men again, Duncan, until the contagion is passed. You will have to send a message to them another way."

"Aye. I will see to it," he said, earning a nod from her before she turned to go. But as she walked to the kitchen, Duncan noted the effort it took her; he saw the shuffling stumble in her gait, and it filled him with alarm. She looked ready to topple from exhaustion.

"How long has she been like that?" he demanded of Bridgid once she'd gone. "How long since she ate or slept?"

Bridgid shook her head and looked down. "Without

food . . . since yester eve, I suppose. Sleep . . . longer than that. And even then she will not use a bed. She sits over there near the fire." She pointed to an uncomfortable looking chair positioned not far from where some of the sick lay. "Of course she doesn't get much sleep that way. If someone groans loud, up she goes, tending to them again." She sighed. "The missy is stubborn, she is. But her healing has saved many already, God bless her."

"Aye, well enough is enough," Duncan growled, more in frustration at Aileana's stubbornness than in anger with Bridgid. "I am sending her to her bed until morning, unless there's reason against it."

Bridgid shook her head. "None that I know."

Duncan nodded. "Good. Can you manage without her until tomorrow, then?"

Swiping a hand over her eyes, the *bailie* nodded. "She's shared with me all she knows of healing those with the plague, and I will carry on fine without her."

Duncan paused, noticing for the first time that Bridgid seemed almost as tired as Aileana. Most likely she'd slept as little. He motioned for her to sit. When she was comfortable, he said, "After you sup, I'll be asking you to show me the methods Aileana taught you. Then you'll be taking to your bed as well. I will assist your helpers for the rest of the night."

Kinnon stepped from the shadows. "I will stay, too. We'll both do whatever is necessary to help."

Bridgid started to protest, but Duncan added, "I am commanding you as chieftain of this clan. No more arguments."

Her mouth clamped shut, though the warmth in her eyes expressed how grateful she was. Her voice cracked as she gestured them toward the kitchen, shooing them along like the fowl in the yard. "Off with you to eat, then. When you're done I will take a quick meal myself and then teach you what I know."

Duncan nodded and motioned Kinnon along with him, quickening his pace as they neared the kitchen. Eating didn't interest him as much as ensuring that Aileana supped well and was tucked safely into bed before the hour passed. Strange warmth cut through the worry that had been gnawing at him. He savored the thought of sitting at table with her again. When he was gone, he'd realized that he'd missed her fiery looks and the occasional sharp rejoinder she offered when he became overbearing.

Duncan suppressed a smile. Even tonight, tired though she was, she'd managed to incite his anger, cutting straight to the heart of the matter. She was a strange, unpredictable woman; she didn't hold back from letting her complaints against him be known quite freely, but at the same time, she'd driven herself to exhaustion tending his people, caring for them while he was away.

Another surge of warmth bloomed in him. Her generosity was a surprise, made all the more pleasant for the fact that it was unsolicited. Be she from an enemy clan or not, she'd made a sacrifice for his people, and because of it, he was going to do something he never thought he would ever do for a MacDonell . . .

He was going to offer her his thanks.

Duncan strode into the kitchen, more eager than ever to find her. But he didn't get the chance to say anything. The room was empty.

He stopped so quickly that Kinnon slammed into his back. His cousin careened to the side, muttering a curse, and without looking, Duncan held out his arm to steady him. He was too busy searching the chamber for sign of

Aileana. "Where the hell has she gone off to now?" he grumbled.

Kinnon brushed off his sleeve and scowled. "Most likely she's at the well, or in one of the pantries. Don't worry, cousin—I'm sure she's no plot to starve us."

"It is not the food that concerns me," Duncan snapped, as he crossed the length of the chamber in search of her. "I just want to make sure she is—"

"Sweet Jesus."

Duncan froze mid-step at Kinnon's exclamation, his heart in his throat at the tone in his cousin's voice. Everything seemed frozen for an instant, suspended in time. He twisted his head and saw that Kinnon was leaning over something. Nay, leaning over *someone*. Someone slender and pale, with flaming gold hair . . .

"Aileana." Her name whispered past his lips, and he spanned the distance between them in a few strides, falling to his knees beside her and lifting her onto his lap. Her head lolled lifelessly, and though the shallow rise and fall of her chest assured him that she lived, her body's heat burned into him, even through their layers of clothing.

"Ach, lass." He rocked her gently, ripping off his glove to touch her brow, her cheeks, and the back of her neck. But it was all the same. She was burning with fever. "Christ, Kinnon, she's come down with the plague." His fingers tingled and his throat ached with dread. Scooping her up, Duncan cradled her against him and strode out of the kitchen, toward the steps leading to their bedchamber. "Get Bridgid and tell her to bring everything she has to help." His final command was uttered in a half growl. "Hurry, dammit."

Cold twisted in his gut as he held Aileana close, murmuring in her ear, trying to elicit some response from her. She was so quiet, her eyes closed, her cheeks flushed from the fever. His anxiety intensified, building with every step he climbed. But as he reached the top of the stone staircase, something broke inside him. It had long been crusted over, but it was released now by the surging flood of feeling that consumed him. When it had happened, he didn't know, but it was clear as day in this moment. He cared deeply for Aileana MacDonell. It was too confusing to make sense of right now, but he knew one thing with certainty: he'd fight with every ounce of strength in him to keep the hand of death from pulling her down into the shadows.

Duncan bowed his head. His lips began to move in an almost forgotten stream of words. He'd sworn never to do it again, vowed to deny it as a worthless waste of breath and time. But he did it now, and with every bit of energy that was in him.

For the first time in thirteen years, Duncan prayed.

"What else? Just tell me what else can be done, and I'll do it. Anything." He grasped Aileana's burning hands in his own and laid his forehead against them. He wasn't sure that he'd spoken aloud, but Bridgid stepped forward. Through a haze of exhaustion, he saw her approach, her hands twisting in her apron.

"There's nothing more that I know of. If I did, I'd be telling you, I swear I would."

He didn't answer, but he felt her hand on his shoulder as she tried to urge him away from Aileana's bed. "You've got to rest, now, laddie—you haven't slept in two days. I promise I'll stay here, sitting by her to bathe her forehead. If she wakes, I'll be quick at sending someone for you right away." When he didn't respond, she added, "If you don't rest, you're going to end up as sick as the missy. Please, let me take over for a little while."

"Nay."

Duncan sat up and reached for the basin. "No one will tend her but me." As he'd done a thousand times in the past two days, he felt the temperature of her skin, sought the swellings that would mark the apex of the disease in her slender body. She remained hot, but the area on her neck and near her groin showed what seemed to be an inflammation where none had been before. The discovery sent a shock through him, making him sit upright.

Aileana moaned and twisted as he examined her, and he wanted to cut off his hands for hurting her. But he had to be sure. Satisfied, he sat back.

Joy mingled with incredible fear; the presence of the swelling showed that the pestilence had almost spent its course, but it also brought them to the crucial point. She'd live or die in the next twelve hours.

"Give me the salve, Bridgid."

"Is it time already?" she whispered, her voice shaky.

Duncan glanced at her. "Aye. I have to apply it now. And bring the wine for her, too."

With a sharp nod, Bridgid left, leaving him alone with Aileana. He reached out, smoothing the thick, red-gold tresses from her brow. God, she looked so small in his bed. Helpless. Vulnerable.

He twisted the cloth in the mint water and unfolded it across her forehead. His eyes burned, and his teeth clenched as he worked, hating that he couldn't take the ravages of the disease onto himself for her. But tending to her and treating her was the best he could do, and he vowed to make the healing work.

"Here." Bridgid pushed through the door and hurried forward with the pot of salve. Kinnon followed close behind with a skin of wine. As Duncan reached for the ointment, Bridgid held back.

"I'm thinking you might want me to do this part, laddie. It's not a pretty sight, what happens, after it is spread over them."

"Just give it to me."

His tone left no room for argument, and, handing the pot to him, Bridgid sidled out of the way. Wordlessly, Kinnon untied the wineskin and set it near the bed.

Duncan propped Aileana in his arms and prepared to help her drink. "You can both leave now."

Lifting his gaze from Aileana only long enough to catch Kinnon's concerned look and Bridgid's frightened stare, he added, "I've got everything I need here. Go now."

As if they both understood the strange force that drove him, they turned to leave. But before Kinnon stepped out he said, "If you need me, just come to the door and call. I'll be sleeping in the hall, a little way off."

Duncan nodded, not moving as his cousin shut the door behind himself. Then it was quiet. Gently, he laid Aileana back down. He washed his hands, readying himself to apply the salve that Aileana had mixed herself before she fell ill. If it went as he'd been told, she would resist the ointment, but once applied to the swellings it would immediately begin to take effect. She would most likely vomit, and the convulsions might start again. Within a few hours, the engorgements would either subside or burst, but with a different outcome for each.

The first meant life, the other death.

Steeling himself for the suffering he was about to inflict on her, Duncan removed the thin linen sheet. He worked with efficient speed, trying to hold her still long enough to smooth the ointment along her neck and on the swelled places below. He cursed when the stiffness in his crippled hand made the task more difficult, berating himself for the additional pain his clumsiness surely caused her. Perhaps he should have accepted Bridgid's help.

But suddenly he was finished. Aileana lay still. Her cheeks remained flushed, though the rest of her was ghostly pale. Moving gently, Duncan covered her again with the linen sheet and set an empty basin near the bed. Then he waited.

He didn't need to wait long. With a sudden motion, Aileana jerked, her body heaving as she retched from the effects of the ointment. Duncan supported her, tipping her sideways and holding her hair from her face as he murmured soft words of reassurance until the violent sickness passed. Then he laid her back against the bolster and bathed her face with cool water again before giving her a few more sips of wine mixed with water.

When she was quiet, he pushed himself up from where he'd knelt by the bed. His legs protested the cramped position of the past three hours, and he stumbled as he walked to the hearth to drag a chair back to the bedside. He sat there like that, not moving except to bathe her face periodically with mint water and encourage her to take sips from the wineskin.

The night faded away. His legs grew numb and his eyes stung. And still he sat. He studied her face, the beautiful, noble features that shifted from wrenching pain to peaceful serenity and back again, more times than he could count as the hours slipped by. Aileana was in truth nothing like her sister, now that he took time to notice. Where Morgana's beauty had been cold and precise, Aileana glowed with inner strength and goodness. He prayed to God for the joy of looking into her vibrant eyes again, vowing to fight any battle, face any enemy for the privilege of it. He'd even go willingly to the bowels of the Tower again and suffer the tortures of the damned.

If only she could live.

For in those still, empty hours of the night, when death hovered round him like a curse, Duncan realized something startling. Somewhere along the twisted path of hatred and revenge, he'd changed. The sweet enemy had come quietly, secretly, tying him with silken chains more solid and irrevocable than any walls that had ever held him prisoner.

And he knew that come heaven or hell, he would give up his life to keep Aileana MacDonell safe.

Chapter 11

Something stabbed her in the eye. Something white-hot. Bright. Twisting her head from the source of the pain, Aileana raised her arm to shield her vision. Her lids felt crusted shut, but she managed to edge them open enough to peek from beneath the shadow of her elbow.

Everything was quiet, the place coated, it seemed, in the scent of mint. Her mouth felt full of dust, and her head throbbed as if a boulder had rolled over it, but still she peered through scratchy lids, desperate for a drink of water. A pitcher and wash basin rested on the table across the chamber, but she felt too weak to get it. Then a more terrible thought wrenched her foggy mind. *Heaven preserve her—she'd fallen asleep and left the sick to fend for themselves.*

With a groan, she tried to push herself up from the bed, but her muscles refused to obey. The throbbing increased in her head and spread to every aching joint in her body, making her fall back limp against the bolster.

Panic swelled. What was wrong with her? Why did she feel so strange?

Then she noticed something odd. Using every bit of effort she possessed, she pushed herself to her elbows and peered over the edge of the mattress. Duncan lay curled on the floor near the bed; his left arm stretched out above him, cushioning his head, his right hand was cradled to his chest as if for protection.

Or defense.

His hand. For the first time she saw his crippled hand without the glove to conceal it. The first three fingers curved in an awkward twist; they'd healed without being properly set. His knuckles seemed strangely flattened, and thick, ridged scars formed a mass at the back of his hand, while his thumb seemed locked at an angle.

She frowned and managed to roll to the edge of the bed, reaching down to gently touch him. It didn't look nearly as bad as she'd feared it would. The sight of it inspired a rush of sympathy for the pain he must have felt with its happening, but she certainly didn't feel disgust as she'd been led to expect, based on the murmurs of his clanswomen. So then why did he bother to—?

Suddenly, she slid and began to tip toward the floor, unable to stop herself in her weakness. She shrieked but the sound came out more like a croak from her ravaged throat. Duncan growled something indistinct as he sprang to a sitting position and grabbed her wrist, twisting it and forcing her back against the bed.

He scrambled atop her and pushed down, and Aileana struggled under the pressure of his hand round her throat. "Dun . . ." she tried to call, "Duncan . . ."

His steel gaze flickered at the sound of her voice, and the scowl faded from his face. In the next instant he dropped to his knees at the side of the bed, releasing her and taking her hand gently in his own.

"Oh, God, forgive me—the dream . . ." he mumbled. Stunned, she saw his eyes welling, watched as cold gray melted to quicksilver. "Thanks be, you're alive," he said hoarsely, before leaning his brow against their entwined hands.

"Duncan," she rasped. "Water. Please."

His head snapped up, and he sprang into a flurry of activity. Soon a cool cup was tipped to her mouth. "Here," he murmured as he urged tiny sips past her cracked lips, "but don't drink too much at first. Otherwise you'll be sick again."

"Again? I was sick?" Aileana frowned as she tried to remember, but only an incessant thudding at her temples rewarded her effort.

"Aye. For almost a week now." Duncan nodded and shifted away from her. She saw his furtive movements as he pulled his gauntlets over his hands again. She wanted to say nay, to tell him to foreswear the unnecessary protection of the gloves, but the words got stuck in the incredible weariness weighing her down.

"So tired," she breathed, trying to resist the urge to close her eyes again. She felt cool and relaxed. An almost forgotten peace lulled her toward slumber. But as the gossamer waves of sleep closed over her and her eyes drifted shut, she felt certain that she must already be dreaming . . .

Because as Duncan leaned over to tuck the coverlet around her, she thought she felt him press a tender kiss on her forehead.

The autumn rain pattered its chill melody against the window, though the fire crackled brightly enough to dispel any dampness. Duncan stood in the shadows of the bedchamber, watching Aileana sleep; myriad emotions filled him with startling swiftness. He followed each rise and fall of her breast, let his eyes slip over the red-gold sweep of her hair on the bolster. His eager gaze absorbed the beauty of the face he'd come to know so well in the tortured, wee hours of those nights when death had lain in wait, trying to claim her.

He'd never thought to feel so about a woman again. Not after Mairi. And certainly not for Aileana Mac-Donell.

But he cared for her deeply, and there was no going back from the truth.

He paused, a kind of incredulity forcing him to review what he'd hardly begun to comprehend. His mind and heart mingled in force, examining, searching. He approached her and crouched beside her as she slept. His head dipped in prayer, the words flowing free and from his heart. God had answered his call, giving back Aileana's life. In time she would blossom again. She'd regain her vibrancy, her sharp-edged tongue and her lush, impossible beauty. She would heal and grow strong and prosper.

But no matter; he could never tell her how he truly felt about her.

The thought broke the spell of his prayer, and he raised his head to look at her. There was so much weighing heavy between them—so much that had the power to destroy them both, were he fool enough to allow it. She was a forbidden temptation, and not only because of her heritage or her connection to Morgana and the clan who'd butchered his people—nay, it wasn't that, though it would have been easier to hold on to that notion. Aileana had proven her character and her loyalty time and again, in sacrificing her own security for her brother's safety, in standing strong against the insults and trials of living as his leman . . . in risking her own life to help his people. He could put down any lingering animosity the others might feel against her, were he to make her his wife. If only it were that simple.

But it wasn't. Even if he were foolhardy enough to ask her to become his bride in truth—to consider the possibility of love growing between them—she would never consent. How could she? What woman would want to take to her heart and her bed the very man who'd led the attack that killed her father and clansmen, a man who'd humiliated her, threatened her brother's life and ripped her from her family to live in subjection with him?

Yet even with all of that, there was still more that made him likely the last person that she or any woman would choose willingly for a husband.

Duncan pulled off his glove to stare at his crippled hand. It was true that it worked well enough, ravaged as it was. He could wield a sword, saddle Glendragon, and help in the repairs of the Castle. But he was damaged nonetheless. His touch wasn't capable of evoking haunting, beautiful music on his *clarsach* anymore, of carving fine lines in a stick of wood . . . of stroking Aileana to the brink of passion and beyond in the way that he wanted to love her. In the way that she deserved to be loved.

He fingered another of his ugly scars, the one that threaded along his cheek and jaw, bitterness twisting in his chest. He was disfigured and flawed. If he lived to be an old man, he'd never forget the look Aileana had given him on the battlefield, that first day, when she'd seen his face up close; he'd thought himself accustomed to such reactions, but her shock and aversion had cut him to the bone.

When she awakened for good from this sickness, it would surely be more of the same; she would continue to hate him, both for who and what he was.

He needed to remember that.

But right now she slept. He stared at her, soaking in the sight of her like a drowning man reaching for a branch anchored on the shore. Uncontrolled need swelled inside him anew. Heaven help him, but he wanted to feel the warmth of her skin against his one last time before he made good on his vow to forsake it forever.

His hand trembled as he reached out to touch her, sweeping his fingers in a reverent path across her brow, her cheek and down to the pulse that fluttered warm at the base of her throat. He savored the moment, storing the sensations for the lonely, barren nights that loomed ahead of him. She was like warm velvet, alluring to him even with the ravages of sickness still evident. Her lips parted in a sigh, and she turned her head toward him, nuzzling into his caress.

The tide overflowed, then, carrying Duncan with it to a place of no thought, no reason . . . only feeling. He leaned over and brushed his mouth across the full swell of her lips, tasting wine and mint. Her lips moved in response, melding to his and softening in surrender. He felt the sweet pressure of her mouth beneath his as he cupped her face gently, letting all that he was feeling through his palms and into her.

But then with a suddenness that almost stilled his heart, her eyes fluttered open, dark pools of liquid yearning that took him by surprise with the force of their intensity. He froze as she raised her hands, bringing them slowly up his arms and across his shoulders until her fingers tangled in his hair. She pulled him closer, burying her face in his neck. She nestled there, and he felt the light tickle of her lashes against his skin as her eyes drifted shut again. When he pressed a kiss on the top of her head, she sighed in contentment.

And he thought his heart would break.

Never. He'd never have this joy, this happiness of a life and love with Aileana. He'd stolen a single moment in hopes of its memory sustaining him through the emptiness of his future. But he'd discovered too late that it brought nothing but lancing pain for what might have been.

Gently, he disentangled her hands from around his neck and tucked them back beneath the blanket. Then he stood, closing his eyes and squeezing his fists tight against the wave of anguished emotion that washed over him. When he'd controlled his feelings enough to command his legs to move, he turned and walked from the room, hardly daring to breathe for fear that a single wrong step might make him fracture into a thousand pieces.

He'd been kissing her. Aileana kept her eyes closed, holding on to the tattered edges of the dream floating through her mind. Only it wasn't a dream; it was true. Her lips felt warm and slightly swollen, and she ran her fingertips across them as if testing for traces of Duncan's touch. A happy tingle wavered in her belly, and the corners of her mouth curved up slightly.

She'd liked his kisses.

Duncan had given her a feeling of peace, of security . . . of passion when he'd pressed his lips to hers.

The memory of it sent a pleasurable shiver down her spine.

Cautiously, she opened her eyes, hoping to see him sitting at her bedside. But only night shadows greeted her; in the gloom she could make out Bridgid's ample frame tucked into the chair before the fire. The *bailie* stirred and yawned, the back of her hand brushing across her eyes as she turned to find a more comfortable position.

"Bridgid?" Aileana whispered. She hadn't intended to whisper, but that seemed the only level of noise she was capable of making at the moment.

Though Bridgid sighed in response, she didn't wake.

Aileana looked up at the intricate stone design of the ceiling above her head, then closed her eyes again as she gathered her strength. She needed some water, and it seemed that she was going to have to get it herself.

Swallowing with effort, she pushed herself to a sitting position on the bed. Her legs felt weak as a newborn foal's. It was a strange sensation, the dizzy weightlessness that came over her when she scooted to the edge of the bed. Her bare toes slipped from beneath the covers, dangling toward the cool floor. Little goosebumps rose on her arms and legs.

Drawing the coverlet around her, she waited until her balance felt stable again. Then she pushed herself up to stand. But for all her thinking she was ready, her legs refused to support her weight. Blindly, she reached out for something solid to break her fall, groping for the table Duncan had positioned next to the bed. Her hand smacked into it, making an empty cup atop it clatter to the floor. Aileana followed soon after, collapsing with a painful thud that knocked the breath from her lungs and made her curl into a ball on the hard stone.

"What is it? Where—?"

Through breathless pain, Aileana saw Bridgid start from her chair. The *bailie*'s eyes opened wide as she cast her startled gaze from right to left, her face still bleary from sleep. But Aileana couldn't call out; it was all she could do to try to stave off her panic at not being able to get enough air.

As she tried to blink away the increasing number of black dots dancing before her eyes, she felt Bridgid's strong hands grip her shoulders. With one swift motion, Bridgid helped her to sit, and before long she was back in bed.

When her breathing calmed, Aileana saw that the *bailie* stood over her, clucking her tongue with disapproval, her hands on her hips.

"What're you doing, missy? You shouldn't be out of bed yet, as I'da told you if you hadn't gone ahead and tried it on your own without a by your leave."

Aileana attempted an answer, but she was forced to swallow again, this time with even less success than before. Her tongue felt thick and dry, like a strip of leather, and her lips twisted with the effort to speak. Pointing across the chamber, she tried to show that she needed some water. Bridgid hurried to comply, mumbling apologies as she shuffled back and tipped the cup to her lips.

Finally, Aileana lay against the bolster and closed her eyes. "You've no cause to scold me you know," she said hoarsely. "I did try to ask for your help, but I couldn't wake you. My voice wouldn't carry that far."

After a moment's silence Bridgid came closer and took Aileana's hand in her own. "Aye, well, I'm sorry for not being here, ready when you needed me." Her brows met in a frown. "It's strange that Duncan didn't wake me to take over the vigil."

"What vigil?"

"The watching over your sickbed."

"What do you mean?"

"The laird himself watched over you the entire time you were sick, even when you were sleeping." Bridgid rearranged the bolster behind Aileana's back. Her kerchief flapped as she nodded. "The whole time Duncan kept the watch. He wanted to be tending you until your fever broke. After that he let me and Kinnon spell him every few hours."

Peculiar warmth spread through Aileana's belly, and she twisted her fingers in the blankets. "Where is he now?" Her voice gave out before she could add that she wanted to thank him for tending to her.

"I don't know, missy. But if you're feeling well enough for the moment, I'll go find him. He'll want to be told now that you're awake."

Aileana nodded and closed her eyes for a moment. Though her arms lacked any real strength, she soon sat up and tried to run her fingers through her tangled hair. If only she'd thought to ask Bridgid for a comb and a damp cloth to wash her face. She smoothed her fingers over her cheeks, hoping to bring up a little color, but as she lowered her hands to the coverlet, she saw that they were shaking.

Frowning, Aileana noticed that she could see the threading of her veins more than usual; her skin appeared almost translucent. It was clear that the plague had laid her low.

"I see you're sitting up."

Aileana looked toward the door; the low timbre of Duncan's voice sent strange warmth flooding through her again. He leaned against the curved entrance to the chamber, a guarded expression on his face. She squinted to see him in the shadows, but still he held back, as if hesitant to actually come into the room.

"I'm feeling much better," she said quietly.

"I've sent Bridgid to fetch some broth for you." He pushed away from the door frame and walked into the chamber. Still he kept his distance from her bed, moving instead to the fireplace. "You'll need to rebuild your strength."

He gazed at her then, a flicker of concern piercing the careful look he'd been wearing since he came into the room. "Bridgid told me about you trying to get your own water, and I'll not have you behaving so foolishly again. You're to stay in bed, on my order. Is that understood?"

Aileana closed her eyes again, weakness overcoming her. "I'm no babe to be coddled." She would have said more, but a fit of dry coughing interrupted her.

"If you insist on being stubborn, I'll resume my own watch of you until I'm convinced that you're strong enough to be left alone." Duncan leveled his gaze on her, his eyes compelling. "It was not so long ago that I feared losing you to the plague. I'll not have you falling sick again for the sake of obstinacy."

She paused, the memory of his kisses flickering through her mind. Her cheeks heated with the sudden rush of blood, making her feel dizzy, and she took another sip of water.

"I heard—" she whispered, "nay, I *remember* you caring for me." She stared with marked intent at the square of stone flagging right in front of Duncan's booted feet. "It was kind of you, and I thank you for it."

Duncan remained silent, and Aileana felt tingles of unease dance across her skin. She didn't dare look at him.

When she finally glanced up, she saw a stricken look in place of the pompous arrogance she'd expected. Yet in the blink of an eye he shuttered the expression in favor of a calm, level gaze.

"What I did was nothing I wouldn't have done for anyone under my personal responsibility."

Aileana's stomach tightened and she resisted the urge to touch her swollen lips again. What he said couldn't be true. She remembered, she'd *felt* his passionate tenderness after her fever broke.

Unless she'd been dreaming.

But then why did her lips feel as if they'd been kissed? Why did she recall the sweet, silken pressure of his mouth, the warmth of his breath against her cheek?

"I thought . . ." She swallowed and tried to focus her cloudy mind. "I thought that there was more. That it wasn't just—"

"It was nothing." Duncan's face looked gray, and he turned his back on her to pace toward the windows while he continued talking. "Plague fevers are known for the delirium they can cause." He spun on his heel to face her again, though he wouldn't meet her gaze. "Bridgid will be up soon. Eat and then rest. I'll be checking on you later."

Aileana forced herself to remain silent as he left the room. Hurt and confusion sliced deep, compounding the weariness she already felt. Ignoring the lump in her throat, she rolled to her side and pulled the coverlet over her shoulder. Something was wrong. The way Duncan acted just now didn't fit. Not with what she remembered.

Her body shook with a shuddering sigh, weariness weighing her down too much to think on it more. When she closed her eyes, welling tears spilled warm onto her cheeks, and she brushed them away quickly. But it wasn't until many hours later that she finally fell into exhausted, troubled slumber.

Chapter 12

Kinnon tossed back the remainder of his ale and wiped his mouth. The sounds of the feasting going on around him in the great hall had risen until the din was almost deafening. Now that the outbreak of plague seemed to have died down, the need to celebrate life had burned strong. With that in mind, a contingent of MacKenzies had arrived three days ago, with a score of men and as many women, and the revelry had increased every night since.

Leaning back against the wall, he looked around the gathering before letting his gaze settle on Duncan. Though his cousin mingled with the company, he seemed none too pleased at the attentions Nora MacKenzie had been lavishing on him all night. The woman had survived her bout with plague, none the worse for wear. Now she seemed intent on luring Duncan back to her bed . . . something she'd been trying to accomplish ever since Aileana MacDonell had come to Eileen Donan. Unfortunately for her, she hadn't yet realized the futility of that effort.

Kinnon let his sights drift along the table, across the expansive stone floor to the corner near the massive fireplace. Aileana sat curled on a chair there, a length of plaid draped over her legs. Though she'd recovered from her own bout with the plague more than a fortnight ago, her face was pinched and wan. He followed the track of her stare; it led back to Duncan, who continued to resist Nora, all the while glancing furtively at Aileana as if he both wanted her near and wished himself far away from her at the same time.

Kinnon sighed. The two of them were like to kill each other with coolness if someone didn't step in soon. They'd circled their shadows for days, and it was ruining them both. Kinnon had pondered approaching Duncan, but he knew from experience that trying to talk to him about this would be tantamount to engaging him in battle. Duncan resisted advice, especially about women. But Aileana might be willing to listen. She'd talked freely in the storage chamber several weeks ago. Perhaps she'd welcome his counsel now.

Smiling, Kinnon weaved his way through the revelers. Before he reached Aileana's side he secured two cups of honeyed wine, bowing as he offered her one of the fragrant drinks.

"May I tempt you with some refreshment, lady?"

Aileana gave him a startled glance. "You've no need to serve me." But after a pause, she nodded in thanks and took the cup from him to sip. Her faint smile dispelled the gloom of her expression a bit. "It's delicious, thank you."

Kinnon swung himself onto a bench near her chair. "Aye. A special brew to mark the arrival of our honored guests." He inclined his head toward the many MacKenzies who celebrated at the banquet table. When he sipped again, he glanced furtively at Aileana, hoping his comment encouraged her to notice the one MacKenzie in particular who was heaping attention on Duncan.

Aileana grimaced. Setting her cup aside, she leaned back again in her chair and pulled her plaid closer around her knees. "The festivities are quite too fervent for my tastes, I fear."

"Perhaps you should retire for the evening what with being ill as you were," Kinnon said shrewdly. "You might take sick again."

"Nay." Aileana shook her head, though her cheeks had paled. "I'm well enough."

"It's a different kind of ache, then, is it?" Kinnon murmured, casting her a sideways look.

Aileana threaded her fingers together, squeezing, he noticed, until the knuckles turned white. "I've never liked revelry." She looked down at her lap to stare at the swath of plaid. "It is the consequence, I suppose, of spending so much time alone."

"Ah, I see. It has nothing to do with Duncan over there, then."

Aileana's gaze snapped up. "Of course it doesn't."

Kinnon shrugged. "I only suggested as much since you seem more awkward with him than usual, of late." He touched her hand. "It would be no crime to talk of your feelings, you know. They'd be safe with me; you've my word on it."

Aileana stiffened and pulled her hand away under the guise of adjusting her plaid. "There's no feeling about it, Kinnon MacRae. I'm Duncan's leman. He's the laird. It's as simple as that."

Her cheeks had heightened in color as she spoke, and

Kinnon ran his hand through his hair as he looked away. *Saints, but she was as stubborn as Duncan.*

After a long silence, he murmured, "I am glad, then, for your peace of mind, lass. Would that I shared it." Pushing himself from the bench, Kinnon bowed again. "I'll be taking my leave now." He looked up long enough to fix his gaze on her, ensuring that she caught the import of his next words. "But know that if you ever wish my advice or support, I'll be more than willing to give it."

After he left, Aileana sat stone still. Dragon's breath, she must be as transparent as water. Kinnon had known her dilemma just by looking at her. The sorry truth was that ever since she'd recovered from the plague, she'd pined after Duncan, and jealousy had been gnawing at her with every additional moment she'd been forced to watch Nora MacKenzie fawn over him. It was enough to make her almost regret having nursed the woman through her illness. Worse still, the wretch was lapping up Nora's attention like a kitten with a dish of milk.

Pulling her gaze from that disturbing scene across the hall, Aileana stared into the roiling flames on the hearthstone. Their twisting gyrations matched her emotions perfectly. Hot, angry, and uncontrolled. She couldn't continue this way much longer, else before long her mood swings would reveal her feelings to every inhabitant of the castle.

She needed to distance herself from Duncan and this unexpected hold he seemed to have on her emotions. Now, before it got any worse.

But how?

Running away from Eilean Donan was out of the

question. Though that kind of separation was sure to ease her suffering in time, she couldn't risk the damage she might cause to her clan or to Gavin if Duncan chose to retaliate for her breach of their bargain. She tipped her head to the side, leaning the weight of her chin onto her hand. She could try to force Duncan to admit he'd kissed her when she was sick. By using every feminine wile she possessed, she might be able to make him forget the existence of any other woman save her. She could tempt him and tease him until . . .

Aileana's cheeks burned hotter than the flames on the hearth as she brushed the wild notion aside. Even if she wished it, she knew in her soul that she could never be so bold when it came to such things. She knew nothing about seduction. Those kinds of triumphs were reserved for a few select women. Women with more obvious physical charms, and the ability to carry on suggestive repartee and exchange flirtatious gestures.

Women like Nora MacKenzie.

Branding her rival with a stare sharp enough to draw blood, Aileana sagged backward. She snuggled her plaid tighter around herself. Self-pity was useless. She'd learned that long ago in the bitter solitude of her bedchamber at Dulhmeny. When Father imposed especially harsh dictates on her, she'd avoided wailing and tears, instead waiting for Gavin or Robert to sneak to her window or door. Then she'd sprung into action.

Action . . .

That was it. She needed to *do* something. Something she knew that she could do well.

She swept her gaze over Duncan once again, her eyes narrowing as she saw where his large, gloved hands rested. Something clicked inside her, then, propelling her to her feet and across the hall. She spared barely a glance at the revelers, escaping under the wide, stone arch to climb the stairs to her bedchamber. Once there, she stretched out on her pallet, letting her mind drift toward the thoughts she'd had on her first night at Eilean Donan so many weeks ago.

Thoughts of revenge.

At first, dredging up those memories stung like a handful of salt on an open wound. But as each inspiration returned full force, a heady lightness filled her. She wasn't powerless. She could do something to ease the suffering she endured thanks to Duncan MacRae and his insensitivity. And the first revenge she took against him would give balm to this most recent wound. Or to be exact, the wound he'd allowed Nora MacKenzie to help inflict on her.

In an instant Aileana leaped out of bed and splashed water on her face. There was no time to waste. Supper was almost over. With a last pat to tuck several unruly waves of hair into place, she raced down the stairs. No one saw her as she ducked into the kitchen; holding her breath in a prayer that her luck held, she slipped into the pantry.

Cool dark surrounded her, thick with the tangy scent of herbs she'd put up for the coming winter. Squinting to see the earthen jars, Aileana fumbled and stood on tiptoe, almost knocking the marjoram to the floor before she found the correct pot. Her hand closed around the vessel, exploring its cool contours, and she suffered a moment's hesitation about using its contents. Never before had she called upon her knowledge of herbs for anything other than aiding the ill.

A woman's laughter rose above the din in the great

hall, drifting to Aileana's ears. She stepped into the light of the kitchen and peeked through the archway at the festivities still raging across the threshold. What she saw made her eyes sting, and her fingers tighten round the pot.

It was as she suspected. The owner of the irritating giggle sat perched on Duncan's lap, tipping her head back to laugh and offering him a calculated view of her two greatest assets; the ones that wobbled only inches from his face. Aileana's jaw clenched, and she darted back into the kitchen, uncorking the pot's lid as she went. Though it wouldn't hurt them, a good dose of this herb would ensure that Duncan and Nora wouldn't soon forget this night—or the view from inside the confines of their privy chamber.

She quelled the tiny prickle of guilt that remained. This was war after all, she reminded herself, and everyone was entitled to use the weapons at her disposal. Nora might have cannons, but Aileana had artillery enough to fell an entire clan.

With a purposeful step, she marched to the trenchers, sprinkling a generous amount of the herb on a portion of stew that she would personally deliver to Duncan, for he and Nora to share when the meal was served in a few moments. Aye, Duncan MacRae was going to feel the sting of her weapons this night. It would be the first attack in her methodical assault against his manly arrogance and pride. The man was doomed to submit sooner or later. For no matter how long it took, she intended to make this a fight to the finish.

Dawn's pink light pierced the window hangings in Duncan's bedchamber, making Aileana sit up on her pallet. He still hadn't come to bed. Worry creased her brow, and her imagination took flight. Was he too sick to climb the stairs? Had she been so eager to dispense justice that she'd laid it on with too heavy a hand? Shaking her head against such nonsense, Aileana rose and dressed. She knew without a doubt that she'd been careful with the herb. Neither Nora nor Duncan would have gotten much sleep last night, but they certainly wouldn't have suffered any danger. Just a bit of restorative purging.

A scratching at the door made her jump. Bridgid's red face appeared in a splinter of light as she entered the chamber. The candle she held cast her features in an almost eerie glow, and Aileana's stomach flopped. Something must be wrong.

"Missy, it's the MacRae. You'd better come. I just found him out in the yard. He's holding his stomach and looking awful gray." Bridgid's eyes rounded further as she whispered, "Heaven preserve us, do you think it could be the plague again?"

Relief bubbled so swiftly in Aileana that she almost laughed aloud. But she schooled her face into a somber expression. "I don't think so, Bridgid. It would be unlikely, with symptoms such as those. Does he have the fever?"

Bridgid shook her head. "Not that I can tell, though it was hard to be sure, seeing as how he growled like something from a cave when I tried to touch him."

Aileana wrapped her plaid round her shoulders and nodded. She followed Bridgid into the hall, asking innocently, "Are any others afflicted?"

The *bailie* nodded. "Aye, but only one. Nora MacKenzie has taken ill, though I'm not sure how bad. It's what made me think it might be the plague again, passed from one to the other, since she and Duncan have been spending a fair amount of time together, and—"

Bridgid clipped off her comment and glanced to Aileana. Embarrassment mottled her skin a more fierce crimson than usual. "I meant nothing by saying that, missy, and anyway, it's no shame upon you if Duncan prefers—" She shook her head as she searched for the words, "—well if he wants to be spending his nights with another, then—" Bridgid clamped her mouth shut and made a strangled, coughing noise.

Aileana tightened her fists, savoring the knowledge of her revenge more fully. "It doesn't matter, Bridgid. Where the MacRae chooses to sleep is his concern." She lifted her chin and muttered, "But his illness is mine. I'm eager to examine him and ensure—I mean *check* his level of discomfort."

Bridgid nodded and hurried along with her until they reached the door to the yard. "He's out there, leaning against the wall." She gestured in the direction and scurried off, murmuring something about looking in on Nora as she left.

Aileana barely paused before marching into the yard and around the corner. She searched the dusky, pink-tinted gloom, trying to find Duncan. A low groan drew her gaze to the spot. He sat on the ground, his back against the wall. Even in the low light, Aileana could see the gray cast to his skin and the sheen of sweat on his face. His head was tilted back, his eyes closed.

"Duncan?" She stepped closer to him. A tiny stab of shame pricked her. Swallowing, she said more loudly, "Duncan, can you hear me?"

"Aye, I hear you," he growled under his breath. "But don't come too near me, unless you want to share in whatever's gripping me in its jaws." He groaned again, wincing as he bent forward. His arm clenched around his middle. "It's got me in the gut."

Aileana took another step toward him, ignoring his weak gesture warning her away. "Don't worry; I'll be fine." Her lips pressed together with guilt she refused to voice. "Can you stand?"

Duncan swung his leonine head, peering at her through tendrils of lank golden hair. His mouth was tight with pain.

"Stay away, Aileana. I'll not have you falling sick again." He grimaced. "Don't make me move to stop you."

Ignoring him, she leaned over and reached out to help him up. As her fingers grazed against the iron-hard muscles of his arm, he stiffened.

"Nay, I said!"

His command reverberated off the walls of the courtyard, making her jump back. A flare of anger shot through her, and she planted her hands on her hips. "Dragon's breath, Duncan MacRae, stop pretending to be so noble, and let me help. I'm not like to die from what ails you."

Her breath caught as he lifted his head in a slow, deliberate motion. His silver stare pinned her to the wall as he ground out, "And how would you be knowing that?"

Her cheeks heated and she looked away, stomping over to the well to draw a cool bucket of water. She didn't trust herself to meet his gaze. "I know enough of healing illnesses to be sure that it is nothing too serious. Even if I did take sick, it would be over in a day. Your discomfort will fade as quickly if you heed my advice."

She knew that he stared at her, until, from the side of

her vision, she watched another pain wrack him. Seeing it, Aileana rushed forward and tipped a ladle full of water to his lips. "Drink, but just sips. It will help what's in you to be flushed out."

Duncan grunted in response, but he drank. When he'd had enough, he waved her away. "Send Kinnon to me. I'm going to my chamber, and I don't want you helping me to get there."

"Nay. I'm here. I'll do it."

He took a deep breath, his hand clenching his belly. "Do as I ask, Aileana. I'll need his strength to help in dragging me up the steps." When she bristled, Duncan tipped his head back and groaned again. "Christ, lass, don't make me beg." His skin took on a greenish color, and his lips tightened.

Another lance of conscience stabbed her. She took two steps backward, driven away by the unfamiliar tone of pleading coming from this strong, unyielding man. There he sat, the giant felled by little David's slingshot. Yet somehow, she didn't think that God was on her side as He'd been on David's. He wouldn't support the kind of trickery she'd used last night.

Duncan's eyes opened, and Aileana's breath caught, so strong was the entreaty in his iron gaze. She could resist no longer. Without another word, she dropped the ladle into the bucket and ran to the kitchen, holding her hand to her breast as if that would help to still the pounding of her heart.

It wasn't supposed to be like this. She wasn't supposed to feel guilty. Duncan deserved it. He'd disregarded her feelings; he'd led her down a merry path, kissing her when she was ill, then denying it later. He and Nora deserved every pang they felt until the herb's effects wore away.

Then why did she feel as if she'd driven Duncan's claymore straight into her own heart?

The question reverberated through her mind with the incessant clang of a kirk bell. But before she would allow herself to consider the inevitable answer, Aileana threw a baleful look at the herb pantry and hurried into the great hall in search of Kinnon.

A soft tittering from the left side of the table drew Duncan's attention. Two of the MacKenzie women sat, heads together, whispering behind their hands. Every now and then one of them glanced at him and fluttered her lashes before falling into a fit of giggling. It was beginning to rake his hard-won calm like the sting of nails down his back.

Shoving his broth away with disgust, he pushed himself to his feet. He knew the root of their laughter; it had been building since he fell ill yesterday. Everyone believed that Nora MacKenzie had finally enticed him to her bed . . . and that she'd given him a dose of sickness in return.

But he knew better. He knew the real culprit.

Duncan pushed himself to his feet and stalked to the hearth, his gaze narrowed on the object of his thoughts. He watched her fiery head tilt forward, her teeth flashing as she laughed at some bit of witticism one of the others offered. She was entirely too jovial. A complete change from the solemn, somber Aileana he'd come to know after the plague.

And he could think of only one possible reason for her sudden transformation.

She'd been the cause of his and Nora's illness. Yet the idea that Aileana would stoop to such foul practices seemed at odds with what he thought he'd learned about her. The contradictory images warred in his mind. Aileana mixing a brew to prevent the plague, Aileana bent over his kin, nursing them until she fell ill herself . . . Aileana standing over him in the yard, her guilt-stricken expression making him feel far more ill than the rolling of his stomach.

The truth couldn't be denied. The facts led to no other alternative. And there was more than just his sudden sickness to make him certain he was right. Though it hadn't been him, Nora *had* bedded someone this week. Young Gil had taken her to his pallet, and she'd gone gladly, stung as she was by Duncan's frequent rebuffs and thinking to make him jealous with a more willing bedmate. Only Gil hadn't taken sick. Just himself and Nora.

And he himself had shared a trencher of stew with her at supper two nights ago. A well-seasoned dish, if he recalled, steeped with an odd taste he'd struggled to place at the time.

Aye, it seemed more than likely that Aileana had brought on his bout of misery. But why?

The answer he'd been resisting as heartily as he could spilled over him now like a shower of ice, making his teeth grate and his fists clench. He'd known it all along but just refused to believe, holding on instead to false comfort. But the truth was that Aileana hated him, enough, it seemed, to incite her to poison him. *But had she wanted him to die?*

She'd wanted him to suffer, that much was clear. Nora was just an unintended victim, stricken because she'd been at the wrong place at the wrong time. *Had Aileana planned to kill him, then?* His throat constricted and his head throbbed, the dark brooding of his own thoughts beginning to bring on a headache. The uncertainties went round and round, torturing him in away that rivaled the unholy skill of his guards in the Tower.

He knew that Aileana had used her herbs to make him ill. But he also knew her to be very skilled with her remedies and knowledge of healing; her abilities were such that if she'd intended for him to die, he'd wager Eilean Donan that he'd not be standing here debating it right now. Relief swept through him with the thought. Aye, she'd dosed him to make him sick, but that was all. It wasn't an attempt on his life.

And yet he'd suffered mightily, curse her brews. But his body wasn't the only thing paining him; something unseen inside of him ached with the wound of her actions as well. Ruthlessly, he stamped down the hurt beneath his anger. Aye, he told himself, the only thing preventing him from throwing her out of the castle gates right now was his knowledge that she continued to hide the *Ealach* from him. And he couldn't—he wouldn't let her go until he had it in his possession again.

"Matters of the heart rarely run smooth, cousin," Kinnon murmured, apparently noticing his black expression from where he stood off to Duncan's side.

"It's not my heart that I'm concerned with. It's my health—or apparent lack of it these days."

Kinnon raised his brows. "You're feeling ill again, then?"

"Nay," Duncan snapped. "But it's no thanks to that hex over there." He nodded toward Aileana. "I want her removed from the kitchens and the brewery. She's to have no more access to the food preparation areas. And in future, she'll be sharing my trencher with me, whether she likes it or no."

Kinnon let out a whistle. "You're thinking she brought the sickness upon you, then." Duncan nodded, and Kinnon cocked his head. "But why was Nora afflicted too? Surely your leman is skilled enough to curse those she chooses, without mistake?"

Duncan could have sworn he saw a twinkle in Kinnon's eye.

Deciding his imagination tricked him, he stared into the fire. "I don't know. Perhaps she decided it was worth a risk to others to lay me low," he mumbled, kicking at a sputtering log that had fallen too close to the hearth. "It's clear how she feels about me. It's been so from the moment she laid eyes on me on the field beyond her family's holding."

Kinnon folded his arms across his chest, remaining silent for so long that Duncan finally pulled his gaze up to look at him again. His cousin appeared to be in deep thought.

"You might be wrong, you know."

Kinnon spoke so low that Duncan wasn't certain, at first, that he'd said anything. But then Kinnon stopped rocking and looked him straight in the eye. Duncan felt the strength of their friendship in his gaze, a bond that reached deeper than ties of blood ever would.

Duncan shook his head. "Nay, I don't think I'm wrong about her, Kinnon, though God knows I wish it otherwise. It's the only reasonable explanation for what happened."

"I'm not talking about her giving you something to make you feel sick," Kinnon said. "That might well be true. I'm talking about *why* she'd be wanting to do something like that."

Duncan scowled. "What other reason could there be?

She despises me. I'll concede that I don't think she intended to harm me mortally, but you cannot deny she intended for me to suffer."

"Why not let her go home, then?"

"I can't release her until she tells me where she's hidden the *Ealach*."

Kinnon shrugged. "But if you fear for your life . . . ?"
His voice drifted off, and Duncan saw a flash of the
twinkle again. "Still, I have to say that the food around
here has been much improved since Aileana began helping with the cooking."

Duncan glared at Kinnon and pushed himself away
from the mantel. "You seem quite at ease with knowing
that my leman may have poisoned me. Have you something else that needs saying? Anything I should know
before I continue to trust my life next to you on the battlefield?"

Kinnon leaned forward, his serious expression wiping
away all traces of joviality. "Aye, cousin, I do have
something to say. I think you ought to reconsider the
workings of the female heart. It is not so cut and dry as
you paint it, I think." He pulled back, then, and cuffed
Duncan on the arm. "But now I'm finished giving advice. Think on what I've said, if you like."

With a smile, he sauntered into a group of MacKenzie
women and set them all to fawning over him. Duncan
watched his cousin's broad back, ire filling him up once
more. He frowned, brooding about Aileana and what
Kinnon had just said. The workings of Aileana's heart?
What *heart*? His leman had dosed him to make him sick
and then had been gleeful about it. It was an act of pure
spite, bred from her hatred of him. What in bloody
blazes was Kinnon getting at with all of his talk about
hearts?

Duncan slammed his fist atop the mantel with a growl of frustration. Then, stalking to the table, he grabbed a full pitcher of ale and a cup, and sank into a chair before the fire. Damn it all to hell. He was done thinking about it—or her—this night.

Hearts, sweet, merciful heaven.

Hearts.

Chapter 13

Aileana glanced to the door again, breathing a silent prayer for a few more seconds of solitude. Another snip here, a tug there, and her task would be complete. She worried her lower lip with her teeth as she cut tiny holes in the last of Duncan's clean tunics. A noise outside the door made her stiffen, setting her heart to a thundering gallop. But soon all was quiet again.

Rolling her gaze skyward, she murmured thanks and slipped the scissors into her sleeve. Then she thrust the rolled tunic into a basket and skittered over to her sewing by the fire. She smoothed her skirt, forcing herself to hum softly, her feet tapping to the rhythm.

In the distance she heard Duncan call for his breakfast to be readied. Moments later he entered the chamber, stamping and dripping water. He moved to stand before the fire as a shudder rippled over him, and he shook his wet hair from his eyes with a hearty growl.

Aileana's heart skipped a beat. His body glistened,

shining like wet gold in the morning light. Aside from his plaid, it was clear that he was naked.

"It is getting a bit cold to be bathing outside now, is it not?" she murmured.

"Nay. It is never too cold to be clean." He watched her for a moment, gray eyes inscrutable. Then he began to unwind the plaid from his torso. "In truth, you might find the practice a welcome change from your heated baths."

"Nay." Aileana kept her gaze trained to the floor, studying the pattern of the thick woolen rug beneath her feet. She tried to look submissive, but her lips kept twitching upward of their own accord. "Such sport is not for me. I prefer to stay indoors like all of the other wee creatures who know when it is time to hide against winter's breath." She glanced up and bit her treacherous lips. "Why just yesterday, I found some of my kin curled in the corner of the hall downstairs."

Duncan's gaze snapped to meet hers, and he ceased rubbing a linen towel over his arms and chest. She added smoothly, "It was a nest of puir, wee mousies. Pitiful they were, though clever enough to nip me with their teeth when I squeezed them too hard."

Duncan stiffened, and she was glad to have reminded him of his earlier insult, comparing her to a tiny mouse caught in the great cavern of his keep. Aileana twisted a bit of yarn round her finger till the tip turned white, trying to keep her thoughts trained on revenge, rather than the expanse of Duncan's naked chest. Scarred as he was, it was still a magnificent sight.

Finally he commented, "I hope you got rid of them all." His gaze flickered. "We've no room for creatures either weak or cunning within these walls."

"Don't fear," Aileana murmured. "I remedied the situation." She chewed the inside of her cheek. "Quite satisfactorily, I think."

Standing, she flapped the skirt she was pretending to mend and folded it atop the ruined tunics in the basket. "Now it is time for me to wash up before breaking my fast. Since you are going to be using this chamber at the moment, do I have your permission to go into the kitchen for the basin there?" She gritted her teeth, forcing the words out in a tone of sweet subservience.

Duncan impaled her with his gaze, making her feel both hot and cold at the same time, before turning his back to her. "Aye, I suppose it will be all right this time." He grabbed a fresh square of linen from the warming rack before the fire and rubbed it over his wet hair.

Aileana felt an unexpected twisting in her belly. He bore scars on his back as well, but the muscles beneath the scarred flesh undulated with every movement in a dance of sheer perfection. She closed her eyes, imagining what it would be like to feel that warmth and strength under her palms.

"Do not linger too long in the kitchens or try to help in serving the meal," he said, jerking her from her reverie. He stiffened when he commanded, "And meet me at the table in time to break your fast with me."

The suspicion in his voice stifled the heat burgeoning through Aileana. She murmured her assent and turned to go, focusing again on her plots and plans, and silently counting the minutes it would take until the seeds of her little surprise blossomed into the sweet fruit of vengeance.

Before many minutes had passed, Bridgid puffed to her side at the table. "Ach, Duncan's coming, missy, and he is looking for you." She shook her head, adding, "Sure he's bringing the storms of hell with him. I haven't seen him so angry since the day he brought you home to live with us." Bridgid colored hearty red. "Not that I think poorly on your living here, mind you."

Aileana concentrated on tearing her bread into chunks. "There's no need to explain. I know how Duncan feels about me, and it does not hurt me to voice it aloud."

Bridgid's face relaxed a little. "Aye, well, be that as it may, he's in a fine fettle. He's got cracks of lightning behind his eyes, so you'd best watch yourself."

Nodding, Aileana picked up her mug of ale and took a big swallow. Heaven help her, but she'd pulled the lion's tail this time. She only hoped she hadn't gone too far. Over the rim of her mug she saw Duncan approach from across the hall, and a shiver swept up her spine. When he stopped right in front of her at the table, she gained the full measure of his appearance, and a choking cough escaped her.

"Is something amiss?" he thundered. More than just lightning flashed in his silvery eyes; it was a full-blown tempest.

"The ale," she choked. "I must have swallowed wrong."

He stood before her, legs planted in a wide stance. Many of the hall's other occupants stopped to stare at the odd figure cut by their fierce leader. The only normal thing about him was the plaid draped across his torso and thighs. His long-sleeved tunic and his leggings gaped from scores of holes. A few large spots were stitched together to wrinkle in bunched folds. He looked ridiculous.

Exactly as she'd intended.

Only she hadn't thought he'd have the gall to wear the ruined garments so boldly into the hall.

"I'm waiting. Have you nothing to say?" His voice echoed quiet and deadly, spreading hot tingles over her.

Blinking up at him, she tried to school her face into impassive lines. "Nay, other than to wonder why you're dressed so strangely this morn." She blinked again.

"I was thinking you would enlighten me on that count." A muscle in his jaw twitched, and he leaned forward. "Now."

Aileana swallowed. After a long pause, she shrugged and gave him a crooked smile. "The wee mousies had a hand in it, perhaps?" Her gaze brushed over his ruined garments. "The mites *were* making a nest with scraps of just that color, now that I think on it."

His jaw clenched again, and she saw him suck in his breath. But then suddenly something in his expression altered. The tightness around his mouth relaxed, so much so that for a moment, Aileana thought he was going to laugh.

"From the look of me, woman, we're housing a ravenous pack of she-wolves."

Relief flooded Aileana. That he could jest boded well. "Aye," she murmured, her expression as grave as she could make it. "It is possible."

"Possible," he echoed, his lips twitching as he sat down next to her, "yet unlikely." Pouring himself a full mug of ale, he took a long drink, then pushed it aside to look at her again. "But wolves or mice, the creatures had better possess skill with a needle and thread to mend the damage they've done."

"And if they refuse to comply?"

Duncan's brows arched at her boldness. He shook his head as he took another drink of his ale. "If the beasties refuse, their own garments will meet a worse fate. Then they will find themselves roaming the castle naked to the skin for all to see." He cast a sidelong glance at her, and her heart pulsed faster.

Aileana looked away, willing her voice to remain steady. "That would be an unkind measure to take considering the chill that's set upon the land." Taking a swallow of ale for strength, she added, "They might catch their death of cold, not to mention their modesty."

"Ah, but what is lost in modesty is gained in pleasure for the rest of us."

"Pleasure?" Her cheeks heated at his implication.

"The pleasure of winning the sport your wee creatures have begun, of course," Duncan answered smoothly. "It's a fine thing to best an adversary in battle."

Aileana remained silent, glancing at him, unsure how to proceed with this new and somehow unsettling Duncan.

He fixed his quicksilver gaze on her. "I, for one, try never to overlook an enemy's strengths," he continued. "Or special skills." He pushed his trencher of food toward her. "Care for a bit of breakfast?"

"Nay, I've eaten."

"Oh, but I insist."

Aileana clenched her jaw and took a finger full of the oat mash. Curse him. Being made to taste his food at every meal was almost as bad as being banned from the kitchens.

"It is fine," she mumbled, standing up to leave.

"I'm relieved."

She scowled and nodded to go. But before she took even three steps, Duncan's voice rumbled behind her, laughter and warning mingling in a rich timbre. "Do not forget to instruct your wee friends on the task that lies ahead of them, now. If my clothing still bears holes by the time the sun sets on the loch, the morning light will be illuminating a great deal more of the guilty ones than they ever thought to show."

Aileana bit back her angry response and stalked on toward the curving stairway—and the room full of mending that awaited her—with Duncan's hearty chuckle sounding in her ears as she went. She tightened her fists and compressed her lips, his amusement pushing her steps to haste and pricking her with the bitter gall of defeat.

Three men crouched in the wooded copse beyond the arched stonework bridge to Eilean Donan. Dusk had descended, and a cold rain trickled down, penetrating the thick plaids that covered their heads. A branch crackled behind them. Almost of accord, they twisted to face the intruder, poised and ready to attack. But in the next instant they sat back on their haunches again.

"It looks the same as the day I left it, thirteen years ago," Colin said as he approached. His blond hair was streaked dark with the wet, and he pulled his plaid closer around his shoulders and squatted near the three. "What news?"

"It's as you said. There's been some repair to the rear. Over there," one of the men said, as he pointed to an outer wall where new masonry was just visible.

Colin shook the damp hair from his good eye and walked past the men to the edge of the copse. He squinted in the misting rain. The castle's position so far out onto the land jutting over the loch made it difficult to tell the quality of the work. "Aye. It's not so long since the clan came back here. Work has just begun." He stood. "What of the girl? Have you learned if she's here?"

"She's here all right," the second man said, barking a laugh. "With all the MacKenzies milling around, it was easy to sneak into the yard and watch for a while this afternoon." He laughed again, revealing, when he parted his lips, several black holes where teeth should have been. "Yet as sure as hellfire, when the girl walked out, I almost thought the mistress herself had come without telling us. The lass took my breath away. She's the very image of Morgana, by the Rood."

Colin raised his brows, a flare of interest lighting in his gut as he made a grunting sound. When he pulled his gaze away from the castle, it was to stare at his informer. "Did she wear the amulet?"

"Nay. At least not out in the open."

"Then perhaps it is hidden, as Morgana's vision foretold. She claims it is beyond any walls." Colin tightened his hand around the handle of his claymore, rubbing his thumb along the smooth leather gripping. "And my dear brother?"

The man shook his head. "I didn't see him. Though I know he's inside by the way those around me were talking. Some of the women spoke of him." He grinned. "Something about him catching sick from one of the MacKenzie wenches."

Colin bit down hard and turned back to stare at the sturdy, square keep rising straight into the misty sky. "Aye, well, *legitimacy* doesn't ensure good taste." He spat the words like dirt from his mouth. "Apparently Duncan isn't much changed by his stay with the English, if he's still after tupping women all the time." He made a clucking sound. "What's the world coming to when you cannot count on the Tower to torture the itch out of a man?"

The three cackled their agreement, then fell suddenly

quiet as Colin faced them again. Thinking of his brother had set him on edge, as it always did, and he knew his black mood drifted off of him like a stench. He watched the men fidget beneath his stare. One man almost made the sign of the cross over himself for protection, but thought the better of it when Colin flicked his gaze to him.

"We've seen enough. Gather the supplies and meet me at the crossing. We'll head back tonight."

The toothless man opened his mouth to protest but the second man elbowed him, making him clamp it shut before uttering a word. The third man grumbled under his breath about a hot meal and shelter. Colin spared them nary another thought. He stalked toward the horses, his boots tramping with a dull sound on the sodden ground.

He'd learned what Morgana wanted to find out. Her sister was here and the MacRaes had settled into Eilean Donan once again. As for the amulet, he couldn't tell, and he'd not risk discovery by prying further. Three years ago, when they'd first tried to steal back the *Ealach* at Dulhmeny, they'd all nearly been captured for their pains. Nay, Morgana would have to determine the rest of what she needed through her sorcery.

Swinging himself astride his horse, Colin aimed for the north. Wind whipped at his cheeks, making the flesh around his patched eye sting with cold. The ruined socket ached. Yet another reason to make Duncan pay. To make him keep paying. He'd lost his eye thanks to his brother's parting blow, delivered right before Gavin MacDonell had knocked Duncan senseless and dragged him to the dungeon where Mairi awaited him.

Colin frowned. He hadn't wanted that part of the plan. Not for Duncan's sake, but for Mairi's. She'd been a gentle soul, kind-hearted and innocent. She hadn't deserved what happened to her. But Duncan had. In the end Duncan had suffered mightily, both in losing Mairi and in the Tower. But it would never be enough. Colin would never forgive him for taking his eye. Or the clan. *His clan.*

A branch snapped back beneath Colin's hand, spraying him with icy drops of water as he urged his mount faster through the glen. He cursed and wiped his face. He needed to think on something else. Already his belly twisted as if it was infested with a thousand burning snakes.

His mind turned to Morgana. If nothing else, she would be grateful for the confirmation of her vision. It would be proof that her powers were strengthening. And when Morgana was feeling grateful . . .

Colin's lips edged upward in a smile. Morgana's inventiveness would be just the relief he needed. She knew how to drive away the bitterness, the rage that consumed him. *A two days' ride.* In just two days, he'd be back at Morgana's side—and in her bed. Then he'd help her to plot their next move.

And when all was in place, they'd spring the trap and seek vengeance against those cursed few who thought to keep them from the power that had always been their destiny.

Chapter 14

"It's your own fault, you know. You shouldn't have done it."

Aileana twisted away from the chest she was trying to drag across the floor and scowled at Bridgid. "Nay, it's *his* damnable stubbornness that's to blame." She tugged at the corner of the massive case, but it remained unyielding. "He's worse than a bairn, wailing at the tiniest bit of change."

Bridgid shook her head and then came over to help her pull the chest into place. "Duncan's a bit peculiar about his things. More so since the Tower." She brushed a sweaty strand of hair from her forehead. "And you know very well that he allows nothing to be altered in his chamber without his permission."

Aileana rolled her gaze skyward and sat hard on the chest's curved lid. "I was only thinking to make the room more welcoming. The way he's crammed all of the furniture against the walls . . . why it's as ugly as it's unnatural."

"Likely it stems from his years of imprisonment. Look," Bridgid gestured. "Windows, candles, carpets, draperies . . . more chests and cabinets than four men could use." She tramped over to straighten the bed. "He craves the comforts denied him so long." She nodded, seeming satisfied with her explanation.

"Tower or no, he didn't need to use such language upon me," Aileana mumbled. "It was as if he thought that I'd changed his room solely to plague him. He wouldn't even listen to my explanation."

"Aye, well after you put those field mice in his boots, his temper was short. You should have waited a few more days to let him recover before you tried another one of your tricks."

Aileana stopped so quickly that her shoes slid on the floor.

Bridgid cast her a sideways glance. "Aye, missy, I know it's you who's been playing all those jests on Duncan. You don't need to pretend innocence with me."

Aileana's mouth opened, but nothing came out. Bridgid's expression was playful as she folded a thickly furred deerskin and tucked it into the corner. "Don't fear—I don't think there's any harm in it. Duncan needs a bit of stirring up, if you ask me. It won't hurt him." She stopped to frown at Aileana. "Unless you be trying more of those herbs on him. I wasn't very happy to learn of that, I'll be telling you."

Aileana's shock melted to shame, and she stuttered, "I never meant to cause him any serious hurt by it, I swear. I only—that is, we—"

"Ach, well, your secret is safe with me." Bridgid looked up over her shoulder. "And with Kinnon, of course."

"Kinnon?" Aileana drowned in a new wave of embarrassment.

"Oh, aye. It was he who told me. Though I suspected as much myself." She puffed over and sat next to Aileana, taking her hand in her own. "Allow an old woman her say, missy. Rattle the MacRae as you like, but leave the herbs and such out of your plans." She shook her head and sighed. "I wouldn't have him feeling poorly again." Then she patted Aileana's hand and stood. "Come now. We've no more time to dawdle. The lot of them down below expect another feast tonight. I've a dozen geese to baste, puddings to stew, and loaves to bake."

Through her tightened throat, Aileana managed to mumble, "But I'm not allowed to help you with the cooking anymore."

"Ach, I forgot."

Aileana looked away. Just a few hours ago she'd been so sure of herself and the little revenges she'd been taking against Duncan. Each action had seemed to restore her wounded dignity a bit more. But now everything seemed more muddled.

"Well," Bridgid shook her head as she gathered her arms full of more blankets, "You can come with me nonetheless. You've no cause to be wasting time in this—"

A clamor rose from the courtyard, followed by shouts and hooting. Aileana and Bridgid went to one of the windows and looked below. Several boys waved their arms and bellowed as they raced in circles. "The MacKenzie himself—he's arrived! The MacKenzie's here!" The lads yelled so loudly that anyone who hadn't heard the call must needs be deaf.

Bridgid put down the blankets and planted her strong

hands on her hips. "This changes everything, it does. Duncan will not be too pleased, I think."

Aileana peered out the window again to see several horsemen ride through the gate. "Why?"

The rider in the lead made an impressive figure; his white hair flowed to blend with a thick beard, and his legs were muscular beneath the distinctive plaid covering him. With the wind snapping his cloak, he appeared regal and in command.

Moving toward the door, Bridgid answered, "Duncan will chafe at having to entertain the MacKenzie. Though his clan is always welcome here, Duncan doesn't feel kindly toward or respect the chief."

"Is he unfit to lead, then?" Aileana stole another glance out of the window. The white-haired man looked distinguished enough. He dismounted and began striding toward the entrance.

"Nay, I wouldn't go that far. And yet Duncan has cause enough against him. It was on the MacKenzie's orders that an army was not raised when Duncan was sold to the English. The chief could have gone to war for him, but he did nothing."

"But the MacKenzie couldn't have possibly attacked England. It would have been suicide."

"He wasn't supposed to attack England." A heavy silence fell between them, and when Bridgid broke it, her voice sounded strange. "He was supposed to attack your clan."

"Oh." For the second time in less than a quarter hour, unpleasant surprise dulled Aileana's ability to speak.

Bridgid continued, "As Chief of Kintail, the MacKenzie should have demanded vengeance for the crimes committed against us. But he chose peace over right." Pursing her lips, she added, "In his favor, he took in those of us who survived after the ambush. He even gave some men for Kinnon to take with him when he tried to free Duncan from the Tower. But he wouldn't raise a force against your people."

"I see." Aileana's back stiffened. "I suppose that gives Duncan another reason to hate me."

"Nay, missy. He doesn't blame you for that," Bridgid said in a kinder tone. "Duncan is just. He always has been."

"Then I would not want to see him when he's behaving *unjustly*."

Bridgid was quiet for a moment. She sighed. "I cannot stay longer to talk about this with you right now. But come and I'll set you to some tasks outside the kitchens to get your mind off what troubles you." She gave a gentle smile. "Come."

Feeling the weight of her shameful position at Eilean Donan settle into her chest once more, Aileana nodded and followed. As she walked alongside the *bailie*, she bit her lip. None of this was working as she'd hoped.

It seemed that it was going to take something much greater than these little revenges she'd plotted against Duncan to ease the ache that grew in her heart every time she thought about him . . . and somehow she doubted that she was ever going to find the means she sought.

The door blew open. Duncan waited a few seconds before pushing himself to his feet. He stood to face the Chief of Kintail reluctantly, but he couldn't risk open insult, not when his clan might suffer the consequences of his insolence.

John MacKenzie, Chief of Kintail, strode into the hall, flanked by four other MacKenzies in full regalia.

He stopped ten paces from Duncan. His wide stance exuded pride and confidence, yet his expression revealed a hint of uncertainty.

"It's good to see you prospering, Duncan MacRae." He spoke loudly, his words echoing in the silence of the great hall.

Duncan clenched his jaw before tilting his head in greeting. "I'm well enough. Though it's safe to say that the English did all that they could to ensure otherwise."

"Aye, well, the English are dogs."

"Dogs with a bite," Duncan rejoined quietly, fisting his ruined hand within its gauntlet.

Kinnon appeared out of nowhere, stepping up behind Duncan and laying his hand on his shoulder. "My cousin is too modest to admit that he fought the bastards in body and in spirit, for which they repaid him in cowardly fashion. But we survived, did we not, Duncan?" Kinnon slapped him on the back and smiled, before raising his cup. "Enough talk of our enemies, now. Come, share some warmed ale and a meal with us on this cold day!"

The MacKenzie nodded. "Aye, a cup would be most welcome after our journey." He moved to a table at Kinnon's gesture. Duncan flicked his gaze to a serving boy, directing him to bring the ale. Then he too sat.

The chief took his place at the seat of honor next to Duncan, refraining from talking while a trencher of venison, turnip, and bread were placed before him. He dug into the repast with relish, slowing only when he'd finished a good portion of the food.

"I would have come to greet your return to Eilean Donan earlier, MacRae, but for the skirmishes these past months with the Buchanans. The sorry bunch of them keep attacking Brahan Castle."

"So you still lead raids against other clans, then?" Duncan murmured the statement half as a question, and the chief paused with a finger full of venison part way to his mouth.

Kinnon threw Duncan a warning glance, but Duncan ignored him and tossed back the remainder of his ale.

Finally, the chief put the meat in his mouth and chewed slowly. After he'd swallowed, he spoke. "Aye. I lead attacks—on those who threaten the welfare of Highland peace. If another way is available, I take that over warfare. It is less costly in both men and time."

Duncan toyed with his empty cup, twirling it between his fingers. "And what of leaving a matter unsettled— leaving a debt unpaid? Are you saying you've never allowed the likes of that?"

"Nay, never." The chief's eyes were steely, his gaze unwavering. "And I'm not daft, either. I heard about your raid two months past on the MacDonells. I cannot condone it, though I understand your feelings in the matter."

Then why did you not retaliate against them for me when I was helpless in the Tower? The question burned in Duncan's brain, but he didn't voice it.

The MacKenzie sat back and picked a shred of meat from his teeth. "It's time now to put aside your thirst for vengeance, Duncan. The MacDonells themselves punished those who wronged you; justice was served many years ago."

"Not all of the guilty were punished."

The MacKenzie leaned forward. "Morgana Mac-Donell was sent into banishment to die, along with two score of her clan." The chief raised one brow. "If I don't forget myself, your own brother Colin was made to join them for his part in the plot." The chief drank and wiped his mouth with the back of his hand. "Let the past go, man."

Duncan stared into his cup, gritting his teeth until he thought they would crack. He could say no more. His duty to the Chief prevented it. Yet knowing that the MacKenzie was willing to sit here at his table and defend his lack of action against the MacDonells all those years ago galled him.

The corrosion of such dark emotions seemed strange to Duncan after the relative peace of these last weeks. But it was easily recalled in the face of the MacKenzie's arrogance. Duncan felt a swelling of the same tension, the same savage rage that he'd experienced before his raid to steal back the *Ealach*. Clenching his fist round his cup, Duncan let the feeling build, let it rise, until it blurred his vision beneath a veil of red.

At that moment his gaze fell upon Aileana. She stood in one corner of the great hall, partly obscured by the others who had come out to see the Chief of Kintail. But she hung back, almost as if she was afraid to be seen. At that moment a wicked thought took hold in Duncan's mind. An idea to toy with the MacKenzie just as the man had played him for a fool. Duncan latched onto it in the heat of his rage, clinging to it, nurturing it until it emerged whole and perfect. Then he swung his gaze to the MacKenzie and smiled.

"I almost forgot. You've not been introduced to someone very important. Someone that I'm sure you'll be interested in meeting." Lifting his arm, Duncan stood and gestured to Aileana. "Come, lass," he called to her across the hall. "The Chief of Kintail has arrived, and it would warm his heart to greet one of those fortunate enough to benefit from his generosity thirteen years ago."

"Duncan," Kinnon said quietly, trying to pull him back into his seat, "Don't do this. Think on it, man, before it's too late."

"Nay," Duncan growled under his breath. He faced the chief again, watching him closely as Aileana stepped into the light that filled the area around the table.

Though the MacKenzie did not gasp aloud, the blood seemed to drain from his cheeks. "What by all the fires of hell is this, MacRae?" he whispered. He could not seem to tear his gaze from Aileana's face, as he set down his cup. "Why chide me when you yourself have resurrected the serpent and brought her to your bosom?"

Duncan watched the flush spread across Aileana's face. He felt a brief flash of remorse, but he doused it. "It's not as you think, MacKenzie." Duncan stood again, pulling Aileana to him. Though she stiffened, her resistance was no match for his temper.

Reaching out, he stroked a tendril of soft, fiery hair that curled over her shoulder. "This is not the sorceress Morgana. It is her younger sister, the fair Aileana."

The MacKenzie stared. Then he seemed to gain control of himself. Stepping forward, he nodded to her. "Forgive me, lady, for my lack of manners. They aren't usually so remiss, but for a moment, I thought I was seeing a ghost."

"It is of no matter, my lord," Aileana murmured hoarsely.

"Is this a reconciliation visit you're making to the MacRaes, then, lass? A gesture of goodwill between your clan and his?"

"Nay," she answered, though her words were barely audible. "It is no visit. I live at Eilean Donan now."

The MacKenzie looked stunned again. But then he shook off his amazement quickly, laughing and slapping

Duncan's shoulder. "You're a scoundrel, to be sure, MacRae, pretending to hold your grudge against the MacDonells when you've arranged a marriage of peace with them. It's a time-honored way to unite warring clans." He sat back and grabbed his cup again. "Who's the devil lucky enough to capture such a bride?"

"I am." Duncan felt another tingle of success as the Chief snapped his gaze to him. He returned the stare. "But I didn't take Aileana MacDonell as my wife . . ."

The hall went silent. Duncan let his hand drift along Aileana's arm, close enough to her breast to make her gasp. He forced himself to remain unmoved when she pushed him back angrily, tears springing to her eyes.

Facing the chief again, he dropped his remaining words like cannon balls. "I took her as my leman."

The silence thickened in the hall, rising up to strangle Aileana. She thought that shame would swallow her whole, leaving nothing but a patch of scorched stone where she'd been standing.

The MacKenzie also looked ready to choke, grasping for words that refused to come. He finally muttered, "I see," then waved his empty cup in demand for something to drink.

With his utterance the room came to life again. A fierce buzzing began in Aileana's ears. She seemed to be viewing the scene from a distance, yet so close that she felt smothered by it. Duncan stood to her right, though she saw only his rigid profile in her refusal to turn her eyes on him. But even through her shock, she noticed that Bridgid cast her a sympathetic look. Kinnon sat slumped in his chair, staring at the table. The hall's other inhabitants moved and whispered in a dizzying swell of sight and sound. Everything slowed for Aileana as she turned to Duncan. Her cheeks burned and her lungs strained with the effort it took to keep breathing, to keep from crying her pain aloud.

In the instant that he met her gaze, she saw the hardness of his expression, took in the almost agonizing rigidity of his beautiful, scarred face. But something flickered in his eyes. A shadow passed through their depths, darkening the cold gray with what might have been a glimmer of regret. Heat burned her eyelids. It didn't matter. Sorry or not, it didn't change anything. Nothing mattered now, except the sense of degradation that Duncan had heaped on her.

Without making a sound, Aileana fled the hall, bursting into the courtyard and not stopping until she stumbled to the ground near the well. Cold scorched her lungs, and, once she was free of prying eyes, cries ripped from her throat, fueled by the swelling sense of injustice and rage. Wrapping her arms around her middle, Aileana edged to the far side of the well, hiding from the view of anyone who might come out of the castle. She rocked back and forth, her now soft keening distant in her own ears, the heat behind her eyes driving, bitter, desperate.

After a while the world started to come into focus again. The pain eased. The tears stopped, and hurt faded to numbness. She sat still now, staring ahead with nothing but a huge, bleak hole inside of her that threatened to smother her in darkness.

It had been so cruel.

Duncan had treated her like a whore in front of his entire clan. In front of Bridgid and Kinnon and the MacKenzies. And it hurt all the more because she'd thought that the two of them had reached an uneasy truce, a certain level of understanding. Thought that he felt some kind of tenderness for her.

She'd thought.

Why think at all, twit? You're his leman, nothing more. That he hasn't made you so in truth is but a trifle to anyone. If they'd even believe it.

Rubbing her hand across her nose, Aileana blinked. But the tears just kept flowing. Duncan's act today had been purposely callous. Worse, even, than his treatment of her that first day in the forest, for she'd been running from him then, concealing what he thought was his. Today she'd done nothing to warrant such abuse. She'd—

"The repaired wall is over there. I'll be but a moment getting the plans, and then I'll meet you loch-side."

Aileana sat up a little straighter, brushing her fingers across her eyes again and twisting around, enough to see who spoke without being seen herself.

Her gaze narrowed. It was as she thought. Duncan led the MacKenzie and a few of his men into the yard. *Overbearing wretch*. She watched as he showed off the work he'd completed on his precious castle. It was the only thing he truly cared about after all—his pile of rock and stone.

Duncan broke off from the others and started her way, alone. Stiffening, Aileana pressed back against the wall and held her breath. He passed less than six paces from her, but he didn't notice her.

It was nothing new. She almost scoffed aloud at the aptness of her observation. She watched from behind, as he ducked his golden brown head to enter the storage room. The breadth of his shoulders filled the doorway an instant before he disappeared into the dark recesses of the chamber.

Before she really knew what she was doing, Aileana had surged to her feet and charged toward the spot. An idea bloomed in her mind like a deadly flower, filling her thoughts with venom. The arrogant boor had a lesson to learn, and an opportunity for instruction had just presented itself. Hot emotions drove her forward. She had to lean halfway into the room in order to grasp the heavy wooden bar that would latch the door from the outside, but she gritted her teeth and pulled until the slab of reinforced beams began to groan and move.

And as Duncan whirled to face her in the shadowed recesses, Aileana paused, locking her gaze for just a moment with his in a glare of grim satisfaction . . .

Before slamming the door shut and dropping the bar, trapping him inside the darkened chamber with a resounding thud.

Chapter 15

Silence settled on Duncan, freezing him with disbelief. *The insolent woman had shut him in.* He took
three steps forward, blinking in the pitch darkness.
When he encountered nothing but blank air, a tickle of
unease lit in his belly. He shook it off, scowling and
reaching to find the door. Hell, it was only a few steps
farther; the chamber wasn't that large.

A lancing pain shot up from his toe as his foot glanced
off a wooden crate. *Damn.* He'd veered too far to the
right. As he rubbed away the ache, Duncan sucked in his
breath and scowled more deeply. He hoped Aileana was
enjoying her jest, because in a few short moments she
was going to pay for it. When he got outside this cursed
little chamber he'd—

His gloved hands hit something hard. *The door.* Relief
filled him, tingling to the ends of his fingers as he found
the hand latch and pushed.

Nothing. It wouldn't budge.

That set Duncan back on his heels again. *Curse her.* She'd thrown the bar home. His mouth tightened. There was only one other method of escape that he could think of trying. But he'd need some luck to accomplish it.

Pressing his shoulder to the resisting planks, Duncan used his entire weight to try to jiggle the bar off its latch. For an instant it felt like the bar lifted and teetered, ready to fall off. But then it clunked back into place. He pushed again, just to be sure. It remained fixed. Unmoving.

"Aileana, open the door," he called. He sounded irritated, and his own voice echoed back at him, mocking him. Silence reigned supreme, emphasizing the knowledge that he found harder and harder to ignore.

He was imprisoned here.

Locked in. *Just like he'd been in the Tower.*

A cold sweat broke across his brow. *No, damn it. He wouldn't think on it.* He stared through the darkness, searching for even a sliver of light—a tiny flicker to hold onto, to help keep it at bay. But there was only darkness. Unending blackness. Duncan fisted his hands and closed his eyes, trying to stave it off, trying to breathe deep and keep his head clear. He needed to stay calm. It was but a prank, plotted in ignorance. Nothing more.

Clenching his jaw, Duncan repeated the phrase in his mind. He willed himself to break free of the memories, to keep steady. To find a way out. But when he opened his eyes, the familiar, sickening jolt sliced through him. God, he couldn't stop it. It kept coming.

Relentless.

Cold sweat spread to the rest of his body. The old weakness began to invade his chest, his arms, his legs, making him sink to his knees on the dirt floor, while the tide of images swept over him with the ferocity of a charging army.

A tiny room. Dark. Cold.

He was there again. Trapped and helpless . . .

Yanked to his feet, his muscles screaming, he was dragged down the hall. His legs scraped across ragged edges of stone, the shackles biting deep into his flesh. They threw him to the floor of the chamber. One of the bastards grabbed his right arm, stretching it out, so that his hand lay, palm down, on the bloodstained, wooden slab at the room's center.

Fear prickled through him. Nausea and impotent rage filled his throat, choking him. He saw the rock lifted high above his hand, tried to jerk away, strained to pull his arm back, even as the nerves of his fingers thrummed in preparation for the impact. But they held him fast. Laughing, taunting.

The rock cracked down, and he started to scream . . .

"Nay!" The primal roar burst from Duncan's lungs as he bolted upright. He slammed his body into the heavy wood of the storage door, pummeling the beams with his fists. He heard a crack . . . and then the solid mass began to give way. Splinters of light shot into the chamber, blinding him as the door burst open with a crunch of wood and metal. He pushed through, falling to the ground and gasping for air.

His heart beat thick in his ears, and he gradually became aware of the harsh sound of his own breathing. Dirt. He tasted dirt in his mouth, gritty and cold. But the crushing weakness began to ebb. He pushed himself up on his hands, raising his head slowly. And he saw them. They were all staring.

The MacKenzie, his men, and Kinnon stood across

the courtyard, stock still, their expressions aghast. Kinnon moved first, running to Duncan to grasp his arm and pull him to his feet.

"What the hell happened?"

"Aileana," Duncan rasped. His throat felt seared with the air he sucked into his lungs. "I'll wring her neck with my bare hands." He shoved past Kinnon. "Where is she?"

"Aileana?" Kinnon's brow furrowed.

"She locked me in there with no light . . ." Duncan's voice grated quieter now, as he swallowed the nausea that had threatened to overwhelm him. "And I couldn't stop it from coming. Everything all over again."

Kinnon went pale. "Christ Almighty . . ."

Without another word, Duncan strode toward the castle, clenching his fists. The rage he'd experienced with the MacKenzie seemed nothing compared to the feelings raking his heart at this moment. He stopped at the well, pulling up the bucket and plunging his gloved hands into the water. He cupped his palms, bringing them up to sluice the icy liquid over his face.

Standing straight again, he breathed deep. A hard, cold calm filled him, driving out the panic, the terror . . . the sense of helplessness that had consumed him. *She'd gone too far this time.* There'd be no more looking the other way. No more humoring her little revolts against him. Aileana MacDonell had declared open war against him this day, and he'd be damned if he'd let her retreat from the battlefield unscathed.

He found her in the great hall, bent over the table, washing a single spot as if she wanted to wear a hole in the wood. His anger pitched higher. How dare she appear so innocent? He tensed as he strode to her, eager to escalate their personal fray. And he knew just the way—

a strategic attack that would shred all of her defenses as completely as she'd just tried to destroy his.

Aileana glanced up from her work and felt a stab of pure fear. Duncan charged through the entryway, looking as he had that day on the field outside Dulhmeny— face pale, eyes icy gray, his expression dark and intense, like one of God's fallen angels. But she hardly had time to gasp before he was upon her, clamping her arm in his wet, leather-covered grip. Wordlessly, he began to drag her to the stairway.

"What are you doing?" Her voice sounded too loud in the unnatural quiet of the hall.

She hazarded a glance at his profile, then wished she hadn't. He stared straight ahead as he pulled her along, not answering. Ripples of fear multiplied in her belly, spreading outward, until they threatened to immobilize her. She began to struggle against him in earnest.

"Where are you taking me?" She braced her heels against the stone floor and twisted in his grasp. But he was resolute. Strong.

Though she kicked and fought, Duncan continued to take her up the stairway. When he reached the landing, she slammed her foot into his shin with a satisfying thud. He stopped, then. But other than the cessation of movement, he showed no reaction. Aileana swallowed and held her breath. As his gaze met hers, her heart stilled, and she cringed. He seemed to stare right through her as if she didn't exist, like she was no more than a speck of dust to be crushed under his heel.

"If you do not come with me peacefully, I swear I'll tie and gag you to get you there if I have to." His voice echoed low and dangerous.

"I'll ask you again, where are you taking me?"

"I'm securing you in my chamber."

Her head felt too light, and a hollow space opened in her belly. "You plan to lock me in?"

Though he didn't answer, his eyes spoke for him, unyielding and furious.

Trying to still her rising panic, Aileana clenched her fingers convulsively in her skirts. "When will I be released?"

"You won't."

Her breath escaped in a rush, followed by a renewed swell of sickness. She despised the pleading in her voice, but she couldn't stop it any more than she could stop herself from taking in air. "You cannot hold me there. Please . . . I—I cannot bear to be confined to a chamber again."

"You've left me no other choice."

Her sob broke off into a shriek as Duncan picked her up by the waist and slung her over his shoulder. All too soon she was set on her feet again inside his room. When she tried to push around him and run out, Duncan stood in her way, his chest as unmovable a wall as any in Eilean Donan.

"Do not try to escape. This lock is strong, and it's a long way down to the loch from the windows." He stepped back, preparing to leave. "I'll be staying here of the evenings as usual. Attempt any more trickery, and I'll have you moved to the dungeons below." His steel eyes darkened. "Trust me when I say that you do not want to be put there."

Aileana's lips trembled. Although she hated herself for it, she reached out, hoping to stop him, to make him pause at least. "Please," she said. "I'm begging you, Duncan. Don't do this. I—"

"I'll be returning after sundown," he broke in, cutting short her plea. She stared at him, her eyes filling with tears. Then, as if in a dream, she saw him avert his gaze. He turned his back to her and drew the door shut behind him.

And as he clicked the lock home, it was with the precision of an expert swordsman striking for his mark . . . landing it directly into the center of her heart.

The shout for departure went up. With the MacKenzie in the lead, the procession of horses, litters, wagons and people started to move. The chief raised his arm in a last farewell, half turning in his saddle to meet Duncan's gaze once more.

Duncan returned the gesture and nodded. An array of feelings assaulted him as he watched his chief pass through the gate and down the causeway. He'd not forgiven the MacKenzie for his lack of action against Morgana and her clan those many years ago, but at least the burning rage had faded.

"Will you be coming inside now? It's a good time for a cup of ale, I'd say."

Duncan looked at Kinnon. "Aye, I'll be joining you, but not right away." He glanced up. As expected, Aileana stood silhouetted in one of the bedchamber windows. Her expression seemed to condemn him. She looked tired and drawn, as she'd been each time he'd seen her in the three days since she'd been confined to his chamber.

Kinnon followed Duncan's gaze up to the window and shook his head. In the next moment she was gone, vanished like a wraith in the mists of the moors.

"You cannot keep her up there forever, Duncan."

"Aye. But I can't let her loose either. Once she gives me the *Ealach*, I'll be sending her home, but not before." Duncan clenched his jaw and stared at the thin layer of new snow blanketing the dirt and grass around the castle. He glanced up again at the dark window, his heart heavy in his chest before starting back toward the castle. By the time he reached the kitchens, Bridgid was in the process of covering Aileana's breakfast tray with a clean towel. Steam rose from a cup of spiced ale she poured from the kettle, and she placed the drink next to the other things on the tray.

"I'll be taking her food up this morning, Bridgid. Give it to me and go on with your other duties."

The *bailie* looked startled, her eyes wide, as she handed the tray to Duncan. "Is everything in order? Are you sure you don't need me to come with you to . . . to help in any way?"

The anxiety in her voice made Duncan wince. It was clear that she cared for Aileana and was concerned for her safety. *Perhaps Bridgid thought him a monster now as well.* After his flare of temper the afternoon he'd dragged Aileana upstairs, he couldn't blame her.

"I wish to speak with Aileana in private; that is all."

Bridgid colored pink. "I'm just worried for the girl."

Duncan's teeth ached he was clenching them so hard. "There is nothing to fear, I assure you." He started toward the stairs. "While I'm with Aileana I need you to prepare food enough for me and four of my men. If all goes as I plan, I'll be taking a short journey before nightfall."

"Aye, it will be done."

With a nod, Duncan carried the tray to the steps, taking each stair slowly, deliberately, to allow himself time to think of what to say to Aileana, and how. They hadn't exchanged a word in the three days she'd been held; each night when he'd come to the chamber, she was already in her pallet, feigning sleep. He'd never pressed the point, though he knew her to be as awake and sleepless as he was. It was the one concession he'd been willing to make.

Halfway up the stairway, Duncan paused. His feet refused to move further. He felt weighted down and unhappy, but his feelings made no sense. If what he was about to do proved successful, he'd finally gain all that he'd wanted, all that he'd dreamed of for thirteen years. Yet it left him empty. Aching.

He reached the top of the landing. Setting the tray on a table in the hall, he pulled the key from the tie at his waist. The lock turned with a rusty creak, and the door swung open to silence. From his position the room looked vacant and cold, though a fire burned in the grate. The faint crackling of the flames was the only sound to break the stillness.

He stared through the shadows. *There she was.* His heart thudded a slow, steady rhythm. Aileana sat with her back to the door, hidden in a corner, her chair a few paces from the window. She'd drawn back the curtain, but he noticed that she'd positioned herself far enough from the pane to avoid being seen from outside.

"I've brought your food." He stepped in and waited.

At the sound of his voice, she twisted around, but the look of surprise lasted only an instant before she masked her expression.

"Have you decided to play nurse to me again, then? It has been weeks now since you first thought it amusing to undertake the chore during my bout with the plague." She spoke quietly, but her words pricked him.

"Nay." Duncan cleared his throat. "Bringing your meal is not the only reason I'm here." He put the tray down, indicating that she should eat if she wished, but she shook her head and remained seated. He walked closer to her, silent, pausing to stare out as she was at the loch, glowing pink and yellow now in the rising sun.

"I'm here because you have a decision to make, Aileana. I've come to discuss it with you."

"Discuss it . . . or direct me to your way of thinking?"

He felt her gaze shift to him, but he didn't trust himself to look at her, to drink in the beauty of her eyes without losing his will to continue.

"Only you can choose the path we'll both be taking."

"Then I wish to be freed from this room."

The anguish in her voice made his heart twist, but he forged ahead. "I'll be releasing you when you give me the *Ealach*, and not before. It's the whys and whens that I wish to discuss."

"Ah, I see. Another attempt at blackmail." A harsh sound caught in her throat. "My father imprisoned me in my chamber in order to protect the *Ealach*, and you lock me inside in order to make me surrender it; the irony of that is almost amusing, don't you think?"

Duncan faced her, steeling himself against the hurt he saw in her face. "Aileana, we cannot go on as we have, that much is clear. Despite what you think, I don't relish the thought of keeping you locked away."

"Then why continue to do it?" Her eyes welled with tears, and Duncan's hand shook as he struggled not to reach up and brush the sadness away. She wrapped her arms around her middle and whispered, "Keeping me in here . . . you're killing me, Duncan, breath by breath."

A stabbing pain pierced him, but he gritted his teeth against it. "Just give me the amulet, Aileana. Then I can release you to your kin and we can find a peace between us."

"I cannot do that. No more than I could those months ago when you first attacked Dulhmeny."

"Why not?" Irritation fueled him again. "Why are you sacrificing your freedom for the sake of something you were made to keep—something you didn't even choose to protect?"

"My life and freedom were sacrificed to the *Ealach* long before I met you." Her voice sounded hard, and his stomach lurched at the shadows in her eyes. "Besides, who are you to ask such a thing—a man whose sole purpose lies in stealing back an amulet you've lived without for thirteen years?"

"It is my birthright. The *Ealach* was my father's and his father's before him."

"My father died trying to protect it."

"It is not the same." Duncan scowled. "Don't try to compare your claim to mine. My entire clan was nearly destroyed and the woman I loved more than my life was slaughtered before my eyes."

That statement pulled Aileana up short, and she felt the dagger-thrust of the reminder pierce her heart. *Mairi.* Of course. She stared at her hands, clasped tightly together on her lap. It was the memory of Mairi that drove Duncan. His murdered love, perfect and irreplaceable to him. Oh, she'd been a fool to think that any softness he'd shown her these past months meant anything to him. He belonged to his slain wife, body and soul.

That knowledge made the dagger press a little deeper, adding to the bite of guilt she couldn't help feeling at his obvious pain. The realization of it startled her. *Why care that Duncan suffered?* After all, she'd had no part in Morgana's attacks and the terrible things he'd endured after. He, on the other hand—he had locked her in this room, a fate almost worse than death after the weeks of freedom she'd been allowed.

Raising her gaze to Duncan again, she tightened her mouth, willing the sting of heat from her eyes. "I cannot keep silent, Duncan. The *Ealach* should be used for good. Your clan exploited its powers. It doesn't belong with you."

"Who told you that?"

"It is a well-known fact."

"It's a lie," he muttered, "and one your sister used to muster your people against me."

"Few in my clan condone the way Morgana took the amulet from you," Aileana answered quietly, "but there was more reason for us keeping it after the raid than simple selfishness, as well you know."

"What do I know? There was no other motive for your people to keep what wasn't theirs."

"You cannot possibly be claiming ignorance. The feud spans three centuries."

"There's no truth to it." Duncan paced near the windows again.

"Aye, there's truth!" Aileana retorted. "The *Ealach* belonged to a MacDonell before any MacRae ever laid hands upon it."

"That is a myth."

"It is a fact. My father gave his life for its sake. And Morgana believed, too, enough to risk all that she had to right the wrong."

"Morgana wasn't interested in *right*," Duncan scoffed, twisting to look at her with dark sarcasm. "She wanted much, much more—and when she didn't get it she happily sent me off into thirteen years of living hell."

Aileana felt herself flush, but she didn't have a chance to respond. All trace of softness had vanished from Duncan's eyes.

"Enough. This bickering serves no purpose." A muscle in his jaw twitched. "What I came to tell you is this. Unless you give me the *Ealach*, in one week's time I will be leading a raid against your people. It is as simple as that."

Shock struck Aileana like a fist to the belly. She popped up from the bench, her hands suddenly icy. "But you can't do that. We agreed that if I came with you as leman, you'd—"

"I agreed that if you came with me, I would spare your brother's life. An even exchange. You for Gavin." Duncan's expression was grim, feral. "And I'm upholding my end of the bargain. I'll not harm Gavin. But every other MacDonell is fair game."

Aileana's breath left her, and she sank back into her seat. Her gaze flew to Duncan, searching, her mind tripping over itself as she tried to reach through the fear to argue with reason. "But you'd be doing battle for naught! No one knows where I've hidden the amulet. Attacking them serves no purpose. No one else can give you the information you seek."

"Exactly. A few months ago you were willing to sacrifice your honor to save one brother. It's my guess that you'll relinquish the *Ealach* now in order to save the lives of the rest of your clan."

A hard knot formed in Aileana's throat. He couldn't be doing this. It was unjust. Cruel. She shook her head, trying to keep away the bloody images that rushed into her mind. "If you attack Dulhmeny, many innocent people will die."

"Aye," Duncan's brow quirked up, "which is why you must—"

A scratching sounded at the door, interrupting him. An instant later Kinnon burst into the chamber. He looked serious, and his stance was tense. He flicked an uneasy glance to Aileana.

"You'd better come down to the yard now, Duncan. A score of riders are approaching from the south—" He shifted his gaze from Duncan to Aileana and back again. "And they look to be a contingent of MacDonells."

Chapter 16

*M*acDonells? Aileana's heart leaped into her throat, and everything slowed as if in a dream. She saw Duncan scowl, saw him lean in while he and Kinnon murmured, their golden-brown heads close together. Then, without a backward glance, Duncan turned and left the chamber. Kinnon started to follow him, but Aileana grabbed his arm, stopping him.

"Wait. I must speak with you."

Kinnon looked none too happy, and he shook his head, indicating his need for haste.

"It will only take a moment, I promise." She clutched his sleeve. "Please."

"All right, then. But you must hurry. I need to stand with Duncan."

She nodded, releasing his arm. "You must help free me from this chamber, Kinnon. I—"

"Nay, lass. I cannot do that," he interrupted.

"But more than anyone here, you know what such

confinement is to me. After all of those years at Dul-hmeny . . . I—I cannot go on like this." A hysterical edge had crept into her voice, but she couldn't seem to quell it.

Kinnon shook his head, though his expression was sad. "I know your feelings, lady, and I sympathize with your plight. But I will not go against Duncan in this. It is his decision to make." He grasped her arm, leading her to the bench and guiding her to sit. "Do you not see the trouble you created for yourself when you locked him in the storage room?"

Bewildered, Aileana shook her head. "Nay. It was un-kind, I admit, but I regretted it almost as soon as it was done. I was planning to return and undo the harm when Duncan burst into the hall and dragged me away. He gave me no chance to explain."

"No explanation would have sufficed." Kinnon stared hard at her. "Do you not realize that when Duncan was captured and taken to the Tower, he was kept in the most vile, filthy dungeon that his captors could find for him? He endured thirteen years of cold, disease and abuse—all imprisoned in a tiny room without benefit of light. He was tortured almost daily, but in between they kept him locked in complete darkness."

The shadow that passed over Kinnon's face gave Aileana just a glimpse of the harrowing memories he de-scribed. "You sent Duncan back to that time and place in his mind when you threw the bar on the storage cham-ber. And you cannot imagine the hell that you forced him to relive."

A sick feeling began to spread through Aileana's body, lodging in the pit of her belly.

"Duncan needs the light," Kinnon added. "He needs

fresh air and freedom. Have you not taken note of the many windows he ordered built into the castle? Did you not remark on his frequent bathing, or wonder at the many wall torches he commands be kept lit, morn, noon, and eve?" He frowned, his expression stern. "What you made him remember was beyond reasoning."

Without waiting for a reply, Kinnon gave Aileana a curt nod. "Now I must go, lady. Fare you well. And when the burden of your confinement becomes too steep, remember what I've told you and be thankful it wasn't the worse for you."

He left, and the key turned to lock her in once more. Aileana sat, stunned, the realization of what she'd done sinking in now with a vengeance. It was awful. Even more terrible than she'd imagined. Duncan had suffered horribly at the hands of her sister and the English. Then she'd brought all of it back to him through her own ignorant act against him.

Be that as it may, a voice inside asserted hotly, *he has no right to coerce you like this. It is evil to make you choose between the* Ealach *and the safety of your clan.*

Her hands clenched, and she felt the satisfying sting of her nails digging into her palms. Aye, it was true. Whether she'd hurt him or not, it was Duncan who was in the wrong now. Keeping her confined and threatening her . . . it wasn't right. And she didn't need to accept his treatment with submission.

She had to find a way to warn her clansmen about what he planned. If she knew her brothers at all, they'd not want her to give Duncan the *Ealach*, even if it meant a clan war to resist. But forewarned, their chances of withstanding a raid would be much better. Aileana scrambled to the bed and knelt, running her hands along the cool, smooth wood of the bed frame. She grasped a strip of knotted fabric there and pulled. A thin rope, one that she'd been twining these past three days from strips of cloth from her bed coverings and underskirts, slipped to the floor with a thud.

She looped the cord around her arm, counting each length and estimating how much more would be needed to provide her means to scale the wall outside the chamber window. She'd have to work quickly if she wanted to get word to her kin before the group of them returned to Dulhmeny.

A noise at the casement made her jump. She shoved the rope back under the bed, stood and made her way to the wall. Cautiously, she peered out the clear, wavy panes, and what she saw made her almost faint dead away. A man was hanging alongside the window, swinging back and forth. For a moment, she thought he was dead. When he jerked, suddenly, her doubt resolved, but the sight of his face made her heart surge with both fear and relief.

Frantically, she worked the latch, tugging until she opened the window enough to allow him inside. With a few grunts and curses he dropped to the floor of her bedchamber, then straightened and pulled her into a hug that threatened to break her ribs.

"Little sister! It seems a lifetime since I looked upon your beautiful face!" He cupped her cheeks in his hands, pulling back to examine her. "How have you been faring these weeks? We've been nigh unto death with worry over you." He scowled. "Has that bastard treated you well, or do I need to gullet him for his pains?"

"Gavin. Oh, Gavin, I've missed you!" Aileana's breathless whisper escaped her in a rush, and she gazed into sparkling, laughing brown eyes that were so much like her own. "I see your wounds have healed." She ran her finger along the reddened creases above his brow and across his chin. "But how did you get here? And where is Robert? Is he well?"

Gavin chuckled, then put his finger to his lips to indicate that they should be quiet. "If we keep asking each other questions with neither answering, we'll never hear what needs to be said."

A noise sounded from below, and his gaze swept nervously around the room, pausing at the door as if he feared someone might open it and come upon them.

"Don't worry," she said. "The door is fastened from the outside. We'll hear it being undone and hide you before anyone can enter."

"The cur has locked you in?" Gavin looked indignant.

"Aye, but only for the last few days. It is a long tale, and of little matter." She shrugged, trying to lighten his mood. "Besides, it's not as if I've never been confined to a chamber before."

"That is beside the point," Gavin mumbled as he pulled her down to sit next to him on the bench.

"I'm fine, Gavin. Truly. But why didn't you send one of the others to come to me here with news?" she scolded. "Why risk coming yourself, when you know how Duncan feels about you?"

"Ach, it's no danger. The MacRae doesn't know that I'm anywhere near Eilean Donan." Gavin fixed his laughing eyes on her again. "I've sneaked past many a wall in my day, little sister, and this one was no harder than any of the others. Easier, actually, because of my purpose. I'm here to spring you to freedom, Aileana. Just like when you were a wee lass."

Before she could respond, he continued proudly, "It was my idea alone. I let it be known that I'd be joining the group to come here, once we healed and gathered enough strength to ride out again. But I told Robert I'd wait behind in the woodland. He'll be surprised to see you, I warrant, when he returns with news and our plan of attack!"

"*Attack?*" Aileana choked. "You're planning to attack Eilean Donan?"

"Aye, of course." Gavin got up and began to pace. "But not until Robert decides our method. He and the men will be leaving the castle shortly, and we'll discuss options in the glen after I've figured how to get you down the wall with me." He stopped pacing, glancing at her with concern. "What is it, lass? You look a little green. Do you need some water?"

Shaking her head, Aileana pulled him to sit beside her again. "Nay—just tell me what foolishness you're planning."

Gavin frowned. "We won't be attacking in the usual sense, if that's what worries you. Robert didn't want to risk harm to you, and there aren't enough MacDonell men that's fit to do it right now." Gavin tapped his finger to his temple and winked. "But leave it to your brothers, lass. We've a few ideas yet. If he was going to be living long enough, the MacRae would curse the day he brought shame on you."

Aileana felt as if she'd been kicked in the stomach. "Dragon's breath, Gavin MacDonell, just what is it you're planning to do?"

"Why, we're going to kill the MacRae, lass," he said slowly, as if she lacked the wit to follow what he'd said. "Honor demands it. From the moment he took you, Duncan MacRae was a marked man."

She shook her head, too horror-stricken to utter a sound.

"What? Why are you looking like that?" Gavin tipped her chin to look at him. "The bastard ruined you, little sister, and I mean to make him pay for his crime."

"But you cannot kill him. I—I won't allow it."

"Ach, feel no tenderness for the scoundrel! He's not worth—" He stopped suddenly, and shook his head in denial. "Don't tell me the bastard's got his child growing in you, already?"

A strange pang shot through her. "Nay, I don't carry Duncan's babe."

"Then why are you so hell bent on saving him?"

She looked away. "It is just . . . it's just that I don't think this plot against him is honorable. I made my bargain with him in good faith. I gave him my word."

"A bargain in good faith! He made you his *leman*, lass. There's nothing good nor faithful about that."

She flushed and looked away. "Not in truth, he didn't," she murmured. "He only wants everyone to think it so."

Gavin looked as though he'd swallowed a school of loch fish. "What exactly are you telling me?"

"Just what it sounds like," she muttered. "In the time that I've been here, Duncan MacRae hasn't touched me even once in that way. I'm as pure as the day I left Dulhmeny, so you cannot kill him for dishonoring me."

Gavin remained quiet, his expression doubting.

Exasperated, Aileana said, "If an oath is necessary, then I swear it on our mother's grave."

Gavin's eyes widened. His gaze traveled over her, and he shook his head. "By the Saints, Aileana . . . sure and that I'm thankful, but—" He looked askance at her.

"Doesn't the man have eyes? He cannot have looked upon you lately, or else I'd have to be saying he's gone daft as well as murderous."

"He's nothing of the sort, I assure you." Aileana flushed again. "And he was honest enough not to kill you. Many a man in his place might have sought vengeance, even after taking me at my bargain. At least he's living up to his side of the agreement." Then she added more quietly, "Or at least he was until an hour ago."

"Why? What the devil did he do now?"

Aileana felt ashamed she hadn't told him sooner. "You must forget about everything else we've discussed and go home quickly, Gavin. Gather as many men as you can." She squeezed her hands tight in her lap. "Less than an hour ago Duncan told me that he's going to lead a raid on Dulhmeny by week's end if I don't give him the *Ealach*."

"The bastard! I knew he couldn't be trusted," Gavin growled and sprang to his feet, his hands clenched to fists. "It's all the more reason to let me kill him. If he's dead, he cannot lead an attack against us." He nodded to Aileana. "You're coming with me. I want to get you out of harm's way before the deed is done, so that none of his clan tries to retaliate against you when they find their chieftain dead."

"Nay!" Aileana tried to control the fear that consumed her every time she considered the possibility of Duncan dying. She didn't know why the thought of it wounded her so, especially considering how he'd behaved toward her these last days, but understandable or not, her feelings on the matter were definite. While she might not be able to stop the chance of its happening if a clan war broke out, she knew she'd be fit for the grave herself if she didn't prevent her brothers from outright murdering him.

"I won't go with you, Gavin." She stood. "Please, just do as I say. Go home without delay."

He shook his head. "We're leaving together, Aileana. We'll settle the rest later." He took hold of her arm and started to lead her to the window. "Come. I'll not have you spending another minute with that lying churl. He's not fit to be called a man."

"Nay, I said!" Aileana shouted and yanked her arm from his grasp. "I will not be pushed and prodded like a sheep to the gate."

Gavin stared at her, stunned. She shook her sleeve back into position. "I've made my decision, and you must abide by it." She glanced to him, softening enough to add, "I'm no longer a child, Gavin. Father is dead. I'll allow no one to take his role of power over me again."

Her brother's gaze hardened, and he gestured round the chamber that confined them. "The MacRae seems to be doing a fine job of it if you ask me."

"Whether that is true or not is my concern," Aileana answered, feeling her cheeks heat. "It shouldn't influence you."

"You're my sister. Anything that happens to you influences me. Christ, you're only in this predicament because of me."

"Nay, I'm here because I chose to be. But if it pleases you to think yourself the cause of it, then you will also admit that I've given much for your sake already. Do this one thing for me now." She took his hands in hers. "Do not kill the MacRae, Gavin. If there's a way to keep him from raiding our clan, I'll find it. I already have an idea. But I don't want him killed."

He looked exasperated, but she saw from his eyes that he was wavering.

"Please," she murmured, pressing her point. "I'm asking you on the bond of blood between us."

"Aye, lass," he said finally. "A bond of blood I'd prefer we keep, without any of yours being spilled."

"The best way to ensure that is to do as I say. Swear that you won't harm Duncan." She stared hard at him. "Swear it, Gavin."

He looked as if he was swallowing something bitter, but when she stepped closer to him, he muttered a curse. "All right, lass! I swear that I won't harm him—for now, anyway."

She nodded. "Good. Leave the MacRae to me and go now to warn the others. Prepare them for his raid in case I fail."

Gavin shook his head. "Nay. I refuse to leave you alone here until you tell me exactly what you're planning to do."

She gazed at him quietly, trying to finalize the nebulous bits of her idea. "I'm planning to escape from Eilean Donan, Gavin—and I'm going to go alone." Her heart lurched at the thought, but she saw no other option.

"Escape *alone?* How?" He scowled. "It would be difficult enough for me to steal you out of here."

She tilted her chin and tried to sound brave. "It will not be so hard. The only reason I didn't leave earlier was because I thought it a risk to your life and the clan if I broke my agreement with Duncan. Now that he's decided to attack whether I break it or no, I'll simply climb from this chamber, swim the loch, and go to our allies at Dumfrie in the north. They'll hide me and the *Ealach* until this is settled peacefully."

Gavin started to argue, but she leveled her gaze at

him. "Just hear me out. If I escape with you and go to Dulhmeny as you wish, Duncan will most certainly follow me there, and people will die. But if I leave alone, he might give up the plan to raid in favor of searching for me and the amulet."

"So you think serving as bait for a murdering MacRae is the answer? That's the whole of your fine plan?"

Aileana winced at his description of Duncan. *Murdering MacRae.* It was what she herself had called him, both to his face and in her own mind during those first few weeks. But something had changed since then. She'd come to see him differently, watching him struggle to rebuild a life for his clan. She'd glimpsed the tenderness that lived along with the rage and the hurt inside of him.

Aye, her feelings for Duncan had changed much in these past weeks. Too much to explain to her brother right now . . .

Gavin made a choking sound and shoved his hand through his hair, bringing his voice to a whisper only when she motioned for him to be quiet. "What will you do, lass? Let the MacRae hunt all over the Highlands until he finds both you and the *Ealach*? He'll do far worse than confine you to your chamber then, I'll warrant!"

"It won't come to that. Not if you complete the rest of my plan as I tell you to."

"Sweet Mother Mary," he muttered, gazing skyward, "give me the strength to hear what's left of this."

She favored him with a dark look. "When the time is right, you will find the MacKenzie Chief and ask for a hearing of the clans. He is Chief of Kintail and laird over Duncan. I met him myself, and it is clear that he is sympathetic to our cause. He thinks our debt of honor long paid to the MacRaes, and I think he would support our dispute and petition for peace."

Gavin looked unconvinced. "I don't feel right about this, Aileana. What if the MacKenzie will not help us?"

"Then we will be no worse than we are right now. There will be a war between the clans, and we will all suffer for it." Fear squeezed her heart as she took Gavin's hand. "At least if we try what I suggest, there is a chance to avoid bloodshed. Please, Gavin, try it my way first. It cannot hurt."

Gavin stood silent for a moment. Finally he shook his head and sighed. "Ah, lass, you wear me down, and in that you're more like our mother than I ever realized." Love shone warm in his eyes. "She would be proud of your courage, Aileana. As am I." He cupped her chin and smiled. "When did you turn into such a fine woman? It seems only yesterday that you stood no higher than my knees and lisped up at me through the spaces in your teeth."

She smiled back at him and kissed his cheek. "Ach, be off with you, now. Our time is running out. But it will all work out in the end, Gavin, I promise. Go and make haste."

Nodding, Gavin climbed half out the window, then twisted to face her again. "I am conceding to try it your way for now, lass, though I do not like it. But understand that if anything goes wrong, or if the MacRae harms one curl upon your bonny head, I will kill him with my bare hands. This I vow."

Aileana nodded, mutely, and he blew her a kiss. Holding her breath, she watched him disappear through the window, climbing up his rope to the battlements again. The twine skittered up after him, retrieved from above. She knew that he'd leave nothing that might be seen and lead anyone to suspect he'd been there.

But once he was gone, cold emptiness settled over her. *It was done, then. She'd have to be leaving Eilean Donan and Duncan. Soon.*

And forever.

As grim purpose faded and reality struck her, she stumbled back from the window. Tears clouded her eyes. The thought of leaving hurt her, more deeply than she'd thought was possible. Duncan bullied her and tried to control her. He'd locked her in this room and blackmailed her.

And cared for you night and day through your sickness, kissing you with whispered words of tenderness . . .

Nay! She covered her face with her hands, determined not to soften, not to think of those moments again. She should be glad to get away from Duncan MacRae's passions and his temper. She should be glad for the freedom she'd gain once she left.

But she wasn't.

All she knew was that from this day forward, the pain inside of her was never going to stop. Never, so long as she was forced to be parted from this man who was both her sweetness and her curse . . . the man who held her heart in the tender cruelty of his hands.

Duncan peered from behind the wall slit, eyes narrowed, watching Gavin MacDonell emerge dripping and shaking from the loch to vanish into the shadow of the trees. The other MacDonells were in the act of leaving as well; Robert's mount had just cleared the gate, and his men were thundering after him.

Duncan fingered his claymore, unsheathing it and running his thumb along the edge. Had Robert's visit been a

ruse, then—a distraction, conceived to divert his attention while Gavin spirited Aileana away?

It was possible, except that Gavin had crossed the
loch and left alone. Besides that, something told Duncan
that Robert knew nothing of the secret visit. He'd been
enraged, actually, when Duncan had denied him the
chance to see his sister. If he'd known of Gavin, he'd
have avoided the request, fearing to let anyone catch his
brother in Aileana's chamber.

Nay, surely Gavin had worked alone this time. He'd
gone to Aileana to pollute her, to pull her into his deceit-
ful snare.

*What had been said? What evil plot laid out for his
demise and the ruin of the MacRaes?*

Anger roiled in Duncan's breast, partly against Gavin,
and partly against himself for being so gullible again. It
mingled with pain as he remembered the last time he'd
allowed Gavin MacDonell to creep past the defenses of
Eilean Donan. Mairi had died that day.

Now Gavin meant to sway Aileana to more mischief.
Fiery, headstrong Aileana, who had somehow worked
her way into his soul and made him care for her, even
though he knew that he could never have her. Gavin had
likely given her advice on how to betray him.

Arrows of heat shot behind Duncan's eyes. Thirteen
years ago the MacDonells had knocked him senseless
in order to accomplish their evil against him. This
time, he had his wits about him, and whether she
wanted him to or no, he was going to protect Aileana
against herself and the insidious pull of her brother's
schemes.

Sending his claymore hissing back into its sheath,
Duncan turned toward the stairs, taking them two at a
time. He stalked toward the chamber that housed his

fiery-haired, impetuous bird . . . the sweet MacDonell nightingale who was about to sing out all of the secrets of her heart to him.

Every one of them. And now.

Chapter 17

Duncan slammed open the door to his bedchamber and stopped still. Cold gushed through the room, and one of the windows gaped open, making the tapestries flap and flutter against the wall.

Something was amiss. Aileana had vanished, as surely as if she'd melted into the misty air. He took a step forward, his gaze slipping around the chamber, noting each piece of furniture, every square of blanket and covering. Nothing was out of place. There'd been no struggle.

Damn her. She must have escaped right after her bastard of a—

A flash of color at the window caught Duncan's eye. Fiery. A waving mass of light auburn, shining with glints of gold. The figure moved into view of the casement, standing on the wrong side of the wall . . . perched on the ledge. Poised. Waiting.

Waiting? For . . . what the devil?

Duncan's mind seemed to slow to a maddening pace.

Each moment lingered an eternity. He saw Aileana twist to look at him. Her cheeks were streaked with tears, her expression grief-stricken.

He bolted forward, lunging for her as he realized her intent. It was like that day at the cliffs all over again. She was going to go over the edge, and he had to stop her. Catch her before she fell to the grinding stones of the loch below. But as he thrust his hand through the open casement to grip her, she tipped forward, throwing herself away from him. His gloved fingertips barely brushed the fabric of her skirts as she slipped from his grasp.

"Aileana! Nay!" The words ripped from his throat. Shock filled his chest and pressed the breath from his lungs. Frantic, he threw himself against the casement, reaching over as far as he could, only to see her fall away from him, down, down, down. To the cold, gray waters and rocks below . . .

Before coming to a jerking halt that forced an unladylike grunt from her lips.

A faint trickle of curses drifted up to his ears, and relief flooded Duncan with a stabbing sensation. His heart pounded heavy and hard. Painful. But with the rush of feeling came strength. And fast behind it, renewed anger.

Taking hold of the knotted cord that held Aileana suspended ten feet above the water, Duncan pulled. He grated his teeth, scowling and concentrating on hoisting her back inside the room. His muscles flexed and contracted, and he forced himself to focus on the satisfying ache that radiated through his arms and back.

When she clambered into the chamber again, she looked meek and bedraggled; her hair and clothing were disheveled, the cord hung limp around her waist, and she held her arm around herself there as if her ribs pained her. It would be no surprise if they did, he thought, waiting for her to speak. But her gaze was fixed to the floor, and with each passing second, the silence weighed heavier between them.

"Damn it, Aileana," Duncan murmured at last. "Why did you let him get to you?"

She looked up at him in surprise, her eyes shadowed and her lashes clumped with tears.

"Aye," he said softly, "I know very well about Gavin's visit."

"How?" she breathed.

"I saw him swimming to shore." Duncan took a step forward, taking her chin in his gloved hand to make her meet his gaze. "I know it has been difficult for you here, but after everything I told you, after everything we—" He broke off and dropped his grip from her, adding in a husky murmur, "By the Rood, Aileana, I never thought that you'd be so quick to do something like this."

"What did you expect?" she retorted. "It was you who betrayed our agreement."

He didn't rise to the bait of her challenge. "Did Gavin devise the plot to sneak into my castle for you, or was the idea yours?"

"Do not turn this on him, Duncan. I was as surprised to see Gavin as you. My attempt to escape had nothing to do with him."

"Then mayhap it was a reason even more insidious," he answered, ignoring her protests before stepping back. "Tell me—if the plan for your escape wasn't just now hatched between the two of you, then what *was* your brother's foul purpose in coming here?"

Aileana's face looked ashen. He watched her swallow,

saw the flicker of pain in her beautiful eyes. "We had the same idea separately, that is all. He came, intending to take me back to Dulhmeny with him, but I refused him in favor of my own means of escape."

Duncan arched his brow in surprise; he was silent for a moment before adding, "I know something of Gavin MacDonell, Aileana. Even had the both of you conceived the same idea of securing your freedom from Eilean Donan, he would insist on doing it his way. He'd have thrown you over his shoulder and carried you away no matter your protests, if such had been his purpose." Duncan's face sharpened. "I want to know what else was discussed. What else was plotted or planned that would give him cause to agree to leave you behind. What was it, Aileana?"

"It isn't important now. I made Gavin agree not to pursue it further."

"I'll hear what it was anyway."

"Fine, then," Aileana retorted hotly, her expression sharp. "It is nothing you wouldn't expect of a brother whose sister had been dishonored. Gavin told me that he was planning to kill you."

Bitter laughter grated from his throat. "How original. A plot against my life." He smiled grimly. "Not much has changed in thirteen years, it seems. But pray tell, how did your foolhardy jump from the window play into Gavin's plans for achieving my murder?"

Aileana sounded exasperated. "I've already told you; my attempt to escape had no tie to Gavin. I was only trying to leave because I thought it might prevent you from raiding Dulhmeny and spilling innocent blood." Her eyes glistened with tears, though whether they stemmed from anger or latent regret, he couldn't discern. "If you wish to know the truth, then you should know that before I let him go home, I made Gavin give me his oath that he wouldn't harm you."

"Please, Aileana, wanting to kill me is bad enough. Don't go so far as to insult my intelligence, too."

Her hands fisted at her sides. "I'm telling you the truth, Duncan—my escape had nothing to do with Gavin. It had to do with us. With you and me and the threats you made not an hour ago to attack my clan if I didn't give you the *Ealach*."

Duncan couldn't prevent his sardonic expression. "Then your timing is more than unfortunate." He crossed his arms over his chest. "You've wanted me dead for as long as I've known you, Aileana, and since poisoning me a few weeks past didn't work, I think you were plotting with your brother to find a way of completing the deed."

She shook her head, and he felt a jerk of surprise at the desolation in her eyes. "I never wanted you dead, Duncan. When I dosed you with those herbs, it was only to make you realize—" She choked to a halt. "The reason doesn't matter now. It is enough to say that they were not the kind of herbs to kill you, even had you taken thrice the amount I gave you."

He leveled a glare at her. "For the hours I spent suffering their effects, I wholeheartedly wished that they were."

"Aye, well, I am sorry for that now." She had the good grace, at least, to look ashamed. "But I never wanted any real harm to come to you." She turned away and added more quietly, "I only wanted you to stop thinking about *her*."

"Who?" Confusion made him scowl.

Aileana glared back at him. "Nora MacKenzie. The brazen woman who flaunts her charms in your face every chance she finds."

"Nora?" Duncan grimaced as he thought of Nora's cloying scent and groping hands. "What the devil could that woman have given you to fret about?"

Aileana made a scoffing sound in her throat. "Pretending ignorance doesn't become you, Duncan MacRae." She flicked him a glance potent enough to shrivel a tree. "Nora takes every chance that comes to throw herself at you, and you encourage it. You will not trick me into saying more by acting like you know nothing of it."

Duncan's body suddenly felt numb. All thinking vanished as his mind latched onto the one possibility in all this he'd not dared to allow, except in his most secret thoughts. Kinnon had suggested something of the sort weeks ago, but he'd refused to believe it. He stared at Aileana again, looking deeper this time, taking in her outraged stance, her tousled, fiery hair, eyes that flashed heat and annoyance . . . and something else.

The hollow feeling in his gut opened wider.

"Tell me about Nora," he murmured, finally, not taking his gaze from her. "Tell me what you feel when you see her being friendly with me."

She paused, then frowned and shook her head. "Nay, I'll be your sport no longer. You can humiliate me with your clan and disgrace me in my family's eyes. You can even imprison me here. But you cannot command me to speak of my feelings. I will not demean myself more by giving you another weapon to use against me."

"I'm not commanding you, Aileana; I'm asking you." He clenched his gloved fists. God, how he wanted to trust, how he needed to believe. "Tell me. Give me a reason for dosing my food and cutting holes in my clothes. For hiding mice in my boots and moving my furniture so that I didn't even recognize my own chamber. Christ, just tell me the truth of how you feel about me."

She breathed in, her eyes widening slightly. All was still for several agonizing seconds. Then, like a beach washed smooth by the ocean, her rigidity crumpled. Her expression softened, and her eyes took on a telling sheen. She shook her head. "I do not think that I can."

"You must." Duncan's voice broke with husky entreaty. "Ah, lass, tell me if what I'm thinking—what I am feeling—is true. *Please.*"

She blinked at him. Her lashes were wet smudges of auburn against her pale skin, and her lips trembled. "It is difficult." She swallowed. Then, straightening, she took a deep breath and brushed her fingers beneath her eyes. "But I suppose it is pointless to keep it in any longer. I did all of those things because I wanted you to notice me, even if it was only in irritation."

She pulled her gaze away to look down at her feet, her arms wrapped around her middle, and the expression of agony clear on her face. "In truth, when I saw you and Nora together I was jealous, and that is why I dosed you both with the herbs. I—I couldn't bear the sight of her draping herself all over you. You can mock me for being a fool if you like, but I've said it."

The joyful shock that shot through Duncan made his knees weaken. *Godamercy.* He took two steps forward, his feet like leaded weights as he slowly raised his hand to touch her cheek. A feeling of awe swept over him, making him speak in a tone more befitting a chapel than a bedchamber. "I didn't think it possible."

"Nay?" She still looked miserable, her gaze downcast, shame suffusing her cheeks. As she spoke, her breath wafted soft across the exposed skin of his wrist, and an answering shaft of desire lit in his belly.

"Aileana . . ." He brought both hands up now, making her look at him, cradling her face with tenderness that flooded from the deepest, most hidden part of him. Her eyes widened slightly with surprise as he pressed a gentle kiss to her brow, savoring the silky feel of her skin beneath his lips, breathing in the sweet scent of her. "You'll never know how many times I wished for just this . . . how many times I longed to hear such words from your lips."

She looked shocked for a moment, her expression of misery vanished under its force. "Truly?" she whispered.

"Aye, truly. I care about you, Aileana. But I never thought—" he broke off and shook his head, a rueful smile curving his lips.

They stood close. Almost touching. He could feel the heat of her body warming him through his plaid and igniting the embers of his passion, kept forcibly banked for so long, to full blaze. But he sensed that she still reeled from the suddenness of this change between them. She needed a little time to realize the truth. To come to him when she was ready. Hell, he needed some time to adjust to it all. Nevertheless, it took much of his resolve to remain motionless and let her make the next move as she willed it.

He watched the rise and fall of her breast. His gaze traveled from the curve of her chin to the full swell of her lips, his breath catching as they parted in soft exhalation. When his stare moved up, finally, from there to the sweetly rounded, freckle-sprinkled tip of her nose, the graceful sweep of her cheekbones, and up to her eyes, he saw the sweet warmth filling her gaze, and his passion spiraled tenfold.

"I cannot believe it," she murmured, still looking at him as if he might melt away before her eyes.

"It is true, Aileana. I don't know how it happened, and I tried to deny it to myself, but the feeling is there."

He smiled. "As with everything else about you, it is persistent, prodding and poking me even when I do not wish it."

"Is that so?" She smiled back at him in response. "And what, pray tell, is it that you wish from me now, Duncan?"

He paused for a moment, the image of what he envisioned full and perfect inside of him. But he'd learned a few things where Aileana MacDonell was concerned, and one of the most important was that it was always better to let her take the lead—or at least the satisfaction of seeming to get it from him. Raising his brow, he murmured, "What do you have in mind?"

"Hmmm . . . I believe I shall have to give that question some thought."

Her tongue darted out to moisten her lips, and his heart skipped a beat. She looked both innocent and yet somehow confident in her feminine allure, and the contrast of the two aspects was nothing less than intoxicating. Though he had handed her the control over what happened next, he suddenly found that the idea of her initiative in this excited him more than he'd believed possible.

"It is unwise to become *too* confident, lass," he answered huskily, trying to keep himself from completely abandoning all pretense of restraint, "or you might find that you've gotten yourself in—"

His words cut off to a groan as she stepped closer and pressed her body full against him. "—over . . ." he murmured, while her hands slid up his arms and to his shoulders, ". . . your head," he finally whispered against her lips, before she wrapped her arms around his neck and pulled him into a soul-searing kiss.

With a growl, he clasped her closer to him, and she

sighed and opened her mouth to him, restraint finally abandoned as she deepened their kiss. The warmth of her, the voluptuous feel of her in his arms threatened to drive him beyond the edge of reason. Through the jolt of sensation, he realized that it was as he'd always imagined it would be. She fit to him. Even through their clothing, her warmth and her contours melded to his as if their bodies were made for each other.

Perfect.

When she pulled back, it was to place her palms flat on his chest. A tentative smile curved her lips as she pulled her fingers gently down his body, her progress unhurried. His body sang under her touch, his flesh burning with tantalizing fire. When she reached his waist, she slowed even more, slipping her hands around behind him and bringing them to a stop only when her palms rested atop his buttocks with a touch that was unbearably erotic in its gentle artlessness.

Then she shyly tugged him to her, leaning in to whisper hot against the skin of his neck and shoulder, "Perhaps you're right, Duncan. I do believe that I'm in far over my head. So far that I do not care if I drown because of it."

Her touch, coupled with the innocence of her admission, sent his desire bubbling over. With a deep-throated sound, he slid his hands down to cup her sweet curves in the same way that she held him, pulling her more fully against him and eliciting a gasp of pleasure from her. "Then it seems we'll be drowning together," he murmured, interspersing his words with kisses along her jaw and across the warm, sensitive point beneath her ear. "But it will be a blissful death, to be sure."

She trembled, tilting her head back as his lips trailed a burning path along her throat. When he could bear the delicious torment, the tempting taste of her no longer without tearing her garments off where they stood, he scooped her into his arms and carried her to the bed.

He stretched out beside her, and she gazed at him with a desire that matched his own. "Hold me close to you, Duncan," she whispered. "Please. After all of those nights when you carried me to your bed—" she broke off, biting at her bottom lip and glancing away for a moment before directing the full and beautiful force of her gaze on him. "In my most secret of hearts I wished that just once during one of those nights you might forget what had brought us together and pull me close to you. Do it now, Duncan. Let me feel you next to me, touch me and let me touch you as I've yearned to for so long . . ."

A tide of love swept through Duncan. But he couldn't tell her of it. Not yet. He lacked the courage, though perhaps in time . . . Heat and joy and tenderness rushed in all at once, and he cupped her face to kiss her again.

But she shook her head even as she gripped his hand, stopping him. "Wait." Lifting herself to one elbow, she pulled off his left gauntlet. "We must be rid of this." She gripped his other hand. "And this."

Before he realized, she'd started pulling the glove from his right hand as well. A thrill of fear shot down his spine. She would be repulsed. It would be a cruel irony to have it so now, when they had just taken this first, difficult step. Roughly, he jerked back.

"Nay. I cannot take this one off."

She sat quiet for a moment. Then she reached out and stroked a lock of tawny hair that fell across his brow, tracing the scar that threaded from there to his jaw. He couldn't meet her gaze, but her voice caressed him with sweet reassurance. "There is no shame in what lies beneath that gauntlet, Duncan. Your captors may have done their worst, but they could not ruin you. I do not care how your hand looks. It is you that I admire—all of you just as you are."

He half sat up. Pain mixed with a vulnerability that threatened to rip him apart inside. "Nay, Aileana; it is an ugly thing. No one who has seen it uncovered has—" He broke off, feeling the old shame twisting deep again, and so he ground it down with vicious determination. "The truth is that any woman who has ever seen my hand has cringed at the thought of my touching her with it, even though some tried well to hide their feelings. Do not ask this of me."

"But it has already happened, Duncan, and it was of no matter. I saw your scars that day I woke after you'd tended me during the plague." Unshed tears sparkled in Aileana's eyes, making them look like gems in the light filtering through the windows. "I tell you that I felt naught but respect and pride for the courage you must have shown to make the English hurt you in such a cowardly way."

Duncan was silent, fighting the hot emotions warring in his heart. But he found that he could resist no further when she lifted his hand and gently stripped the glove away. His gaze locked to her face as she raised his ruined fingers to her lips and kissed them, letting the drops of her tears splash hot, now, onto his skin. She pressed his palm to her cheek, whispering, "I see you for all that you are, Duncan MacRae, and if anything I esteem you more because of this. Please say that you'll forgive me for closing you in the storage chamber. I did not know, until Kinnon told me, what such a place would make you remember."

A broken growl rumbled from his throat, and he pulled her fiercely into his embrace. "Hush, lass . . ." The rush of emotion choked him. "It is no worse than what I've done to you, confining you in here, and I am truly sorry for it." He brushed the hair from her face, watching her suck in her breath at the promise he knew that she read in his eyes.

Tenderly, gently, he stroked his scarred fingers from her temple to her mouth, reveling in the sensation of his skin against hers with no barriers remaining. When his thumb rubbed across her lower lip, her eyes fluttered closed, and she leaned more fully into him. A tingling heaviness burgeoned, hardening him and intensifying when he replaced his thumb with his lips to feel the silky heat of her pliant mouth beneath his. His kiss was deep, probing, and he lingered for a long moment, wanting to taste his fill. She pressed closer to him, burying her face in his shoulder as his hand slid around to cup her breast. He relished her sweet fullness, the gently rounded warmth of her in his palm, and he nuzzled her hair as he touched her, her delicate fragrance filling his senses.

Easing her back against the bed, Duncan kissed her eyelids, the freckled bridge of her nose, along the curve of her jaw and neck as he deftly loosened her plaid and unlaced her tunic. It fell away to reveal the creamy expanse of her that had haunted his imagination since that very first day in the glen.

Leaning over, he brushed gentle kisses around each of her breasts, and she breathed in, arching against him. When he captured a taut peak in his mouth, suckling gently, Aileana clung to his shoulders. But he kept her prisoner of the pleasure until a soft cry of surrender spilled from her throat. "Please, Duncan . . . it feels wonderful, but you make me ache for something more—"

"Soon, Aileana," he murmured, flowering kisses across her stomach and dipping his tongue into the tiny hollow there, until she shuddered with the pleasure of it. "But not too soon. I want to savor you, lady, and it is our good fortune to have an entire afternoon ahead of us . . ."

With a gasping laugh, she stroked her hands over him as he kissed all the way back up her body to take her mouth again, his passion surging as he realized that she was helping him to remove his clothing. Soon he was as naked as she, and when she brushed her hand across the now bared skin of his chest, he felt a jolt of pleasure that was almost painful.

"By God, Aileana," he said raggedly, "you've bewitched me." He sucked in his breath as her hand slid down the expanse of his chest to his abdomen, his muscles tightening under her, stroking to an almost unbearable tautness. Burning need pulsated like flames as her fingers edged ever closer to where he ached most for her touch. A groan wrenched from his throat when her hand finally closed over his erection. Her grip was silk and fire; she stroked him, her touch tentative and innocent, and he struggled with the desire to bury himself deep into her in the way that would make her truly his.

"Ah, Aileana," he whispered, "it's been so long, and I don't think I can hold back more. Are you ready for me?" As he spoke, he nestled his fingers in the soft curls between her thighs, groaning again when he felt her slick wetness. When he parted her swollen folds and stroked upward, rubbing the sweet nub of flesh hidden there, she whimpered and arched into his touch.

"Aye, Duncan, please. I cannot wait longer either," she breathed against his lips. Her hips squirmed deliciously as he stroked her, her own hand gripping reflexively around him in similar rhythm, until he thought he would explode from the pleasure of it. She tangled her other hand in his hair, pulling him closer. "I want you now, Duncan. Right now."

In one, fluid motion he positioned himself between her legs, but he forced himself to pause, lifting his head to gaze at her. Her breath was soft against his cheek, her beautiful eyes trusting, filled with a need and passion that matched his own. "I want you more than I've ever wanted anything, Aileana," he murmured, "and yet I do not want to hurt you. There may be some pain in this first time."

She placed her finger to his lips, hushing him even as she shifted to open wider to him. He held his breath at the exquisite sensation of his turgid flesh sliding against the heated, wet silk of her.

"I fear nothing with you, Duncan," she whispered. "I want to be yours, in every way. Yours completely . . ." She rocked her hips up against his a little more, and he thought he'd go senseless from need. Teeth gritted with his struggle to keep his control, Duncan nudged against her entrance and slipped inside. Then he pressed deeper, inch by tantalizing inch.

He felt her tense beneath him, felt her nails clench into his back as he pushed with one, smooth stroke through the barrier of her innocence. She made a muffled sound against his shoulder. He slid a little farther inside, her woman's flesh wrapped with tight, smooth heat around him. Desire beat in his blood, feverish and throbbing, and every instinct told him to drive himself deep. His muscles strained to take her in the wild abandon that burned in him—but he held still, giving her time to accommodate to the feel of him inside of her.

She began to relax a little, and when he thought the

pain had eased enough for her to feel pleasure again, he began to move slowly, rocking against her gently. The muscles in his arms corded with effort, and his sight hazed with need as he struggled to hold back. But then Aileana moaned and arched against him, pulling him deeper and splintering his mind into shards of raw sensation. Bracing his weight on his palms, he deepened his strokes, matching his rhythm to the throbbing beat of their hearts, to the pounding urgency of their bodies joined together.

"Look at me, Aileana," he growled soft in her ear, "I need you to look at me now. To know that you're mine, as I am yours."

She tipped her head back against the pillows, meeting his gaze, her eyes heavy with passion and something softer, too. Her hands crept up to cup his face, pulling his lips down to hers in a kiss of surrender and abandon, as she clung to him. He squeezed his eyes shut, reveling in the beauty of what was happening between them, feeling his passion spiral higher as her whimpers became murmurs of entreaty, and then cries of fulfillment.

Her woman's core began to pulsate around him an instant before he lost the battle with self-control. Aileana's name burst from his throat as he gave in to the devastating pleasure. And with a wordless roar of pure ecstasy, Duncan spilled himself into her soft, welcoming body, surrendering at last to the only sorceress who had proved powerful enough to banish the demons that had haunted him for thirteen long years.

Steady. Reassuring. Aileana listened to the slow, even tempo of Duncan's heart. She lay nestled into him, her legs twined with his, her head resting on his chest. His eyes were closed, his arms wrapped snug around her, and she felt the warmth of his breath through her hair.

All was quiet.

Peaceful.

She breathed deep, savoring the vague throbbing between her legs; she was Duncan's in truth now. When she closed her eyes, a trickle of wetness slid down her cheek, and smiling, she nuzzled closer to him. His skin was warm and smooth, and he smelled of pine and sunshine . . . and of her. The scent of their lovemaking lingered with his natural fragrance, making her heart twist with unbearable love.

"What's this?" Duncan murmured in a soft, teasing lilt. "I hope I did not disappoint you, then."

"It was wonderful, as you know very well. I am happy, that's all."

"Ah. Well, in that case, I'll have to strive harder to make you sad, so that I can see you smile."

She laughed then and jabbed her knuckles into the ticklish area of his side until he rolled onto her with a shout of laughter, playfully dragging her wrists above her head.

"Mutiny, is it?" He grinned, his eyes crinkled at the corners, their silvery depths caressing her. Then he tilted his head toward her ear to breathe the seductive threat, "You do not realize, I see, that I have methods of taming such a rebel as you. Ways like this . . ." He nipped tingling kisses down the side of her neck, lingering with sweet, hot tenderness at the sensitive skin beneath her jaw. "And this . . ." His mouth feathered up over her chin to brush across her lips.

When he deepened the kiss, Aileana opened to the subtle pressure. She made a little sound deep in her throat when his tongue slipped inside to gently stroke hers, rising up to meet his passion with the force of her own.

"Ah, Aileana, I cannot get enough of you," Duncan said, finally, releasing her hands to brush her hair back with his fingers. He pressed another kiss on her forehead, murmuring, "But before I give in to the pleasures of loving you again, there's something I must do first."

Surprise edged through the happy, sensual haze Duncan had woven around her with his kisses and his touch. She sat up a little as he slid off of her and out of bed to pad across the chamber toward one of the massive wooden chests that stood along the wall.

The afternoon sun streamed between the edges of the tapestries, making his naked skin tawny and his honey-brown hair lit with gold. He moved with an inborn grace, his muscles sleek and powerful, even in the simple act of walking, and Aileana smiled at the shiver that tingled up her spine. But when he turned to face her, having found what he'd sought, she felt a rush of love so strong that, were she standing, she knew her knees would have failed to support her. She tucked the cover under her chin, trying to get a glimpse of what he held in his hand, as he came back to bed and slid under the blankets.

"What is it?" she couldn't resist asking.

"You'll be seeing soon enough."

Aileana's curiosity spiked. "Aye? And why is it such a secret, then?"

"It's not so much a secret, really." He slid closer, and she felt a delicious tingle when his naked thigh brushed against hers. "At least not one meant to be kept. It's meant to be given," he said, grabbing her hand under the blanket.

Then, pulling it above the covers, he dropped something heavy into her open palm. Something round that had warmed in his grip. She stared at it, gasping. It was a ruby ring, delicately made, with a smooth band of gold that glinted in a shaft of afternoon sun. And it was very old by the looks of the black edging on the heavy gilded pattern near the gem. She took it between her fingers and turned it this way and that to examine it more closely.

"This cannot be your ring, Duncan. It is too small."

He nodded. "You're right. It would never fit my finger. It belonged to my mother, given to her by my Da. I remember her wearing it when I was a child, as she stroked my brow till I fell asleep." Then his voice quieted. "Only one other besides her has worn it since, and then but for a single day."

A bubble seemed to rise in Aileana's chest, preventing any air from coming in or escaping. She just looked at Duncan, questioning, uncertain.

He gave her a look that was almost pained with its intensity. "It is my betrothal ring, Aileana. It has been in my family for generations, and I'm giving it to you now because I'm asking you to be my bride."

She felt almost incapable of speaking, but she managed to stutter, "You—you want me to *marry* you?"

"Aye, if you'll have me. You once offered that very choice to me several months ago, and though I know much has changed since then, I am hoping that you'll still consider it."

She sat silent, frozen in the cascade of emotion that overwhelmed her. It was what she'd secretly longed for, and yet . . .

Her hand, cradling his ring, began to tremble, and she lowered it to her lap.

"Why do you not answer?"

She shook her head, struggling to find her voice. "I—I don't know what to say. It is so sudden . . ."

"What's happened today is sudden, perhaps, but not the possibility of a union between us." His expression looked serious, as if he were steeling himself for something more. "I want you to know that I do—that is I—" He shifted his gaze away from her for a moment before glancing back to finish, "The truth, Aileana, is that I care about you, deeply. More than I have for any woman since Mairi. Tell me that you'll be mine in name as we are in body."

Aileana swallowed the sudden rush of pain; he hadn't—he couldn't say he loved her. That didn't seem too much to want, did it? He'd loved Mairi, she knew that. Dragon's breath, it seemed she'd suffered the sin of the woman's death a thousand times over. But could Duncan ever allow himself to love again—and could she live as his wife if he didn't?

"What of the feud between our clans?" she settled on asking him hoarsely.

"A marriage between us is the solution your own brother proposed that day at Dulhmeny. He will support this as a means of mending the rift. My overlord, the MacKenzie, will as well. You have nothing to fear from that quarter."

She nodded but remained silent. His assertion was undoubtedly true, but there remained another dark shadow over them, still. A stumbling point even greater, perhaps, than his love for Mairi or their clans' feuding, and she couldn't accept his proposal until she'd acknowledged it.

"And what of the *Ealach*?" she whispered, her throat tight. "Will you still wish to take me to wife if I continue in my refusal to give it over to you?"

For a moment she wasn't sure that he would answer, and her heart plummeted anew when he averted his gaze. A muscle near his temple twitched before he breathed in and exhaled in a deep sigh.

"Aye, Aileana, I intend to marry you even so," he said firmly at last. "I want to be with you, lass, with no more anger or bitterness or contention between us. I want to be with you under the law, as your husband. You deserve no less. We'll find a way through this last trouble as well, and we'll do it together."

Heat rose behind her eyes. His offer of marriage didn't depend on getting back the *Ealach*. He cared for her; he'd said the words earlier, but this proved it. And it was enough for now. More marriages than not were based upon friendship respect, affection . . . and if the couple was fortunate, physical attraction. They had that aplenty—this afternoon had made that very clear. The caring he felt might deepen to love in time. Until then, she'd just have to love him enough for both of them.

With a bittersweet smile, she cupped his jaw, brushing her hand back into his hair before settling her palm gently on the back of his neck. "I accept your proposal, then, Duncan MacRae. I can think of nothing that would make me happier than to become your wife." She tipped her face up, sweeping her lips across his, tasting . . . loving him as no words could.

With a murmured endearment, Duncan returned her passion, easing her back against the pillow. Her hair fanned out beneath them, releasing her sweet scent, and he buried his face in her neck.

Suddenly, his kisses stopped. "Wait," he murmured against her, his voice husky with desire. He pulled back, and from his expression she deemed that whatever had intruded on the seductive magic he'd been weaving was something very important.

"What is it?"

"There is still one thing left to do."

Aileana felt his hand close over hers again, felt him slip the ring over her finger. Its contours were heavy and smooth. As solid and strong as Duncan himself, she thought, her heart giving a little twist.

"We'll speak the words before a priest later, but as of this moment, I consider myself yours, Aileana Mac-Donell."

Tears threatened to choke her again, and she swallowed hard. Her smile was tremulous as she whispered, "I am yours as well, Duncan MacRae. I belong to you and no other, from this day forward."

When he smiled and leaned over to take her mouth in another kiss, spiraling them into renewed passion, Aileana knew that whether or not Duncan realized it yet for himself, she'd finally found the answer to what she'd been seeking all of her life. She knew, suddenly, that the desolation, the emptiness, the hurt—all of the pain she'd felt in her lonely childhood was part of her past, now. She'd found a comfort and sense of belonging far more wonderful than any she'd ever dared to imagine . . .

For she knew that in Duncan's arms she'd finally come home.

Chapter 18

The Northern Highlands

The wind blew its chill breath through the ruined keep. It sent tingles of pleasure down Morgana's back as she lay on the fur-covered bed next to Colin. She'd always loved the wild shriek of the storms that battered round the old stone walls. It reminded her of her own powers, wild, fierce, and strong.

Colin chose that moment to exhale a loud snore, and Morgana grimaced. She rolled away from him, restless and impatient. It seemed like an eternity before morning. Tucking the silken bolster more comfortably beneath her cheek, she stared into the coals of the dying fire. Sleep was out of the question. The events looming ahead of her tomorrow were far too exciting for her mind to rest.

With a sigh, she looked round her chamber, soaking in the extravagance of her surroundings. Beauty had always been important to her. Being surrounded by perfection of sight and sensation had been one of her driving needs since she was a child. It was why Father had spoiled her as he did. He'd indulged her every whim. Expensive tapestries, velvet and fur-lined gowns, a tiny golden knife for her meals . . . complete freedom to do as she willed.

Father had been surprised when she'd taken up with old Biddy Ferguson. Yet he'd turned a blind eye, never realizing that she was practicing the Black Arts in the crone's smoky hovel at the edge of the glen. But Morgana had known from an early age that power bought what goodness could never hope to gain—and that sorcery was the most potent power in the world.

Narrowing her eyes, Morgana played a little game with the last tiny flames in the hearth, changing her view of the shadows as they jumped and danced. And she remembered. Remembered how eager Biddy Ferguson had been to teach her, how eager she herself had been to learn. But Biddy had tried to control her, keeping some of her spells and magic back to insure that Morgana would always need her. So Morgana had watched in secret to learn the rest. When the old woman discovered her duplicity, she'd flown into a rage and threatened to tell Father.

The choice, then, had been clear, though not easy that first time. Morgana had simply silenced her.

Biddy's death was the start of it, but when Duncan had betrayed her, she'd found the real joy of her new powers. A feeling like none she'd ever experienced had flowed through her the day she had shattered his future and decimated his clan.

And Mairi. Fair, delicate, accursed Mairi. Remembered bitterness washed through Morgana, and she dug her nails into her pillow. She never would have needed to attack Duncan's clan, if not for Mairi. Duncan should have been hers, not Mairi's. *Her* husband, her man. She'd set her sights on him from the first time she'd seen him in the woods. And he'd wanted her, too, she *knew* he had; she'd almost enticed him to kiss her that day— she'd been closer still in the days that followed, when she'd sought him out in the forest . . . until he'd learned who she was.

Then everything had changed. By the time she was able to meet with him privately again, he'd found his precious Mairi—become *betrothed* to her. And nothing Morgana could say would convince him that a marriage between the two of them would be far better—a way to unite their warring clans. *A way to bring the* Ealach *finally into her grasp.*

She'd gone to Mairi then, hoping to warn her off, telling her not to interfere. But the stupid chit had just cast those big, soft eyes at her, murmuring something about Duncan having already spoken his pledge in front of the Council. And she'd begged Morgana to leave them alone, claiming that she couldn't give him up, because she loved him more than her own life.

Morgana smiled. Mairi had kept true to her word, she'd grant her that. She'd forfeited her life when she'd crossed Morgana and tried to keep Duncan for her own. All of it had seemed so logical and crystal clear to her. But Father hadn't felt the same. He hadn't looked the other way, then. Even without Mairi, the dead had been too many. Scores of her own clan were lost in the bloody attack she'd led against the MacRaes on Duncan's wedding day.

Morgana squeezed her eyes shut, hoping not to see Father's face as she last remembered it, red with fury, his eyes cold and condemning. He'd turned on her. He'd allowed them to banish her—*her*—his pet and his favorite. Even after she explained how Duncan had betrayed her. How he'd deserved what had happened, and how the Tower was too good for him after the way he'd rejected her.

But Father hadn't listened. He'd told her that the only thing preventing the clan leaders from hanging her for consorting with the English was that she'd reclaimed the *Ealach*. He told her to feel fortunate in keeping her life . . .

Right before he'd slapped the back of her horse and sent her into the oblivion of exile and near-certain death.

Shoving herself to a sitting position, Morgana ground her teeth and knocked her pillow to the floor. Satan's bones, she knew better than to let such memories consume her. It should be enough to know that she'd had her revenge.

Colin made a snuffling sound and stretched his arm to the empty place on the mattress. "What's wrong?" he mumbled, still half asleep. "Why are you getting up?"

"What difference does it make?" Morgana snapped, standing up in one fluid motion. "Just go back to sleep."

Colin grumbled under his breath, something about needing a spell to tame her wicked tongue, but he didn't argue. With a curse, he rolled himself over and was soon snoring again.

Morgana wrinkled her nose at him and paced to the hearth. *Ungrateful wretch*. It was only because of her that they lived in opulence, with none the wiser. From outside, the old keep looked as it always had, ruined and crumbling. An abode fit for beasts and rooks. But thanks to her means of persuasion, she'd filled the central rooms with treasures.

Like the pearl within a shell, she liked to think.

She breathed deep of the scented air, calming her nerves. Tomorrow. Tomorrow she would begin the journey that would increase her wealth and powers twentyfold. It had taken weeks to lay her plans after she'd learned that the *Ealach* was finally unprotected. Ages, it seemed, to summon the power that had finally revealed what Colin hadn't been able to discover when he rode south with his men . . . days of invoking spells, of sweating and toiling, seeking that last grain of truth in the contorting flames of her conjure fire to show her just where the amulet rested. And tonight she'd found success. She'd seen a vision of the *Ealach*, bright and glowing in its little den. In the secret grotto. Safe and sheltered from the eyes of men.

But not from the eyes of a witch. Nay, not from that.

Laughter began to bubble up in her, rich and full of spite, dissolving the painful memories. Covering her mouth with her hand, she slipped into a robe she'd left warming near the fire. Only when she'd let the heavy weight of the door close behind her did she allow her mirth full rein. It started as a chuckle and then built to a full-blown shriek of laughter. When it was over she wiped her eyes, relishing the hard, dark feeling that remained in its wake.

Morgana pulled her robe tighter round herself and started down the hall to gather her provisions. Tomorrow couldn't come soon enough, for tomorrow she'd begin her journey to revenge.

They'd pay. All of them. She'd make them rue the day they'd banished her to this place of cold nothingness. The day they'd hoped for her death. When she finished with them, they'd be begging for an end to their misery, and her power would reign supreme. As she imagined the moment, her heart beat faster and her breath came shallow.

Thirteen years. She'd waited thirteen long years to taste this vengeance. Nothing could stop the wheels of destruction now. Only one last piece still needed to be gathered, and with it secured, her powers would be complete; the true and final cycle would begin.

Success was a foregone conclusion.

For in a few days, the precious *Ealach* would be hers again.

Chapter 19

"**I**'m glad to see you finally came to your senses, man." Kinnon grinned from his position next to Duncan at the banquet table. Sounds of revelry and celebration clanged around them so that he had to speak louder than usual to be heard. He picked up another piece of roasted duck in his fingers and nibbled at it before leaning back with a sigh. "I'd hoped you'd see the light and ask her to marry you. I was beginning to think I'd never get a decent meal again."

Duncan laughed softly, cuffing his cousin on the shoulder. "I wouldn't let Bridgid hear you say that."

"Aye, I'd better watch my tongue," Kinnon agreed. But the silly look on his face spoiled any attempt he made at seeming fearful. He straightened, adding, "Where is Aileana? She should rest and eat. She's hardly touched her food."

"Aye, well, I've been too busy cooking it."

Duncan twisted to see Aileana approaching, feeling

the same burst of happiness he'd felt each time that he looked at her in the days since she'd agreed to become his wife. He'd spoken true when he'd told her how deeply he cared for her, choosing his words carefully for fear of how she might feel. Though they'd made love, he'd been afraid that she'd never accept him as her husband; so much darkness had come before for them, so much hurt.

It had been the greatest joy of his life when she'd said yes. Casting up a silent prayer of thanks, he'd promised to be patient—to do all he could to help her grow to love him as he loved her. When the time was right, he could speak the words to her without worry, and know that she felt the same.

A smile pulled at his lips. At least there was one place that needed no help in their life together right now; aye, they'd made a fine start in the bedchamber this past week. A *very* fine start . . .

"I don't know if it's proper to let the bride prepare her own betrothal feast," he teased her softly, as she came near enough for him to reach around her waist and pull her close to him.

"Better this than on the day we wed," she clipped. "Besides, I've grown accustomed to being worked to the bone in this keep." She grinned when Duncan pulled her across his lap in retaliation, resisting tickling her only when he realized that holding her was bringing up a familiar, pounding heat. And though he'd like nothing better than to disappear upstairs and indulge in some other, more pleasurable pastimes with her, he knew it wouldn't be fair to those gathered to celebrate their betrothal.

"Saucy lass," he whispered so that only she could hear, "you'll pay sweetly for that tongue of yours once we're alone tonight."

"Truly?" she asked, her brows raising in mock alarm. She wrapped her arms round his neck as she sat on his lap and leaned over to whisper, "Well, mayhap my tongue will find other, more pleasurable pursuits this eve. Then you won't wish to curb it, I'll warrant." Before he could answer, she scrambled off of him and skittered away, leaving him laughing and reaching to swat at her retreating backside.

"She's a lively one, sure," Kinnon said, raising his cup of ale in salute.

"Aye, she is, and glad I am of it." Duncan picked up a sugared berry and popped it in his mouth before asking, "Any word from Dulhmeny yet?"

"Nay, nothing. When Gil returned from delivering your message, he said they'd received it without comment."

"After what Robert MacDonell saw here little more than a week ago, I doubt he knows quite how to take a message telling him that his sister and I are going to wed." Duncan ate another berry. "Just keep the guards posted as we discussed, in case he decides to disagree with the idea and attack us. I do not think he has the manpower yet to try it, but I cannot be sure."

"It seems unlikely—a marriage is what they wanted at the start, isn't it?"

"Aye, but after hearing about Gavin's plot against me and their plans to seek retribution, I don't want to assume anything."

Kinnon nodded, and they fell silent until a sudden scuffling at the end of the hall drew their attention. A burst of long, red hair popped up at shoulder height, then two flailing hands. When the gathering people shifted, Duncan could see a laughing Aileana being hoisted up in the air by some of his kinsmen. Gil and

Ewen led her pack of captors, with several of the women following behind, waving bits of plaids and making loud calls and jests.

"Bring on the nuts! The nuts must be tossed," they called, as they carried Aileana to the massive open fireplace.

"It looks like you'd better join her." Kinnon bit back a smile as he took another swig of his spiced ale. "You don't want to miss such an important ceremony."

"You put them up to this, didn't you?"

Kinnon merely shrugged and stood. "It doesn't matter much, now, does it? It cannot hurt. It's only for sport to read the omen in them." He winked. "Just think of it as an early present in honor of your union."

"Aye," Duncan answered wryly. "Just what I needed." He stood. "With my luck both of the fruits will explode before they've sat in the coals for five seconds."

Kinnon just laughed and grabbed his arm, dragging him toward the festivities that were building to uproarious levels near the fireplace. By the time Duncan reached Aileana, a selection of nuts had been laid out across the hearthstones. "It appears as though we'll have to partake of this ancient and noble custom," he murmured to her.

"Aye, so it seems."

Duncan felt another warm jolt go through him when she looked at him. Her eyes sparkled. She was enjoying every moment of this revelry, he realized with delight. A far cry from her demeanor the last time they'd had a large celebration in the hall, when the Mackenzies had been visiting. Duncan grinned and soaked in the sight of her. He never thought he'd be able to feel this way about any woman again. He loved everything about her—her spirit, her fire, her beauty, her tenderness. The passion she was capable of feeling. She'd stolen his heart, and he realized that he never wanted to be free.

Clasping her hand in his, he said, "Shall we choose, then?"

Smiling, she nodded, and they knelt down at the hearth. His clan folk gathered in a huge semicircle around them, leaning in and pressing closer, calling out advice on the best nut to pick. Duncan made a great show of choosing and discarding one after another, until he finally settled on a small, firm-looking acorn with a tight brown cap. Aileana picked a fine hazelnut, and a cheer went up as they held their choices aloft for all to see.

A hush came over the group, and many of the women murmured blessings behind their hands. Then, at the signal, the gathering began to count the way to the casting of the nuts. Only Nora hung back, sour-faced and unwilling to participate. When they reached the lucky number seven, Aileana and Duncan both rolled their nuts into the coals of the fire, then leaned away to watch if they would burn slow and steady or if they would crack and explode too quickly.

The moments ticked past, and with each second, the excitement in the hall built higher. "It's a good omen! They're burning together in the light o' love!" some of the women began to whisper.

"Aye, they're burning in love, all right," one of the men called out loud with a laugh. "And a good marriage it'll be, if that burning love lasts every night for the rest o' their lives!"

The gathering erupted into shouts and cheers, and Duncan helped Aileana to her feet, laughing with the rest and delighting in the blush on her cheeks. Gil stepped forward to slap him on the shoulder, nodding his congratulations. Several of the men moved closer as well, only to be stopped by someone's loud command at the hall's entryway. Duncan stood still. He recognized Robert MacDonell's booming voice.

And as he turned to face his future brother-in-law, his gaze swept past the hearth to see that his acorn had burst into flames.

"Is it true, MacRae? Are you planning to marry my sister, or is this another ploy to make a mockery of my clan?"

Aileana felt a shock go through her. *Robert was here?* She looked questioningly at Duncan, and he nodded. "I invited him with my message to Dulhmeny. Don't worry, Aileana; we'll convince him to support our union."

She didn't have time to question further. A path cleared, revealing the new chieftain of the clan Mac-Donell, her eldest brother, Robert. He looked impressive, standing in his full regalia as laird, with a jaunty bonnet on his head complete with a plume jutting out to the side. Without the dirt and blood of battle, as she'd last seen him, he looked a new man. Startled, Aileana realized for the first time how much he resembled Father.

Robert's stony expression softened at the sight of her, and she went running into his arms.

"How have you fared, lassie?" he murmured, cupping her cheeks in his palms and tipping her face up.

"I've been well. In truth, I'm the happiest I've ever been."

Robert's brow shot up. He released her gently. "That is much to say, the happiest in all your life. The MacRae . . . he's treated you well, then? I couldn't tell as much when I visited last, since the wretch wouldn't let me see you."

"We've had some difficulties, it's true, but Duncan has never done ill to me. I—I've come to care for him, Robert."

Robert frowned. "Then the news of your betrothal is true?"

"Aye. Duncan has asked me to be his wife, and I've accepted." She took his hand and began to lead him back to where Duncan sat waiting on a bench near the hearth. "You needn't look so stern. I'm only going to be married, not disappear forever." She spoke the rebuke as if in jest, but she sensed the troubled undercurrent in him.

"I don't like the lateness of MacRae's decision. He wouldn't accept the offer of your hand when I made it at the beginning of all this." Robert frowned. "Though I suppose as things rest, late honor is better than none at all."

Aileana felt the flush grow warmer in her cheeks. Until seven days ago, her honor had been intact, no matter what the world had thought true. But now she could no longer deny Robert's reference to her lack of purity. Shaking off the momentary guilt, she said, "Duncan is a man of his word, Robert."

Her brother stopped her ten paces from Duncan and stared at her. "His sudden claim to want a wedding isn't because you're with child, is it? I've heard of rogues who'll tell a woman almost anything to keep her happy until the babe arrives. Then they take the child and abandon its dam."

"Aileana isn't with child, so far as I know, Mac-Donell." Duncan had stood and was approaching them, looking like a thundercloud. Robert fixed him with a glare, and Aileana shuddered, wishing that her brother had thought to ask such an indelicate question while they were still out of Duncan's earshot. A devilish glint came into Duncan's eyes, and he directed an equally pointed glance at Robert. "However, I am looking forward to the time when Aileana will bear the future heir to the clan MacRae."

Irritation lit in Aileana's breast as she viewed her brother and her betrothed, facing each other down and discussing her like a possession of war. She stepped up between them. "I do not much like serving as the unseen subject of your conversation. If the two of you cannot speak to each other and to me in a civilized way, I'm going up to my chamber. *Alone*," she added, as she flashed a sharp look at Duncan, "to leave you both down here wallowing in your foolishness."

The heat in her chest began to abate with her outburst, and she saw with satisfaction that both Duncan and Robert had stopped still to gaze at her. Robert looked puzzled, but Duncan's blank stare soon turned to wry amusement.

Finally, he crossed his arms over his chest and rocked back on his heels. "I think if you needed proof that I haven't mistreated your sister, MacDonell, you've just witnessed it. She's found her temper and the will to voice it in the time she's lived at Eilean Donan with me."

Aileana lifted her chin, refusing to let Duncan make her feel the slightest bit embarrassed for what she'd said. She looked at her brother. "What Duncan means to say is that I've learned to defend myself against his oafish behavior." She heard his choked laugh behind her and fought the exasperated smile that suddenly tugged at her lips.

She struggled to maintain a serene composure as she slipped her hand beneath Robert's elbow, steering him closer to the fire. "Come. You must be hungry. I'll bring you a bowl of stew. We can talk more after you eat."

Robert nodded, casting a searching glance between her and Duncan, as if trying to read their swift exchange of emotion. Aileana felt the tension relax from his arm, finally, as he too gave into a smile and allowed her to lead him to the bench. Duncan came close behind, and Robert slid over to allow him room to sit.

"Come join me near the fire, MacRae," Robert said, slapping the bench. "We've much to discuss." He gave Aileana a sly wink. "In truth, I'm starting to think that this match between you and my sister might be a good one. A very good one indeed."

The date of the wedding was set. The ceremony would take place soon, shortly after the passing of *Samhain* at the end of October. But for all of the preparations that consumed the days and exhausted everyone by nightfall, Aileana still lay awake, staring up at the stonework of the ceiling. It was near dawn, already; she could tell by the leaden cast to the light outside the shutter. With a sigh, she turned on her side in the vast emptiness of the bed, missing Duncan's warmth and wishing that he'd not had to leave for another of the seemingly incessant raids he'd been forced to lead against some of the rogue clans that kept plaguing them. He'd said he planned to be home by dark today, though, so she'd resolved to be patient.

But it was for more than just missing him that sleep would not come easily, she knew. Every time she began to relax and her eyes began to drift shut, it was the same. The same startling, disturbing image shot through her mind, jolting her to complete, stark awareness again . . . *The Ealach falling, its golden chain twisting in the speed of its descent. Then splashing into water, cold, gray and deep, floating down, before disappearing into the murk of the ocean.*

Her logic told her that she was only reliving the horror of that day when she'd jumped over the bluff's edge to elude capture. But her heart thrummed a different story. Something deeper inspired this vision; she knew it in her soul. It was almost the same as the odd tingling she'd gotten the morning she'd realized that the *Ealach* was in danger. The morning Father had taken it out to the battlefield. Only this feeling was even more persistent. It compelled her. But why? The amulet was hidden in the grotto, safe from harm. Or was it?

Sitting up in bed, Aileana shuddered. What if the *Ealach* had been taken from the security of its hiding place? She gripped the blankets tightly to her chest, looking toward the shutter to see the light of dawn peeking through the cracks. It was enough to see her path back to the grotto; if she set out soon she could be back before supper. Then she could rest easier about its safety—perhaps even bring it back and make a gift of it to Duncan. A sign of her faith in him and the rightness of their union . . .

Scrambling from beneath the coverlet, Aileana hurried to dress and ready herself for the journey. She needed to do this alone and yet she knew she'd have to tell Bridgid of her plans to take one of the horses and be gone for the day. Perhaps she could hide her true purposes under the guise of seeking out some mandrake for their herb supplies, she thought, as she hastily plaited her hair. Likely none would wish to accompany her then, fearing as they did the darker magical qualities associated with cultivating the roots of that plant.

Aye, that was a plan. It would serve to protect her true reason of retrieving the *Ealach*. Now she just had to hurry to set everything in motion so that she could return to Eilean Donan before Duncan did.

Nora crouched deeper into the shadows behind the cart near the stable, watching through narrowed eyes as Aileana MacDonell led a haltered pony out into the misty dawn light. A sour taste filled her mouth as she studied her rival, trying to see just what it was . . . what gift Aileana could possibly possess that had allowed her to claim such a resounding victory with Duncan.

She was beautiful, aye, but Nora herself had turned many a head in her day. It had to be more than that. It had to be something powerful enough to entice the laird from Nora's bed, blinding him to the truth of what the MacDonell traitor was. Something that would have compelled him to elevate Aileana from the humiliating position of leman to one as his honored betrothed.

Witchcraft.

She'd long suspected it. Aileana MacDonell was surely practicing the black arts, just as Nora had heard her cursed sister did before her. It had to be that. Nothing else could explain the change that had come over Duncan within days of the conniving wench's arrival at Eilean Donan.

Oh, Aileana had pretended to be innocent, and within a few weeks of coming to live with them, she'd even mastered the pretense of caring about the MacRaes. She'd lured Bridgid, Kinnon, and many of the others into believing, even going so far as to cleverly using some of her skills to aid the clan when the plague struck.

That she herself had fallen sick after nursing them all was the only fly in the ointment of Nora's conviction, but she wagered that Aileana had used her ungodly arts to feign symptoms of the illness in order to garner Duncan's sympathies and attention. And it had worked, damn her eyes. Her spells were potent.

Now, finally, Nora had a chance to prove it. Aileana had been up earlier than usual this morn, intending to go off on her own to collect more herbs before winter snows fell in earnest . . . or so Nora had overheard her saying to Bridgid. She sought mandrake, she'd told the *bailie*, and so she would go alone, to prevent anyone else from becoming tainted if aught went awry as she collected the dangerous root.

But Nora knew that was a ploy; she was sure Aileana was leaving the confines of the castle grounds to practice more spells. Spells to keep Duncan by her side.

Aye, the time was right. She'd follow Aileana this morning to see just what she was up to—and when she caught her at her witchery, then at last she would be able to prove to Duncan, once and for all, that he'd made a terrible and dangerous mistake . . .

For he would finally see that when he'd asked Aileana MacDonell to marry him, he'd taken a snake to his bosom instead of a bride.

Chapter 20

The glen looked dim, even in the mid-morning sun. Aileana suppressed a shiver. She'd felt strangely all morning, but she'd be finished here soon enough. She squinted, searching for the spot. It was hidden well. Dragon's breath but she wanted nothing more than to find the amulet and bring it and herself home to Duncan and their warm bed. A smile teased her lips. Thoughts of Duncan had sustained her through the dark hours of travel. Even when the rain began, soaking her to the skin, she'd kept on, driven by an image of his face and the memory of his touch. She loved him, and giving him the *Ealach* would be a final act of trust, a gift to ensure he never need doubt her commitment to him again.

But first she needed to find it.

Pulling the old, frayed plaid she'd brought with her as a cloak more firmly over her damp hair, she stepped into the chill of the glen. Bits of sun sparkled through the copper and gold leaves still clinging to the trees, belying the storms of the night. Mist rose from the mossy ground, making her shiver. It was cold. Much cooler here than along the barren stretch of road she'd followed from Eilean Donan. Her breath hung around her in white puffs, dissolving almost as soon as it took shape.

Then a jutting boulder caught her gaze, and she paused. Its brown and red contours looked familiar. A twisted root nearby seemed to point to a mossy patch of earth, just as she remembered. *This was it. The spot that—*

A chill raked up her spine an instant before she heard it. Soft laughter, tinkling over her like a shower of ice. Whirling to face the sound, Aileana gasped. Her hand flew to her throat, and she took a step back. Ten paces away, half hidden in the gloom, stood a disembodied vision. A haunt like those of a thousand Highland stories told round the fire of a cold winter's evening. Only this spirit was more frightful than any anonymous fiend she might have faced. She knew this shade's identity.

"Morgana?" She breathed her sister's name, fear and awe closing her throat so that only a whisper escaped. She almost expected the vision to melt before her eyes into the mists of the glen.

"You remember me, then, little sister."

Aileana swallowed. She'd never known spirits to speak. Yet this could be nothing but a phantom. "Why have you returned here? Is something troubling you that you seek me out?"

Morgana laughed again, throwing back her head, and the rippling cascade of sound filled the glen. When her amusement abated, she stepped closer to Aileana, directly into a shaft of sunlight that shone through the branches of the trees. It kissed the glossy waves of her red hair, her luminous blue eyes . . . the *Ealach* amulet that hung shining around her neck.

"Ah," Morgana said, cocking her head, "it's a fine story I'll be telling, what with you thinking me a ghostie come back to haunt. How delicious, when the truth is nothing more otherworldly than that you came upon me here just as I was readying to return to my holding in the north."

Bewilderment, joy, and uncertainty all blended in a torrent as Aileana faced the sister she'd last seen more than thirteen years before. It seemed a dream. Unreal.

"They told me you were dead."

"Aye, as I made certain they would. I had word sent that I'd died from the privations of banishment, and it was nothing our dear clan leaders hadn't expected to hear." Morgana arched one brow wickedly and smiled. "It went just as I planned. But as you can see, little sister, I'm as alive as you are, and I have many tasks yet to accomplish— many dreams to fulfill." She stepped closer, reaching out to chuck Aileana under the chin, a gesture reminiscent of their childhood. Tilting her head to the side, she studied her. "It is true what they say," she murmured finally. "You do share an unusual likeness with me. All except for the eyes . . ."

Aileana's plaid fell to her shoulders, and she shrugged herself away from her sister's touch. "Why have you come back?"

Morgana's expression hardened, and she brushed her hair back from her face. "To get the *Ealach*, of course. But first I had to determine where you'd secreted it." She gestured around her. "It took me a deal of time to find it once I arrived here last eve, but in the end it was a certainty. And deliciously ironic, wouldn't you say? I couldn't have chosen a better spot myself."

"But the amulet isn't yours. Father took it from you, and for good reason."

"Father is dead," Morgana stated flatly. "May his soul burn in everlasting hell."

"How can you talk so about him? He loved you more than the sun."

"Not enough to stop the clan elders from banishing me," she snapped. After a moment, a knowing, sinister look came into her eyes. The negative force of it drove Aileana back a step. "But come, little sister. Don't tell me that you never cursed Father for all those long years he locked you away in the tower chamber. He was a meddling fool who got what he deserved."

Anger and shame clouded Aileana's mind. It was true; she'd sometimes wished Father dead—wished so heartily for freedom from the four walls of her room and from the keeping of the amulet that she could taste the need. But Morgana couldn't know that. It was impossible for her to know that.

Aileana lifted her chin. "What would you care for how I felt? It was because of you and your ways that I was kept under watch and key at all."

"Be that as it may, I've learned much these thirteen years, Aileana. Much to make me strong." A fierce light shone in her eyes, making them pierce the shadows of the glen like sapphire blades. She stroked the *Ealach*'s opalescent surface. "And now my time has come. *Samhain* is fast approaching, and on that day all of the Highlands will be forced to acknowledge me. Your arrival here is unfortunate, sister, but it confirms what I'd suspected; you've cultivated a connection with the amulet as well. Such a thing might prove useful to me. If you wish to share your gift in that way, I would make sure that you shared also in the glory that is to come when I use it to gain my power."

"I could never use the *Ealach* for ill, Morgana."

"Why? Are you so loyal to those who mistreat you? Our father imprisoned you and our brothers sold you as leman to the MacRae; he is no better than they, keeping you in shame and captivity at Eilean Donan." She arched her brow. "I admit to being rather surprised at the news that Duncan lived; I'd thought I'd taken care of him when I gave him to the English those years ago." She shook her head, making a clicking sound with her tongue. "You'll have to forgive me for that one, sister. By rights he should have been dead and of no threat to anyone anymore."

"It is only because he still lives that I am able to bear any forgiveness for you, Morgana. What you did to him was nothing less than—"

"After all he's done, you can still feel pity for him?" Morgana broke in sharply.

"Nay, not pity." Aileana swallowed, the softer part of her nature not wishing to cause her sister pain even now, after all she'd learned about her. "Duncan has asked me to wed him, Morgana, and I have accepted. I am to be his wife."

A deadly silence settled over the clearing, and Aileana felt a shiver up the back of her neck.

"His *wife?*" Morgana broke the quiet, hissing the words with vehemence. "You must be jesting. Duncan would never offer to marry you. Not after everything that happened between our clans."

"And yet he did. We are to be married."

As Aileana spoke, Morgana's face tightened, sharpening to a look that was almost painful in its bitterness. "I see," she answered, her voice both harsh and echoing hollow through the chill of the wood. She glanced around them. "You've come to this place alone, haven't you, little sister? Duncan could not know of your journey, else he'd never have allowed you to make it without escort, especially with so important a prize as the *Ealach* at stake," she added, her palm drifting up to stroke the amulet.

Aileana remained quiet, the sudden, painful memory of what Duncan had told her about Morgana's cruelty and lack of conscience lodging in her chest. She worried the edges of her plaid almost absentmindedly, feeling the frayed weave loosen. It seemed she'd been foolish to eschew all company this morning, and now she was forced to do what she could to conceal her mounting uneasiness.

Her sister's gaze slid back to her, piercing as she leaned in to say with soft menace, "It would be wise of you to answer. Your silence will be deemed an attempt to thwart me—and believe me well when I say that you do not wish to do that."

Tendrils of fear unwound in Aileana at Morgana's tone, and to mask her reaction she gripped the plaid tighter to her chest, cocking her head at a mutinous angle. "If you know as much about me as you claim, you would realize that I am not easily intimidated. Just what do you think you can do that would force me to comply with any demand of yours?"

"Not what I can do," Morgana said with a dark smile, "but what I'll let *him* do."

As she finished speaking, she jerked her chin toward a place just past Aileana's shoulder, and Aileana whirled in that direction, gasping as she came face to face with what seemed to be another haunt—only this one in the shape of a strangely familiar man.

He stood a bit taller than Duncan, with hair the same golden brown color and a jaw square and firm. He even had a scar, though not as severe as the one on Duncan's face, disappearing beneath a black eye patch. The similarity ended there. This man's visible eye held a hard expression in its dark depths.

He stared down at her, his gaze sharpening more with each passing second, the lines around his mouth tightening into a cruel grin that reminded her of a wolf. The answer to his identity clicked suddenly in her mind.

"You must be Colin," Aileana said, her voice barely a whisper.

"And you're Aileana MacDonell." Colin grinned wider and the wolfish image intensified. "So, my brother's been talking to you of me, has he?" A moment later he scowled. "But Duncan is supposed to believe us dead." He reached out and gripped her arm painfully. "Tell me what he's learned of us."

"He knows nothing," she countered, trying to pull away.

Colin jerked her closer, raising his other hand, and she flinched, sure he was about to strike her; but in the next instant Morgana snapped an order for him to release his grip, and mercifully, Colin obeyed. Aileana stumbled back a step, rubbing the bruised place above her elbow.

"There is no need for that, Colin," Morgana said silkily, stepping around him to peer into her face again. "Aileana is telling the truth, I think. If Duncan had had any inkling about us, he'd have led a search long before now, to finish what our exile was supposed to have accomplished. His damned MacRae pride would have demanded it—no insult intended toward you, of course, darling," she continued quickly, flicking her gaze toward Duncan's half brother as she spoke the last bit.

Until then he'd been glowering like a thundercloud, but now he swiftly laughed, and Aileana nursed a fleeting thought that perhaps Colin MacRae was daft, his moods shifting like the wind.

He fixed his gaze on her when his mirth had passed, his expression making her feel both dirtied and exposed. "I'd not be surprised, her trying to protect Duncan. She's probably soft on him, what with him tuppin' her all this time."

Aileana remained silent, enfolding herself in icy calm as a defense, but Morgana hissed in her breath. Colin only chuckled again. He walked away a few steps, leaning over to retrieve a leather pack from behind a pile of stones nearby as he added, "But be that as it may, you'd best decide what to do with the chit and soon, Morgana. We've a goodly distance to cover before nightfall and little time to spare."

"It will be quite simple," Morgana answered flatly, clearly not amused with Colin's observations about Duncan. "My sister will be making the decision herself," she said, swiveling her head to look at Aileana again. "You see, Colin and I must keep the secret of our continued good health safe from the MacRae or anyone else, at least until *Samhain*. After that day, Duncan can lead all the clans of the Highlands in chase of me, and I'll care naught. But until then, I cannot have you running back to him, telling tales that will interrupt my plans."

Morgana nodded to Colin, and he grinned as he came back toward them, pulling from his pack a thin strap of leather twice the length of his forearm. Aileana felt like some kind of prey, cornered in the den of two hungry wolves; her gaze darted between the two of them, uncertain which was more imminently dangerous.

"Your choice is this then, sister," Morgana intoned. "You can come with me peacefully, to remain at my holding in the north until my plans reach fruition—or Colin will have to ensure your silence by other means . . . a decision which I am afraid will be far less enjoyable and infinitely more permanent."

Colin had wrapped the ends of the leather strap around his meaty fists, and now he snapped its length tight, pausing to stand in readiness of Morgana's command.

"You would order me strangled?" Aileana rasped, even though the horrible truth was staring her in the face.

"I will order whatever is necessary," Morgana answered sharply, her expression dark and powerful. "I have waited many long years, Aileana. Years of endless privation and suffering while I watched and planned for this chance, and nothing—not even a sister—is going to stand in my way now. The choice is yours."

"Do not think to run," Colin said quietly, as if sensing the instinct that rose in her for impending flight. His voice was all the more menacing for its seeming gentleness, as he added, "I *will* catch you if you do, sweet . . . and then I will surely demand additional recompense from you for my efforts, before you breathe your last."

Even for all her pretended calm, Aileana couldn't suppress the shudder that rippled through her. Colin gave her a knowing grin, driving his point home with unmistakable meaning as he blew her a mocking kiss.

Revulsion swept through her, and it was all she could do not to slap the smirk from his handsome, scarred face. Instead, she concentrated on pulling herself to-

gether, letting anger override the panic that was burgeoning with each passing moment. The two of them had
won this battle, it seemed, but all was not lost. Not yet.

Looking back to her sister, Aileana thought quickly.
Going to Morgana's holding was preferable to death;
that much was certain. And if she feigned cooperation
cleverly enough, she might still have a chance of stealing
the *Ealach* away from their grasp and finding her way
with it back to Duncan. It was worth a try, at the least.
She refused to dwell on what Duncan would likely feel
once he realized that she wasn't returning to Eilean Donan—that she had vanished without a trace during her
foray to the woods. He'd either worry that she'd been
taken off by beasts . . . or worse yet he'd decide that
she'd betrayed him at long last, sneaking away to retrieve
the *Ealach* when she'd claimed to be innocently gathering herbs.

Her heart plummeted, and a sick sensation filled her.
Would he think she'd been pretending what she felt for
him all along in order to fool him—or would he harbor
doubt about her disappearance and forestall an attack on
Dulhmeny until he'd investigated it further?

There was no way to know what he would think. She
only knew that Duncan had been betrayed once before
because of the *Ealach*; and though they'd recently come
to an understanding, the tenderness they'd confessed to
each other was so new and fragile that it was likely to
waver in the face of this apparent—

She closed her eyes, forcing herself away from such
tormenting thoughts. After taking a deep breath, she
tightened her jaw, resigned to commence what needed to
be done. "I will come with you, Morgana, without struggle. Lead on."

"A wise choice, sister."

"Aye, but not nearly as entertaining as the other," Colin murmured, earning himself another glare from Morgana.

In an apparent attempt to distract her from her ire, he added, "You do realize that when Aileana fails to return to the castle, a search will be sent—and when no body is recovered, my arrogant brother may decide to broaden those efforts . . . which in turn might lead him to stumble upon something that brings him to us. He is betrothed to the wench, after all; he is sure to consider her his and will be unlikely to relinquish her easily." He grunted, his expression a mixture of derision and reluctant admiration, "There will be hell to pay if he's anything like he was with Mairi. Christ—he had to be knocked senseless in order to get him away from her, even after she was dead."

"Aye, I remember," Morgana murmured, her eyes icy enough to send another shiver up Aileana's spine. "We will need to have a care, both in the path we choose to return home and in how we travel so that if Duncan does pursue a broader search out of stubbornness, he will find naught but a cold trail."

Colin nodded. "I'll fetch her mount, then, so we can be on our way."

With an answering nod, Morgana turned away from Aileana and bent to gather a small bundle of provisions from the ground, wrapping the tools in a length of plaid she used as a pouch. Then she straightened to offer a shrill whistle. At the signal, a silver-streaked palfrey cantered up from the opposite direction of the mist-enshrouded woodland, followed by a larger bay stallion. Colin rejoined them with Aileana's pony in tow, securing it to his steed and jerking his head in a silent order for her to mount up.

She did as she was bid, and when they were all astride, Morgana twisted to look at her once more, a strange and almost unholy light filling her gaze. "It is time, Aileana," she called out softly, "time to right the wrongs of the past and fulfill my destiny. From this moment onward, there will be no looking back." Then her lips parted in a smile, her teeth flashing white in the shadowy forest, as she dug in her heels to urge her steed into motion.

Colin broke into a canter behind her, pulling Aileana's pony to follow; she held on tightly with one hand, tugging with the other once more on the frayed edge of the plaid she'd been fiddling with all morning. After a final yank, a tiny piece tore off. A thrill of victory shot through her, but she knew she had little time to rejoice; they were almost out of the clearing. Staring straight ahead and keeping as still as she might, Aileana carefully opened her fingers, releasing the hard-won scrap of wool. It fluttered on the waft of air caused by the horses' movement . . .

Floating down to rest upon the dead leaves that stirred and rasped over the barren ground below.

Chapter 21

The council had been summoned hastily, and now Duncan sat in his accustomed place as chieftain at the middle of the long table near the northern end of the great hall. Kinnon had taken a position to his right, Callum, as clan elder, to his left, with another half dozen men serving to even out the group.

The hall itself was nearly full to the bursting with people from the castle and village, and yet a dead silence had descended over all. There had been no other reaction possible after Nora had stood up moments ago and called out her accusation. She'd insisted that Aileana MacDonell had committed blatant treachery against Duncan and the entire MacRae clan that very morning, using her newfound freedom as his betrothed to sneak away and meet with two accomplices before running off with the *Ealach* amulet.

Nora's words had fallen like hammer blows on Duncan's soul. At first there had been an outburst of voices, with those who were more than ready to believe in a MacDonell's treachery—even if the MacDonell in question was the chieftain's chosen bride—arguing with those who felt they knew Aileana better. But eventually all had fallen silent out of respect for Duncan. Only *he* could decide what should be done next, not only as leader of the MacRaes, but as the betrothed of the accused.

And so the stunned silence stretched on, broken only by the crackling of the fire in the massive hearth along the wall.

There was one glaring problem, however: Duncan couldn't bring himself to speak. Not if his life depended on it. He felt numb, suffocating. What Nora had said *couldn't* be true. He knew it deep in his bones, but still he struggled with a shadow of doubt. For as much as he wanted to deny it, he couldn't pretend that there was no history to her accusations. Aileana had wanted revenge on him and the MacRaes in the past. She'd considered betraying him only a few weeks ago. And though he believed with every fiber of his being that they'd gotten past all that, today's events had called it into question again—and it was that which played havoc with his ability to speak.

There was no overlooking that Aileana had not returned from the forest today. Nora had offered up additional details as well that had made Duncan's stomach churn: She claimed to have followed Aileana secretly, compelled by a feeling that the search for mandrake was a ruse to cover something more insidious. Her suspicions had proven true, she declared, and she'd watched from a safe distance as Aileana had entered a glen somewhere between MacRae and MacDonell land. There, Aileana had consorted with an unknown man and woman who had conversed with her at length—even seeming to laugh and jest with her—before she left the clearing with them on horseback.

The information had left Duncan feeling sick at heart. An unknown man and woman had met with Aileana in a glen beyond Eilean Donan . . . a man and woman working together for a devious purpose, God help him. An innate sense of these strangers' identities, impossible as it would seem, burned in Duncan's chest, but he couldn't bring himself to ask anything that would give him the confirmation he dreaded. Not yet.

"Do you believe that Aileana knew the people she met with in the glen, Nora?" Kinnon finally called out, sparing him the need to speak. Duncan threw him a grateful glance.

Nora nodded. "She talked with them and made no effort to run away. She followed them from the glen freely as well, allowing the man to lead her pony behind his."

"And the *Ealach* seemed the purpose of their meeting, based on what you witnessed?" he continued.

"Aye."

"Did you see the amulet with your own eyes, woman?" Kinnon pressed, exasperation clear in his voice. "These are serious charges you bring against the MacRae's betrothed. Are you sure beyond a glimmer of doubt that what you're saying is factual truth?"

"I saw the *Ealach* myself, there's no mistake," Nora returned hotly, raising her chin as she faced him. "I'd never laid eyes on it before this day, having come to Eilean Donan little more than seven years ago, but I know its description as well as any in our clan. Aileana MacDonell snuck away from here and then ran off with it—for though she didn't carry the talisman in her own hands, the woman who rode out of the glen alongside her was wearing it around her neck, clear as water."

Duncan closed his eyes, then; nausea swelled in him, and he fisted his hand against the scarred surface of the wooden table as the buzz of angry voices rose again in the chamber.

The hum grew rapidly to shouting, with several from the crowd demanding that a raid be planned to make the guilty parties pay, others disputing that no one knew where to lead an attack, unless it were to Dulhmeny, the seat of all the traitorous MacDonells . . . and still others urging restraint and calm, until more could be learned. Kinnon stood up in an appeal to keep the discussion peaceful, and the rest of the council did their best as well to deal with the various arguments and cries of dissension coming at them from the floor.

Through the uproar, Duncan forced himself to open his eyes, look at Nora, and call out in a strong, clear voice, "What did she look like?"

Nora seemed confused for a moment, but the hubbub began to die down as people started to realize that their laird had spoken at long last.

Frowning, she faced him. "Aileana? I'd have thought you'd care little about how she was faring once you heard what I had to say. But if you must know, she looked the same as she always—"

"The *second* woman," Duncan broke in, his words clipped and icy in the near silence that had blanketed the hall once more. "Describe her—and the man who was with her."

"Oh." Nora's cheeks reddened and her expression looked more pinched than usual. "Well, it was obvious that the other woman was of the MacDonells as well, which is one of the reasons I know Aileana played traitor against us all today. The two women shared a marked likeness, with red hair and fair complexions; they even seemed similar in height, though the other one stood a bit taller than Aileana. The man with them may or may not have been of their clan. He was tall as well, and strong-looking, but his hair was tawny rather than red."

"Is that all?" Duncan managed to ask past the sudden constriction in his throat and the pounding that had begun in his temples.

"Aye—no wait," Nora corrected herself, frowning more deeply, and looking away as if to hone her recollection of the morning's sights. "The man with them . . . he had an eye patch and what looked to be a scar below it, though I can't be sure of that part, since I was a fair distance away. I was close enough to see the *Ealach*, though—and to watch Aileana ride off with it and her conspirators!" she finished with a spiteful glare.

"Nay, not her," Duncan answered huskily, pushing himself up to stand and face the people of his clan. "Aileana MacDonell may have been in the glen, but she was not in possession of the *Ealach*. Her elder sister Morgana was. It was that cursed witch and my half brother, Colin MacRae, who took the amulet again. We thought them long dead, but it seems we were wrong. It can be no other than they, from your description."

After a moment of stunned silence, chaos bloomed anew in the hall, with many people crossing themselves for fear of the dead returned, and others shouting for the overdue spilling of blood—whether it be Morgana's and Colin's, Aileana's, or the MacDonell clan's as a whole, it didn't seem to matter. The prayers and cries for vengeance blended into a cacophony of sound. Everyone began to surge forward, many of the men offering themselves for positions on the raiding party while the coun-

cil rose and prepared to hear Duncan's plans for retaliation.

As they readied to leave the hall for that purpose, Kinnon paused to glance at Duncan, his face ashen. "Do you
really think it is Morgana and Colin, Duncan?" he murmured. "Still alive after all these years?"

"Much as I'd like to deny the possibility, it would
seem so. You heard Nora. The two she described can be
no others," Duncan answered, his jaw tight as he turned
away. But Kinnon placed a restraining hand on his arm,
and Duncan swiveled the look at him again.

"And Aileana? Do you think, then, that she is—?"

Duncan shook his head. "I would wager my life
against Aileana being involved in this willingly or betraying me, Kinnon, and yet . . ." He glanced away, his
throat aching. "Well, it appears by Nora's testimony
that it could be otherwise."

He swallowed, looking out over his people, most of
whom were still clamoring with each other for retribution and the return of the *Ealach*. "In truth," Duncan
continued hoarsely, "either possibility chills me to the
bone. But regardless of which it is, I must ride out within
the hour and try to track where they've gone, for I'll not
risk Aileana's safety if Nora is wrong . . . or allow Morgana and any who aid her to escape without retribution
if she is right."

Kinnon nodded, his expression more serious than
Duncan could ever remember having seen it. They
clasped forearms to show their solidarity, before finally
separating to stride from the hall to their individual
preparations.

Duncan headed off to gather his war gear and send a
message to Dulhmeny. And as he went, he steeled himself for the upcoming battle. He knew it would be far

greater than any he had fought in his life. For this would
be a conflict undertaken on a field of sharp contrasts,
with uncertainty and dark suspicion warring against
blind, trusting love . . .

And with the spoils of victory being nothing less than
a final judgment on the survival of his own, battered
heart.

"I don't think we should be stopping," Duncan said.
"We're too close."

Kinnon squatted next to the newly kindled fire and
threw another handful of sticks onto it. "The men cannot continue. Besides, it's dark now and harder to find
the witch's path."

"All the more reason to keep going. We may lose her
altogether if we don't push on. By morning the signs of
her may have faded." Duncan paced round the edge of
the fire. Though they'd been traveling for hours and his
body was weary, he knew he'd not find rest this night.

And yet he needn't have dissembled with Kinnon. His
cousin was well aware of the real reason he couldn't bear
stopping: his fear for Aileana. Duncan's remaining
doubts concerning her innocence had vanished with the
first scrap of cloth they'd spotted along the trail. It was
from an old swath of plaid Aileana always wore as a
shawl when she worked in the garden or foraged for
herbs . . . any time she would be digging in the dirt.

That plaid had gone missing with her, and so when
that first bit had been found, his heart had leapt with renewed hope—and lancing fear. Had there been a struggle of some kind, one that Nora hadn't witnessed? There
was no blood to be seen, no sign of crushed bracken. But
the bit of cloth he'd found had been torn away from the
larger piece; there was no mistake.

When they'd stumbled upon two more scraps of the same pattern along the way, Duncan had known that Aileana was leaving him intentional signs. She'd gone with Morgana and Colin against her will, regardless of what it had seemed to Nora. Kinnon agreed, though some of the other men still expressed doubt, saying the cloth could have snagged on branches as she fled to the north. But Duncan knew better. Aileana was in danger, and she was trying to let him know it.

Suddenly, the impulse to find and punish the two people who had orchestrated so much misery for him those many years ago burned hotter and deeper.

"Morgana's tracks will be as clear in a few hours as they are now," Kinnon said, pulling his thoughts back to the present. "Actually they will be better, for the fact that we'll have daylight to show the way—and help us spot any new clues." He cast Duncan an understanding look before getting up and calling to Ewen, telling him to bring a few of the spitted hares they'd prepared for roasting over the coals. While they waited, he added more quietly, "Try to curb your impatience, cousin. It will not serve Aileana to try to fight Morgana when we are tired and hungry. The men need rest. At the first sign of light, we'll resume our way."

Duncan's jaw clenched in frustration. He felt afire, his body consumed with a heat and energy that drove him to action. But Kinnon was right. The men were exhausted. He shook his head when Kinnon offered him a bannock cake. He couldn't eat. Not yet. Too many thoughts cluttered his mind, and he had to clear them before he could do anything other than envision his goal.

His cousin stiffened beside him, pulling him again from his musings. Aileana's brother Robert was approaching, and Kinnon glanced at him before murmuring, "I'm not convinced it was such a good idea to include him on the hunt for his own sister. How can we be sure he's to be trusted?"

"I've taken care of it. Don't worry."

There was no time for more talk, once Robert came within hearing distance. Kinnon busied himself setting the hares to roast, and Duncan nodded to Robert, who crouched next to the fire with a troubled expression on his face.

"Is something amiss?" Duncan asked, tossing him a bannock cake before sitting on a chunk of log near the blaze.

"Nothing other than that I don't relish thoughts of what's to come on the morrow."

Kinnon raised his brow and caught Duncan's gaze. "I hope you're not having second thoughts about joining us against your sister, MacDonell."

Robert shook his head. "Nay. Morgana must be found; I know that—for both our clans'. sakes as well as for Aileana." He sat down near Duncan and sighed. "I want to help you, MacRae, in any way that I can." He twisted a twig in his fingers until it snapped, then tossed the pieces into the popping flames. "I just need to know what you're planning to do with Morgana once you find her."

Duncan remained silent, staring into the fire and watching it lick at the wood, devouring it. His imagination ignited with similar force, producing visions of what he'd like to do to Morgana once he found her. What he'd wanted to do to her for thirteen years.

She'd ruined his young life. Stealing the *Ealach* had hurt him, yet it wasn't the worst. He might have forgiven her that. But she'd destroyed his clan and killed Mairi out of spite. She'd murdered innocent people simply for the pleasure of hurting him, and he'd had to relive that agony every day since. Now she'd taken Aileana. It was a pain worse than any the English had inflicted on him in the Tower, and he'd never forgive her for it.

The only thing stopping him from cornering her like a vicious beast and driving his claymore through her evil heart was the thought of Aileana. How would she feel if he sought final vengeance against her sister? Her family's blood already stained his hands, her father having been killed by his men during the initial battle to retrieve the *Ealach*. Aileana seemed to have made peace with that sin, it was true, but would she be able to forgive him a second time?

And then there was the fear of what Morgana might do to Aileana if he ordered a direct attack once he located their hiding spot. Aileana was in the deadly grasp of a witch who had already proven herself capable of base murder and betrayal. She'd had Mairi killed; who knew how much more vindictive she'd be with her own sister as the object of her resentful hate? Nay, a downright attack on Morgana's holding in an attempt to kill her was too dangerous, much as he'd like to order it. He couldn't risk the woman he loved any more than was absolutely necessary to free her.

Dark fear for Aileana gnawed at him, but he forced himself to push it aside in order to concentrate on what he could do to bring this nightmare to a just and safe conclusion for them all.

Looking at Robert once again, Duncan leaned his forearms on his thighs. "What do *you* think I should be doing with Morgana once we catch her?"

From Robert's expression, Duncan could see that he'd thrown him off guard. He met Duncan's gaze, finally, searching, perhaps, to see if he'd been in earnest.

"I think you should bring her back to the High Council and let them decide what is right, both for the *Ealach* and for her. They banished her once, and she stayed in seclusion, as dictated." His tone dropped a little lower as he added, "Though she did lead us all to believe her dead." Straightening his shoulders, he glanced to Kinnon then stared at Duncan again. "But Morgana hasn't done wrong to either of our clans since then. She threatened to seek vengeance when she left, aye, but she has not acted upon it. And while it is true that she may have coerced Aileana into coming with her, it was my understanding that we're riding after her to find out the truth of it and to prevent her from doing anything unjust or evil with the *Ealach*."

Duncan leaned back. It took him a long time to answer, but when he did he spoke evenly, with resignation and finality. "I agree, MacDonell. And that's what I'm planning to do. Bring her back to face the Council."

"What?" Kinnon shot to his feet, the question slicing across the space between them like a blade. "What the hell do you mean, you're going to bring her back to the Council? After the crimes she committed against you— after all that she did to *us*?"

If he hadn't prepared himself for such a reaction, Duncan would have bristled at being questioned so, even by his cousin. But all he felt was guilt. He'd known Kinnon would protest. And the unwritten law of the Highlands supported Kinnon's instincts. A life for a life. If they followed the code, Morgana needed to die in order to repay the lives she'd ruined and the evil she'd wrought.

But he couldn't go through with that. His heart would no longer allow it. His soul was tied, now, to something stronger, something more important than vengeance.

"I cannot seek retribution as I'd like, Kinnon, or allow it to be taken under my leadership. If the Council decides for her execution, then so be it. I will not be sorry for it." He glanced to Robert. "But I cannot kill her. If I do, I'll only be allowing her to commit another crime. Her death at my hands would sow the seeds of destruction between Aileana and me, and I will not allow that to happen. The witch cannot be given the means to destroy my life again."

"But she killed Mairi, for God's sake. She had you locked in the goddamned Tower for thirteen years. She's taken Aileana to do Lord knows what. Does none of that matter to you any longer?"

Duncan stood up, his back tight, his chest aching. By using Mairi's memory and questioning his loyalties—by bringing Aileana into this—Kinnon was dangerously close to crossing the line. "I've not forgotten any of it, Kinnon, nor will I ever," he growled. "Forgetting is not the reason Morgana won't die by my hand. Loving Aileana is."

Kinnon didn't answer. The flickering light from the fire illuminated his face, showing the sweep of emotions that passed through him. Duncan waited, watching him, and their gazes met. God help him, but he hoped Kinnon would understand. He had to understand. Their friendship, their bond was no small thing, and it would be one of the most difficult and wrenching dilemmas he'd faced yet if his cousin refuted his decision.

Finally Kinnon shifted, breaking the silence when he glanced away, murmuring, "Aye, well, do as you see fit. I've supported you from the time we were lads, and I'll not be changing that now. If capturing Morgana alive is what you want, then I'll do what I can to help you make it happen."

Duncan reached out and gripped Kinnon's shoulder, the gesture speaking his thanks with more eloquence than any words could.

Suddenly, something crackled in the brush just beyond the clearing's edge. Duncan stiffened, gazing warily into the dark. Robert and Kinnon heard it too and stopped, half turning toward the noise as their hands slid to their claymores.

Without uttering a sound, Duncan gave a quick nod, and Robert walked away, pretending to go for another wineskin as he warned the men who sat at a fire farther off. Kinnon met Duncan's gaze, and understanding flashed between them. As of one accord, they slung arms round each other's shoulders, raising their voices in feigned laughter and talk as they worked their way ever closer to the area beyond the clearing. When they reached to within five paces of the spot, they bolted into the brush, drawing their weapons and standing to each other's backs as they tried to flush out the hidden intruder.

But there was nothing. Nothing but a few broken branches and a place where the coating of fallen leaves looked to have been disturbed. Robert and the others had joined them by this time. Several of them carried torchlights, and they all searched, looking more thoroughly for a sign of the unwelcome visitor.

"Must have been an animal, attracted by the scent of food," Gil said.

Duncan let the branch he'd been holding aside swing back and returned to the clearing.

"A fox, mayhap," Kinnon suggested, following close behind.

"Aye, a fox." Duncan squatted near the fire, looking over the dancing flames into the shadows of the glen beyond the trees. "Or a witch," he added quietly.

Kinnon sank down beside him. "You think it possible that Morgana watches us from the cover of the woodland?" He spoke so that only Duncan could hear him.

"Though she thinks us unaware that she is alive, she had to consider the possibility that I'd be coming to look for Aileana."

"Then why would she not make herself known and attack us here in the forest rather than lead us to her hiding place?"

Duncan shook his head, standing and gesturing for Kinnon to come with him as he walked to check their mounts. "It may not have been her at all. If it was, it could be that she has other plans for us. Perhaps she wanted to learn what she'd be facing in numbers so that she could muster enough of her own to help her in defending her position."

"Should we initiate a search now, then?"

Duncan weighed the question in his mind. The same thought had occurred to him. But he couldn't be sure it had been Morgana. He'd been dwelling so heavily on wrenching memories and tortured thoughts that he could be imagining what wasn't even there.

Finally he shook his head again. "Nay. If it was Morgana, we'd gain nothing by following her now, as you pointed out. She's clever enough to hide in the dark. We'll track her down in daylight as planned and corner her in her lair."

Kinnon nodded. Together they headed back to rejoin the others. Yet though all settled into quiet and soon slept, Duncan couldn't rest. He found it impossible to relax. Everywhere he looked he seemed to see eyes glittering at him from the dark, preventing him from dispelling the notion that Morgana MacDonell planned to out-smart him . . .

That she plotted to make him commit a tactical error that would cost him dearly in the end.

Chapter 22

The ruins of Carlisle Castle
Northern Highlands

The rattling of the door warned Aileana of her visitor a moment before the heavy wooden slab swung open. Colin stood in the open portal, a half-grin on his face and what looked to be the same leather cord he'd threatened her with in the glen, dangling from his grip.

"Come," he said, walking toward her. "I must bind your hands to take you from this chamber."

"Why? Where am I going?" Aileana asked, backing up and turning her face away when he attempted to stroke his fingers down her cheek.

In retaliation, he took her chin in a cruel grip, forcing her to look at him. "You've been a naughty little lassie, Aileana MacDonell. Your sister is not very happy with you or the tricks you've played. And while I'd almost convinced her to let me punish you properly," he leaned forward to breathe the words, hot and moist, into her ear as he pinched her buttock, "she denied me the pleasure at the last moment in favor of speaking with you herself."

Yanking herself away from his groping hands, Aileana made a sound of disgust, which only made Colin laugh. None too gently he spun her away from him, making quick work of lacing her wrists together with the leather cord. After tugging the knots several times to ensure their hold, he gripped her arm, dragging her along to keep pace with his strides.

Soon they entered a dark, musty corridor where water seeped in rivulets down to the slimy stones of the floor. Aileana fought the urge to wrinkle her nose with the odor pervading the enclosed area, a revolting blend of urine, decay, and sweat. It was worse, even, than the chamber in which she'd been held. But before long they reached an archway, blocked by a wooden door bound in bands of steel. After Colin made a series of taps on it, it swung open, bathing them in golden light.

When Colin pulled her through to the brightness on the other side, Aileana had to squint. As her vision adjusted, she saw that she was in a room as startling in its opulence as the corridor had been for its deterioration. At the far end of the chamber, across a floor of expensive wood inlay, sat a golden chair on a dais. And reclining in the chair sat a poised Morgana. All that lacked for a completed portrait of royalty was a golden circlet for her sister's head.

She was dressed richly in blue velvet trimmed with ermine, her glossy hair falling in loose waves to her waist, unencumbered except for a sapphire-trimmed comb that held the weight of it back from her face. But she wasn't wearing the *Ealach* anymore, Aileana noticed at once.

Without further delay, Colin pushed her forward, his fist to the small of her back, urging her closer to her sister's seat of power. He moved so fast that Aileana thought she might trip with the pace. But she kept her footing, holding herself stiff and proud as she approached the dais. Then he jerked her to a halt, and Morgana met his gaze before shifting to look at her.

Facing her now, Aileana felt stung by her own uncertainty and fear. Morgana refused to speak. She just sat, studying her. When Aileana could stand the silence no longer, she blurted, "Where's the amulet, Morgana, and why have you brought me here?"

Her sister didn't answer for a long moment. She seemed to be struggling with her thoughts, her expression softer now than it had been in the glen. Then she leaned back and sighed.

With false courage Aileana took a step forward, but Colin's hold on her upper arm tightened. His fingers dug into her flesh, forcing a small gasp from her as the pain of his grip radiated down her arm and into her wrist.

"Cease, Colin. Unbind her hands," Morgana snapped, flicking her wrist in a motion of annoyance. As Colin hurried to obey the directive she added, "Aileana will not attempt any further foolishness." She pierced her with her gaze, her brow arching. "Will you little sister?"

Rubbing her arm and wrists, Aileana swallowed the nausea and fear that had climbed into her throat. She shook her head. "Nay. I only wish to speak reason with you, Morgana."

"Reason?" Morgana's blue eyes widened slightly, and a smile curved her full lips. "How quaint . . . and how stupid as well. I warned you in the glen; there is much more at stake here than you realize."

Looking away, Morgana rose from her chair to walk

over to one of the beautiful tapestries hanging on the wall. The fabric of her skirts whispered in velvety folds as she moved from the dais down the tiny, gilded steps to the delicately embroidered wall hanging. Aileana watched in silence, glad her sister didn't know of her dread, of the way her heart skipped along at a speed that made her breathless. She didn't know what to think or do at this moment. She couldn't force Morgana to tell her where she'd hidden the *Ealach*. And yet strangely enough, she was having difficulty sensing its presence now herself.

Morgana ran a pointed fingernail over the figures woven into the tapestry, teasing the image of a unicorn about to impale a warrior at full tilt. When she turned to face Aileana again, her arm dropped to her side. "Your little games have placed me in a difficult position, sister. One of my scouts found this, not a mile from my holding."

As she spoke, she held up a scrap of the plaid that Aileana had been leaving all along their path north. Then she lifted the ruined shawl of the same fabric, casting a dark look at its tattered edges, which were clearly jagged from where numerous bits of cloth had been torn away.

"Care to explain, Aileana," she asked smoothly, "or should I simply release you to Colin to do with you as he pleases in order to make you confess the information?"

Aileana felt herself blanch. But she wouldn't show weakness in front of either of them. She couldn't; not if she wanted to survive. Stiffening her back, she fixed a superior gaze on her sister. "There is no need to explain anything, Morgana. You're very well aware of what I did and why I did it—and furthermore, I'd warrant you'd have done the very same thing had you been in my position."

To Aileana's surprise, Morgana threw her head back and laughed, only looking at her again when the mirth had passed, though its shadow remained in her cold, cruel eyes.

"Well said," Morgana replied at last, "and likely quite true. But that is neither here nor there. Your ploy still presents me with a problem that I'd tried my best to avoid, and yet—" She broke off her comment to glance away, tapping her fingertip against her lips as if in thought. "It might be turned to our advantage, even so . . ."

Sliding her gaze back to her, Morgana strolled over and, reaching down, brought Aileana's left hand to eye level.

"What an interesting design," she murmured, shifting for a more thorough view of Duncan's betrothal ring. "I only saw it closely once before, and for but a few moments. Mairi was already dead, then." She blinked, looking Aileana straight in the eye and making her flinch involuntarily at the cold hate spilling from her gaze.

"It is clear that you've been busy in more ways than one, Aileana, and if Duncan takes the bait you've left for him, it will prove to be your downfall, as well as his." She released Aileana as if her touch had dirtied her.

"What are you talking about?" Aileana barely found her voice to croak the question.

"Ah, you haven't guessed?" Morgana lifted a finger to her mouth, tilting her chin down and smiling as she peered at Aileana. "Well, I suppose it cannot hurt to reveal it to you now. You're powerless to stop me anyway. It is simple, really. I never felt that the Tower was enough punishment for Duncan after what he did to me, but I'd accepted it as all I was likely to get."

Morgana shrugged. "His coming here, though, will

change everything." Reaching out, she smoothed back Aileana's hair with unexpected tenderness, her expression sweet, innocent, and deadly. "Because then, little sister . . . then Duncan must die."

An hour later, Morgana leaned on the window opening in her chamber, her side pressed against the delicate, arching curve of the stonework. She held the curtain back with one hand, tilting her head to see through the slit in the shutter. Beyond the courtyard, the glen looked quiet. Undisturbed. But it wouldn't remain so for long. Not if her scout was accurate in the information he'd reported back to her. Duncan was on his way to the ruins of Carlisle at this very moment, coming to finish what he'd started—and he'd brought more than two score warriors with him.

With a muted swish, she let the curtain swing back, cutting off the slash of daylight. She paced over to the hearth, basking in the glow of the huge logs that burned there. The warmth enveloped her like wool, and she breathed in the heat as she curled up in a chair nearby. Tucking her silken overdress secure round her legs, she rested her head against the chair-back.

Duncan's approach was but another momentary inconvenience. It would all come to fruition soon. The waiting was almost over. She drew her knees up, and the movement made Duncan's betrothal ring dig into her thigh. Reaching into her pocket, she pulled out the circle of gold to study it in the firelight.

A frown weighted her lips. She'd almost failed to get the ring from Aileana's finger. Her sister had struggled to prevent her taking it, even after the sleeping herbs had been administered. Such resistance to the herb's potency was unusual and indicative of a strong will, and it cast an ill omen on the day's work.

But all that would change once Duncan arrived. Then her prophecies would come to pass. Duncan might come by stealth or charge the very gates, but come he would. And she would be ready.

Slipping the ruby ring over her finger, Morgana clasped her hand into a fist and squeezed her eyes shut. The metal branded her skin. It circled her finger, solid, heavy and perfect, just as she'd envisioned it. As it had been meant to be.

But it was too late for such imaginings.

Yanking it off, she dropped it into her lap, watching as its muted gold shimmered with reflections of orange and amber flames. Her dream of a life with Duncan had died more than a decade ago. Faded away, but for remnants of desire that flickered to the surface every now and again. Colin had always proved useful at such times, providing the comfort she'd needed to keep her focus. To help her proceed with her plans. And now it was time. Duncan would come, seeking her out in his quest for Aileana and the *Ealach*. But he'd never guess what he was going to find once he reached her castle.

Morgana pushed herself from her chair and tossed the ring up in the air, following it with her gaze, until it dropped heavily back into her palm. Aye, Duncan would come, and she couldn't wait to watch his reaction. It would be as enjoyable, perhaps, as watching him find the gift she'd left stretched out dying beside him in his own dungeon thirteen years ago. Except that this time, the woman he'd claimed as his own wouldn't be offered as a passive reminder of his sins. Nay. Aileana would serve as the live temptation to draw Duncan into her gilded trap.

Morgana dropped his betrothal ring back into her pocket. With Duncan secured and helpless, the real amusement could begin. This time, when the trap door snapped down, she'd see that it was done with expertise, crushing him with force enough to extinguish the last spark of life from his strong, unyielding body . . . because if she couldn't have him, no one could.

She would make sure of it.

Chapter 23

Duncan reined Glendragon to a halt and dis-mounted near the edge of the pine copse. Kinnon and Robert followed his lead, tethering their mounts to nearby branches.

"What news from the men?"

"My scouts have not returned yet," Robert answered.

"Nor mine," Kinnon said. "Though I saw a glimpse of Ewen through the trees not far back. They should be meeting with us here shortly."

Duncan nodded. "It will be none too soon. Morgana's path leads straight through this bit of woodland, and be-yond it rest the ruins of Carlisle. She's chosen a noble place to hide herself and any followers she may have gathered." He uncorked his water pouch, tipping his head for a long draught before giving the skin to Kin-non. "We'll remain here long enough to make final plans, but I want to move against her before the sun reaches its peak."

Kinnon wiped his mouth with the back of his hand and tossed the water sack to Robert. "The men will welcome an hour's rest. It is wise to hold off the attack until then."

Duncan looked around, searching the barren woodland for any sign of life. He found none. Only the wind, wailing its forlorn song through the black, wet trees. Peering straight ahead, he imagined that he could already see the ruin where Morgana was hiding, concealed there like a rat in a trap. He wouldn't allow himself to think too deeply on Aileana and her condition—or even whether or not she was still alive. He couldn't; not if he wanted to be able to concentrate on what needed to be done next. He burned with a need to finish this, to bring Morgana to justice, but he knew that he couldn't rush. They needed a strategy. He would not fail in bringing the witch down this time, not if his very life depended on it.

He glanced at Kinnon. "The attack must be undertaken secretly. Once we're inside you must find Aileana. I will lead another group to overpower Morgana and Colin. After she's cornered, I'll give her the option of surrender."

A scowl darkened his cousin's face. "And if she refuses?"

"Then I will be compelled to try to take her by force—though I will have to do what I can to prevent her death."

"Why? What care we if Morgana MacDonell dies in the fighting that's to come? Her death is our only hope for true justice," Kinnon scoffed.

"Aye, and yet it will not be at my hand if I can help it. We'll find our satisfaction by bringing her back to face the Council for her reckoning."

Robert had remained quiet throughout the exchange.

Now he stepped forward, murmuring, "MacRae, I've something to say to you. Alone."

Duncan nodded, and Kinnon cast a cautious glance at them before moving away to check their horses. When they stood apart, Robert spoke again. "I want to give you my thanks."

Surprise tingled through Duncan. "Thanks? It's strange to hear you say it, considering what Kinnon and I were just discussing."

Robert's expression twisted with his clearly conflicting feelings as he admitted, "I'll not pretend that this has been easy, but I can see that it is the just thing to do. Morgana has hurt and coerced too many, including even Aileana, it seems." A muscle in his jaw jumped. "And so I'm thanking you for the restraint you've shown. Knowing what happened those years ago, most men wouldn't blame you if you charged into that ruin and took her life without blinking. I'm grateful that you've chosen to do this with honor—with mercy, even."

Duncan's jaw tightened. "I've no mercy where Morgana is concerned, MacDonell, make no mistake. But I'll not risk losing a drop of Aileana's blood—or her respect—because of Morgana if I can help it."

"Whatever your reasons, I'm thankful."

Their gazes connected for an instant, and Duncan nodded before his attention was drawn away by the activity occurring near the horses. Some of the men had returned, and they looked none too happy as they gestured and talked with Kinnon. Robert followed close behind as Duncan approached the group.

"What is it? What news?"

Gil stood with his arms folded across his chest, a little behind Ewen, whose face was flushed and strained.

"A message was tied to an arrow and shot into the

flank of Hamish's horse." Ewen glanced away and shifted uneasily. "It demands that a single messenger from our group be sent, unarmed, to the gates of the ruin to receive further information concerning Aileana."

Duncan fisted his hands and burst into motion, pacing toward the edge of the clearing to look at the castle ruin, just visible through the trees.

"Are you going to comply with the demand?" Kinnon asked, his face pale. "Any message from the witch cannot be trusted. We cannot even know for certain that Aileana is there."

"And yet I have little choice," Duncan answered grimly. "We'll do as she asks. Perhaps we can strike a deal with her—learn what she wants. We'll sort out the rest of it later."

"I'll go as messenger," Gil offered. His chest expanded in anticipation of the important task, and he fixed his gaze on Duncan with an intensity that made him look older than his eighteen years.

Kinnon gestured toward the ruin. "Hold for a minute, Gil. How far do you think to bend in bargaining with Morgana, Duncan?"

Duncan's heart thudded heavy and slow in his chest, and he felt an expansion of the burning sensation that had lodged in his gut ever since he'd first realized Aileana was in danger. "I'm willing to do anything, Kinnon, including letting Morgana go for now, to prevent Aileana coming to harm. I do not like it, but it is what I must do."

Kinnon looked like he'd swallowed something bitter, but he remained silent for a moment before finally nodding, "So be it." Kinnon looked round to the others, calling, "Did everyone hear that? Any mistake can be deadly." The men called out their agreement, and at

Duncan's signal, they fell into place behind him, riding into the clearing near the gate. Gil tied a white flag onto his spear, and with one last look to Duncan, kicked his horse to a gallop.

Duncan watched, back stiff, as Gil approached the crumbled wall of the castle. A sudden movement flashed behind the rotted portcullis gate, and instinctively, Duncan reached for his claymore. The others followed suit, the air hissing with the sound of swords clearing their sheaths.

A moment later a tiny bundle was thrust through the opening, fastened to the tip of a spear. Gil took it, then wheeled his mount around to come riding back to them.

"Someone was waiting for me." Gil pulled his horse to a halt beside Duncan. "But he wouldn't exchange words. He only handed this over, then disappeared round the corner, into a dark passageway beyond the inner court." Gil held out the offering to Duncan.

The linen square felt weighted. It was more than a simple message, sure. Duncan unfolded the fabric so quickly that he almost dropped the object that fell from its creases. With a jerk, he caught the token and then opened his gloved hand to view it. Cold sliced through him, followed by a shock so deep that his hand froze in its outstretched position. He couldn't tear his gaze from the object in his palm.

Kinnon cursed softly as he too caught sight of it.

"What is it?" Robert asked, pulling his mount in closer.

"It's the MacRae betrothal ring. The one Duncan gave to Aileana not two weeks ago."

Robert grabbed at something that fluttered from the linen that had encased it. Unfolding the parchment, he said, "It's a message, instructing you to come to the gate and enter alone, MacRae. The rest of us are to go back to the forest and forego an attack of the ruin for three days."

Kinnon made a scoffing sound. "Not likely, that."

Robert looked at him, his expression grim. "Aye, well it also says that if these conditions are not met, Aileana will die. The ring has been offered as a token of Morgana's esteem—and as a reminder of what will be sacrificed if you do not heed her will."

Duncan heard each of Robert's words as if from a distance, though every syllable fell on his ears with the weight of death. He felt a grinding in his gut that he hadn't experienced since that night many years ago, when he'd woken after the massacre to find Mairi so still and silent beside him. "I'm going after her. Now," he said hoarsely, shifting Glendragon toward the gate and preparing to dig his heels into the stallion's sides.

"Wait!" Kinnon grasped his bridle. "You can't go in there, Duncan. It's suicide to go alone."

The muscles in Duncan's arms twitched, and he wrenched Glendragon free of his cousin's grip. "I'm going."

"What can it serve, if this be nothing more than a ploy to entrap you?"

"It *is* a trap, about that there is no doubt, but I'd rather face it and die than not try at all and have Aileana suffer for it."

"And what if—" Kinnon paused, his eyes shadowed with pain. "I hate even to think it, and yet if I did not voice the possibility I would be remiss as your kinsman . . . and as your friend."

He shook his head, his expression grim. "God forgive me, Duncan, but what if Aileana herself is working with Morgana for some reason? What if this ploy is the one she knows will be most likely to bring you in—the one that will leave you most completely at their mercy?"

Duncan scowled and steadied Glendragon, who seemed to sense his master's leashed fury, pawing and wheeling about as if to break into stride. "If Aileana is that corrupt of heart and I am so mistaken in my belief of her, Kinnon, then I would rather be dead, for never again would I be able to trust my own judgment in anything or anyone," he said, all the force of his passion and love for her filling his voice. "But she is true, man; I know she is. And I cannot stand idly by while her devil of a sister destroys her in order to get to me."

Robert broke in. "If you've a mind to go in after her, MacRae, I say do it."

"It is my intent." Duncan loosened his hold on Glendragon's bridle a fraction; the stallion felt the change and lunged forward, prancing in a circle as Duncan issued his final command to Kinnon, Robert, and the others. "Do as the message dictates, up to one point. If I haven't returned with Aileana by nightfall, don't wait. Attack and take the castle. By that time I'll have succeeded in gaining our freedom or else it will be over."

His gaze locked with Kinnon's for an instant before he nodded and let Glendragon have full rein. With a whinnying cry, the stallion broke into a gallop, crossing the outer courtyard and approaching the gate. The wind whipped Duncan's cheeks, and he clenched his jaw with impatience and anxiety. Before long he reached the portcullis. Dismounting, he dropped Glendragon's reins to the earth to keep him still and peered into the courtyard.

Nothing. All looked overgrown. Were it not for the messenger who'd given Gil the ring, he might have believed himself mistaken in thinking the place a home for naught but daws and spiders. He leaned in further, searching for signs of life. Out of the corner of his gaze he saw the movement an instant before a hand darted from an alcove in the castle wall to grip him by the plaid on his chest. As he was yanked into the courtyard, he caught a glimpse of the man's arm.

In reflex, Duncan shifted his gaze to his attacker's face. Golden-brown hair and a scowling mouth flickered into his conscious mind, then an image of an eye patch and a stare that was hard and remorseless . . .

Recognition slammed home, making Duncan suck in his breath. *Colin. He should have known his brother would be the one to greet him.* But before he could voice a word, a fist hurtled at his face, connecting with a sickening thud and dropping him into a darkness that was as all-encompassing as the flat chill of his bastard brother's gaze.

Chapter 24

Duncan awoke, gasping, and snapped up to a sitting position. His arms lashed out as he tried to fight his way from the fetid, black hole that had been swallowing him again. It had been the same as always. Darkness. Pain. The hell of the chamber they'd kept him in. Only this time there'd been something different. This time others besides the guards tormented and tortured him . . .

Colin. Morgana.

As their names uncoiled into his conscious memory, the remaining fog of his nightmare lifted. He became aware of his surroundings and of the throbbing ache in his head. Rubbing his sore jaw, Duncan looked around the dim contours of the room that confined him. If nothing else, it was cold and damp. No wonder, then, that he'd had the dream . . .

He blinked, and as he lifted his hand to rub his forehead, he brushed against something warm and soft.

Time seemed to stand still, and all movement ceased. His chest ached with tightness, as his gaze focused on what lay next to him on the pallet. She was stretched out in graceful repose, her fiery hair accentuating the pallor of her skin with unearthly contrast.

Sweet Jesus, Aileana . . .

Frantic, Duncan twisted to kneel beside her, a groan of agony welling in his throat. *Just like Mairi.* Holy God, she lay just as Mairi had in the moments before she'd died in his arms, so still and silent, with her life's warmth seeping from her like blood. His vision clouded and his hands trembled as he reached toward Aileana, the past and present colliding horribly in his mind. Tensing, he tried to prepare himself to stroke the hair from her brow, to see if a mottled bruise marked her tenuous hold on life as it had with Mairi. *God, no . . .*

Pleas that seemed locked in Duncan's own mind spilled from his lips in a litany of anguish and grief. He couldn't bear losing Aileana. Not now. And especially not like this.

"I see you've found my surprise, Duncan," a voice purred from behind him.

Half turning, he tensed as she continued, "I must confess that this little scene is almost as entertaining as the first time I arranged it for you. My sister's imminent recovery, however, is an unfortunate change that mars my enjoyment a bit." Morgana stepped from the shadows of the corner, a smile flirting over her lips.

Duncan spared her less than an instant before leaning over to cup his hand over Aileana's neck. The witch had said she'd recover, but he wanted proof. Hope and a kind of harrowing joy jolted to the ends of his fingers as they encountered the warmth of Aileana's skin, the steady beat of her pulse against his palm. No bruise hid beneath the sweep of hair at her brow. But she didn't wake.

"Damn you, Morgana. What have you done to her?"

Morgana's laughter tinkled through the chamber, piercing him. "Don't fret so, Duncan. It is nothing that will harm her. Only a sleeping potion to keep her quiet until your arrival. She'll come to herself soon."

Rage caught up to the shock that had stilled Duncan earlier. It coursed from a deep well inside of him, slashing through his body like a cannon shot. In one fluid motion he lurched to his feet and grasped Morgana by the throat. "Your lackeys made sure that I never got my hands on you thirteen years ago, Morgana MacDonell, but there's nothing to stop me from taking my vengeance now."

He watched her expression waver. But her eyes spoke the truth, showing him that she had no fear, though his grip was tight enough to prevent her from speaking and to force her toes from the floor. It was pure physical reflex that made her dig her fingernails into his hand and kick her feet against his shin. Yet he knew that only a few more seconds of this and she would be senseless from lack of air.

He had to make his decision. Unless he wanted to kill her right here, he'd have to let her go. Anger pulsed through him, making him shake. The need to strangle the life from her was so strong that he felt it in every fiber of his being.

"Release her," a low voice rumbled from behind him. "Or I'll run you through."

Colin. No wonder she'd had no fear.

Stiffening, Duncan calculated the possibility of taking on his brother and Morgana both, with no weapon and while trying to protect Aileana in her senseless state. It wasn't promising. With a growl, he shoved Morgana away from him, deciding to bide his time until he could find the chance to finish both of them for good. Morgana staggered against the wall, gasping for breath, and he turned slowly, coming face-to-face with the razor-sharp edge of his bastard brother's claymore. Colin lowered the point, leveling it directly at Duncan's heart and adding, "A good decision. I would have hated to waste the chance to have you look me in the eye and know who it was that was killing you."

Duncan arched his brow. "Why? Stabbing me in the back never seemed to trouble you before."

Colin's gaze darkened, and his blade sliced into Duncan's skin with a sting that drew blood. But Morgana stepped up and knocked the sword away, hissing, "You waited long enough to stop him, Colin."

He shrugged. "I enjoyed seeing your tender reunion after all of these years. But I have to say it wasn't nearly as satisfying as this is going to be."

Duncan sensed a tensing in Colin's arm an instant before his brother pulled back and slammed a fist in his gut. Too late to stiffen against the blow or deflect its force. Every scrap of air rushed from his lungs and pain ripped through his belly, making him fall to his knees. Shaking away the black spots swirling in front of his eyes, he coughed and willed himself to his feet. Raw anger made him start forward, but the tip of Colin's claymore dug into him again, forcing him to pull up short.

"You'll be moving when I tell you to, little brother."

"Issuing commands does not ensure obedience, Colin," Duncan answered hoarsely. "A lesson you've clearly yet to learn."

"Enough of this bickering," Morgana snapped, pushing Colin aside. "I didn't arrange for your being here only as entertainment, Duncan. I brought you here to give you a choice."

"A choice?" He had trouble focusing on what she was saying; he kept glancing in worry to Aileana. He had to come up with a plan to overpower Colin and Morgana so that he could get her out of here and to safety.

"I suggest that you listen carefully."

Something in Morgana's voice pierced him. He met her gaze, struck anew by the emptiness in her eyes, and wondered how he could ever have allowed himself to think that Aileana resembled her in any way.

"It seems that you've been stupid enough to fall in love with my sister."

Morgana offered her tight comment almost in the form of a question, but Duncan sensed the underlying bitterness in it and remained silent, unwilling to give her any more ammunition to use against him or Aileana.

"Your refusal to answer will not save either one of you," Morgana continued, as if she'd read his thoughts. "Aileana admitted to your betrothal—and of course the presence of your ring confirmed it." Morgana's mouth twitched then and she wrapped a length of her own red-gold hair round her finger.

"I was going to finish you both once I got you here. I'd already decided, even, on how it should happen." She glanced to the cot. "But I kept bumping into the realization that killing my own sister might be less difficult, if someone else bore the true responsibility for her death." She smiled. "And that's where you come in."

Duncan kept his gaze neutral, not asking her to explain. He knew he'd hear her plans soon enough, and the less he revealed about the depth of his fear for Aileana, the safer he might be able to keep her.

Morgana tipped her head to one side, fingering the tendril of her hair once more. "Aren't you curious about your role in killing or saving the woman you love?"

A sick feeling rolled in his gut, but he kept quiet, refusing to give in to her manipulations. Clenching his fists, he mentally calculated the distance between himself and Colin. His brother stood a few paces away, partly blocking his view of Aileana. If he could reach him in time to kick the claymore from his grip, he might find means to disable him before Morgana could . . .

"I understand that your stay in London Tower was a memorable one, Duncan. My spies tell me your recollections of the place are so vivid that even little reminders bring back a sense of . . . coming home, so to speak?"

Duncan snapped his gaze to her, reading the twisted satisfaction she was feeling as she spun her web of hate and vengeance around him. At the mention of the Tower, the sickness in his belly intensified, billowing into an ache. He tightened his jaw, refusing to answer. *Christ. She was enjoying this the way his torturers had relished each new victim brought to their keeping.*

"Aye, Duncan. I see that you remember. And that—" She flicked her gaze to his scarred hand, which was exposed he realized suddenly to her view, his gauntlets having been removed while he was unconscious. "That must be a delightful memory in and of itself."

He felt rooted to the spot as she turned her attention from him to walk with measured steps toward Aileana. After staring down at her sister for a moment, she fixed her gaze on him again. "Since you will not ask, I will simply tell you. Your choice is this. You will submit to imprisonment in my dungeon, or Aileana will die right now in front of your eyes. Painfully."

Her ultimatum ripped through him, shredding his protective cloak of silence. "You're a murderous bitch, Morgana."

"I am only what you and your kind have made me," she answered smoothly. "But come, come. The decision is yours, and we haven't much time to waste. Prove your love for Aileana by sacrificing yourself to my mercy, or condemn her to death."

"Damn you," Duncan rasped, his throat aching and tight. He clenched his fists, wanting to destroy this evil creature who dared to play with their lives. Who dared to taunt him with the hell she'd condemned him to for thirteen horrifying years.

Before he could react, the hissing arc of Colin's claymore swung through the air, its point veering to within a hairsbreadth of Aileana's neck. "Don't try to do anything stupid, brother. Not unless you want me to sever the lass's head from her pretty neck."

Impotent rage coursed down Duncan's arms, making them tingle. Every fiber of his body strained to shield Aileana, to protect her from the filth and danger she faced in this viper's den. He took a moment to steady his breathing, resisting the weight of fear for her that bore down on him. Finally, he looked at Morgana. "You cannot think me fool enough to take you at your word. Even if I agreed to go into your cursed dungeon, what assurance would I have that you'd not kill Aileana anyway, once I was safely imprisoned?"

"None," she said, "other than my oath that I'll let her live." She arched one brow, her smile wicked. "Then again, if you do not submit to me, you can rest assured that she will die. And I will arrange for you to watch, chained to the wall like an animal and knowing all the while that you could have stopped it if only you'd chosen differently."

A war raged within Duncan, a struggle with no out-come. His own safety didn't concern him, but allowing himself to be imprisoned would leave Aileana exposed to Morgana's treachery. And yet, if he could occupy Morgana's perverse imagination with torturing him, she might leave Aileana alone. She might live long enough to escape or to await rescue when Kinnon and the others launched their attack at nightfall.

Temporary surrender seemed to be his only option.

Duncan's muscles relaxed as he accepted his fate. He tried to resist thoughts of what was to come, of the hor-rors he would know again once Morgana interred him in the bowels of her ruined keep.

Once she began to play with him as a cat does a mouse.

He knew that his first breath of fetid air would send him spinning back into hellish memories of the Tower, and it would take all of his strength to stave off the mad-ness that was sure to follow. He shifted his gaze to Aileana, soaking in her beauty, the purity that shone from her, even though she slept with almost unnatural stillness. If he held on to that, if he kept this and the thousand other cherished memories of their time to-gether in his thoughts, he might survive. He had to sur-vive, to save Aileana.

Slowly, Duncan looked up. He nodded. "I'll go where you bid me, Morgana, if you give me your vow that Aileana will not be harmed."

"She'll live. You have my oath." Morgana moistened her lips, her pink tongue darting out, and her eyes sparkling. "And I'm pleased with your decision. It will be far more entertaining this way." She nodded to Colin and soon Duncan felt the sting of rope as his brother yanked his wrists behind him to bind him. "A necessary precaution," Morgana added when she read the question in his eyes. "Though you've agreed to go, I'd hate to have instinct take over once you reach your destination."

"Nay, we wouldn't want that," Duncan answered in a voice thick with sarcasm. "Your lover might end up dead if it does."

Colin jerked up hard on his bonds, making Duncan grit his teeth. Without further remark, Colin dragged him toward the door, slamming him into the stone wall that flanked the entry before pulling him around to face Morgana one last time.

She stood poised in the mellow light, looking wistful, and he couldn't help but acknowledge that, though she was of an age with him, she wore her years well. She was still beautiful. But her proximity to Aileana only called attention to the qualities she lacked, traits that bloomed from a deeper source than physical beauty. They were attributes she'd never know, of a soul unsullied, sprung from the kindness and love that colored Aileana's spirit.

As if she'd seen the slant of his thoughts, Morgana flinched, and a tiny scowl marked the smooth line of her brow.

"Memories are powerful things, Duncan." She stood quiet, her presence almost otherworldly. "Those we wish most to forget are very often the ones that will not cease." She leveled her gaze at him, and he saw that her eyes held no light. A shock went through him. They looked like the eyes of a corpse. Lifeless and evil.

Her soft voice billowed across the chamber, winding around him, suffocating him with tendrils of hate. "You'll be learning that lesson as thoroughly as I have before I'm finished with you."

Chapter 25

The stench slammed into him, making his stomach tighten. Duncan forced himself to take shallow breaths as Colin shoved him the rest of the way down the narrow corridor, into the bowels of the dungeon, trying to concentrate on anything but the dark reality of where this little journey was going to end. They'd not seen another living soul along the way, a fact that had surprised him; if Morgana had any followers, they weren't large in number, and that gave him hope that Kinnon could overcome any there were and face Aileana, if Duncan was still imprisoned here come nightfall.

His brother's torch shone off of the wet slime on the walls as he pulled Duncan along, the wavering light revealing all of the filth and rot that coated the floor and lay caked along the edge of the passage. With every step, Duncan heard the skittering of rats running for safety from the sudden illumination.

Yet it was better than the dark.

A sharp pain sliced into his shoulders, as Colin yanked him to a halt from behind.

"We're here. I chose your new home with care, Duncan, to ensure that your stay would be everything you deserve."

He unlocked a massive door, turning the key in its rusty slot. Without hesitation he shoved Duncan into the unyielding wood. It opened against the force of their weight, and Duncan stumbled to his knees inside the chamber, landing in a pile of straw that reeked of excrement. When something squirmed against his leg, he jerked upright, choking back the growl that rose in his throat.

Swinging around to face the doorway, he instinctively lunged forward, but with his hands still bound, he had no weapon other than his own momentum. Colin grunted at the impact, then recoiled in time to land a glancing blow to Duncan's jaw. The shock of it sent Duncan careening into the wall, a blinding pain radiating through his head and neck.

Before he could recover, another hit slammed into his midsection. He doubled over, feeling the edge of Colin's blade against his arm. With barely a whisper the blade sliced. His arms were dragged over his head, and the cold steel of shackles clamped onto him, securing him with his back pressed against the wall.

"Damn you, Colin," he muttered, coughing and trying to regain both his voice and his breath. "Will you never fight like a man?" His chest heaved, and as if from a distance, he heard the muffled sound of his own blood dripping to the straw.

Colin stood a few paces away, holding his torch aloft in one hand, his other hanging loose at his side. Even in the damp chamber, his muscular arms gleamed with sweat, and he breathed heavily from the effort it had taken to subdue Duncan. The startled expression on his face was the only sign that he'd heard him. But that emotion shifted quickly to bitterness, and then to anger.

"Codes of honor do not affect me, *brother*. They have not from the day that Farqhuar MacRae denied me as his heir."

Duncan's jaw tightened. "You're still a MacRae, whether either of us likes it or no. Da acknowledged you as his son. We were raised as brothers in every way." Colin remained silent, and his obstinacy made Duncan's anger flare. "Christ, can you overlook all of those years? We did everything together. I trusted my life to you, then, and you to me!"

"We may have been together in much else, Duncan, but we were not together in *legitimacy*. Da made that clear when he overlooked me in naming his heir."

Duncan clenched his jaw. It was what he'd always known. The shadow that had always lurked between them. He'd accepted its ugly truth long ago, but he'd never seen it in his brother's eyes. Never until the day Mairi had died. His gaze locked with his brother's again, part of him filled with a hate spawned by the horror of the last thirteen years, another piece of him sickened by the circumstances and the suffering that had led them to this.

"Da did what was needed when he made his choice," Duncan answered, his voice low and steady. "You know as well as I that the clan would not have accepted you as their leader. Not with the knowledge of what your mother was."

"Aye, I was told as much from the time I was a lad." He sneered. "But I did not accept it, then or now, which is why we're here today." He looked as if he might say something more, but then he shook his head and barked a laugh. "It is pointless to discuss further." He walked to the door, and the light of his torch flickered, then seemed to dim.

Duncan's muscles contracted. His mouth went dry. *God it was going to happen again.* As soon as Colin left, the dark would come, and the nightmare would swallow him whole. Strong. He had to stay strong. He'd resist the horror. *Sweet Jesu, he'd have to resist if he was going to survive.*

Colin stood in the doorway, and Duncan could see that he relished the prospect of the torment he was about to unleash. With slow deliberation he transferred the torch from his left hand, which was still in the chamber, to his right hand in the hall.

The effect was immediate. Gloom swept over Duncan, the last precursor of utter black, and with it a cold terror that seemed to grip his innards, twisting and wrenching without mercy. He pressed himself harder against the cold stone, struggling to stay calm, to keep his expression even. He'd be damned if he'd allow Colin to have even a morsel of satisfaction in this sick game. He could stay strong, as long as there was even a little light. Until his brother walked down the hall and took that final bit of salvation with him.

Duncan strained to see in the darkness as Colin leaned into the chamber one last time. "Enjoy your solitude, Duncan. You can be sure I'll be thinking of you while I'm enjoying myself aboveground."

He saw a last, flashing glimpse of white as Colin grinned, and then the door slammed, the lock grated shut . . .

And it surrounded him. Stifling, choking. Wrapping him like a grave shroud. Panic hit almost immediately, made worse by the fact that his hands were secured to the wall. At least when Aileana had locked him in the storage chamber he'd been able to lash out with his fists. It was how he'd gained his freedom. Now he was completely helpless to fight it.

He felt his breath come faster, steeled himself against the dizzying whirl of images, the brutal phantasms that began to form, creeping out of the dark to beset him. He slammed his head back against the hard stone, gritting his teeth as they attacked, blocking his lungs until his chest began to burn with the need to take in air. But still they came. Relentless. *God, no. Not again, not again . . .*

His eyes squeezed shut, and in the blackness of his own vision, he was surprised to see a tiny light. A thought he'd all but ignored in his dread of what was to come. It wavered and took shape, gaining strength, and Duncan focused on it in desperation, latching onto it. It came as a whisper, reminding him of how he'd gained his freedom once while buried in the blackness. Reminding him of what he had to lose if he didn't find a way now. In his mind's eye he saw Aileana, her pale, still form stretched out on the pallet. The image flashed into his thoughts, giving him added courage and strength.

He could do it. And not just for himself, this time, but also for Aileana. To free them both from the prisons that held them.

With a growl that built into a roar, Duncan tightened every muscle in his back, chest and arms, flexing all of his strength against the hard rock and chain. He felt the manacles bite into his wrists as he pulled, endured the cutting pain that made the blood flow faster down his arm. He heard a harsh rattle, the grinding, metallic sound of his bonds, as they strained to keep their moor-

ings within the stone wall against his yanking and tugging.

The chains held.

Duncan paused to rest, his breath harsh, in the silence.
He kept his eyes shut against the blackness, willing himself to focus only on the goal before him. On the reason
he needed to succeed. Taking a deep breath, he gritted
his teeth and pulled again. And again. And again. Until
the weakening chains groaned and screeched.

And began to bend.

"Damn you, Morgana." Aileana hunched over, her
head cradled in her palms. The throbbing in her skull
intensified as she spoke, so she left off condemning her
sister.

"I don't know why you're acting so abused." Morgana leaned against the wall near Aileana, her arms
folded. "It's not as if I gave you something deadly. If
anything my actions protected you." She sniffed and
looked away, feigning a concern that Aileana knew to be
superficial at best.

Squinting at her in light that pained her eyes, Aileana
scowled. "How do you think giving me that potion was
protection?"

"I made sure that you did not have to see something
you'd have certainly thought . . . unpleasant." Morgana
gave her enigmatic answer with a kind of muted glee,
making tingles of worry slide down Aileana's back.

"What are you talking about?" Her headache made it
difficult to think, and she closed her eyes, trying to concentrate. "Be plain or do not speak to me."

"Oooh . . ." Morgana made an exaggerated gesture.
"You've gained defiance in the months since you crawled
from beneath the weight of Father's fist, haven't you?"

"Do not mock me."

"It is just surprising. Duncan never struck me as being the gentle sort. I'd have thought you apt to cower even more under his authority, especially considering that he made you his leman."

She said the last bit with a tone of superiority that brought Aileana to her feet. She faced her sister, trying to stand firm against the wave of dizziness that swept over her. "Duncan may be many things, Morgana, but tyrannical is not one of them."

"How touching. Such faith in a man. I would not have deemed you quite so naive, despite your years of seclusion."

"Believing in Duncan is not foolish."

"I'm so glad that is how you feel. It will make everything that much more . . . satisfying." Morgana's brow arched wickedly, and she paused, the silence pregnant with an emotion Aileana couldn't name. Then, as if she'd suddenly decided to tell a secret, Morgana murmured, "Did you really think I'd waste my time keeping you alive without profiting by it?"

Aileana made a scoffing sound, then groaned as the effort sent a stabbing ache behind her eyes. "I don't know what game you play, Morgana, and I don't care. You disgust me, with your plans and plots. It is all for evil." She straightened, determined to show a strong front. "Didn't your spies tell you that I've spent the last decade trying to be sure that everyone realized I'm nothing like you?"

"Mayhap it would have been better for you if you were," Morgana snapped. "As it stands, your stupidity has made you a lure for catching the one person you'd most wish to keep safe." She grinned. "But now I have him and you, too. It's only a matter of what I'm to do with you both after I've had my fun." Swinging a key on a silken rope, Morgana swayed to the door.

"Wait!" Dread filled Aileana as Morgana stopped, turning to her with a smirk.

"Ach, I've finally gotten your attention, have I?" She shook her head and made a clicking sound.

Aileana kept silent, driven to let the taunt pass by her need to know if what she feared was true.

Morgana's expression took on a diabolic light. "I think you know what I'm saying to you." A slow smile spread across her face. "The truth is that your beloved Duncan is here as we speak. Secure in the dungeon below and suffering the torments of the damned."

When Aileana sucked in her breath with horror, Morgana laughed. "The greater beauty of it is that I got him to surrender without a fight. He came in alone, without Kinnon or any of the others."

"Why would he do something like that?" Aileana breathed the question, not wanting to believe Morgana's lies, not wanting to hear any more. She knew better than anyone that Duncan would never have attempted Morgana's castle alone. Not without good reason. Not unless . . .

"I offered you as bait, of course. It was why I took his betrothal ring from you, as proof that I had you imprisoned here. I told him that if he wanted to keep you alive, he would go willingly into my dungeon." She scoffed. "Of course he did. A lamb to the slaughter, it was so easy."

Sinking to the pallet again, Aileana threaded her fingers together. "Nay," she whispered. "It cannot be."

"Aye, Aileana. Revenge is in my blood, as much as any man's in the Highlands." Morgana yanked open the door, pausing for an instant to take hold of the bar she would use to lock it from the outside. "Now all of my plans are complete. After today, I'll have my vengeance on everyone who tried to stop me," she skewered Aileana with her gaze, "including you, little sister."

A shadow passed over her features, then, but vanished before Aileana was even certain she'd seen it. "Enjoy your remaining moments of solitude. You'll be having a visitor soon enough, while I'm working with the *Ealach*." A flat smile contorted her face again. "I'm sure you understand."

And then she was gone, the door locking with a hollow thud of the bar dropping home. A shudder rippled over Aileana, caused by a chill deeper than the temperature of the damp chamber. It was something else . . .

A tingle of shock shot through her. *Samhain!* Memory snapped back into place, and with it a quick calculation of days. There was no mistake. Today was *Samhain*— the sorceress's high holy day. The day Morgana would invoke the *Ealach*'s power.

Heaven help her, but she had to free Duncan and stop Morgana before it was too late.

Wrapping her arms round herself, she let her gaze sweep the room. It was empty, but for a small table with two candles and the pallet. A single window broke the monotony of gray wall, its view facing west, if her sense of direction held true. Hurrying over to it, Aileana unlatched the shutter to peer out, hoping to find a means of escape.

Chill wind rushed at her through the casement, almost robbing her of breath with its bite. It forced her to squint to see what lay beyond the castle boundary. She crossed her hands to her shoulders for warmth, gritting her teeth as she stared at the barren landscape of rock and salt-crusted sea grasses that stretched to the edge of a cliff not thirty paces from the wall. Beyond that she saw waves, their white tips curling above the gray surf. They seemed to pull back and crash, again and again, into the ragged rock that formed the land here. It was as cold and unforgiving a landscape as her sister's black heart.

Another shiver tore through her, but when she tried to pull the shutter closed, the brittle wood snapped in half. Securing what remained of it over the gaping hole, Aileana stepped away, looking at the sun through the broken portion. It was at the edge of its arc, preparing for final descent on the horizon.

Her time was almost up.

If she couldn't escape, find Duncan, and stop Morgana before the sun set, all would be lost. When darkness fell, Morgana would cast her spell with the *Ealach*. And heaven help them all, but no one knew what damage Morgana might be able to wreak with the amulet at her will.

Panic twisted her heart, followed by guilt. *Duncan.* His name ripped through her with a vengeance. She remembered his torment the day she'd locked him in the storage chamber. Morgana's dungeon would be much worse, surely. Like the Tower all over again, and it was all her fault.

Shaking her head to stop the voices, Aileana wrapped her arms round her waist. Recriminations weren't helping. She needed to find a way to get to Duncan and—

"That worried pose becomes you."

Aileana whirled to face her intruder; the bar must have been lifted so quietly that she hadn't heard it. Colin leaned against the door, his large, muscular shape filling up the entire opening. He'd crossed one foot over the other, and his bulging arms folded across his chest. Tilting his head, he smiled, but the expression failed to reach his gaze. The black patch covering his missing eye added to his sinister aura.

"Why have you come here?" she asked. Her voice sounded strangely loud in the empty chamber.

Colin's smile deepened. "My reasons are personal." He pushed off the door and took several steps into the room, making Aileana move back until she felt the wall behind her. Fear rose in her throat. She swallowed, pressing her palms flat to the cool stone. Her heart thudded painfully in her chest, struggling, it seemed, against the confines of her ribs. She felt trapped.

"What do you want of me?" She fought to sound normal, to keep her tone calm.

"I don't want much, Aileana MacDonell. Only to know you better." He moved a step closer, and a smile flirted over his lips. "In the same way that my dear brother does."

He stood less than three paces away now, and Aileana sensed the energy, the coiled strength that rippled beneath the surface of his massive frame. She feared him in a way she'd never feared Duncan. Even at the beginning, even that first day with Duncan, when she'd stood naked in the glen . . . even the first night at Eilean Donan, she'd known that he would never take pleasure in hurting her. She'd sensed that in him.

But Colin would; she could see that clearly. He'd enjoy every second of pain and terror he could make her feel.

Mustering the tattered remnants of her bravado, Aileana pulled back her shoulders, balling her hands into fists at her sides. She called upon a haughty stare, reminiscent of Morgana's, and leveled it at Colin. "I'm in no mood for conversation. I'm tired, and I wish to sleep. Leave me."

For an instant she thought her ploy had worked. Colin's mouth slackened, and a shadow of doubt darkened his eye. But then he scowled and made a low noise in his throat, and Aileana knew she'd failed. Glaring at her like a wild boar preparing to attack its prey, Colin narrowed the distance between them.

"Do not think to toy with me, wench. You're no Morgana." He pierced her with his gaze, his stare hard and dark. "And I am no Duncan. Haven't you unraveled it yet? You're to serve as your sister's peace offering to me—a boon to repay my efforts on her behalf. You're my prize, to sample at my leisure. So if any commands are issued between us, they'll be coming from me."

Aileana couldn't stop the nausea that rolled up from her stomach. Her mind spun through what he'd just said, but his words jangled like music out of tune. "Morgana *gave* me to you?"

"Aye, she did." He grabbed her by the upper arms, pulling her to him. "And I never turn my back on a gift."

Struggling to keep his mouth from finding her own, Aileana twisted and writhed. It was like struggling in the grasp of a demon. His chest felt immovable, his arms clamping her into position. Only she sensed that Colin didn't plan to kill her right away. Nay, he intended to play with her first.

Frantically, she wedged her foot against the wall, trying to gain enough leverage to push him away. But he was too strong. He grasped a handful of her hair and yanked, making tears spring to her eyes and forcing her to arch sideways. Then he pressed his mouth to her exposed neck, lavishing her with wet, brutal kisses, and pulling back his lips to nip her with his teeth as he got closer to her ear.

"You've the taste of a glen breeze, wench," he whispered, the sound grating harsh into her brain. "And your skin feels of silk. I wonder if it is as smooth elsewhere." Without further warning, he dipped his hand into her tunic to clutch crudely at her breast. His fingers found her nipple with practiced skill, and he twisted the tender flesh, sending a lancing pain deep through her.

She stiffened. A burst of anger spiraled past the hurt, dispelling the shock she'd been feeling since this nightmare began. With a hiss of rage, she snapped herself upright, struggling and scratching like a wild cat in his grasp. She fastened her teeth onto his wrist, biting down hard, intent on gaining her freedom from his loathsome touch. Colin shouted and released her, but before she could dart away, he swung his arm and struck her a backhanded blow across her cheek.

A wall of agony fanned from her cheekbone into her head, making the chamber explode into fragments of colored light. She was only vaguely aware of the hard stone floor rushing up at her face before she landed against it with a dull thud. Her breath burst from her, and she tasted blood in her mouth. She lay on her belly, her palms splayed on either side of her head, as she gasped for air. Black warred with the sparks of color, threatening to overwhelm her and send her into blessed dark. To a place of escape, where she need not think. Where she need not feel.

But a tiny voice prodded, urging her to get up. To stay awake and fight the demon who assaulted her. It continued, relentless, until she could ignore it no longer. With a blast of pure will, Aileana pushed with her arms, trying to force herself to her knees.

Nothing happened.

A low, sinister breath fluttered soft against her ear,

making the hair on the back of her neck prickle. For the first time, her mind cleared enough for her to notice that Colin's thickly muscled arms were positioned on either side of her, pressing her into the cold floor. His groin pressed into her buttocks, and he began to grind himself lewdly against her. Bile surged into her throat. With a whimpering cry, she writhed in a renewed effort to escape.

"That's good, lass. Fight me. I like a wench with spunk, though I wasn't sure if I'd get such pleasure from you."

As if from a distance, she heard her own cries. She struggled harder, feeling her thighs scrape along the rough stone beneath her. He began to yank her skirt above her hips.

No! Her mind screamed for salvation from this degradation. Her nails clawed at the unyielding stone, and the muscles of her legs burned as she fought to keep her thighs together. But Colin only dug his fingers deeper into the tender flesh there, forcing them wider apart.

His knees took the place of his hands, the heel of his palm pressing with unbearable pain into her back, keeping her pinned and helpless. Sobs ripped from her throat as she felt him position himself. She squeezed her eyes shut. An instant more and he'd accomplish his foul deed. He shifted, and then . . .

The weight was gone. Aileana heard a growling roar and a thump. She rolled instinctively to her side, her knees tucked to her chest. Her eyes flew open, but tears blurred her sight. Through the haze of hurt, she blinked, disbelief filling her as she stared at the man who stood between her and her attacker—the avenging god of destruction that towered over Colin.

Duncan stood primed for attack, his chest heaving.

Shocked, Aileana realized that chains dangled from both of his wrists, still attached to manacles that had cut into his flesh so deeply that blood stained both of his arms like some kind of primal Celtic war markings. But it was the look on his face, the silver ice of his eyes that made her cringe and push herself back against the wall, out of the path of that gaze and its unfortunate quarry.

And when he finally broke the silence, she couldn't help but shudder again at the doom in his voice.

"Prepare yourself for hell, Colin MacRae . . . because brother or no, I'm going to kill you for this."

Chapter 26

Rage coursed through Duncan as he lunged forward and hauled Colin to his feet before pounding his fist into his brother's face with a satisfying crack. Colin reeled, blood spurting from his nose, and Duncan landed two more bruising blows to his jaw.

Pulsing fury robbed him of reason. Robbed him of anything but the desire to kill this wretch for defiling the woman he loved. When his brother whipped a six-inch dagger from the sheath strapped to his waist, it had little effect in slowing Duncan's charge against him. He tackled him, slamming him against the wall just as the dirk sliced home. Though it cut deep, their crashing momentum made Colin's aim falter. Instead of sinking into Duncan's chest, the blade gouged a burning path into his shoulder.

And with the blossoming pain came renewed rage. Growling, Duncan grappled with his brother.

Blood.

Vaguely, Duncan realized that he was bleeding heavily from the wound on his shoulder. He struggled to keep Colin from burying the dirk in him again, fighting a sudden light-headed sensation that was caused as much by his fury as from his wound. His fists found their mark on Colin's resisting flesh again. And again. With each blow, with every groan his brother uttered, Duncan felt a greater desire to continue. He wanted him dead. Wanted to feel his life pulse to a finish beneath his hands.

With a bellow of fear, Colin managed to break free. He lifted the dirk, jabbing down in blind panic, but Duncan grabbed a silver candlestick from the table and raised it just in time. Metal sparked on metal as blade and silver collided. He followed through his upward motion, catching the edge of the weapon with the candlestick's footed bottom, sending it spinning away to clatter on the floor out of reach.

"Now there's nothing left to hide behind," Duncan growled, gripping his brother round the neck. He twisted, and they fell to the floor.

"It doesn't matter, so long as you end up dead at the end," Colin retorted, though his voice sounded strangled with Duncan's arm around his throat. Duncan squeezed tighter, closing his eyes against the pain that surged through his shoulder. He had to hold firm. If he could just keep him like this a little longer. Colin was weakening, he could sense it. Just a little longer . . .

Stabbing pain jabbed into Duncan's midsection, spreading additional layers of agony over the already bruised area. Again Colin's elbow slammed back, and the agony intensified, making Duncan loosen his hold. Through the blurring hurt, he saw Colin roll away, hands to his throat. Heard him gasping for breath. He threw himself forward, knocking Colin to the floor. He heard his brother's head collide against the stone with a sickening thud . . .

And then all was still. He lay unmoving.

In the beats of silence that followed, Duncan heard the harsh rasp of his own breathing. Gradually, his blinding rage cleared, and he pushed himself up to a sitting position. His shoulder burned as if with fire, but Aileana was there, her cool hands moving over him to check his wound. Her soft voice whispered endearments and little panicked sounds of worry.

Gently pressing her hands away, Duncan twisted to look at her. Anger surged anew when he saw her cut lip and the bluish, painful-looking swelling along the graceful arch of her cheekbone.

He brushed his fingers over the spot, and guilt welled up to choke him. "Forgive me, Aileana. I didn't stop the bastard in time to keep him from hurting you."

She shook her head, her eyes filling with tears. She gazed at him for a long moment before answering. "You saved me from much worse." Tears slid down her cheeks, then, and she clasped his hands as if convincing herself that he was whole and safe.

Duncan pulled her close, wincing at the pain it caused him. He tried to ignore the black spots dancing across his vision.

Then suddenly, he stiffened. A strange, keening sound rose up from outside. "What the hell?" His gaze snapped to the window, and he noticed for the first time the crimson streak of light that spilled into the chamber like a river of blood.

"God preserve us," Aileana whispered. "It's Morgana." She pushed herself to her feet, hurrying to the window, and Duncan saw her pale before his eyes. "She's got the *Ealach*, Duncan. The sun is going down, and she's starting the incantation."

"Christ." Alarm filled him, followed by cold certainty. If all of the legends about the *Ealach* were true, then what Morgana was about to do posed a danger far greater than anything they'd faced thus far.

He shoved himself to his knees, almost falling over as dizziness engulfed him. Through sheer strength of will, he made it to the window. Black clouds rumbled on the horizon, seeming to build and roil with greater force as the seconds passed. Morgana looked the picture of ancient evil, standing along the cliff. Her arms were upraised, her hair whipping in the wind as she called the timeless words to invoke the *Ealach*'s power.

"We have to go," he said. "We cannot let her finish the incantation."

Aileana was running for the door, with Duncan just behind her, but he was jerked to a halt by a punishing grip clamped to his ankle.

"You're going nowhere," a voice grated.

Disbelief made Duncan pause long enough for Colin to yank hard, sending him toppling to the floor. In an instant, his brother was over him, his fist cocked. As if from outside of himself, Duncan saw the punch coming. He tried to tighten against it . . .

The impact sent shafts of pain into his jaw and up behind his eyes. Instinctively he lurched upward, throwing Colin off balance, reversing their positions. He gripped Colin round the throat, squeezing and fighting through tearing splinters of pain that shot into his shoulder and arm.

"Go, Aileana!" Duncan twisted his head for an instant to meet her gaze. "Stop her before it's too late! I'll be right behind you." As he spoke, Colin renewed his struggles, and Duncan shouted as his brother slammed his fist into his wounded shoulder.

"I cannot leave you like this," she cried. "I won't—"

"Go!" He twisted to glance at her again, desperate urgency in his gaze. "I cannot hold him down much longer."

With a strangled cry, Aileana paused. Then with a last, torn look, she nodded and ran out the door.

At that moment, Colin broke free. He slammed another punch into Duncan's face, knocking him onto his back. Through the pain, he saw Colin roll to his side. His brother coughed, and Duncan shook his head, trying to clear away the double images that floated across his vision.

With deliberate concentration, he forced himself to his knees. Suddenly, Colin stiffened. He was staring at something, and Duncan followed his gaze to a spot near the wall. To the place on the stones where the bloodied dagger lay.

Uttering a choking growl, Colin began to drag himself toward the dirk, and Duncan's mind screamed in protest. He had to stop him. He pulled himself forward, ignoring the pain. His muscles ached, and his bones throbbed. He had to finish this, or Aileana would pay the price for his failure. Lurching to his feet, Duncan stumbled toward the dagger. He fell onto his hands, shouting with the agony that tore into his shoulder as it jarred. Colin was ahead of him, trying to stand, preparing to lunge for the blade himself. With desperate effort, Duncan threw himself forward. His bloody fingers slipped on the dirk's golden handle, and it slid another inch away.

Time seemed to slow. As if in a dream, Duncan felt every breath, every beat of his heart. His senses tuned to a fine pitch. His mouth tasted bitter, and he smelled the sweet, sickening scent of his own blood. He could hear a rustling sound behind him, over him, heard his brother's growling roar as he leapt to grab the dagger. In that instant, Duncan found his grip on the ornate handle. He twisted in reflex, onto his side, the blade up . . .

Colin slammed into him. His brother's eyes widened. A gurgling, choking groan breathed past his lips, and he stiffened. Then without another sound, he slumped over, a dead weight, his body sprawled over Duncan and the floor.

With a guttural moan, Duncan pushed him away, rolling from beneath him. But releasing the pressure from his shoulder unfurled a wave of pain so sharp that he sucked in his breath. Black spots converged on his vision, threatening him with oblivion. Precious seconds ticked by as he struggled not to give in to the temptation of unconsciousness.

He had to get to Aileana.

He took a deep breath, preparing to stand, and as he did, he looked at Colin for the first time since their struggle. His brother lay on his back, the dirk protruding from the spreading, crimson stain beneath his lowest rib. Its handle wobbled sickeningly to the rhythm of his heart.

He was still alive.

Cursing again, Duncan burst into motion, heading for the door. If Colin died before they could bring him back to face the High Council, then so be it, but he'd not purposefully aid that end before its time.

In the next moment he secured the chamber and ran for the stairs. But when he reached the end of the corridor, he saw that piles of rubble that had fallen long ago blocked the stairway. He had to find another way out.

And then he heard it. The sound floated up to him, raising the hairs on his neck and sending a shudder of foreboding up his back. *Eerie.* The wailing howl rose in pitch, until it trailed off into the shriek of wind that whipped round the castle walls. It came again, followed by an answering shout, and Duncan stilled. *Sweet Jesus.* The second voice was Aileana's. She'd reached the cliffs.

Racing to a window at the end of the hall, he looked out, frantic, searching for a sign of her. What he saw made his heart skip in his chest. Aileana and Morgana struggled on the ocean bluff.

They were too close to the edge, damn it. At any moment one or both of them were going to careen over it.

God help him, but he couldn't lose Aileana like that again. He wouldn't.

Mentally gauging the distance between the window and the ground, Duncan pulled himself up onto the ruin's open stone ledge and jumped down. The impact shook his bones, though he had foresight enough to tuck his legs and roll when he hit the earth. Still the force of it stunned him. A thousand new hurts sliced through the old, and his arm felt as if it had been ripped from his shoulder. But he pushed through the pain, surging to his feet and racing across the salt-encrusted grass to reach them—to reach Aileana before Morgana hurt her any more than she already had.

Something glittered on the ground a few paces from them, and Duncan lurched to a halt. The *Ealach* lay untended, its chain bunched from the way it had apparently been dropped during the women's struggle. Its opalescent surface beckoned him like a siren's song. Leaning over, he scooped it up. It fit in his palm as if all of the years without it had never passed, but its weight failed to bring the comfort, the sense of completion he'd been certain he'd find once he held it again. And he suddenly knew that nothing but the feeling of Aileana in his arms could do that for him now.

"Hold, Morgana," he shouted, holding the amulet aloft so that it dangled from his hand. "Hold or lose the *Ealach* forever!"

He could see the madness in Morgana's expression. The wind whipped her hair in a wild fury, accentuating the aura of evil that surrounded her. When she heard his voice, her gaze snapped to him, and had he not been a man of courage, a man who'd faced the horrors of hell and lived, he might have flinched at the unadulterated malice she leveled at him. Her pupils were narrowed down to pinpricks, lending a supernatural appearance to the icy glaze of her eyes.

In one, fluid motion she twisted Aileana around, her arm circling Aileana's neck. Duncan saw the gleam of a tiny blade in her grip. It pressed against Aileana's throat, and he saw a shadow of fear pass across the precious, beautiful face of the woman he loved.

"How dare you interfere with me?" Morgana hissed. Her grip tightened around Aileana's neck enough to force a choking sound from her. Duncan took a step, and Morgana jerked Aileana back. "Don't think it will be so easy, Duncan. I've fought too hard to give up now." Unblinking, she looked past him, her expression wary and cold. She obviously sought something. Or someone.

"Colin won't be coming to aid you, Morgana."

She met his gaze again, and her eyes narrowed. "You've killed him."

"Nay." Duncan approached cautiously, trying to get close enough to pull Aileana away. "He's not dead. Only wounded. I've secured him where he cannot hurt anyone else."

Morgana sneered. "I don't believe you." Pressing the edge of her blade harder against Aileana's neck, she snarled, "Come no closer. I've no more fear of dispatching my dear sister than you had in murdering Colin."

Impotent rage churned in Duncan as he watched a trickle of blood slip from beneath Morgana's dagger to slide down Aileana's throat. He raised his palms as if in surrender, the *Ealach* still clasped tight. "He was alive when I left him, I swear it. Go and see for yourself if you doubt me."

Morgana laughed, and Aileana flinched as she felt the knife bite deeper. She tilted her head up, trying to shrink from the stinging pain, but it only made Morgana tighten her hold.

"Be still, sister." Warm breath burned Aileana's ear, and fear pounded in her veins, making her feel faint. Duncan's blank expression only reinforced the understanding that she teetered on the edge of a terrible death. One flick of Morgana's wrist, and she'd either go spinning off the cliff or have her throat slit like an animal at slaughter.

"Duncan, take the *Ealach* and go while you can," she called out hoarsely. "You must keep it from her now more than ev—!" She sucked in her breath and winced as Morgana dragged her closer to the edge. With skittering scrapes she heard stones and pebbles falling, pushed over the precipice into the narrow line of rocks and crashing waves below. The dizzying height swung suddenly into her vision as Morgana shoved her so close that her toes tipped over the brink. She squeezed her eyes shut and leaned her weight back onto her heels.

"I don't think you'll want to be doing that, Duncan. Not unless you're craving the sight of your beloved lying broken on the rocks below us." Morgana gave her another shake, and this time Aileana couldn't prevent the moan of terror that escaped her. She saw Duncan start forward, and in a panic she twisted her head to look at him, silently pleading that he stay back.

Their gazes locked, and in that instant, Aileana felt calm descend on her. It was as if Duncan spoke, but not aloud. His message sang to her heart alone. It seemed to say that all would be well, that together they would conquer this evil. He lowered his hands slowly to his sides. His gaze reassured her, and love shone through the silvery depths of his eyes.

Aileana barely breathed as she watched Duncan slowly lift his right hand to eye level again, the *Ealach* dangling from his fist. Strands of hair blew into her eyes with the wind, but she dared not try to push them away. Duncan's gaze swung to Morgana, intensity and leashed power sculpted in every inch of his taut frame.

"Here." He spoke in a calm, deadly serious voice. "I'll give you the *Ealach*. Only you must release Aileana to take it."

Morgana stilled behind her, and the pressure of the blade at her throat lessened. Duncan took one step closer, then another, all the while holding out the amulet as an offering, a treasure to be exchanged for the prize he sought himself.

Morgana's left arm fell from Aileana's waist so that she could reach for the powerful talisman. She nudged Aileana from behind, pushing to get closer to what she wanted. Closer . . .

At the moment that Morgana's fingers touched the *Ealach*, Duncan lunged to the side, swinging his arm and uttering a growling curse. He flung the amulet, and it spun through the air, up until it formed a silhouette against the crimson sky.

With a bloodcurdling howl, Morgana lunged. Aileana used that instant of distraction to push away, and Duncan caught her against his chest as Morgana fell from the bluff in a vain effort to recover the vanishing talisman.

Burying her face in Duncan's chest, Aileana tried to block her ears to the sound of her sister's fading scream. It ended abruptly, and she squeezed her eyes shut, feeling Duncan's warmth and the steady pounding of his heart against her cheek as she tried to slow her breathing. They were both filthy, covered with blood, dirt and sweat, but she'd never felt so relieved, so safe in her life. He pressed gentle kisses to her head, and she clung to him, wanting to anchor herself to his strength as the tears finally came. They spilled down her cheeks, wetting his skin.

Tipping her face to his, Duncan brushed his thumb over the liquid tracks. "It's finished. You've nothing more to fear, I swear by my life."

"But the *Ealach*—you've lost it forever now—"

"Far better that I lose it than you, Aileana. Nothing is more important to me than you. Nothing."

She looked at him in silence for a moment, overwhelmed by the feelings coursing through her. Love swelled, warm and life-giving, driving out the cold that had been gripping her so tightly these past hours. She nodded, blinking back her tears and reaching up to cup Duncan's cheek in a tender caress before stepping back. Still holding his hand for support, she peered over the ledge, needing to be certain that it was really over. A bitter ache unfurled in her belly as she stared down at Morgana's broken body on the rocks below. So pointless.

Perhaps it had been inevitable, after all that had happened, but she couldn't help remembering earlier times. Times when she was still a child, and knowing Morgana had been good and happy. Her beautiful sister, so full of adventure. She'd adored her, then. Wanted to be like her.

Aileana stepped back into Duncan's embrace. "God, I just want to forget that all of this happened. I want to go home and never look back."

Duncan's eyes clouded. "Home . . . ?"

A shout came from the castle ruin, making them turn to look. Kinnon and several MacRae clansmen charged into the open area, claymores drawn. Duncan stepped away from Aileana for a moment to intercept his cousin.

"What happened? Where's Morgana?" Kinnon's breath came hard, and when his gaze flicked to Duncan's wounded shoulder, to the bruises on Aileana's face, he clenched his fists. "We charged the fortress not long ago and took a handful of men and two women as prisoners."

Nodding toward the cliff, Duncan said, "She's dead. She leapt from the bluff trying to get the *Ealach*."

"Christ." Kinnon cursed under his breath. "It is a brutal death, though in her case, I suppose it was just." He glanced to Aileana, and guilt colored his cheeks. "I'm sorry. I meant no disrespect to you."

"You don't need to explain. Morgana's evil earned its own end."

Kinnon nodded, his eyes filled with gratitude. After Duncan dispatched a group of men to retrieve and bury Morgana's body and search for the *Ealach*, they spoke briefly again, deciding that they should seek shelter in the castle. The dark fell fast around them. Only a rim of sun remained on the horizon, painting the sky crimson and purple. As they walked to the ruin, Duncan told

Kinnon where to find Colin, and several of the men went ahead to gather up his body, or if by some miracle he still lived, to secure him for travel back to Eilean Donan and the judgment he would eventually face before the High Council.

When they reached the castle, Duncan left to make some arrangements, and Aileana settled into one of the empty, inner chambers to await final preparations for the journey ahead. Men bustled about, gathering those valuables that they could carry for the clan's use back home. Aileana watched it all in a kind of daze, empty, detached, and lonely for Duncan's touch. She looked up when he came in a few minutes later. His shackles were gone and his shoulder was bandaged, but her welcoming smile faded at his serious expression.

He paced to the window, turning to face her, finally. He stepped close. So close that she could see the torchlight glint off the golden strands in his hair. Close enough to feel his warmth. More than anything, she wanted to reach up and stroke his brow, to kiss away the hurt and worry in his eyes. But she held back.

"Did they find the *Ealach*?" she asked softly at last, gazing up at him.

"Nay. They found nothing but Morgana's body. The waves must have carried the amulet away."

Silent, she nodded, uncertainty filling her at the troubled look in Duncan's eyes. He had something on his mind, and it wasn't good, that much she could tell. Perhaps now that the *Ealach* was gone he'd decided that he didn't need her in the way he'd thought he did. That he didn't feel—

"I need to ask you something, Aileana," Duncan murmured, breaking into her thoughts. "I was going to ask you when Kinnon and the others came." He looked away, and Aileana stepped forward, unable to stop herself any longer from being near to him. She took his hands in her own.

"What is it? Tell me, Duncan. Please."

"Ah, Aileana . . ." He breathed her name like a prayer, and she felt her heart lurch with hope. He gazed at her again, his eyes bright with unspoken emotion. "I need to know what you meant when you said you wanted to go home. Whether you mean to come home with me to Eilean Donan, or go back to Dulhmeny with your brother Robert."

Aileana almost laughed with relief. "Is that all? *That's* what made you look like the sky was about to fall on you?"

With a scowl Duncan mumbled, "I didn't think it was so small a matter."

Aileana reached up, caressing his stubble-roughened jaw, the scar that threaded along his cheek. She pressed herself firmly against him, so that he couldn't help but feel her warmth, her need to be close to him. He felt so strong. So right. They fit together, soul to soul, and she knew that she'd never allow anything to come between them again. She smiled, her brow arching slightly as an idea came to her for helping him to understand that truth.

"Ah, Duncan MacRae. When will you learn to trust what stands right in front of you?" She leaned in, breathing soft onto the exposed skin of his chest. "It's as clear as glass, if you ask me." She punctuated her words with gentle kisses to the hollow above his collarbone, along a heated trail that finished just below his ear. A throaty chuckle bubbled up in her as she slid her fingers up his chest to tangle in the golden-kissed waves of hair at the back of his neck.

Duncan stilled under her tender ministrations. His arms tightened, holding her, rigid and uncertain. "You wish to make your home with my clan, then?"

"Nay, not exactly."

Pulling back, Aileana pressed her fingertips to his mouth to quell the confused protest that rose to his lips. "What I'm saying is that I want to be with *you*, Duncan, wherever that might be. Whether it is at Eilean Donan, or the other side of the world, it will be home to me, as long as I'm with you."

Love shone from his gaze, so profound that he seemed transformed by it. His gray eyes took on the quicksilver light she'd come to recognize so well. Right now, he appeared to waver between tenderness and playful exasperation.

One corner of his mouth quirked into a smile. "You had me worried for a moment, love. I keep forgetting that my wee mousie has teeth with which to bite me if she chooses."

She gazed at him, eyes wide-opened and innocent. "Ach, it was just a nibble."

With a growl, Duncan bent his head, taking her mouth in a kiss of love and passion. She responded in kind, reveling in the powerful give and take of pleasure as he slid his hands down her back to cup her more fully against him.

She was breathless when he released her mouth, still hungry for the taste of him, the feel of him beneath her hands and along the burning length of her body. Duncan held her close, and she settled into his embrace, lulled by the steady beat of his heart. When he spoke, his voice caressed her, soft and tender.

"It was true, you know. What you said before."

"What?" Aileana lifted her head from his chest.

He gazed down at her, and again she felt bathed in the warmth of his love. He looked into the very recesses of her soul, and it was as if she could feel him melding to her, becoming one in a way that could never be broken by time, age, or any power on earth. He traced his finger over her lips, brushing his mouth along the same path before he spoke again. "You were right when you said that I looked as if the sky was about to fall in on me. It was. Because if I lost you, I'd lose everything." Duncan's gaze caressed her, pulling her deeper into the mystery of his heart. "I love you, Aileana. You are my heart, my soul, my eternity. You and no other."

A swell of love rose up in her, bringing tightness to her throat and burning behind her eyes. "With all that I am, I love you as well, Duncan," she murmured through tears of happiness. "You and no other, until the end of time."

He touched his forehead to hers. "Always, Aileana," he whispered.

"Aye, my love." She gazed into his beautiful gray eyes and pressed her lips to his. "Always."

Epilogue

Nine years later
Loch Duich, near Eilean Donan Castle

Mama was going to be so surprised.

Rowena smiled as she clutched the crumpled spray of flowers tightly in her small fist, watching where she put her feet as she clambered up the slope heading back toward home. Bridgid shook her head and called from the top of the bank for her to come along, but Rowena needed no further encouragement. She was too excited; aye, she might be three years younger than snooty Fia, but it didn't mean she hadn't done a fine job in seeking out a present for Mama anyway. In fact, she'd found *two* presents to celebrate their new baby sister's birth.

Scrambling the last few paces up the slope leading to Eilean Donan's causeway, Rowena slid to a halt. She panted with her exertions, disappointment spilling through her at the sight that greeted her. Fia was dancing around Da and Bridgid, her arms filled to bursting with flowers from the wood beyond the glen. Because she was eight, Fia could go to the edge of the wood now by herself, while Rowena was only allowed to walk the rocky edge of Loch Duich within sight of Bridgid or whoever else had been placed in charge of her at the time. They treated her like a baby.

Her eyes stung as she looked at the wilted stalks in her hand before catching a last glimpse of Fia skipping up the causeway with her bountiful present for Mama clutched to her chest; Bridgid followed close behind. Walking slowly forward, Rowena met Da, feeling a little less sour when she saw his smile and the twinkle in his eye. She couldn't help smiling back, certain in her heart of hearts that he was the most handsome, wonderful Da in the whole wide world. He impressed other people, she knew, by the very fact that he was Duncan MacRae, laird of the mighty clan MacRae. But to her he was finer than the sun and the moon together, and he always made everything better when she was feeling worst.

"And how's my wee sprite, this morn—did you find some pretty flowers for Mama, then?" he asked with a grin, reaching down to swing her onto his shoulders.

Rowena giggled, wobbling precariously as she clung to his head, which made her drop her handful of wilted blooms.

Da laughed and righted her, preparing to lower her again to retrieve them, but she patted him to stop him, calling, "Nay, Da, go on. I've another present in my pocket for Mama. I found it next to the loch. Now gallop me to the castle yard, please? I want to give it to her right now. Oh, let's gallop!"

He twisted his neck to look up at her, making such a

funny face that Rowena giggled again. "You found a pretty pebble for Mama, did you, lass?"

"Aye, it is very pretty," she murmured, nodding and patting the necklace in her pocket. She felt excited again, thinking of the cool, milky stone with those sparks of color shining from it. That it was circled in gold only added to its magical beauty, she thought. It was going to be great fun to give Mama such a fine gift. "It's not as pretty as Mama, though," she said, finishing her thoughts aloud.

"Right you are in that, lassie." Da chuckled and faced forward again as he prepared to gallop her to the yard. "There's nothing in this world as beautiful as your mother—except you and your sisters, perhaps." He gave her a little jounce and set her to laughing again. "Are you ready for your ride now, milady?"

"Aye, Da—giddy up!" And as he galloped forward Rowena squealed with delight, one arm wrapped around his head and the other hand pressed tight to her pocket . . . keeping safe the precious, opalescent gem resting inside.

Author's Note

Eilean Donan Castle is, of course, a real castle at the meeting points of three Scottish lochs—Loch Long, Loch Duich, and Loch Alsh—and is one of the most photographed and recognizable of Scotland's castles. Its history reaches back into the mists of time, with evidence of a Pictish fort uncovered there during various excavations. In terms of documented history, it is clear that at the beginning of the seventh century a religious hermit known as St. Donan lived on the island, lending it his name; Eilean Donan literally means "Isle of Donan." According to tradition, Robert the Bruce was given refuge there in the early fourteenth century by John MacKenzie, second of the Kintails—and the MacRaes, who were known as "MacKenzies Coat of Mail," first became Constables of the Castle in 1509.

Of course, I didn't know any of this when I began conceptualizing Duncan and Aileana's story; at the beginning, I had simply stumbled upon a few anecdotal pieces about certain members of a clan MacRae, piecing together some history that seemed to indicate they had been in conflict, at various times, with clans connected to the Donalds. To that initial inspiration, I added in a mystical amulet, some passionate, loyal characters, and several dark familial betrayals, and all the ingredients for *The Sweetest Sin* fell into place.

Speaking of amulets . . . I decided to call the talisman of my story the *Ealach*, for though I am not a speaker of Scottish Gaelic myself, I was told by a reputable source that it is the Gaelic word for "moon." That seemed a fitting moniker for the opalescent stone I'd envisioned—the inclusion of which sprang from research indicating the deeply ingrained superstition and folklore that abounds in the Scottish Highlands.

In fact, it seems that many Highland families owned what are known as "family charm stones"—amulets handed down through the generations that were said to have supernatural powers. One of the most famous of these was that of the Brahan Seer, Kenneth MacKenzie, who lived in the seventeenth century; his stone was small and white with a hole in the center of it. When he looked through it, legend has it that he was able to "see" into the future.

Another aspect of Highland folklore I chose to utilize was the festival of *Samhain*; it seemed the perfect time for Morgana to attempt to invoke the amulet's powers, since traditionally, *Samhain* was believed to be the month that heralded the rule of darkness, the most magical time of the year—culminating in a night during which the great shield of *Skathach* was lowered, allowing the barriers between our world and the Otherworld to thin, and the spirits of the dead (as well as those yet to be born) to walk freely among the living.

As an interesting aside, though the influence of Christianity eventually subdued many of the pagan concepts behind this festival, it nevertheless continued in the minds and hearts of the people, morphing over time into what we now recognize as Halloween.

One final note, concerning the episode of plague I wove into the story: as nearly as possible I tried to replicate the actual symptoms and progression of the disease, according to my research. The buboes, the fever, the ointment (which was written almost as a "recipe" in a very old set of encyclopedias I was fortunate enough to find), and the outcome for the patient, depending on whether or not the swellings burst or subsided, are all as factual as I could discern from my readings on the subject.

And lastly, of course, I would be remiss if I didn't say at least a few words about Duncan and Aileana. These two characters were probably the most purely fun couple for me to write thus far, since they were both so passionate, stubborn, headstrong, and noble. They sometimes seemed to take on a life of their own, coming out with phrases, comments, or actions that I hadn't planned on at all, and it was very satisfying to help bring them to their well-deserved happy ending together. I can only hope that you enjoyed their story, too. As always, thanks for coming along on the journey.

—MRM